# THE LEGACY

Book One of The Legacy Chronicles

by

Luke Romyn

Editor: Chuck David

If you are interested in more writing by Luke Romyn, be sure to visit
http://www.lukeromyn.com

For my father.

See you soon.

# Acknowledgements

Special thanks to Michael de Wee of Groovyways Design in Holland who consoles me when I'm bashing my head against the keyboard, frustrated at photos, trying to design covers. He always answers my pleas and offers great advice.

My proofreaders, Karen Hansen, Sarah Dougherty, Claude Bouchard, Joanne Chase, and Kendra Williams. You are all wonders in my world.

Thanks to Chuck David's editing skills I am certain to never believe I'm omnipotent.

Enormous thanks to reviewers and readers, you help fan the flames.

"But if it is preached that Christ has been raised from the dead, how can some of you say that there is no resurrection of the dead?"

1 Corinthians 15:11-13

# -PROLOGUE-
# THE DREAM

"HE IS COMING!!!"

The words echoed around the room. A small Indian boy's eyes flared open, and he sat bolt-upright in his bed, his throat raw from the scream. Wrenching aside sweat-drenched sheets, he struggled to slow his thundering heart, which seemed to be sitting at the base of his throat. The intense vision had fled, but the memory lingered, its claws retracting, but not fully retreating. Night slithered around young Aadesh like a shroud, escalating his fear.

The dream had begun normally. Aadesh had been playing with friends in the marketplace within his home town of Bhinmal. He'd been sprinting between the timber and canvas fruit stalls, focusing on the uneven cobbles to avoid tripping or crashing into the multitudes of people. Suddenly a tall, azure-eyed stranger had stepped in front of him, halting him with his gaze. The man had kneeled down, whispering seriously, the way adults spoke to each other. The scene around them had melted away as the stranger spoke, his rich voice drowning out the market's cacophony, becoming the crux of the young boy's focus. Aadesh couldn't remember the features of the man, nor could he recall the words he'd spoken, and as such it was a particularly frustrating dream. He knew something of vast importance had been imparted to him, and he would need to remember it eventually. For the time being, though, the information was gone, lost in the haze of his memory.

Aadesh's door burst open, and he blinked against the light streaming in, barely discerning the features of his father.

"What is wrong, Aadesh?" his father demanded in Hindi. "You were yelling in your sleep."

"I had a bad dream, Papa."

1

His father entered the small room and sat on the edge of the bed, holding Aadesh's hand comfortingly. "Tell me of it."

Aadesh shrugged. "I don't remember."

"Then it can't have been too bad, can it?"

"I think it was important. A man told me to remember something, but I can't."

"If you are meant to know, it will return in time," replied his father, smoothing his hair as Aadesh laid back down. "For now you must get some sleep."

"Thank you, Papa."

"It seems your studies are going well, at least," said his father, rising to leave.

"What do you mean?"

"Well, when you called out, your English was perfect." His father paused. "I thought you weren't to start learning foreign languages until next year."

"We haven't started, Papa."

His father stared down at Aadesh quizzically. "That is strange, I could have sworn you yelled out 'He is coming' in English before I came in. I must have been mistaken; or perhaps it is all those American movies you watch. I think they're corrupting your mind." He smiled gently.

"I don't know. I just remember the man in my dreams talking to me. He said it was very important that I remember what he was saying, but I can't now. Will I be in trouble?" Aadesh's chest tightened at the prospect.

His father chuckled in the semi-darkness. "It will come back to you when the time is right, my son. If it is truly important, the words are merely waiting within you for the moment when they must emerge once more. But for now you need to get some sleep, because tomorrow is another day of school."

Rolling over, Aadesh groaned, "Yes, Papa."

His father left the room, and Aadesh pulled his blanket up to his chin once more, staring hard into the darkness, attempting to free his mind from worrying about the message. The man had been so persuasive, so adamant Aadesh remember his message, but all the boy could think of were his eyes. They had been like ice, burning coldly within the sockets of the man's face. But unlike ice, they had seemed alive with emotion – charged – especially when he'd spoken the name.

*Name?*

What was the name? It had sounded odd, perhaps a western one from the movies his father chastised him for watching so often. The unfamiliar language held little meaning, generally ignored as the action blasted across their small television.

What had the name been?

It teetered on the tip of his tongue. So foreign, and yet something that felt comfortable within his mind, as though it bypassed language barriers, becoming much more than merely a moniker.

*Chris?* No.

*Christine?* He shook his head, frustrated.

And then it came to him, and Aadesh smiled, knowing he could finally get back to sleep. He rolled over on his side and closed his eyes, breathing deeply and evenly.

The name was *Christ*.

## -CHAPTER 1-
# REVELATION

The wave, near invisible on the moonless night, smashed into Jacob Hope's face like a salty fist. Gasping in shock, he began to cough and splutter, the seawater burning like acid in his throat. His mouth had been only partially open, but that was enough. The incessant pounding of the inflatable boat against the waves had distracted him, or perhaps he felt simply awestruck by what was taking place; regardless, he now sat choking and drenched. Water dripped into his intense blue eyes, stinging remorselessly, and he swiped at them with the sleeve of his wet canvas spray jacket, doing little more than aggravating the situation.

His first deployment into a hot zone was not proving anywhere near as glamorous as Jake had hoped.

The United States Navy supercarrier USS Gerald R. Ford had transported them as close to land as it could, and a Black Hawk helicopter had been provided to convey Jake the rest of the way. It had managed to fly half the distance before mechanical issues forced them down on a desolate slab of rock just off the Pakistani coast known as Charna Island. Their options at that point had been to wait for another chopper to fuel up and carry them the rest of the way to Karachi, or they could brave the distance to the mainland in one of the inflatables the SEAL teams used to covertly land during missions.

The decision had ultimately fallen on Jake's head. Their mission was urgent. The time saved might mean the difference between people living and dying. He needed to get to Karachi as soon as possible, before the situation got any worse. After a brief conversation with his superiors via satellite phone, the choice had been made. The SEALs had inflated the boat which appeared barely more seaworthy than a blow up doll....

Jake's Kevlar helmet slipped down slightly for the umpteenth time, dropping in front of his eyes. He pushed it back impatiently, only to catch another surge of salt water in his face. The flickering lights of the shoreline weren't too distant now, indicating an end to this hellish sea voyage, and his spirits lifted slightly. The SEAL team supposedly knew people here, and had radioed ahead, arranging to meet a locally-based team of specialists. Jake wasn't sure who they might be, but they were due to meet in Mubarak Village, a dusty collection of random huts splayed at the very edge of the Pakistani shoreline.

The inflatable bounced over yet another wave in the darkness, and Jake's helmet smacked down hard on the bridge of his nose. Cursing softly, he unstrapped it and removed it from his head, running a hand through his blond hair as he did. Pushing the dripping fringe away from his face, he felt grateful that the crimson birthmark on his pale cheek was barely noticeable in this low-light. The mark was something he'd always lived with, but it still caused him discomfort when strangers stared at it. He couldn't help the shape, curved like a bloody teardrop. It was such a clear similarity, yet people always felt the need to point it out. If he could have it removed without fear of scarring he would have, but no doctor had yet been able to promise such success. So he endured it, cringing when eyes fixed upon it, yet holding strong under each scrutiny, anticipating the oft-repeated litany.

Azure eyes stared down at the aqua-blue Kevlar helmet. Jake traced the white UN printed on the side of its coarse surface with his finger. Grinning slightly, he recalled two years before when they'd told him he was being promoted to senior advisor within the United Nations Democracy Fund, a rapid advancement which had upset many and surprised even more. He'd just turned twenty-eight.

That had been a very good day.

The low-noise electric outboard made surprisingly good progress through the churning water, and they soon slid up onto the sand, the underside of the boat rasping softly. The SEAL team crept onto the shore, weapons up, searching the darkness for any sign of a threat. Jake hoped the six-man team had been able to navigate correctly in the darkness – the last thing he wanted was to get lost in Pakistan given the current state of affairs.

The situation in Islamabad had started out routinely enough, but the proverbial shit had hit the fan six days beforehand, as the country geared up for parliamentary elections. The United States had somehow become entangled in Pakistan's latest political ballot, and wild protests had broken out among the populace. Claims of election rigging and accusations the US was trying to worm its way into the Pakistani government through a puppet leader were inflamed in the press. Riots had erupted throughout the country, and United Nations representatives had been called upon as unbiased mediators in an attempt to avoid any more unfounded claims, hopefully heading off the looming military coup. Negotiations such as these were hardly Jake's forte, but for the time being he remained the UN's best option, and he'd readily agreed if it might help stop unnecessary bloodshed. Sometimes just a physical presence could prevent disaster – or so his superior had told him.

Jake remained dubious as to the accuracy of the rumors. Bullying as the United States could be at times, there really wasn't anything in Pakistan worth the trouble of twisting an election around. And besides, if they wanted to rig an election, they'd do it in such a way that few people would ever know. It wasn't like they were amateurs at duplicity.

The SEALs' boots crunched softly on the light, yellow sand. Their night-vision goggles gave them the appearance of heavily-armed insects. Each moved wordlessly into position, securing the area. Jake glanced around nervously, taking in the sinister shadows, each one seemingly an enemy about to rear up and slay him for having the effrontery to set foot upon such foreign soil. His very breath sounded like thunder in his ears, and he felt sure at any moment they would be discovered.

Once given the go ahead, Captain Chenoweth silently motioned for Jake to follow him. The man moved like a ghost, assault rifle aimed and ready, up the darkened beach.

Chenoweth was a career soldier, his strong jaw and fastidiously trimmed mustache setting him as a poster child for the American military. Closing in on forty years of age, the SEAL captain was physically imposing – broad shouldered, narrow around the waist – yet appeared fit enough to run all day. Back on the ship, Jake had asked him why he'd joined the SEALs. The captain had looked at him as though he were a moron.

"I didn't *join* the SEALs. I *am* a SEAL. It's in my blood. It's what I was always meant to be. People can't become something they're not and remain happy. You need to find what you're supposed to do in life and throw everything you have into it. Consequences are irrelevant. That's who you are."

The extended speech from the normally reticent captain had surprised Jake, but he'd nodded appreciatively, at the same time wondering why the words left him feeling so lacking.

As they crouched on the foreign beach, he found his mind drifting back to that moment of inadequacy, wondering why he had felt it so strongly at the time. What he did was important; the United Nations performed a lot of good work in the world, but sometimes Jake sensed it wasn't enough.

A sizzling, red flare shot into the sky right beside their position, illuminating the entire beach in its fiery glow. The sand appeared almost molten. The SEALs whipped off their goggles to avoid any vision impairment. The ramshackle houses of Mubarak Village were lit up clearly, as if a crimson spotlight had been focused upon the poverty of the region, bathing the scene in blood.

"Dammit! Someone must've hit a tripwire," hissed Captain Chenoweth. "*Move!*"

Jake was practically dragged along by the SEAL as the team sprinted up the scarlet beach, their black uniforms sketched starkly against the flare-lit sand. Scores of armed figures surged out of the village, running down the sand toward them.

"Hold your fire!" Captain Chenoweth barked to the other SEALs. "Our objective is to keep the advisor alive. We can't risk losing him in a firefight."

The armed locals rapidly surrounded them, nervously spreading out. Jake scanned the group, trying to keep his thundering heart under control as he did. They made a motley bunch, not a militant among them, but their few guns were aimed at the SEALs and Jake, and that was cause for major concern. Pitchforks, hand axes, and crude, hand-made spears glinted in the wavering light. Jake sensed these people were not normally aggressive. Something – or someone – must have made them wary, hence the tripwire set up on the beach. Though he had little experience in such matters, Jake suspected such a defense was neither cheap nor easily obtained.

A tall, paunchy villager angrily pushed his way through the throng of locals and stared challengingly down the barrels of the SEAL team's guns, finally turning his malicious gaze toward Jake. The man appeared unarmed.

"What you want here?" he spat in broken English.

Jake cautiously stepped forward. "Um… we're here as representatives of the United Nations."

"Why?"

"Well… I'm part of the delegacy –"

"What this word?" snapped the villager.

"Delegacy?" Jake wiped his sweating palms on his thick cargo pants. "A group of people chosen to aid… to help… during a crisis."

"You American?"

"Er…."

Jake weighed his answer carefully. If these people were angry with the United States and blamed it for their current political crisis, they might attack without question. The last thing the United Nations needed was to be embroiled in a fiasco involving a massacre of villagers by Navy SEALs defending themselves – and him.

"I work for the United Nations – you know the UN?" hedged Jake. He reached up to tap his blue helmet and suddenly realized he'd left it back in the landing boat.

Great.

The rest of his uniform was decidedly plain – standard black fatigues and combat boots supplied by the SEALS for their stealthy beach landing. Regular clothing was to be supplied once they'd successfully made it into Karachi undetected.

*If* they made it.

The leader stepped toward Jake, and Captain Chenoweth slipped smoothly between them, his Heckler and Koch MP5 submachinegun's laser-sight glued to the forehead of the villager. The local man froze in his tracks.

"W-we kill you all," he said, his bravado evaporating like smoke in a hurricane.

"Not before I blow your skull open like a melon," growled Captain Chenoweth. "Now tell your people to back off."

The laser-sight seemed to bore directly into the man's skull. He nervously licked his lips.

Seconds ticked by.

Finally, after the longest minute of Jake's life, the man babbled something and waved his hand to the rest of the locals. The group of disgruntled villagers parted like the Red Sea before Moses. Captain Chenoweth kept the leader of the group covered, and the other SEALs hurried Jake through. The captain was the last to follow.

The villagers closed in behind them, but their leader remained silent. Perhaps he'd seen something within the captain's gaze which had broken through his bluster. Whatever the reason, it was enough to keep him silent. The group faded back into the shadows, and the illusion of safety slowly returned... for the moment.

They trudged through the dark for perhaps half an hour, Jake constantly tripping on hidden objects in the gloom. The SEALs couldn't risk revealing their position with lights, and were hesitant to use their night-vision goggles again – the threat of another flare blinding them apparently more of a risk than stumbling upon hidden combatants. Jake kept quiet, trusting in Captain Chenoweth's judgment.

The terrain wasn't difficult, slightly hilly with sparse trees and uneven ground, but the inkiness of the night proved their greatest obstacle. Occasionally Jake would hear something in the darkness, but the captain would murmur that it was merely cattle moving through the knee-high scrub, or the rustling of the breeze. How he knew this Jake had no idea, but it gave him some reassurance as they traversed this sightless nightmare.

"We should hit Mauripur Road any minute now, sir," said a SEAL whose name Jake couldn't remember – a short, thickset, bulldog of a man with dark, thinning hair and a clean-shaven face.

"You already have," growled a voice from the shadows.

Figures emerged from the darkness, and suddenly Jake's group was blinded beneath the illumination of a dozen or more handheld flashlights.

"Settle down, Fletcher," grunted Captain Chenoweth casually, striding forward and pushing aside the flashlight closest to him, its beam dropping slightly before flicking off. "We've already had enough drama on this babysitting run as it is – no offense."

"None taken," replied Jake. "I appreciate your babysitting."

The captain nodded, turning back to Fletcher. "We were ambushed on the beach by some locals, but managed to get through without any conflict. Things seem more hostile here than we were led to believe."

Fletcher, a hulking bear of a man, boasted a bushy, brown mane atop his cinderblock head which fell down his back in a rough mullet-cut. He also sported a decidedly non-military shaggy beard, its gray flecks catching in the light. Beneath faded army fatigues, his open jacket revealed an ancient AC/DC t-shirt; an AK-47 – hardly standard issue for US troops – hung carelessly over a shoulder. The giant shrugged broadly, rubbed his bristly cheek with a grimy hand, and then dug a finger deep into his nose. Quickly glancing at what it removed, he wiped his hand on his pants and flicked on his flashlight once more, shining it briefly at Jake's face, causing him to squint against the intense glare.

"Hmm. I thought you were injured. Is that a tattoo?" He pointed at Jake's cheek. "Looks like you're crying blood."

Jake grimaced. "Nobody's ever said that to me before," he muttered sarcastically. "Can you please turn off the flashlight?"

The light blinked out. "So is it a tattoo? You know the red will fade, right?"

"It's a birthmark," Jake answered.

"Probably won't fade, then," Fletcher said, his voice like grinding gravel. "Do you believe in God?"

"I – um – *what?*"

"God. Do you believe in Him?"

"What's that got to do with anything?" asked Jake defensively.

"It's got a lot to do with everything. Some reckon you can judge a man by his religious beliefs, what his hopes and dreams might be, whether or not he's likely to get you killed. Some of the worst wars this planet has ever seen have been fought in the name of some sort of deity, people chopping each other up in the hopes it'll gain them access to Heaven. You're American, I don't have to remind you of the dangers of religious fanatics. So it shouldn't be too shocking that I ask if you believe in God, should it?" Despite the gloom, Jake got the distinct impression Fletcher was glaring hard at him, his gaze burning through the darkness.

"I find it impossible to believe any god could sit by allowing so much pain and suffering to happen," Jake admitted, fighting to keep his eyes from revealing his dark secrets.

In his memories it was the Bible that had hit him, had lashed his back and buttocks until his throat bled from screaming. The Man had ignored his screams, quoting extracts Jake no longer recalled, words which supposedly excused his actions.

"Hmm. Interesting answer," said Fletcher, looking thoughtful. "Anyway, the locals are definitely pissed off. You Yanks tend to do that to the neighborhood, running all over the place when you're not invited."

It was then that Jake noticed Fletcher's odd accent. He sounded Scottish, though his voice was much more guttural than the usual lilting tones of those from the land in the north of Britain; like Sean Connery if he'd gargled battery acid.

"You're not American?" Jake asked, and both Fletcher and Chenoweth turned to look at him.

"No, sir," responded Captain Chenoweth. "Fletcher is a paid combatant."

"You mean he's a mercenary."

"Titles are nasty things," commented Fletcher. "I like to think I provide a service to embattled nations."

"And arms dealers," put in Captain Chenoweth, his teeth glowing as he grinned wryly.

"Aye, them too."

"Captain, do you really think we can trust this man?" asked Jake.

"Probably not. But he smells less and fires a gun better than that cow over there... barely."

Fletcher laughed good-naturedly, the noise deep and rumbling, like thunder.

"I thought we were meeting US troops," said Jake, determined not to let the issue go.

"Fletcher and his men can get us through to Karachi better than any American team, and they've promised to do it without bloodshed. Right, Fletcher?"

"Sure, yeah, whatever. You guys pay me enough, and I'll swing around a pole in a g-string for ya. Get a bit squeamish around wet-work?"

"Wet-work?"

"Aye. Killin' people."

Jake stared incredulously through the dark at Captain Chenoweth. "He's the best in the game," said the captain defensively. "Don't blame me for his rough edges."

"You think death is a *game*?"

"Of course it is," said Fletcher, strolling toward one of three trucks Jake could now make out in the shadows. "Why do you think they invented chess?"

"He's got you there," said the captain, following Fletcher. Jake jogged slightly to catch up as Captain Chenoweth continued. "These guys are exactly who we need to get you to your destination. They've got contacts throughout the area, and we should be able to slip through without anyone even knowing we're coming."

"But why should anyone care?"

Captain Chenoweth pointed back the way they'd come, toward the coastal village. "Those people down there didn't know us, but they were ready to kill you. Now, no matter what started this little conflict, don't think for a second anyone here cares which side you're on. In their eyes America is their enemy, and they're likely to kill us all simply to vent their frustration. Either that, or they'll capture us and hold us for ransom – maybe do what those wannabe terrorists did and chop our heads off, posting it on the internet for shits and giggles. We're not sitting in your little ivory bubble anymore. Highly polished principles won't wash well here."

The words felt like a slap in the face. "You think I'm that naive?" he eventually mustered after an awkward pause.

Captain Chenoweth gave a short whistle, and the SEAL team dropped back from their defensive positions, jogging up the short hill and clambering into the rear of one of the virtually invisible trucks.

"I think it's time to go, sir."

And with that simple statement, Captain Chenoweth relayed volumes to Jake, who nodded silently and walked toward the large truck, its rear covered by a canvas roof stretched over a high, metal frame. Jake saw the SEAL team seated alongside Fletcher and three of his men, two bench-seats running the length of the tray.

He climbed awkwardly into the back of the truck as its engine roared to life. The tray reeked of livestock; the musky scent of animal feces mixed with grass or hay and wet fur. Jake gagged, but otherwise remained silent, still stinging from the captain's indirect rebuke. Complaining of the stench would only serve to lower him further in their esteem. Captain Chenoweth climbed in alongside him and pulled the flaps of the canvas awning closed, tying them together and locking in the odor even more. The truck lurched forward and, as if on cue, Fletcher unceremoniously lifted one leg and farted.

"Hah! Sorry about that, lad. I seem to have left my manners in my other pants – the less stained ones." Several men chuckled.

"I'm sorry about what I said to you back there," said Jake, suddenly realizing the deep need he felt to express regret. "I never meant to insult you or your profession. I appreciate your help in getting me safely to Karachi."

Fletcher chuckled. "It would take a lot more than a snotty politician like you to insult me. I just get annoyed when a stranger – someone who knows nothing about the way life works outside your Garden of Eden – decides to lay judgment without even knowing me first. It hurts my feelings."

"Seriously?" asked Jake.

"Nah, not really. But I had ya goin', didn't I?" Fletcher's laughter roared through the rear of the truck, and Jake felt flushed with embarrassment, not for the first time since landing.

"Anyway, I'm sorry."

Fletcher seemed to appraise Jake, his dark eyes glinting in the dull light slipping through several tears in the canvas canopy. "Fair enough," he finally grunted.

"How long until we reach Karachi?" asked Captain Chenoweth, thankfully diverting the conversation.

Jake sensed Fletcher shrug, the rough fabric of the hairy man's jacket rustling like canvas. "Two, maybe three hours. Depends on traffic – the local military are more twisted than the Matterhorn at Disneyland, pulling over anyone they reckon they can screw for a penny."

"Is that true?" asked Jake.

"Anything's possible," replied Fletcher. "This country's rapidly turning into a puddle of crap."

"The United States denies any involvement in the election."

Fletcher's reverberating chuckle echoed over the intense growl of the truck's diesel engine. "Of course they deny it. When don't they deny crap like this? But in this case I reckon they're being honest – at least partially. General Sharmeer Khalili is probably the one behind all the trouble over here. He's the guy most likely to wind up president if there's a military coup. His troops have been supplying local villages, like the one you lads just navigated. In exchange for weapons and explosives, and kissing their arses, they get locals on side."

"But what about the Election Commission of Pakistan?" argued Jake.

"What about them? They know which way the wind blows, and they also know when to step aside before that wind turns into a shit storm. If the full army backs Khalili they'll just get rid of anyone who opposes them, and by starting the widespread rumor that it was the United States who played around with the election instead of Khalili, any direct action from America will be seen as an invasion and admission of their guilt. General Khalili has effectively tied the hands of the nation most likely to cause him problems while he tries to take over. He's a cunning bastard, alright."

Unease gnawing at his belly, Jake mused over what Fletcher had just said. The UN had relayed similar information to him shortly before he'd taken off from the USS Gerald R. Ford, though theirs was much more diplomatically phrased. This entire action could merely be a smokescreen for General Khalili to take over the country, and Jake might be walking into a mediator's worst nightmare.

Jake hadn't been the first choice for this situation, far from it, but he was the closest UN representative on hand when the call had come through. Since then, things had not exactly gone to plan, but he was determined to do a good job.

Assuming they ever made it to their destination.

He was beginning to regret his decision to push on after the chopper had broken down. The thought of traveling in the second helicopter instead of this daredevil land approach seemed like a dream realized. What had he been thinking? It'd sounded so simple when Captain Chenoweth had relayed the options to him: a short boat ride, followed by transport via military escort.

Shaking his head, he grimaced futilely. Regret was an empty shell which could never be filled, and Jake was determined not to dwell on any mistakes he might have made.

The truck rattled loudly along the bumpy road, making further conversation near-impossible without shouting, and Jake's mind began to wander. He recalled his first job with the United Nations as a junior advisor in New York a mere three years before, at just twenty-seven years of age. Much study and many sleepless nights had been rewarded with his advancement to Senior Advisor for International Democracy the following year, but the excitement had swiftly worn away as the politics of it all had emerged, like compressed swamp mud rising from beneath slivers of diamond. Life was supposed to be about making a difference to the world, not sitting in an office shuffling through endless stacks of paperwork! But Jake had persevered in the hopes he might eventually be promoted to more field positions.

Such as this one.

No paperwork here. Instead, he sat in the back of a putrid truck in the middle of the night in Pakistan, surrounded by a motley bunch of Navy SEALs and paid mercenary thugs who seemed just as likely to kill him as protect him.

His mother would be so proud – or at least she might be, if he knew who she actually was. Infant Jacob had been abandoned at an orphanage without any knowledge of his birth parents. At three years of age he'd been adopted by Wendy and Gary Hope, an outwardly gentle couple who'd brought him into their home in the small town of Owensville, Indiana. A house with no close neighbors: nobody nearby to hear the cries for clemency, or the bellowing condemnations.

He'd grown up in that dark dwelling; the memories of his adoptive father's Bible and cracked leather belt forever intermingled with the sound of his adoptive mother's whimpering –

The world exploded. The entire truck flipped sideways.

"IED! IED!" a voice hollered.

A fragment of Jake's mind registered that they'd hit an improvised explosive device, blasting the side of the truck, and knocking it over like a toy. The bomb mustn't have hit squarely, otherwise they'd all be playing harps by now.

Talk about luck.

But there are two types of luck, and Jake doubted this incident included any of the good kind….

Ears ringing, he pushed himself up from where he'd landed, face pressed against the scratchy canvas awning of the truck. Panicked cacophony rose amidst the other jumbled figures trying to get to their feet. Had the other two truckloads of paid troops fled without them? Jake wondered if one of them had hit the IED, and the resulting explosion had capsized their own transport.

"Sir, you need to stay here!" ordered Captain Chenoweth grimly, stepping out into the night.

Jake nodded, his mind numb, too shocked by what had happened to fully grasp the ensuing chaos around him. The night air erupted with gunfire. Screams of men dying or wounded pierced the darkness, each one wrenching Jake's heart. These were men fighting to protect *him*, sacrificing themselves while he hid like a petrified rodent.

Forgetting his promise to the captain, Jake bolted from the back of the upturned vehicle, stepping out into Hell.

Enemies hunched or flitted on the edge of illumination, nightmarish lumps in the darkness, their automatic weapons thundering from all sides. Foot-long flames spurted from the barrels of their assault rifles. To Jake it seemed they were surrounded by demons, spraying fire toward them from the shadows. The carnage seized Jake, and he stood dumbly in the open, utterly exposed, powerless to move amid the horror surrounding him.

The shadowy enemies seemed somewhat disorganized, shooting haphazardly at whatever moved. Bullets struck the ground all around him, but mercifully none managed to so much as scratch his flesh. The SEALs and mercenaries returned fire in controlled bursts. The SEALs couldn't use their night-vision goggles given the blinding muzzle-flashes and flames all around them, but still seemed to inflict significant losses against the opposing force, the majority of tortured cries echoing from outside the circle of death.

Something heavy hit Jake from behind, crash-tackling him to the ground.

"What the hell are you doing?" hissed Captain Chenoweth as bullets whizzed through the air over both of them.

Jake suddenly realized the stupidity of his action. "I – I have no idea. I heard the gunfire, men were screaming, and –"

"And what? You thought you'd go for a stroll?"

"I guess I panicked."

One of Fletcher's mercenaries collapsed under heavy gunfire, his body flopping to the ground beside them like a marionette with its strings cut, half his face torn away by an exiting bullet. His remaining features confronted them, the undamaged eye staring accusingly at Jake. He didn't recognize the man, but that just made him feel worse. Here was someone whose name he didn't even know, who'd just died trying to protect him. Others might argue the semantics of the situation, but in Jake's mind it was simple: this man's blood was on his hands. Guilt surged up within him, and Jake found himself unable to tear his eyes from the dead man's lingering stare.

Captain Chenoweth cursed and rose to a squat. "Stay down!" he growled. The captain swiftly took up the defensive position the fallen mercenary had held, his weapon blasting out into the night.

Jake lay frozen, transfixed by the corpse's hollow gaze. There seemed so much left unspoken in the dead expression, such loss and sadness, and Jake wondered who this man had really been. He'd been paid to work as a mercenary, but who was he *really*? Did he have goals and dreams beyond the violence surrounding his life? Did he have a family? Would anyone miss him?

Amid the blood-drenched clash encircling him, Jake felt a deep and profound sadness for the fallen mercenary. He'd never witnessed the bitter finality of death before, and the brutality of it chilled him.

*This* was the reality of battle; not the glory referred to in storytelling and movies. This dead mercenary was the true image of war, his solitary orb unblinking, condemning Jake as blood and gore oozed from his open skull. A disgusting odor hit Jake's nostrils, and he realized the man's bowels had released upon his death, his final act on the planet, a scene of humiliation.

The battle around him faded into the background as Jake thought about the enormity of what had just occurred right before his eyes. A man, possibly one with a family or others who relied upon him, who loved him, had just been killed... and for what? What was so important that a life – *any* life – should be snuffed out so abruptly and without thought?

Something dropped down behind the body of the mercenary. It took Jake a moment to focus on it. What in the world...?

"GRENADE!!!" someone hollered.

Jake's eyes fixed upon the small, black, cylindrical object....

*Oh –*

***

Jake awoke face down on a dirt floor, his brain thudding against the inside of his skull. He tried to raise a hand to check himself for injury, only to discover his arms were immobilized, securely tied behind his back. Raising his head slightly, he peered around, registering the rough-hewed walls of a shoddily constructed timber shack. Thin shafts of sunlight pierced narrow gaps between the planks, leaving long slices of light across the ground, like the bars of a cage spaced across the floor. There were no windows and only one door.

"They hit us with some kind of concussion grenade."

Jake twisted his head toward the voice, regretting the motion instantly as more pain rocketed through his skull. Even so, he recognized the speaker as Captain Chenoweth. The captain was secured to the wall, both hands stretched above his head.

"You were the closest to it when the grenade went off. You're lucky to be alive," said the captain.

"Who attacked us?" Jake's throat felt raw.

"No idea," replied the captain, "but I think it's a safe assumption to say they were tipped off by those people back at the village. There's no way they could have known our route unless they'd been forewarned. I'd hoped Fletcher might be able to get us through unscathed. Obviously I was wrong."

"But why would they attack us? We're here to help solve the problem."

"They don't know that. As far as the people of this country know, we're here to make things worse for them. They don't understand the politics of the situation – to them, America might as well have invaded Pakistan. And we're American, so we're the enemy."

"But –"

"There is no *but* in this situation," snapped Captain Chenoweth. "We've stepped into a highly volatile event, and even though you believe you're working as some sort of Jedi crusader, you need to realize how serious this shit really is. They'll come in here soon and quite possibly torture and kill us for no other reason than they're angry and need an external source upon which to vent that anger. I've heard about the good stuff you try to do through your work with the

UN, but that doesn't mean shit right now. You're from the USA – these people are angry with the USA. *You* are the enemy."

"There has to be something we can do," argued Jake, unable to accept the crude reality the captain presented to him.

"Do what? I'm open to suggestions. As far as I know the rest of my team is dead, along with Fletcher and his boys. If you have any ideas I'd really like to hear them."

"Can't you be a little bit more optimistic?"

"I deal in reality," replied Captain Chenoweth bitterly. "On a day to day basis I face things politicians like you couldn't possibly comprehend. Today, for instance, I need to face the reality that five men who were closer to me than brothers have possibly been murdered for no other reason than because they were doing their duty and protecting you."

"*Me?*" gasped Jake. "You don't blame me, do you?"

"Why not? You opted for this route, didn't you?"

"I –" Jake found himself lost for words. Usually a persuasive debater, the accusation caught him completely off-guard, and he found he had no response whatsoever. He stared at the man tied to the wall, noticing that despite his words, there seemed very little animosity in his attitude.

"And *that* is how these people feel toward the USA."

"Huh?" Jake shook his head, completely nonplussed.

Captain Chenoweth grimaced. "They're lashing out at the most obvious target simply because they're angry. They don't really hate us, but they're upset about the unfairness of their lives, and that resentment needs a focal point. General Khalili has given it to them by manipulating facts, making the United States out as the bad guys."

"So… you don't really blame me?"

"I never said that," replied Captain Chenoweth, "but I needed to make a point as well. Do you understand?"

"Their anger needs an outlet, and we're it."

Captain Chenoweth nodded, seeming to sag a bit, as though his contained fury had been the only thing supporting him. He'd vented his frustration and now felt empty, drained far beyond the point of physical exhaustion. The unknown hovered over both of them like a noxious cloud.

The door to the shack slammed open, the streaming daylight obscured by the silhouettes of two large men, the skin on their arms heavily tanned, testament to long hours beneath the hot Pakistani sun. Both men wore coverings over their hair; the larger of the two, a thick, black pagri headdress, worn like a turban, the smaller sporting a dark-blue bandanna. The smaller man covered the lower part of his face with a scarf, obscuring his features. Perhaps more daring due to his size, his companion's face remained fully exposed, his bushy, black mustache greasy and unkempt, his cheeks and chin peppered with stubble. Both men's eyes chilled Jake with their frozen detachment. His heart began to hammer against his ribs, his breath catching in his throat. They strode directly over, hauling Jake to his knees, and then his feet, steering him toward the door.

"Let him go, you bastards!" bellowed Captain Chenoweth. "He doesn't know anything!"

As touched as Jake was by the captain's valiant effort to save him, terror rapidly engulfed him, and he swiftly forgot about anyone besides the two hulking Pakistanis dragging him out into the brilliant light. Blinded by the brightness, Jake stumbled across the rocky and uneven ground. His two escorts held him erect, easily hauling him over to a large upright pole fixed securely into the middle of a flat expanse of dirt.

Before Jake even realized it, they'd untied his hands from behind his back and strapped him expertly to the pole: both his arms pinned behind him, secured with what felt like a leather belt at the elbows, rope tightly binding his hands once more. Jake tensed at the extreme discomfort of the angle of his arms and the tightness of his bindings. The ligaments in his shoulders felt close to snapping, and the rope cut harshly into the skin of his wrists. But the panic coursing through his veins brought with it huge amounts of adrenaline, and as such the pain became a secondary issue, something he ignored for the moment. Other concerns took priority right now.

Jake blinked away tears. Not tears of fear, despite its intensity, but more the result of his eyes still trying to adjust to the sudden brightness after the poorly lit shack. Squinting, Jake could barely discern the shapes of several people around him. His eyes slowly refocused to the point where he was able to make out their features.

He swiftly wished he hadn't.

His two escorts rapidly retreated, heading for a large, but dilapidated building situated opposite the shack Captain Chenoweth remained imprisoned in. Jake turned his watering eyes toward the half dozen or so other figures arrayed before him.

They all sported pagris, with scarves wrapped around their faces, masking their features. Three carried machine guns. Two others wore long, sickle-like knives at their hips. The last man clutched the most terrifying thing of all: a digital video camera.

They were an execution squad.

The camera lens pointed directly at Jake's face, and he knew what was expected from him: begging, pleading, humiliation. The script would follow with various parts of his body getting hacked and sliced off. He'd seen similar videos during his induction into the UN, highly censored versions, but he'd still felt scarred forever after watching them.

And now he would star in one.

A fist smashed into his stomach, causing Jake to sag, but the strap securing his elbows prevented him from sliding down. The camera loomed closer, catching every agonized expression etched upon his face, silently beseeching him to cry out.

He refused.

The last thing Jake intended was to give these men what they wanted. If this was to be his last act upon the face of the planet, he'd fight in the only way he could. Men who sought fear thrived on the creation of terror, and so Jake did the only thing he could think of to combat their intimidation. Calming himself with great difficulty, Jake stared directly at the camera, focusing on the blackened iris of the lens…

… and smiled.

Confused babbling erupted among his captors, swiftly escalating into arguments, the men apparently unsure of how to proceed. Obviously a reaction like Jake's wasn't something they'd counted on.

Somehow this eased Jake's fears slightly, and his smile became more genuine. Even when one of the captors approached him and threatened him with his horrifying knife, Jake locked his features and held the smile in place, refusing to let them daunt him.

Only one of the men appeared unmoved by his odd reaction. He stood, gripping his AK-47, staring at Jake, his unsettlingly dark eyes peering through the small slit in his headdress. There seemed something very knowing within that gaze. Jake found it nearly impossible to hold eye contact with the man while still maintaining his smile – almost as though the lie of his grin could find no ground against the scrutiny of the stare.

The argument finally ceased, and the cameraman stepped back into position, his camera up and aimed at Jake, recording once more. Both knife wielders moved to stand beside him, saying something Jake felt sure was at odds with the peaceful lilt of their silky Punjabi words.

Understanding suddenly blossomed within Jake. The hair on the back of his neck prickled and he felt the intense need to throw up.

This was it; they were about to kill him. It took all of his willpower not to break down.

A great sadness flowed over him – a sense of loss for many things. He'd wanted to achieve some amount of good in his life, leave some lasting reminder of himself for history, but instead his existence could best be described as thirty years of mediocrity. His first chance to achieve something of worth had met with failure. Sorrow hit Jake quite profoundly, and his smile turned to one of melancholy. He raised his eyes once more to the solitary figure, motionless within the maelstrom of activity around them. Jake nodded silently to the man, hoping to receive some tiny reaction from the one person present he sensed might not detest him for something he hadn't done. The figure remained motionless.

Wrenching Jake's head back, someone pressed a curved knife hard against his throat. The blade rasped slightly against the tiny bristles on his neck as the assassin lined up the killing thrust. In a moment his masked executioner would turn the tip of the knife in and plunge it down with all the vehemence he could muster, swiftly slicing through to Jake's carotid artery. Jake didn't want to think about would happen beyond that – the choked squealing from the training videos still haunted him. He closed his eyes, clenching his teeth, determined not to beg.

Gunfire erupted, shattering the tension, ringing out in the lonely valley.

Jake's eyes flared open, his panicked gaze searching. Five bodies lay on the dusty ground, the silent gunman wordlessly slipping the strap of his rifle over his shoulder and striding toward Jake. The gunman cut through his bonds with the knife that had only moments before been readying to kill him. The situation had changed so dramatically in the space of a couple of heartbeats that Jake was left unsure of whether he was now better off or not.

His bindings fell to the dusty ground, and Jake stepped free on tremulous legs, cautiously moving away from the post and turning to face his savior. The man promptly dropped the knife and raised his assault rifle to his shoulder once more, aiming it directly at Jake's head.

"Get down," said the disguised man calmly, his English perfect.

Jake dropped to the ground, and two more shots cracked out, the sound reverberating from the high canyon walls surrounding them. Twisting around, Jake saw the two bodies of the unmasked men who had dragged him from the shack.

The shack!

"We have to save my companion," insisted Jake, painfully aware as the words escaped his mouth that he was in no position to be making demands.

"Relax. Those two were the last here. You are safe… for now."

"What do you mean 'for now'?" asked Jake cautiously, bitterly aware of the assault rifle the man still held.

"You will never be truly safe," replied the man cryptically. "Not for the rest of your life."

He calmly turned away from Jake and strolled toward the wooden shack. Jake stooped to pick up the knife, carrying it surreptitiously as he followed the mysterious figure. His mind brimmed with questions, but he felt unsure of how to voice them to a man who thought nothing of killing his own companions.

As they approached the shack, Captain Chenoweth's yelling became audible, and Jake realized the SEAL captain would have heard the gunshots and not realized what was happening. Entering the timber shed, Jake strode swiftly to the dumbfounded captain and cut the ropes binding him. In a move of astonishing alacrity, the captain snatched the knife from Jake's hand and slammed their rescuer against the wall of the shack, the blade pressed hard against his throat.

"What's going on?" growled the SEAL over his shoulder to Jake.

"They were going to execute me, but this man saved my life. Let him go." The words were not a request, and Captain Chenoweth seemed to realize it. He reluctantly released the disguised man who, despite the intensity of the situation, seemed highly amused.

"Who are you?" demanded Captain Chenoweth.

The man stepped back. "Let me apologize, in the urgency of the situation I forgot my manners. My name is Aadesh Ranjan. I am not native to this land; these people employed me. As such, I am not your enemy. I'm from a small village in India called Bhinmal." He sounded extremely eloquent despite the poverty of their surroundings, his English perfect, affording only the hint of a slight accent. Aadesh might be an enigma, but he seemed a highly educated one.

"You're a long way from home, Aadesh," observed the captain, his visage tense, distrust still evident. Recalling that Aadesh's companions had slaughtered Captain Chenoweth's SEAL team members, Jake wondered how long the tenuous leash of honor would restrain the captain, if he thought this man might be responsible.

"Perhaps," said Aadesh, "but I have a feeling I am in the perfect place at the perfect time." His gaze rested on Jake, and he slowly pulled the scarf away from his face, exposing swarthy, clean-shaven features, his eyes so shadowy they appeared almost black. Jake felt himself unable to look away from the man's near-hypnotic stare, a gaze so profound it seemed to be burrowing deep within him, searching for something. But what?

"Are you two in love?" snapped Captain Chenoweth, glancing between Aadesh and Jake. "Would you like me to give you a moment?"

Jake snatched his gaze away, ignoring the comment. "What's going on, Aadesh? Why did you rescue us?"

"You would not believe me if I told you."

"How about you give it a go?" said Captain Chenoweth. "Prove to us you're not just a terrorist piece of filth."

The Indian's face suddenly became gravely serious, all traces of humbleness vanishing like early morning mist. His expression became set, and he glared at the SEAL captain. Jake was reminded in that moment of the coldness with which this man had killed his companions. Aadesh's gaze slipped back, resting again upon Jake, softening slightly, but still with an edge of steely determination beneath the surface.

"I was sent to find you," he said, his tone void of emotion.

"Find me? Who by?" asked Jake.

"Some would call it God. Others have different names."

Jake swiftly glanced to Captain Chenoweth, his own surprise mirrored in the SEAL's face.

"Uh huh," said Captain Chenoweth eventually. "God sent you to find us."

"Not you," replied Aadesh. "Him." The man pointed directly at Jake, his expression composed.

"I don't believe in God," said Jake hurriedly, the unwanted memories from his childhood breaking through time-hardened barriers. His adoptive father's sandpaper-like stubble against his cheek; whisky-sour breath preaching unremittingly about the King of Kings, the almighty God. He self-consciously gripped his elbows, hugging his chest.

"Your belief is irrelevant," said Aadesh. "You are the One reborn." Once more Jake glanced at Captain Chenoweth who merely raised his eyebrows and shrugged.

"The One?" asked Jake. "What's the One?"

Aadesh smiled at him the same way a parent would regard a child who had asked how the sun rose into the sky each day. "The Christ. You are the Christ reborn."

Nothing, no answer from this man they had just met, could have been further from Jake's expectations. "Riiight…. And God told you this." This conversation was beginning to feel unhinged. Aadesh's AK-47 still hung over his shoulder, and Jake had already seen how proficient the man could be with it.

"I was told you were coming – whether I was informed by the one called God or by another is debatable, but it has come to pass, and so it must be true."

"When were you told?" asked Captain Chenoweth.

"When I was five," he replied calmly.

Captain Chenoweth chuckled hollowly, though Jake noticed his knuckles whiten as his grip around the knife handle tightened.

"When you were five?" the captain repeated. "That's a long time to be waiting here."

"I have not been here the entire time. I have only been in this place for six months, and did not mean to become involved with what was going on in this country, but circumstances contrived to bring me to this place. My usual lifestyle is somewhat more… sedate. However, I became implicated with these people for a reason totally uninvolved with what the two of you have witnessed here today, and was on the verge of leaving them. Such fanatical zealotry is not for me. I am not a man who can live surrounded by the hate and lust these men harbored like virtues. Yet something forced me to stay, some inkling convinced me to remain here among filth when all good sense begged me to flee. I now see why." The stranger's eyes burned Jake with their power, their inky mystery piercing him like thorny teeth. Compulsion drove Jake to grip his elbows once more, but he fought off the urge, standing upright and facing down Aadesh's glare. The Pakistani seemed to smile slightly, though Jake could have been mistaken; the expression disappeared in an instant.

"And how did God convey this wondrous message?" asked the captain.

Aadesh smiled slightly, but the movement was one of reflection, and held little humor. "It was in a dream I had as a child. I do not remember the details, but the moment I saw your face, I knew you were the Christ reborn. There is no doubt."

Jake had remained silent throughout the entire exchange between Aadesh and Captain Chenoweth, trying to get his mind around what the man was saying. Was Aadesh a fanatic of some kind, latching onto him in some strange delusional hope of fulfilling a childhood dream? What he was saying sounded insane, but the Indian seemed otherwise perfectly rational. Then again, Jake had little experience with such people; Aadesh might be as crazy as Tom Cruise for all he knew. The man showed a total lack of remorse for his killings outside, so he might just be completely sociopathic.

"Aadesh, you've got the wrong guy. If you knew anything about me, you'd realize how laughable such a suggestion is," said Jake. "There's absolutely no way I could be Jesus."

"I never said you were Jesus," replied Aadesh calmly. "I said you were the Christ reborn. This is a different concept altogether."

"Care to explain that in a way that doesn't sound completely nuts?" snapped Captain Chenoweth.

Jake shot him a glance, and the SEAL's intensity subsided. Aadesh ignored the jibe.

"Jesus was a man – a person, just as you are. He died and sent out a message of hope to the entire world which has lasted for centuries. That was his task upon this planet, and he succeeded against great odds. Christ is in that message, but it has become warped and corrupted through the actions of mankind, as even the purest of all things are apt to do. *You* are the Christ reborn, a new message waiting to be shouted to a world on the brink of destruction. It does not mean you are the same man with an identical path before you, but it also means more than you can possibly envision at this time. Perhaps the end of time itself looms, or maybe you are merely here to see mankind through some slight darkness, I do not know. There is nothing predestined, but your coming was foretold in the stars. Your fate is inevitable."

Jake and Captain Chenoweth stood within the grimy, broken-down shack, their breaths rasping in the dead air. They each stared, absorbed in stunned silence at what Aadesh had just said.

"Christ reborn?" said Captain Chenoweth finally. "You're freakin' nuts!"

Aadesh shook his head sadly. "I said you wouldn't believe me."

"What do you think this means, Aadesh?" asked Jake carefully. "I mean, it's a pretty incredible thing to say, you have to admit that."

"Of course I know; I have lived with this my entire life and have fought against it with every fiber of my being. I have walked through paths of sin which have scorched my soul, perhaps beyond redemption, in the hopes that this fate would not befall me. And yet today you were brought here. I saw the look in your eyes as my companions prepared to slay you. At that moment, during that precise fragment in time, I knew the thing I had run from my entire life had finally caught up with me. There was no escaping it. I was put here, in a place I abhorred and among people I detested, to save you from death, and set you upon the course of your destiny. The rest lies in your hands. I cannot make you believe me if you choose not to, but I feel there will be other indicators along your journey which will show you the truth of what I have spoken here today. For now I must go and leave you to your fate. I hope one day we meet again, because that will mean you have accepted the truth and there shall be hope for the world once more."

Aadesh smiled and turned, striding from the shack. Jake and Captain Chenoweth watched him go, the captain exhaling an exasperated breath.

"Whoa! What the hell was that?"

"I'm not sure," replied Jake, "but he saved my life out there. They had me tied to a pole with that knife against my throat...." He swallowed heavily, still feeling the sharp edge against the skin of his neck, unable to finish the tale.

Captain Chenoweth nodded anyway. "The guy might be a nut, but thankfully he was a nut on our side," said the SEAL with a shrug.

The door to the shack smashed open with a thunderous crash, practically flying off the hinges. Captain Chenoweth instinctively thrust Jake behind him and stepped toward the giant figure, the execution knife held expertly in his right hand. The intruder froze.

"You two are alive, then?" growled the newcomer, standing motionless beneath a shaggy tower of hair. "What the hell is going on?"

"Fletcher?" asked Captain Chenoweth cautiously, struggling to see the figure clearly against the sunlight streaming in behind him.

"The one and only, laddie. Did you know there are a lot of dead bodies out there?"

Captain Chenoweth nodded. "Yeah, it's a long story. Where are the rest of your men?"

"None of my lads made it. Yours neither. They all got cut down in the ambush."

"How'd you get out?"

"When that concussion grenade went off, we got rushed by those lads with the hoods – the ones outside, the dead ones. I managed to fight my way clear with two of my guys, but everyone else got slaughtered. Some chased us, and my two lads copped it in the dark. I managed to get away, hid until they gave up looking, and then circled back. Must have dozed off up on the hill, because the next thing I heard gunfire, sounded like an AK-47. And now here I am. I should wear a fucking cape."

"You just came for the money, didn't you?" argued Captain Chenoweth.

"Of course," replied Fletcher, beaming a reckless grin. "Why else would I crawl into this flea-hovel?"

"Men died out there, and you're joking about it?" gasped Jake.

Fletcher glanced at Captain Chenoweth who shrugged. "He was just told he's Jesus."

"Huh?" The giant's face suddenly turned pale.

Captain Chenoweth laughed hollowly. "Some local guy – the one who killed those men outside – told him that he's the reincarnation of Christ or something."

Instead of laughing, Fletcher's face became deadly serious. "Are you sure he was a local man, or was he from India?"

"Actually, now you mention it he did say he was from India. How'd you know?"

"Will you two please just let this go?" interrupted Jake. "That guy was obviously deranged or something. But I'm glad he liked me, because I definitely wouldn't want him as an enemy. He killed those men –" Jake shuddered. "Let's just say it was terrifying, how proficient he was."

"Did you speak to this man?" asked Fletcher. "Of course you did; how else would you know he came from India?" Fletcher leaned heavily against a rickety bench table which groaned under his weight. The parts of his face not covered in hair were creased with concern, and he rubbed his weary eyes with a massive hand. "Did he tell you his name?" The question sounded tentative, as if Fletcher were afraid of the answer.

"Um... Aadesh," replied Jake. "Are you okay?"

Fletcher cursed under his breath, his eyes seeming to lose their focus, as though he stared at something far off in the distance. "Aadesh," he repeated softly. He shook his head, regret creasing his features. "This name means *the message* in their language; did you know that? Are you positive this was what the man who spoke to you called himself?"

Jake glanced at Captain Chenoweth who shrugged. "Yes. Who is he?"

"Aadesh is widely renowned as the most proficient mystic in these parts, among a people who have almost perfected such things to an art. Did he truly say you were Jesus, though?"

"He said Jake was the Christ reborn," said Captain Chenoweth. "In fact, he got pretty upset when I referred to him as Jesus; something about not being the man, but the message. You're not going to tell me you believe this mumbo-jumbo are you?"

"I'm not sure, lad," replied Fletcher softly, and Jake noticed his knuckles whitening where he gripped the edge of the bench.

"What do you mean?"

"Was Aadesh actually *with* the guys who were going to execute you, or did he come into the scene late?"

"He was there the whole time," said Jake. "What's going on?"

Fletcher stared hard at Jake, his gaze piercing. "That man, Aadesh, may or may not be a psychic; I don't really know. But I met him a while back, and he scared the shit out of me."

"How so?" asked Jake.

"He knew my name, which might not seem so weird to you. A man of my proportions in the game I play gets recognized easily enough. But this was different – he knew my *first* name, something nobody on this continent knows. Hell, I can barely remember the damn thing!"

"What is it?" asked Captain Chenoweth.

"None of your fucking business," replied Fletcher swiftly.

Not willing to let the conversation slip off track, Jake persisted. "There must have been more to it than that. A man in your profession has surely seen a lot of what this world has to offer; surprises would be rare. What else did he say that scared you?"

For a moment, Jake thought Fletcher would refuse to answer him, but finally the gigantic Scot submitted.

"He told me I was going to die protecting Christ."

For such a large man, his voice became suddenly very small, like a child's. All his bravado fled for the briefest of instances, and the look upon Fletcher's face was one of abject terror.

"I laughed at him, of course. I mean, what else could I do against something so ridiculous? But he wasn't joking, and something in his eyes told me he wasn't lying. I've never felt like that before and hopefully never will again. It was like he could stare into my soul, and he made no judgment of what he saw there."

Captain Chenoweth cursed. "So Aadesh, the psycho who just single-handedly slaughtered seven killers right outside that door, is some kind of a prophet, is that what you're saying?"

"I dunno," replied Fletcher honestly. "But the guy put the heebie-jeebies into me, and nobody else has done that for... well... I don't know how long."

"Can you hear what you're saying? He killed those guys outside like they were nothing – does that sound like a holy man to you? Of course it doesn't. The guy's insane, and he somehow found out your real name; maybe he guessed it, maybe he found your Facebook page

– I don't know. But to say that the senior advisor here is Jesus Christ reborn is several steps past ridiculous, don't you agree?"

Fletcher shrugged reluctantly. "I guess," he mumbled.

"You're not going to die protecting 'Christ' – unless by Christ he meant *my* holy ass!" Captain Chenoweth chuckled.

Fletcher forced a smile, but still looked far from convinced. He turned toward Jake, and his grin faltered slightly before slipping into place once more, perhaps somewhat more strained now. Jake smiled in return, certain his own terror was hidden as badly as Fletcher's.

If anyone could understand what Fletcher meant it was Jake. He'd seen the same look the hairy mercenary had described, and the piercing gaze of the Indian had shaken Jake in a way he could never explain. As he stared at Fletcher, the two seemed to exchange some unspoken acknowledgment.

The memory of what Aadesh had told him whispered in Jake's soul like a tiny warning, a flickering flame, a precursor of risks yet to come. He understood what Fletcher was talking about when he spoke of the commitment in the man's eyes, and try as he might, Jake couldn't help feeling that his feet had just stepped onto a path not of his choosing.

\*\*\*

The negotiations in Karachi proceeded much smoother than anyone expected. Jake managed to bring the opposing parties together, helping them recognize their true enemy was not the United States, but General Khalili. He did not resolve the situation completely and at times feared the task might prove too onerous, but he managed to prevent things from deteriorating into civil war until peacekeeping troops arrived, and the boiling situation in the country gradually reduced to a simmer.

"Well done, Mr. Hope," the Secretary General had congratulated him, shaking his hand. He'd already been praised by the Director of the CIA along with various other US Government officials, but this was the conversation he'd been looking forward to most. "You managed the situation incredibly well, far exceeding many expectations. Now, about this incident involving the SEAL team, what happened there?"

Jake swiftly explained what had occurred, hazing over the part following their rescue by Aadesh, especially the subsequent conversation. The last thing he wanted was for the United Nations Security Council to think he'd lost his mind. The fact he'd received praise from the Secretary General himself illustrated how well they considered he'd done on his mission, and he didn't want to diminish anyone's opinion now.

"There were some who thought you too inexperienced to send into a situation so volatile on your own, but it was vital we intervene before things escalated. Pakistan is a nuclear power, after all, and the threat of things getting out of control was too great to be ignored."

"Yes, sir," replied Jake. "I just feel bad about the men who died."

"Of course you do, but don't worry about it; we'll put a shine on things, so you don't need to worry about any backlash from your decisions. They'll be declared heroes in the media. Sometimes tough choices have to be made, and people die as a result. I'm certain it's not your fault, and we'll make sure the world knows it, too."

Jake stood silent, momentarily stunned and unable to believe the callousness of the comment. "Sir, I meant it's a shame they're dead. Those men died trying to protect me, helping to ensure my mission succeeded. I don't care about looking bad in the face of that, and I'm saddened you'd think I would."

"It's the nature of the world we live in, Mr. Hope," replied the Secretary General, his tone unwavering. "Every action can see our image shine or dull, depending on how the media portrays our actions. You might do the most heroic thing imaginable, and yet still look like a fool if they choose to spin it so. Representing the UN is more than just doing the best job possible, you also have to understand what our real priorities are. Sometimes it's more important to *look* like we care, than actually caring. You will go far in our organization, Mr. Hope, but you need to remember that sometimes we have to negotiate with the Devil for the greater good to prevail."

Stomach lurching, Jake excused himself, feeling as though his world had just flipped. For three years he'd been striving to rise through the ranks of the United Nations, but now it seemed like he'd stepped through the mirror, viewing things from the other side, and the scene took on a putrid taint. He'd always thought the UN represented good guys in a world full of greed, but their conversation, despite its praise, had opened Jake's eyes to reality: they were caught up in politics, just like everyone else. He was living a lie.

What the hell was he supposed to do now? He loved the work he did within the UN, but for too long he'd blinded himself, shutting out the truth because he hadn't wanted to see it. The conversation with the Secretary General shattered any illusions Jake still held, and all he had left was a choice. Did he stay with the United Nations, doing a job which could see him do a lot of good in the world, but ultimately seemed based on a lie, or did he leave and potentially do nothing of worth for the rest of his life?

Upon arriving in Karachi, Captain Chenoweth had been whisked away for debriefing without even a farewell, and Fletcher had disappeared into the city along with his payment. But Jake couldn't forget the parting look the Scottish mercenary had thrown him: a mixture of fear and regret. Did the man truly believe what he'd been told? Instinct told Jake he did.

The prophetic words of Aadesh hung over him, weighing heavier with every day that passed.

The claims the man had made seemed ridiculous, beyond anything credible, but a tiny voice within Jake whispered about how much good he'd be able to achieve if such a thing were true. How much pain could he alleviate if he truly were the one Aadesh had claimed?

Jake shook the thought away. Of all the people on Earth, he would be the last one chosen for the role Aadesh had prophesied. The memories he had buried were but the edge of the nightmare that formed his youth. Nothing glorious could happen to him, he didn't deserve it....

Gripping his elbows forcefully, Jake pushed away his shame. Wishful thinking was something he avoided at all costs; it became a train of thought which led down a pathway to hopelessness. Long ago he'd learned to deal in realities, things he could use and manipulate in order to achieve an outcome he desired. The daydream of what Aadesh had promised was something he simply couldn't allow himself to dwell upon.

And, of course, there was also the reality of the situation. While such a thing might open some doors for Jake, if he came out making bold claims of being Christ-reborn, he'd find himself swiftly dismissed as utterly insane! The only people who would believe and follow him would be fanatical nuts, further reducing his credibility.

Shaking his head, Jake grinned at the mere notion he was considering something so absurd. He needed to stick to reality, and the reality of his current situation sucked. He'd thought he was working for a group that acted for the betterment of humanity, when in reality it seemed more concerned with its own ends than the people it employed. The Secretary General's reaction to the deaths of the SEAL team members, along with the unknown mercenaries, was more a response to an inconvenience, rather than something truly tragic. Jake could argue that the man had larger issues on his mind than the life and death of soldiers, but the end result was still the same: he simply hadn't cared.

How could Jake, a man driven to leave some mark of good upon the planet, follow the mandates of the United Nations when he'd just glimpsed the truth behind it all? It seemed a lie, a fabrication, but what else could he do? The problems of the world were immense, and he was just a man. At least with the UN behind him he had some sort of power with which to act. Look at what he'd accomplished in Pakistan; there was no doubt he'd saved lives through his actions.

Was it worth promoting a lie in order to see out the greater good? Could he continue his career within the United Nations knowing what the Secretary General truly thought? Were such feelings mirrored throughout the organization, with only Jake on the outside, like some ignorant schoolboy?

Sighing as he sat on the edge of the bed, the empty hotel room cold to his misgivings, a part of Jake wished for nothing more than to return to the naivety he'd once held. His ambitions before this mission seemed a lifetime ago, and he felt like he'd stepped out of childhood into the maturity and knowledge of adulthood in mere days.

And he wasn't sure he liked it.

## -CHAPTER 2-
# ABADDON

"Mister Hope, I certainly hope you know what the hell you're doing."

Jake nodded silently, offering what he imagined to be a reassuring smile. The truth was, Jake really had no idea what was going on, nor did he have any kind of expertise for what he was supposed to be doing, but he figured bluffing his way through was the best option for the time being. Brought in as a consultant for the Red Cross to organize the rebuilding of several villages in Northern Uganda, along with distribution and management of first aid supplies and food packages, the immensity of the task terrified him, and several times he didn't trust himself to talk for fear of merely squeaking.

It spoke volumes about the lack of manpower within the Red Cross that he was here unsupervised, and Jake's nervousness had peaked at an all-time high. Part of the reason such trust had been placed upon him was the stellar report they'd received regarding his work in Pakistan – his final mission with the United Nations. Apparently a personal endorsement from the secretary general went a long way. As such, the Red Cross held few qualms about sending Jake off in charge of a mission which would normally be run by a senior member of the organization. The pressure increased constantly as he began to sense how many people were actually depending on him.

It wasn't just the fact he was in the middle of war-torn Northern Uganda, based a few miles outside a town called Pader, but he was also representing the Red Cross, one of the largest relief organizations in the world. Granted, some might call it a step down from his previous position, but after glimpsing the political shades at work behind the scenes within the Security Council, Jake felt hopeful for this new course in his life.

Much like the UN, the Red Cross worked as an international society designed to assist humanity at every turn, having been around since midway through the nineteenth century. Their mandate to provide aid in all parts of the world where conflict existed, without bias or favoritism, truly appealed to Jake's yearning toward a more selfless calling. The organization seemed less interested in politics and more concerned with helping people.

And right now that meant Northern Uganda.

The war had been raging in Northern Uganda for nearly twenty years, and despite several ceasefires, no lasting peace had ever been established. Initially, Jake had been intrigued with the idea of somehow aiding peace in the area, but he'd soon discarded the notion completely. He was here to help the people hurt in the conflict, not become involved with whatever malevolence had caused such prolonged bloodshed.

Jake glanced around the compound, taking in the seven-foot-high chain-link fences surrounding the dozen or so single-story buildings, most either barracks or medical structures. The eighteen foreign volunteers included four doctors, six nurses and a variety of specialists chosen for skills specifically required in the area. The ground between the canvas and metal frame structures was predominantly hard-packed earth, stamped down by decades of local foot traffic, but sparse clumps of grass ringed the low, spiny acacias edging the camp, adding welcome touches of green and yellow to the sandy countryside.

The thing which had struck Jake most about this land was the capacity of its inhabitants to smile. The dark skin of the locals contrasted with their vibrantly white smiles, and from what Jake had learned of the horrors being visited upon the country, this beauty was a miracle in itself. How could such wonder be present amid so much carnage? Jake couldn't imagine the strength of will required not to be cowed by the daily terrors these people endured, but surely if they could still smile, some hope must remain.

"What was your name again?" Jake asked the man who had spoken to him.

"I'm Phillips. Steven Phillips," replied a crisp British accent.

Phillips was a short, slender man, wearing thin-rimmed circular glasses beneath his creased and tired-looking brow. Jake's initial impression of Phillips had been that the man was arrogant, but on reflection, perhaps he might simply be so tired as to lack the energy for anything beyond short, clipped answers. Phillips's receding hairline shone with sweat, which trickled down over his wrinkled forehead, occasionally slipping past the frames of his glasses, dripping into his heavily-bagged, eyes which currently fixed on Jake's left cheek.

"It's not a tattoo," said Jake, forestalling the impending question. "It's a birthmark."

"Oh! Sorry if I was staring, it's just that it looks so much like –"

"Yeah, I know. What do you need me to do first, Phillips?" asked Jake.

The small man gave him a strained smile. "Stop this pointless war; can you do that? I'm sick of them bringing in the bodies of children forced to fight for the LRA, or the ones simply caught in the crossfire."

"I was quickly briefed on the LRA before I left," said Jake, frowning slightly, "but what can you tell me about them?"

"The *Lord's Resistance Army*," began Phillips, as though reciting from a textbook. "They're led by the notorious Joseph Kony, currently one of the top ten most-wanted men on the face of the planet. Kony claimed he wanted to unite the country under the Ten Commandments laid out in the Bible, but the practices of the LRA have included such things as child slavery and prostitution – hardly the actions of the holy figure Kony tries to portray himself as. It's widely speculated he wants to completely destroy the Acholi people – an ethnic group centered in this region."

"How do the LRA get away with such things?" asked Jake.

Phillips shrugged. "Might is right. Like anywhere else in the world, the strongest man makes all the rules, and right now Kony holds that strength, and has for a very long time."

"But why can't the army defeat him?"

"They've been trying, but whenever they get close, Kony and his troops merely retreat across the border into Sudan, where the LRA have their rear bases, and the Ugandan army cannot follow without risking war with Sudan. In 2002 they came close to catching them, when Sudan allowed the army to cross the border in pursuit, but had to retreat when the LRA increased their attacks back in Uganda behind them. Corruption is abundant throughout Uganda's army, and organization among their ranks is almost non-existent."

"Well, I don't think I can stop the war," said Jake. "Not yet, anyway," he added with a grin. "How about we have a look through your supplies and get a full list of what we have to work with before continuing."

"Sounds like fun," muttered Phillips. "How about —"

A sodden impact made Jake look around, wondering if somebody had just slapped the ground with a wet mop. It wasn't until Phillips lurched sideways and collapsed in a heap that Jake saw the small hole in his right temple and the gaping space where the left side of his skull had been only moments before. The thin-rimmed circular glasses lay askew on his demolished face, his empty gaze now peering at nothing.

Jake gaped at the body dumbly, unable to fully register what had just happened. In a heartbeat which felt like a lifetime he stood frozen, shaken to his core, staring at a corpse which had, just a moment beforehand, been a walking, breathing human being.

And now he was gone: just like that.

The sound of gunfire exploded around the camp, and Jake snapped out of his trance. Shouting sounded, and several troops, many sporting Rastafarian dreadlocks, some dressed in jungle camouflage, and all carrying weapons, rushed into the Red Cross encampment. The wire gates had been left open following a supply delivery, and the one thing designed to keep them safe had ultimately failed. There seemed no discrimination in the carnage; volunteers and villagers alike fell before the onslaught of gunfire.

Jake ran directly toward the attackers, certain they'd made some sort of mistake. No one would attack a Red Cross camp, unless…

… unless they were after the drugs and medical supplies stored here.

Freezing in his tracks, Jake swiftly ducked behind a building which offered him no real protection other than concealment. His shoulder rasped against the canvas wall as he fought to gather his thoughts, silently reprimanding himself for his stupidity – running directly toward frenzied gunfire was definitely not the secret to a long and healthy life. Even here, cowering behind a wall with as much shielding power as a paper napkin, it was likely he'd soon be just as dead as Phillips.

Several explosions reverberated from the opposite side of the camp. Jake's mind worked furiously. He needed to figure out a way to stop these men from attacking; to capture their attention and hold it, without getting killed, for just long enough to reason with them.

Bullets smacked into the dirt on the path just beyond where Jake hid, and he knew he couldn't stay where he was for much longer. He needed to make a decision before he ended up caught – or dead. Every second he remained here saw more people slain. He had to do something.

Jake made his choice.

Holding his hands high in the air to show he held no weapons, Jake stepped out from behind the wall, into full view of those assembled. There was no turning back now – if they opened fire, his former hiding spot would be useless; their bullets would tear it to shreds in seconds. The glare from the sun hit Jake's eyes, and he squinted against it, trying to make out who the leader of the group might be, but he couldn't get a clear view.

Excited yelling rose, as several of the attackers ran toward him. One of them punched him fully in the face, a crunch emanating from his nose; stars lit up in front of Jake's eyes. He stumbled, dropping to one knee, but quickly rising, unwilling to show weakness. Blood gushed down his lower face from his broken nose, but Jake staggered forward toward the jeering men.

The glare subsided momentarily just as a roofless, black jeep rumbled through the front gates of the compound. Pictures from his pre-deployment briefing flashed through Jake's mind. The image of the jeep had been burned into his memory, char-black with its mounted M-60 pointing out like a finger of death. The sun reflected brightly from the windshield, a lone figure lurking in the passenger seat, a malicious grin flashing out beyond the glass. The reflection made identification impossible, but Jake feared he knew exactly who that grin belonged to.

Surrounded by about twenty rebels, Jake couldn't flee, couldn't hide. He could only stand and stare, horrified, as the vehicle skidded to a halt, the barrel of the machine gun peering intently at him like a horrific cyclopean eye. For a moment, Jake had the impression it would open fire, bullets shredding him, blowing him from the face of the Earth for the simple effrontery of not cowering. Apparently the rebels around him feared the same thing, edging away and leaving Jake standing alone in the center of a wide horseshoe. No one stood behind him, and he could have tried to flee that way, but his legs refused to move.

The engine abruptly cut, and deathly silence filled the camp, broken only by occasional echoes of distant gunfire and screams for mercy. In that instant, Jake's senses seemed more intense, as though in knowing that death drew close, they wanted to experience every last ounce of life possible. He could suddenly feel the cool breeze upon his face, smell the light dust in the air, and see every tiny fleck of death surrounding him.

The surprise attack had done exactly what it was designed to do: inspire mute terror. The people within the Red Cross medical compound – both foreign volunteers like himself and locals giving aid or seeking it – had been cut down mercilessly. Bodies sprawled everywhere, and Jake felt tears running down his face, intermixing with the blood from his shattered nose. He spied a small boy, no more than five years old, blood congealing around a deep, hacking gash in his neck, his eyes lifeless.

A lone LRA rebel casually leaned against a nearby shed, cigarette dangling from weathered lips, his machete dripping blood and gore. Staring up into the man's face, Jake knew this was the unknown child's killer. The smile said it all, both evil and mocking, as though he could taste Jake's death on the breeze and yearned for it.

Jake returned his gaze to the boy's limp body once more, silently lamenting the loss of someone so guiltless. War always claimed innocent victims, and from what he'd been told this conflict was darker than most, but to see the evidence with his own eyes proved almost more than Jake could bear.

Rage suffused him, forcing all fear aside. The killer's mocking grin morphed in his mind, becoming the face from his memories: the face of the Man. Jake roared and charged at the murderer, no plan except to exact some sort of revenge for the child now dead at his whim.

He made it two feet.

One of the militia men darted forward, his rifle butt smashing into Jake's gut, sending him collapsing to the ground, choking and retching. Hands roughly gripped his upper arms and hauled him to his feet once more. Hanging limply, he waited until his gasping breath returned to normal against the guffawing of those around him. He shook his arms loose from those holding him. They seemed to feel no need to restrain him. In this world of killers, he stood powerless.

Stiffening his resolve, Jake wiped the already drying tears from his face. Blood from his shattered nose smeared across his cheeks, but he resolutely refused to face the director of such a massacre with tears streaming down his cheeks. The man he suspected watched from the Jeep would not intimidate Jake, with his talk of reshaping the country according to the scriptures of God. If such a God existed who would stand by while such horror occurred, Jake wanted nothing to do with it; he would rather cease to exist than join such a pathetic deity. His anger helped quell the shaking in his hands, and Jake turned his hollow gaze back to the jeep once more.

The door creaked as it swung open, and Jake's heart began to pound, though he fought hard to suppress any change in his expression. A lanky figure emerged, features obscured by a camouflage-mottled cap as he stepped lightly to the dusty ground. But Jake knew who this would be. Only one man was allowed to travel in that Jeep. Only one man wore the uniform striding toward him.

The head rose up –

And Jake's blue eyes stared into a face of horror.

Joseph Kony grinned wickedly, like a soldier of the apocalypse. Beneath the cap swirled a nightmare. It was as though a dark, oily liquid, mixed with blood, floated mist-like above the skin – flesh which appeared melted by an explosion or massive inferno. There was nothing even remotely human about it. The figure had no ears. Where the nose should have been, a jagged chunk of skin covered two vertical slit-like holes. The mouth opened in a ragged gash carved in the lower portion of the visage, broken and shattered teeth poking from split and diseased gums. And yet the eyes that stared back at him were as clear and blue as a summer sky. What drifted within that gaze, however, made Jake tremble with terror, wanting nothing more than to flee from such a stare. Still, he held himself firm, staring back, envisioning his own approaching death with each and every moment that passed.

And then, for no reason at all, Jake smiled.

Joseph Kony seemed to pause mid-stride before continuing forward. Jake glanced at Kony's hands and saw they too were coated in the strange, dark, viscous liquid which seemed to ebb and flow without dripping, their skin charred and raw, the fingers ending in ghastly black claws.

Glancing back at the eyes – those terrifyingly beautiful blue orbs beaming from within the putrid nest – Jake suddenly realized there was no way the figure before him could be human. This wasn't merely a disguise or grievous injury Kony bore, it was something else entirely.

"Who is this meat-sack that dares smile at me?" snarled Kony. His perfect English rose accent-free, the words dripping with malice so intense Jake had to devote all of his willpower not to drop his gaze.

One of the rebels murmured something Jake couldn't understand, and Kony grinned coldly, his gaze never shifting, its hold on Jake relentless. "This man says you bleed like a young girl. I think he is right. I wonder if your pathetic smile will remain if we break you the same way we break the spirits of the children chosen to serve God."

"And which God would that be?" asked Jake, thankful his voice did not shake.

"Why, the same God who influences us every day, of course! The Alpha and the Omega, the beginning and end of all things."

"And He tells you to rape children?"

Kony snarled, his horrific visage twisting to expose his rotting gums. In that moment, Jake realized none of the militia around him recognized what it was they served. Not a single one of them looked upon Kony as anything other than a man – albeit a man who demanded their utmost loyalty and respect. Jake wondered what it was he was dealing with, and why only he could see Kony as he did.

"The children must be taught to obey; there can be no other way. If they do not comply with my word, then they must be broken upon the spear. The Holy Spirit tells me this is the Truth and the Word, and I must obey," hissed Kony, his blackened tongue flicking out, split down the middle like that of a snake.

"What the hell *are* you?" asked Jake, so softly only Kony could hear him.

Joseph Kony's azure eyes narrowed. "What do you mean?"

"I see you as a monster," replied Jake. "You bear the face of a demon, but I can tell that these men who follow you, depraved though they are, can't see you the same way I do. So, what in God's name are you?"

At Jake's mention of God, Kony flinched slightly. This confused Jake because the man had uttered the name only moments beforehand without a problem. Perhaps it wasn't the name, but the way it was referenced that mattered. By applying it as… what? How had he applied it? Was it a command?

"In the name of God I command you to tell me who you are," snarled Jake.

Kony cringed, covering his face with his clawed hands and mewling like an injured cat. Jake's confidence soared while the men around them looked on curiously. The mewling turned to a kind of crying, and Jake took a step closer, intending to make his demand once more, when the crying suddenly snapped to laughter.

Joseph Kony's right hand shot out and gripped Jake by the throat, his strength so intense Jake was lifted completely off the ground. He hung there, breathless, battling helplessly against the steely grip. Kony's laughter cackled out, maniacal and cold.

"I do not know how you managed to see through my disguise," Kony hissed into his ear, "but you can rest assured it will be the last thing you see in your wretched life. You cannot call upon the power of a god you despise, human, and I can taste your contempt for Him in every word you utter. Say hello to God when you finally see Him, and tell Him that I, Abaddon, enjoy corrupting His name. It no longer holds power in this dominion. His fallen seraphs will consume this world He loves so dearly, and we will leave His precious mortals in our wake as ash upon the breeze. We are all here now, a veritable army of corrupt angels, and God cannot touch us without destroying this realm He watches over so dotingly."

The world spun as Jake choked and fought against the immutable strength of the self-proclaimed fallen angel. He barely heard Kony – or was it now Abaddon? – call out to one of his men. A pistol found its way into Abaddon's left hand and without preamble he pressed the muzzle against Jake's chest.

Jake never heard the gunshot, never sensed his body falling limply to the ground, his lifeblood pouring from the hole in his chest.

He felt nothing – he was gone.

-CHAPTER 3-
# SEARCHING FOR ANSWERS

The slow, rhythmic beep began as something minor – a nagging annoyance easily blotted out. Through its persistence, however, the sound drove deeper into his mind like the steady drip, drip, drip of a Chinese water-torture device, and soon Jake became aware of thoughts swimming around within the murkiness of his mind.

Where was he?

He'd have to open his eyes to find out, and Jake found himself intensely reluctant to leave the peace of oblivion.

*Beep.... Beep.... Beep....*

Drip.... Drip.... Drip....

Against his will, Jake felt himself drawing closer to the world, and though he might fight against it, he knew it was futile. He would wake up whether he liked it or not.

The annoyance of the beeping was soon joined by an intense burning pain in his chest, one which seemed to radiate out from a single, tiny point. Like rising through an oil-slicked ocean toward a blazing surface, the closer Jake drew to consciousness the more painful it became.

Finally crashing through the surface of awareness, he heaved in a huge gulp of air, and agony erupted through him. An inferno of suffering engulfed his chest, flaring out from his ribcage to the very tips of his fingers.

What the hell had been done to him?

Grasping and scraping at jagged memories, recollections drifted barely beyond his grasp. Jake struggled on, fighting to recall what had occurred.

Excited shouts sounded, and he heard feet running into the room. In a flood, Jake suddenly remembered – *everything*.

Like Dorothy's house landing atop the Wicked Witch of the East at the start of The Wizard of Oz, the memories fell heavily, their pressure compressing Jake's psyche, threatening to crush him completely with their force. Unprepared for the sheer power of the recollections, he gasped as every moment of his life replayed in the space of milliseconds, concluding with his shooting by Joseph Kony in Northern Uganda.

Jake tried to sit up in the bed, but gentle hands gripped his shoulders and pushed him back down. A kindly face hovered above him, shining a light into his eyes and murmuring something Jake couldn't quite understand. Shaking the remaining fog from his mind, his hearing finally kicked in.

"– lucky to be alive, Mister Hope," the man was saying, his accent British.

"Whe – where am I?" croaked Jake, his throat raw.

"You're in hospital, Mister Hope."

"Call me Jake."

"Well, Jake, you're in London – London Bridge Hospital to be precise. I'm Doctor Harold Scarski, the cardiac surgeon who operated on you."

"How did I get here? I was in…." The memory of the gunshot and the demonic eyes flashed through Jake's mind once more. He swallowed heavily. "I was in Northern Uganda."

"Yes. You were flown here once they stabilized you enough for travel. If they hadn't done so you would have died. As it was, we almost lost you three times on the operating table. The removal of the bullet from your spine was performed by another surgeon, and I am told you came perilously close to permanent paralysis, but at this time it seems you have avoided any major damage to your spinal cord. I was in charge of the surgery on your heart –"

"My *heart*? He shot me through the heart?"

"Not directly," replied the Doctor, "but your attackers must have thought you were dead. I'm told they left your body in the Red Cross compound when the Ugandan army unexpectedly arrived, and they were forced to flee. You're extremely lucky to be alive, Mr. Hope. Your survival is due to the fact they shot you *within* the Red Cross camp. You were treated on scene by a doctor who returned to the compound once the LRA were driven off. With help from some local medics, they stabilized your vitals and transported you to the closest hospital. Your body shut down completely, and you've been in a coma for the last two weeks. You'll probably feel immensely weak for a while, but I expect eventually you'll make a full recovery."

Jake pondered the doctor's words, digesting the information he had imparted. "How many people were killed? In the Red Cross camp, I mean."

"I have no idea. Do you want me to find out?"

Jake shook his head slightly, suddenly realizing he didn't really want to know. "What about Kony – Joseph Kony? He's the one who attacked us. The one who…." Jake trailed off, unable as yet to discuss that horrific moment when the gun had gone off, and his life had fled. "Did they catch him?"

"I don't believe so. As far as I know they drove the LRA out of the area, but the Ugandan army didn't have the manpower to pursue them very far."

"Thank you, Doctor," said Jake. "Thank you for saving my life."

Doctor Scarski smiled gently. "That's my job, Jake." He stared at Jake's face momentarily. "That's a very interesting birthmark you have there. I've never seen one so clearly shaped. At first I thought it was a tattoo of a teardrop."

Jake smiled wanly. "I get that a lot." The doctor turned to leave. "Before you go, can you do me a favor?"

Doctor Skarski turned back, his gaze concerned. "What's that?"

"Can you turn off that damn beeping?"

The doctor's polite laughter lifted Jake's mood slightly, but not enough to make him forget those eyes, and the name which had accompanied them.

Abaddon.

***

"Thank goodness for Google," muttered Jake, tapping in his search and pressing [ENTER].

The entire page filled with references to the name Abaddon, and dread surged up within him. Scanning through the list of websites, Jake's worst fears slowly came to the fore. The first web entry called Abaddon 'The Destroyer'. That really didn't sound too promising – not that Jake expected him to be called 'The Flower Lover' or anything, but something less ominous would have been preferable.

Clicking on the link, Jake discovered that Abaddon had been one of the angels cast out of Heaven when Lucifer attempted to overthrow God. One thing seemed quite clear from Jake's early research: Abaddon was truly one of the Devil's most dangerous allies, and his cruelty seemed boundless.

Sitting silently in his own study, the light from the monitor illuminating his cheeks, Jake suddenly realized he was at an impasse. Researching these things resurrected the image of his adoptive father's Bible, the small, leather-bound book searing brightly in his memory. He could even see the small bourbon stain across the front cover where the Man's glass had tipped onto his lap one night when he'd passed out.

If Jake were to accept that Abaddon truly was one of the Fallen, the existence of angels must also be acknowledged. And if angels were real….

God must exist.

The Man had been right.

Jake's stomach turned and bile filled his mouth. Rushing to the bathroom, he ran the tap in the sink, holding his face above it, ready to heave, but nothing erupted. After several minutes, his stomach settled. He splashed water over his face, feeling the heat of his skin, and wishing he could shed tears for the things he fought against remembering. None came. He'd become too proficient at guarding such emotions.

Lifting his gaze to the mirror above the sink, Jake stared at his reflection. His eyes retained the same weakness of the boy he had once been. With no tears forthcoming he satisfied himself by grimacing.

He had no choice. He'd have to let go of the past... or try to.

Returning to the computer he dropped into his chair, staring insensibly at the screen, forcing himself to continue searching for something, anything, which might be of use.

Most of the other entries seemed like meaningless nonsense, written by idiots with nothing better to do than invent stories in an attempt to make themselves sound cool. The only other website of worth that he discovered contained a biblical reference to Abaddon from the Book of Revelations:

*"And they had a king over them, the angel of the bottomless pit, whose name in the Hebrew tongue is Abaddon, but in the Greek tongue hath name Apollyon."*

"What the hell does that even mean?" muttered Jake.

Typing in another search, this time Jake sought the chapter and verse of the biblical reference he had just seen: Revelations, chapter 9, verse 11. As the results popped onto the screen, something clicked within Jake's mind.

Chapter 9.

Verse 11.

9/11.

The coincidence seemed huge. The fact that the reference from the Bible led back to the date of the most horrific terrorist attack America had ever seen left Jake's mind reeling. Such a thought was ridiculous, and yet....

Jake stared at the monitor for an age, rereading the passage from the Bible over and over, as though doing so might reveal some deep inner meaning. But they were only words written by men during a much more superstitious time. They held no prophecy, no great forecast.

Biting his lip in frustration, Jake cleared the search. Down that road lay the path of conspiracy theorists, blaming the Muppets for the assassination of JFK, and claiming the moon was made of Swiss cheese and didn't actually exist. Anything could be linked to anything if you chose to believe it.

Determined not to give up yet, Jake continued hunting for references to the name Abaddon, finding several by teenage gamer geeks on their blogs and other such inane stuff, but nothing else of real worth. Frustrated after hours of searching, with head pounding and eyes stinging, he admitted defeat. Whatever was going on, he wouldn't unveil its secrets right now, not with Google as his only assistant.

The enormity of the idea that the thing he'd faced in Northern Uganda, the creature posing as Joseph Kony, was some sort of demon – one of the Fallen cast out of Heaven – proved too much for him.

He recalled Aadesh's prophecy back in Pakistan all that time ago. How long had it been now? It seemed like a lifetime. The promise of Jake's foretold destiny threatened to flow up through his memories, but he forced the idea away. Why was he being surrounded by such nonsense? What was happening to him? The world seemed to be spiraling into madness, insane fantasies threatening to overwhelm his life at every turn. He wanted the rational world to return: where trees were green, the sky was blue, water was wet, and fallen angels didn't tread the Earth.

Pushing his chair back from the computer, Jake stood, stretched his arms above his head, and winced. He'd been home in Seattle for over a month now, following many months of rehabilitation in the London hospital, but the wound in his chest still ached.

Glancing around his single-bedroom apartment, its only window staring directly onto the wall of another building, Jake grimaced. Towers of plates encircled the sink, rising like irregular ceramic columns surrounding a stainless-steel pond. Worn clothing lay in mounds at assorted locations about the room. Two overstuffed trash bags were beginning to reek. He'd really have to do some cleaning soon; but not today. He just couldn't seem to get motivated enough to do the normal household chores, not with something like Abaddon hanging over his head. The memory of his near-death haunted Jake, gnawing at his mind like a rat at electrical wiring, and he feared he might blink out at any moment if he didn't find a solution.

But then again it could have been worse. Not many people survived getting shot point-blank in the chest, left the hospital in just a few months, and then found themselves Googling demons in hopes of avoiding a breakdown for fear of what might be lurking out there.

Somehow, Jake sensed part of himself would have preferred lying crippled in hospital rather than having to face the reality of what had happened... and was still happening. Replaying the events surrounding Joseph Kony over and over in his memory, he knew his mind hadn't cracked yet. Kony's disguise had evaporated under his scrutiny, and Jake had witnessed the monster hiding beneath the façade, heard the words it had uttered. The man was not actually a man; Kony was some kind of demon, a self-proclaimed member of the Fallen. When combined with the strange prediction from the allegedly prophetic man named Aadesh....

It couldn't just be coincidence, could it?

It became harder and harder for Jake to discern what was real and what wasn't. For a time he'd contemplated the possibility that he had simply imagined Kony's appearance – there really was no way the man could look like that, was there? And why had nobody else noticed?

The doctors were certain Jake hadn't suffered any sort of brain damage, so the chances his memories had been distorted were slim. And while he had suffered a traumatic experience, Post Traumatic Stress Disorder appeared unlikely, especially after so many grueling hours speaking with the therapist in London as part of his rehabilitation. He hadn't mentioned Kony's threats or monstrous visage to the shrink, mainly because he didn't want to be locked away in a padded room wearing a nice jacket that always gave him hugs.

Still, he doubted himself. Perhaps his childhood was returning to traumatize him yet again, his mind playing tricks on his vision, the glare somehow combining to affect what he'd seen that day. The miasma may have been something else – Jake didn't know what, but perhaps such phenomena existed around the planet. But none of this could alter the words uttered, nor could it explain the power it had taken for Joseph Kony to lift him so effortlessly from the ground.

Jake didn't want to believe it, the mere concept of a figure from the Bible striding the Earth terrorized him in a way he could never explain, but when everything conspired against him, what else was he supposed to believe? He wasn't insane... or hoped he wasn't. Perhaps he was dead, lying in the dust of Northern Uganda, his bones drying in the scorching sun while his soul floated through some sort of limbo trying to discern answers for a dilemma which made no sense. He didn't *feel* dead, but what was that supposed to mean exactly?

He savagely pinched his left forearm, his nails digging into the skin so hard they drew blood. The spike of pain shooting up his limb was instantly recognized by his brain. He released the pinch with a gasp. None of the stories of near-death experiences he'd heard ever spoke of souls stubbing their toe on the stroll down the bright tunnel and having to stop to rub it better.

*Once you eliminate the impossible, whatever remains, however improbable, must be the truth.*

The quote, paraphrased from Sir Arthur Conan Doyle's Sherlock Holmes, cut into Jake's mind. He'd eliminated the impossible, so what remained? Jake could only rely on his instincts, and they told him one thing.

Kony was not a man; he was Abaddon, one of the Fallen.

\*\*\*

"Mister Hope, what do you think you will achieve here today?"

"Please, Father, call me Jake."

The elderly priest nodded, though it seemed he scowled harder, additional wrinkles creasing his already furrowed brow. He adjusted the spectacles sitting low on his nose and gazed over their rims at Jake, his gray eyes piercing. "I don't know how I can help you. What you are talking about is impossible, and you must think me a fool if you imagine I believe you. Is this some sort of joke?"

"It's not a joke, Father. It's right there in the Bible. I *saw* the demon Abaddon. He was as close to me as you are right now. He's hiding within the body of General Joseph Kony in Uganda!"

"Fallen angels and demons cannot act in such a way," Father Deans pronounced stubbornly. "God would not allow it. And for you to question His might in such a way within His house is approaching blasphemy." The words echoed through the otherwise-empty Seattle church, rising to the ornate ceiling and reverberating from the saintly stained images frozen within the window glass.

"God lets a lot of things happen that shouldn't, Father, believe me." Sour-breath memories from his childhood tried to push in on Jake's focus, but he thrust them from his thoughts.

"I've just about had enough of this. Do you have any sensible questions?"

Jake sucked down his anger. He'd expected skepticism from anyone else, but not from a priest. It was like going to a doctor, suspecting you had cancer, only to have him turn around and tell you that cancer didn't exist. Priests were supposed to be the experts about this kind of stuff, not the naysayers. Weren't they the people you went to for exorcisms? A brief image of Father Deans' head twisting around in a full circle popped into Jake's mind, and he suppressed a grin.

"Is there anything you *can* tell me about Abaddon?" asked Jake finally.

The priest stared at him, seeming to assess if Jake were merely being disrespectful, or if this were a genuine question.

"Well, for a start, Abaddon is not what would generally be classed as a demon – he is a fallen angel."

"What's the difference?" asked Jake.

"A demon is consummate evil whereas a fallen angel is a creature of benevolence converted to evil. There is a definite distinction."

"And what else?" prompted Jake.

"Otherwise, Abaddon is what you described. He is known as *The Destroyer* as well as *The Angel of the Bottomless Pit* among other things. My studies rarely focused on such things, but he was supposedly a supremely powerful angel, even after being cast from Heaven. He –"

Frustrated, Jake cut in. "Yes, yes. I can learn all of this from the internet. How do I kill him?"

Now the priest looked worried. "I have already told you, Abaddon cannot possibly enter the realm of Earth. Whomever you might be planning on killing is innocent. My son, before you hurt yourself or someone else, I beseech you to seek help."

"Right. Sorry," said Jake, realizing the futility of pointing out that he had come here to see Father Deans for help. He had to change tactics before the priest decided he was utterly demented – and possibly dangerous. The last thing he needed was for this guy to call the cops. He quickly gathered his thoughts, conjuring a story he hoped might convince this fool. "I lied about seeing Abaddon. The truth is I'm writing a book about this kind of stuff and was worried if I told you about it you might not help me."

Father Deans' attitude instantly changed. "A book? Well why didn't you just say so? That's a different story altogether." His eyes gleamed, and Jake thought he glimpsed some kind of hidden desire within them.

"Can you help me out with my research, Father?"

The priest gave him a surprisingly warm smile. "I'll do what I can, as long as you include me in the credits, or whatever it is they put in books."

"You've got it," said Jake, mustering a stiff grin, trying hard to conceal his contempt. "Now, what can you tell me?"

"Well, from what I can remember, Abaddon was – or is, depending on your point of view – an angel banished into Hell by God and the Holy Host along with many of his brethren after their failed attempt to take over Heaven. He is, like you said, referred to as the Destroyer –"

"I don't mean to be rude, Father," interrupted Jake, "but I already know all this stuff. Is there a way – some theoretical artifact which nobody knows about – that Abaddon might be killed? It would be awesome to include that in my book."

Dust motes flitted through the colored light from the stained-glass motifs, dancing within the air, glinting mischievously, taunting Jake's impatience. Father Deans seemed to regard them for a moment, his expression thoughtful, appearing to weigh how much he could tell Jake. His eyes moved from the light to the birthmark marring Jake's cheek, staring at it for an eternity. Jake refused to shatter the silence despite his anxiety.

"If I tell you this thing," the priest offered in a hushed undertone, "you must assure me that nobody will know it came from me. Do you promise not to divulge my identity?"

Jake nodded, conscious of how this was almost a complete negation of what the priest had requested only moments beforehand. He leaned in eagerly, reluctant to divert the priest from whatever he was about to reveal.

"Well… there was once talk – specious nonsense if you ask me – of a sword guarded within the gates of the Vatican itself. These rumors – and remember they are mere gossip – say that… that the sword… but it's preposterous, and you don't want to hear such nonsense."

Jake gritted his teeth, controlling his frustration with effort. "Please tell me, Father. It's vital… for my story."

"Yes, of course. Your story. Is it a work of fiction?" asked the priest, seeming to stall for time.

Jake smiled warmly. "Yes, it is."

"Well then… I suppose telling you about the – the, er, sword shouldn't matter, then. Since your book is fiction, after all."

"Entirely fiction. It doesn't matter what you tell me; nobody will believe it," said Jake. "And I promise never to mention your name, or tell anyone where I got the information."

This seemed to reassure Father Deans slightly, but when he continued he spoke swiftly, like he was tearing off a verbal Band-Aid. "The sword is referred to in Genesis 3:24." He quoted, "*After he drove the man out, he placed on the east side of the Garden of Eden cherubim and a flaming sword flashing back and forth to guard the way to the tree of life.*' This explains the expulsion of Adam and Eve from the Garden of Eden. God placed guards called *cherubim* –"

"What are they?" asked Jake.

The priest looked upset at Jake's interruption, but refrained from chastising him. "Cherubim are similar to seraphim, which is to say we know very little about them other than they answer to God and aided him during the war against Lucifer."

"So they're angels?"

"I did not say that. They support our Lord and are referred to with deliberate obscurity throughout the Bible. For the purposes of our discussion you merely need to understand they have great power and were set as guardians around the Tree of Life."

"What's that?"

The priest sighed heavily. "What is *what*?" he asked testily.

"The Tree of Life, what is it?"

Father Deans shook his head in disgust. "You have obviously never studied the Bible."

"Not really," replied Jake, biting his tongue, forcing an easy smile despite his frustration.

"The Tree of Life was planted in the Garden of Eden, set alongside the Tree of Knowledge of Good and Evil. God Himself was said to have planted these trees. Some, of course, argue they are one and the same."

"And that's the tree with the forbidden fruit, right?" said Jake.

"Yes," replied Father Deans. "After Adam and Eve were expelled from the Garden, the cherubim were set as guards and a Flaming Sword was placed within the Garden to protect it."

"And you think the sword at the Vatican is the same one?" asked Jake incredulously.

"Like I said, it is only rumor. A tale told among the seminaries – to pass time more than anything. The truth of it all is that nobody really knows if there even is a sword in Rome, let alone one with such extraordinary properties as the one from the Garden was rumored to have."

"Properties? Like what?"

The priest suddenly looked like he had swallowed a bone, an expression of panic jarring his features, and Jake guessed he'd said more than he'd initially intended. Finally a look of resignation settled upon the man's face, and he shrugged.

"You are sure this book you are writing is fiction?" asked Father Deans yet again. Jake nodded. "Well, it is said the sword had the power to kill angels. All of this is highly speculative, however, since such a sword could not possibly exist. It is only referenced in that one small part of Genesis and is never spoken of again throughout the entire Bible. So if it ever did exist, I would guess it still resides within the gates of Eden, guarding it for all eternity."

"Then why would a rumor exist that it was in the Vatican?"

The priest shrugged. "All these stories start somewhere. Perhaps it began as a mere tale that the entrance to Heaven lay within the word of the Bible – whose heart resides in Rome."

Jake smiled, the fakeness of it hurting his cheeks, but the priest didn't seem to notice. Thanking the man for his time, Jake rose and strode from the gloom of the church and into the sunshine, wondering if the entire wearisome conversation had been worth his time. The eyes of Abaddon burned within his memory, and Jake gritted his teeth, squaring his shoulders once more as he moved down the street.

\*\*\*

Withdrawing the last of his savings was a huge risk, but something inside Jake drove him relentlessly onward, forcing him to chase the hope there might be some way he could combat the evil he'd witnessed in Uganda. The memory of the small child's neck hacked open while the grinning man stood untouched, returned to haunt Jake again and again. The blood dripping from the machete echoed through his conscience, each drop of crimson symbolizing another life torn to shreds with every moment Jake did nothing.

This one action, more than anything else, revealed Abaddon's ability to contaminate others with his evil. The machete-wielder had been as human as Jake, yet he'd smiled gleefully after cutting down a child, an innocent. What could make a man do such a thing? The external influence of the fallen angel, or just human nature unfettered by morality? Jake didn't truly know. Evil could flower anywhere, within men and women who appeared reasonable on the outside, but whose hearts were rotten through, filled with hatred.

Maybe true demons hide within people's hearts, waiting for an excuse to emerge.

Jake pushed the problem aside for the moment. He needed to focus on the malevolence he'd witnessed, the most tangible evil having emanated directly from the figure of Abaddon himself.

The idea of chasing after one of the Fallen terrified Jake. He focused instead on the notion that Abaddon was a living creature – albeit one with vast and unknown power. His relentless research had extended for days, probing countless old tomes claiming knowledge of such things. He'd studied a range of Biblical tales. Not just stories from the actual Bible, but near heretical interpretations – some by qualified theologians and some not.

A lot of the studies he'd read had been written by highly educated and recognized history professors, some specializing in religions, but to Jake it often seemed they read too much into things. Contrasted against this were the unscholarly conjectures ranging from theories on aliens to parallel dimensions. Most of these sounded more like science fiction than anything factual. And again, they rested heavily upon the opinions of the author.

The one damning thing which kept plaguing Jake was the fact most of these theories stemmed from one book: the Bible. Putting aside his own mistrust in a deity who sat back and watched heinous atrocities committed upon innocents, Jake admitted he could believe sections of the Bible might have actually occurred. Not the ridiculous parts, of course. But it seemed plausible that an external force – whether in reality, or simply through an individual's desire and belief – had touched certain people's lives in ways to make them act for the benevolence of others.

But the Bible was written by men, *mortal* men, highly susceptible to primitive superstition.

This was the thing which frustrated Jake the most. He was searching for facts, but the majority of his information came from a book written during a time when people still thought the world was flat. As nice as the idea of peace on Earth and all that was to Jake, he had looked into the eyes of the evil. It seemed possible Abaddon had somehow always held Kony's form, but that mattered little in the scheme of things. Jake needed to discover how to stop him without all the mystical nonsense surrounding such things.

Frustrated, Jake had turned to books regarding the occult. If anything, these held even more nonsense than the religious studies, with all sorts of supposed rituals designed to make people do what you wished. It was ridiculous.

Disappointment bogged him down, so much so, he considered trying a different course. On a whim, he visited a side-alley bookstore mentioned on several occult websites. Towering shelves housed many ancient-*looking* books, but Jake suspected they were merely designed that way. Theatrical props for the ignorant shopper. Discouraged after searching through several useless shelves, Jake had almost decided to leave when he finally discovered something.

A time-worn, leather-bound title, *Precursors of the Final Conflict* struck Jake with an immediate curiosity. Touching the cracked cover neither tingled nor tortured the flesh of his fingers, and to most it might seem nothing more than another book. After flicking through a couple of pages, Jake recognized information he might finally use.

The black leather cover seemed very old, almost ancient, and the paper felt dangerously fragile, its contents written in beautiful, calligraphy-like script. Despite its appearance, Jake sensed the book was not as old as it appeared. What was contained within the pages had corrupted it, drawing every ounce of life contained within the bindings.

Excited by his discovery, he studied the pages, noting the scholarly way they were put together, more like a technical journal than a novel, the dates running down a column on the left, and the main body of writing laid out clearly and succinctly like lab notes, completely at odds with the flowery writing style.

For someone merely perusing the ancient text it might have seemed mere superstition, but this book dispensed with a lot of the ridiculous claims others speculated upon, and instead relayed a very detailed account of the Apocalypse through the eyes of a demonic worshipper. Whereas the Bible offered vague allusion to events which could possibly be linked with many things occurring during modern times, *Precursors of the Final Conflict* gave specific predictions, including the approximate decade the author expected they would transpire.

Jake's hands shook slightly as he fumbled through the pages containing references occurring within the current decade. They were tucked almost at the very back of the book – falling on the last few pages; not a good sign for a tome predicting the end of the world.

Running his finger down the date column, he found the current decade and scanned the entry:

*And the day shall come when the Supplanter will walk among us, and his name shall make brave warriors quake. The moments until the end of all things will be numbered within counting when the Supplanter draws forth his lieutenants to fight by his side against the forces of right and blood. None who walk the path will be safe from his vengeance, and he shall destroy or condemn those who choose to stand against him.*

*Blood shall flow in Abaddon's wake when he strides as a king upon the Earth with his brethren Fallen, and their power shall be incredible to behold. The only thing they fear will be the Flaming Sword from the Garden Eternal, for it is all that can defeat them within this world of beasts and men. Hell –*

"WHAT ARE YOU READING?" The very walls seemed to shake with the outraged voice's ferocity.

Jake was so startled he dropped the book and spun around, spying the wizened, old shop owner hobbling toward him, a vintage pistol grasped tightly in his shaking hand, one eye fixed on Jake, the other a milky-white orb. A long, angry scar ran from the man's furrowed brow, through the top and bottom lids of his sightless eye, and down his right cheek. It looked to Jake as though a huge talon had forever marked this man, blinding him in the process.

"I – uh – nothing," muttered Jake, his heart pounding, confusion threatening to overwhelm him. How had such a seemingly-feeble old man been able to bellow like that? And why was he carrying a gun?

"Ya said ya was looking for a spell ter make a girl love ya! So watcha doin' here in the *Accursed* section?"

Jake sneakily slid his foot along the ground, knocking *Precursors of the Final Conflict* under one of the heavily laden bookshelves, hoping the man's one working eyeball missed the action. It seemed to work, the blind orb kept staring at nothing while the functioning eye remained fixed on Jake's face.

"Er, sorry," said Jake, "I thought there might have been something here. Can't I look at this stuff?"

He'd known he wasn't allowed; the cranky owner had made it blatantly clear when Jake had asked to browse the shop. The miserly old attendant had snapped and snarled, telling him at least six or seven times that these shelves were completely taboo. "Members only," he'd muttered. Such a warning had only spurred Jake to search through the titles, thinking that if answers hid anywhere, they'd surely lurk on those dust-cloaked shelves.

Jake hadn't even considered telling the truth of what he searched for, blurting out the love-spell nonsense on the spur of the moment, just to get his foot in the door. Something about the half-blind vendor had told Jake the old man wouldn't likely be very forthcoming if he'd revealed what he was really doing.

"I told ya not ta come back 'ere," the old man grumbled, though he seemed somewhat placated by Jake's lie. At least he hadn't used that booming tone again. What the hell had that been?

Jake peered around at the shelves, trying to appear ignorant to what surrounded him. "What is this stuff?"

"It's none of ya damn business!" snarled the old man, motioning with his gun toward the front door. "Now get out!"

"But what about the love-spell?"

"Jus' get out!"

And so Jake left the store with no option of going back. The little tidbit he'd read in *Precursors of the Final Conflict* had convinced him to follow up on an idea. Rather than risk another trip into the strange shop with its psychotic owner and his pistol from the dawn of firearms, Jake searched for reference of the author of the book on the internet and discovered the man had most recently lived not far across the Canadian border in Vancouver. He found no contact phone number, merely an address.

***

$317.45.

That was the total amount of cash in his bank account. Jake chuckled hollowly at the receipt stub which spat out from the ATM. His account had $7.45 left after he'd withdrawn as much as he could, and now his wallet bulged with just over three hundred dollars to get him up to Canada and....

*And what?*

Truth be told, Jake really had no plan for what he was doing, none at all. That probably had more to do with his drive to meet the author of *Precursors of the Final Conflict* than anything else: he needed some direction for this entire crusade. A small part of Jake hoped that by meeting this author, a stranger named Albert Pointreid, he might get some idea of how to fight Abaddon. At this point, Jake really didn't have a clue what to do to combat the fallen angel, apart from odd references to a flaming sword in the Garden of Eden. How was he supposed to formulate a plan with that as his goal? He blew out a frustrated breath.

For staring into the eyes of the monster, he'd paid a high price: a hole blasted through his chest. Miraculously, he hadn't died, but he was certain that if he went up against the demonic Abaddon again – for Jake no longer deluded himself, it definitely wasn't a man he had faced – he'd end up dead... or worse.

The logical thing to do was flee, to find somewhere safe and try to forget everything that had happened in Uganda, but that was something Jake knew he could never do. He felt driven to act. Some deep inner need to face down the evil he'd seen compelled him onward when a more sensible person might have stopped.

At the same time, the task before him seemed insurmountable. Joseph Kony was one of the most wanted men on the planet; entire campaigns had been orchestrated, trying to capture or kill him, all of which had failed miserably. A whole army was set against his military minions in Uganda, and had been fighting his forces for close to twenty years without any success. On top of all this, Jake was, as far as he knew, the only person alive who knew Kony was actually Abaddon, a fallen angel with untold power. Nobody would ever believe him, he was on his own.

Bitterly alone.

So what hope did Jake have of success? What possible chance did he have to stop this thing?

He truly didn't know, but deep inside, Jake knew he had to try, if for no other reason than for the dead boy with his neck slashed wide. That child – all the unnamed children – deserved some sort of justice. Jake had seen evil with his own eyes, not just in the figure of Abaddon, but in the actions of the men who followed him, and he couldn't ignore it. Maybe if he hadn't been there and witnessed such things for himself he could have turned a blind eye like so many others, but Jake *had* seen the corruption dwelling there, and it haunted his dreams, his every waking moment. How could he live, walking the same Earth, breathing the same air, as such corruption?

The memory of Aadesh informing Jake he was the reincarnation of Christ, or whatever it was the bizarre Indian had said, came back to Jake, and he chuckled humorlessly, the sound hollow in his own ears. It would be nice to have Christ around to tell him what to do right now; such a man would certainly have the perfect answer for any calamity. To suggest Jake was Christ seemed utterly laughable. His own past condemned him, prohibiting anything even remotely righteous.

His foster father's chanting rants echoed in wisps through Jake's memory, the scent of bourbon strong, blending with the Biblical verses Jake could not clearly recall the words to. He recollected the pain that had come with such discourses – pain and humiliation. Jake swallowed heavily and rejected the memory, thrusting it down, deep down, where it couldn't pursue him.

When faced with the evil of Abaddon he'd frozen, unable to even speak. He was no Christ. And here he was contemplating going to battle against the fallen angel, a being so powerful it thought it could triumph against the supposed creator of the universe.

Damn. The scope of what he was thinking felt so huge it made Jake's stomach churn, his heart skipping a beat each time he contemplated it. Nobody was ever going to believe him, let alone help him. They'd all be like Father Deans, dismissing the idea without thought.

Shaking his head, Jake focused his thoughts on the road ahead. He had a plan, albeit one so flimsy it seemed likely to shatter at any moment. After traveling to Vancouver by bus he'd *hopefully* meet Albert Pointreid. From there they would discuss the man's book at length, *hopefully* uncovering more about potential weaknesses he could exploit against Abaddon.

Hopefully.

A pathetic strategy, but it was all he could come up with at the moment. It would have to suffice, because the more time he wasted, the more horror would likely be visited on someone at the hands of a beast disguised as Joseph Rao Kony.

\*\*\*

The hiss of the air brakes sliced through Jake's slumber, shattering the pleasant dream he'd been having. The memory of it blew away like mist before a hurricane. Raising his bleary eyes, he looked out the window of the bus. VANCOUVER. This was his stop.

Jake's heart suddenly went into overdrive at the thought of meeting Albert Pointreid. The author of *Precursors of the Final Conflict* – a man who, if still alive, must by now surely be ancient – the record of him residing in Vancouver had only been a couple of years old, so Jake's hopes were high that Pointreid still survived and hadn't moved.

Pounding in his head threatened to overtake his concentration as his pulse raced, and his palms began to sweat. He wiped them on his denim jeans, but within seconds they were clammy again. Shrugging at the futility of it, he dragged his mind once more back to Pointreid.

The concept seemed simple enough, but facing the actual man would be something completely different altogether. Pointreid would almost certainly be unlike any person Jake had ever met, a demonic worshipper, his writing outlining deeds so appalling they stretched the boundaries of nightmarish imagination, predictions which should have been restricted to fiction. Yet Jake feared these tales might prove all too real. He'd already seen one such nightmare walking and breathing in Uganda, and it had been tangible enough to put a hole in Jake's chest.

The fact Jake had traveled all the way here in the hopes of discovering some method of destroying Abaddon could not be let slip, lest he lose his one and only lead. The memory of the cantankerous shop owner returned once more, the wavering pistol barrel like a shaking head negating the promise of his survival. If Jake screwed up this meeting, if he let on that he might be an enemy to this zealot's beliefs, then the murder Abaddon had attempted in Uganda might be accomplished right here in Canada.

Pushing aside his paranoia and shouldering his bag, Jake exited the Quick Shuttle bus, slipping slightly on the wet concrete sidewalk. It felt cold, but nowhere near the pillowcase full of icy needles he'd expected in Canada. Dropping his canvas bag to the ground, Jake jerked open the zipper and removed his parka, swiftly donning it.

Staring around, he gathered his bearings. Jake felt hesitant to pay for a cab given his already dwindling finances, and his research had shown the distance to Albert Pointreid's house wasn't very far from the bus station. Glancing around, Jake reached into his back pocket for the map he had printed along with the directions he needed to get to –

*Oh crap.*

In his excitement at arriving in Vancouver, he'd forgotten the bus first stopped at the International Airport, before traveling into the city. He'd seen the sign mentioning Vancouver and jumped off prematurely.

He spun around just in time to see the Quick Shuttle bus departing, a plume of gray-blue smoke from its exhaust billowing like gas from a flatulent bull mocking an incompetent matador. He considered chasing after it, but watching it accelerate, rumbling away from where Jake stood, he realized such action would be futile. Turning back, he stared at the building mocking his stupidity. Vancouver International Airport, located on the opposite side of the city to where he needed to be. Blackley Street in Queensborough was a long walk away.

Jake cursed softly, his frustrated breath misting the air.

Now what?

A swift query confirmed his fears: a taxi across the city would cost close to the $50 he had left in his wallet, leaving him destitute should it turn out to be a dead-end. He stared grimly at the jacket he wore. It had seemed such a wise purchase at the time; wasn't Canada supposed to be freezing? The air felt cool, but not a speck of snow appeared on the ground anywhere. So much for smart shopping. The train would only take him part of the way there, and he was leery to try his hand at public transport so soon after his most recent debacle with the bus – he might end up anywhere. Things were looking grim. He leaned back against a chrome handrail, rubbing his chin as he stared at the ground, dejection threatening to overwhelm him.

"Hello?" inquired a voice to his left, cutting into his thoughts. Jake turned, lazily wondering what new mishap might be about to befall him.

Where there'd been empty pavement only a moment before, a gorgeous woman now stood, her intense blue eyes tearing aside his every defense, her flawless alabaster skin crowned by sensuous blonde hair cascading down over her shoulders like a waterfall. For a moment, Jake's tongue doubled in size, and he felt unable to talk. Realizing he was staring, he snapped his mouth shut with an audible pop and searched his blank mind for something to say.

"Er... hi."

The girl smiled, her features, already attractive, transforming into beauty so radiant Jake's breath involuntarily stuck in his throat. Jake gasped, choking, struggling to inhale while still trying to retain some measure of composure. He failed miserably.

"You're American?" she asked, the words dripping with sensuality while her eyes continued to grip him remorselessly. He was hers, and she knew it.

Jake nodded mutely, unwilling to trust his voice. It almost hurt just to look at her, but he couldn't tear his gaze away. The tiniest hint of her perfume drifted across the gap of air between them, tantalizing Jake with promises of pleasure.

"Well then, I have a flight to catch and do not need this taxi voucher. You look like you could use it; am I correct?"

She handed him a card, and Jake managed to pull his focus away from her long enough to flick a glance at the voucher.

"Are you serious?" It would easily take him where he needed to go.

"Of course, I don't need it."

"You're an angel!" exclaimed Jake gratefully. "You have no idea how much I could use this today."

The girl giggled, the sound like tinkling crystal, turning on her heel and strolling sensually toward the terminal. Strangely, she carried no bags, but the oddity only barely resonated with Jake. He felt the strange compulsion to call her back and never let her go.

"Wait!" he shouted. The mysterious woman stopped, half-turning toward him once more.

"Yes?"

"I – um... my name is Jake," he stammered lamely.

She stepped back over to him, cupping his right cheek with her hand as she kissed him on the left. Her lips touched his birthmark, and a jolt of electricity shot all the way to his toes. His breathing shuddered once more.

"My name is Anael," she whispered into his ear, her voice husky. Jake caught another hint of perfume, enough to make his head feel light. "And it is nice to meet you, Jake. Until we meet again... someday."

Jake felt her fingers slip from his cheek and glanced around as though waking from a dream. Anael was gone. The automatic doors to the terminal swished closed, and he sighed.

Wondering at this amazing change in his fortune, Jake stooped to pick up his bag, and strolled over to the nearby taxi stand.

Settling into the back seat of the taxi, Jake pushed thoughts of the strange and lascivious seductress from his mind, mentally trying to prepare himself to meet the author of a book predicting the end of the world....

Jake's mood soured rapidly at the thought, and he stared out the window of the taxi at the pavement, noting the light rain spattering it, thankful he hadn't been forced to walk.

*-CHAPTER 4-*
# DARK AUTHOR

The black door beckoned, calling out silently in the still air. The street remained quiet, the traffic noise muted. No birds sang. Jake yearned to escape, to scurry away and just keep going, but he forced himself to stand fast, though his left leg did twitch slightly, as though tempted to disobey and flee.

It wasn't just the thought of what might lay beyond the door that set his nerves on end. There seemed something innately foreboding about the simple structure of the entrance. It sat at the top of the five steps like the maw of the building, ominously anticipating its prey. The ancient knocker adorned with a gargoyle-like face appeared to want nothing more than to swallow the hand of any person who dared grasp it. Jake stared at the door for a long time, trying to summon enough courage to approach what was rapidly beginning to feel like the next chapter on his path toward doom.

Shaking away the ominous sensation, Jake trudged up the five steps and seized the knocker, rapping it heavily three times, the echo reverberating deeply within the three story house.

Every single hair on the back of Jake's neck suddenly shot up. Once more he was hit with an intense urge to flee, and his stomach threatened to leap from his throat and escape, but he gritted his teeth and held his ground.

Footsteps boomed inside the house, and Jake's trepidation doubled, his heart pounding like a drum within his chest. What would Pointreid look like? Images of a horribly disfigured face and body flashed through Jake's mind as the footsteps thundered ever closer to the opposite side of the black door. The gargoyle's face on the knocker seemed to leer at Jake in anticipation. He forced himself to stand firm.

The door creaked open....

"Hello there!"

A smiling man in his mid-thirties wearing circular glasses stood in the open doorway, his receding brown hair swept back, one hand on the doorknob, the other casually avoiding the chill by hiding within the pocket of the man's caramel-colored cardigan.

Jake stood stunned, completely taken aback. "Um… I'm looking for Albert Pointreid… this is supposed to be his address… I think."

"Well it was, until about ten years ago when he died," said the man. "I'm his grandson, Wallace Pointreid. Can I help you?"

"Er…." This wasn't something Jake had been prepared for. "Do you know anything about a book he wrote?"

Instantly the man's expression dropped, becoming dramatically colder, much more guarded. "What book?"

"It was called *Precursors of the Final Conflict.*"

"Who are you? Are you a reporter? The stuff surrounding what my grandfather did back then died along with him, and you people just need to let it rest."

"I have no idea what you're talking about," replied Jake, caught off guard by the rapid change in the man's attitude. "My name is Jacob Hope, and I need to know some information regarding the contents of that book. It's more important than you could possibly imagine. Can I come in?"

"You should have called first," complained Pointreid.

Jake was beginning to think the same thing. Perhaps if he'd researched a bit more he might have found a phone number, but he'd also wanted to catch Albert Pointreid off guard. Instead, he'd probably just wasted the majority of his dwindling funds.

"I understand. I'll explain everything, I promise. But for now can I please come in out of this horrible damp?"

Wallace Pointreid seemed unsure of the request, but eventually nodded and ushered him inside. Stepping through the door, Jake looked around and almost stumbled; the interior of the house was in direct contrast to the ominous entrance. Bright, vibrant pictures adorned the walls, and striking light décor colors radiated throughout.

"This is a beautiful home you have here, Mr. Pointreid," said Jake earnestly.

Pointreid stared at Jake's birthmark momentarily, but refrained from commenting on it. "Please call me Wallace."

"I'm Jake." The two shook hands, and a bit of the frostiness seemed to lift from the air.

"Come through here. We can talk without getting interrupted by my family. My wife should be arriving home soon with my two boys."

Wallace led Jake down a short hallway into a richly-appointed study, its heavily-laden timber bookshelves reaching almost to the ceiling, a rolling ladder situated in front of them, pushed almost to the end of its runners. Three plump, leather chairs were placed around a low coffee table, and Wallace indicated Jake should take a seat. Jake sank into the luxurious chair like he had just dropped onto leather-bound marshmallow. A rare beam of Canadian sunlight pierced the outside gloom, shining brightly through the far window, brightening the room, shadows from the tree outside filtering the illumination nicely. Wallace moved to a cabinet arrayed with several bottles of exotic liquor, reaching for a bottle of amber liquid in a crystal decanter.

"I have a feeling I'm going to need a scotch, would you care to join me?"

Jake shook his head, preferring to keep his mind clear – at the same time remembering the home had once been owned by a man who'd worshipped evil; who knew what his grandson might put into the drink? For all appearances, Wallace Pointreid seemed a genial host, but looks could be deceiving, and Jake wasn't willing to let his guard down yet.

"Now, what can I do for you, Jake?" asked Wallace, gracefully seating himself in the chair opposite.

Unsure of how to proceed, Jake took a deep breath, steadying his nerves and gathering his thoughts. "I read part of a book by your grandfather called *Precursors of the Final Conflict*, and it concerns something I'm dealing with at the moment."

Wallace chuckled, taking a small sip of his scotch. "Somehow I doubt that. You seem like a nice chap. I don't think there would be anything within the pages of that maniacally delusionary old book which could possibly concern you. The memory of that nasty bastard is the darkest blot on my family's otherwise golden history. I mean, you should have seen this place when I inherited it – full of loathsome knickknacks and disgusting artifacts. The man really was a loon."

"At the door you mentioned something about stuff he did before he died, things the newspapers were interested in. What kinds of stuff?"

Wallace stared intently at Jake, the man's eyes once more flicking down to his left cheek, but again he abstained from comment. The silence in the room grew intense. Jake refused to avert his gaze, returning the stare imploringly. He needed to know what had happened here. Wallace finally dropped his eyes and took a deep swallow of scotch.

"My grandfather... he was a... a nightmare. The things he wrote about in that book will haunt my family name until the end of time, and the crimes he committed –"

"What crimes?" asked Jake.

"He... *experimented...* on people. If you read far enough into that nonsense he wrote, my grandfather spoke about opening the gates sealing Hell and unleashing the Fallen once more upon the Earth."

"I never got that far. What exactly are the Fallen?"

Wallace stared at him once more, his look imploring, begging Jake not to make him continue, but Jake remained unrelenting. The walls themselves seemed intent on hearing the answer, the bookshelves seeming to lean closer. The very air dripped with tension while Jake waited, his heart quavering for fear of what it might be.

"The Fallen are the angels who fought alongside Lucifer when he tried to overthrow God," said Wallace grimly, his eyes averting Jake's gaze, staring deep into the crystal glass in his hands. "They were all cast into Hell alongside Lucifer as punishment, to exist in torment forever. Once there they became warped: horrific parodies of the beauty they had once represented. They now exist only to visit anguish upon those they blame for their banishment: the humans."

"Do you know if your grandfather managed to open the gate?"

Wallace's gaze snapped up. "Why do you ask?"

The moment of truth; the time when Jake needed to decide how much to disclose. The man sitting opposite him, tense despite his best attempts to look comfortable, was the one person who might know how to help him... or who might laugh himself silly before calling the men in white coats to lock Jake in a nice padded cell forever. It was hard enough admitting these things to himself. The thought of sharing such madness brought flashbacks of Jake's previous debacle conferring with the priest about Abaddon. People didn't *want* to consider stuff like this – Jake himself hadn't even believed in such things before seeing them with his own eyes.

"I met Abaddon," he said swiftly, the words tearing the silence, like ripping off a Band-Aid.

"You.... *What?*"

"He's in Northern Uganda, masquerading as Joseph Kony." Jake sat back in the thick leather chair, certain Wallace would start laughing at him.

Wallace didn't laugh; he quietly stood up and moved over to the cabinet once more, pouring himself another measure of scotch, downing it in a single swallow.

"You saw him? Abaddon?" Wallace poured himself a third drink and walked slowly back to his chair, crumpling into it and placing the glass on the low table. Jake noticed the man's hands were shaking. "What did he look like?"

Jake outlined what he had seen, leaving out nothing about the incident, from the moment he'd arrived at the Red Cross aid station until Abaddon had shot him through the chest.

"He shot you?" said Wallace, his brow frowning. "And you think his own troops couldn't see what he truly was?"

"They didn't act like he was anything but human."

"Then how is it you were able to see him differently?" asked Wallace.

"I –" How *had* Jake been able to see Abaddon? "I really don't know. But there was no mistaking what he did; he lifted me clean off the ground using only one hand, like I was a kitten."

"Please don't think I don't believe you," said Wallace. "I'm not asking all these questions because I doubt you, in fact it's quite the opposite; I know you're telling me the truth. Your description of Abaddon in human form is too close to what my grandfather wrote about to be mere conjecture."

"Was that in the book I saw?"

Wallace shook his head, reaching forward and taking a sip from his glass. "It was from his... *other* writings; works which never left this house."

Jake's heart began to hammer in his chest. "Could I see them?" he asked hopefully. Those writings might hold the answers he was looking for.

Wallace shook his head sadly, and Jake's hopes crashed. "I burned them all when I inherited this place, along with anything else relating to my grandfather's obsession with the occult. I couldn't risk their taint corrupting my family. I wouldn't have moved in at all, but we had little option due to our finances at the time; part of the will specified we had to live here in order to receive the money left to me. When we had finally finished renovating this building, the place had become our home; it's the only house our children have ever known. So we stayed."

"Damn," muttered Jake. "I need to know how to stop him."

"Stop who? *Abaddon?*" asked Wallace, alarmed.

"Yeah."

"Y-you can't! He is one of the Fallen – immortal and unyielding to us. Only one of the Host from Heaven can stop him."

"Well, they're not here right now," replied Jake dryly, "and Abaddon is. I can't just disregard what I've seen. How could I live with myself, if I simply ignored what's going on?"

Wallace stared intensely at Jake, his eyes occasionally flicking down to Jake's crimson birthmark, as though it in some way influenced whatever decision he was trying to make.

"If you continue on this course, you may find the price is more than you could possibly imagine," he said.

"What do you mean?"

"You are dealing with powers you cannot possibly comprehend. The thing you saw in Uganda was a fraction of what is out there. It could tear your spirit from your body on a whim. We are talking about a literal fate worse than death: unending torment for your soul throughout eternity if you fail. My grandfather may have been warped in many of his ideas, but he was also brilliant. He quite possibly knew more about what we are discussing than anyone else has ever discovered. Forget the fairy tales you've read in the Bible; Hell is very real, and the creatures there are not like what you may have seen in the movies.

"Imagine an evil man, possibly the most malignant person the world has ever seen – Vladimir the Third from Russia, for instance. A man notorious for his evil, his full name, Vladimir Draculya, would later become synonymous with the Devil through local folklore."

Wallace sighed, taking another sip from his glass before continuing his tale. "Vladimir Draculya became known as Vlad the Impaler, and became the basis for the story of Dracula, the infamous vampire. Draculya had a penchant for impaling perceived enemies upon sharpened stakes, watching them twitch and writhe – sometimes for hours – before dying in horrible agony. His victims would be thrown to the ground, their ankles strapped to a horse, and a sharpened stake fixed in place, the tip pointing between their spread legs toward the anus. The horses would then be forced forward and – "

"I get it," said Jake hurriedly, not needing a more graphic description.

"Well, anyway, Vladimir became a figure of terror during his reign. Thousands were tortured and killed in a manner you can't even bear hearing about, others through methods still more horrific. Stories abound of the terror which took place during his reign. But that's beside the point; what I am trying to get at is the level of evil within the man. Would you agree?"

Jake nodded, unsure of where this was heading.

"My grandfather's writings spoke of a soul which arose during one of his séances, his early attempts to break through the veil into the netherworld. He described this spirit as being that of Vladimir Draculya, the very same man who had taken so much pleasure in witnessing the anguish of others. Some would think such a beast would be at home within the torments of Hell, but my grandfather's writings indicated the anguish of Draculya's soul was palpable during the séance. He begged to be exorcised rather than returned to the Pit. Do you understand what this means?"

Jake shook his head slowly, though he sensed he should have known the answer.

"If one of the most evil men ever to walk the Earth is treated in such a way in the realm we know of as Hell, what do you think would happen to you? If you decide to face down Abaddon and fail, he will tear your soul from your flesh, and you'll discover first-hand what Vladimir Draculya begged to be released from."

Such a fate shocked Jake, dousing him with an icy bucket of reality. To die was one thing, but this?

"Did your grandfather exorcise him? Did he kill Draculya's soul?"

Wallace stared at Jake incredulously. "Have you garnered nothing from what I've told you about my grandfather? He laughed and pushed the soul back down into Hell, writing afterward of the glee it gave him to do so. Beware of what you are about to face. It is beyond anything you could ever imagine, things any *sane* man would never want to imagine, let alone try to combat. Hell is more than chains and fire. It captured the Fallen – former angels with more power in a single thought than anything on our entire planet – and it drove them insane with the torment it unleashed upon them. What would it do to a mortal soul?"

Jake stood up and moved to the drinks cabinet, pouring himself a healthy measure of scotch and downing the entire glassful, wincing as it burned his throat.

What should he do?

He remembered the dead boy in Uganda, killed by a man led by one of the Fallen. Jake could ignore this Hellish tumor, living out his mortal life watching the malevolence in that place swell and multiply, as he knew it would, or he could risk his very soul and face down something which had no right to walk the Earth.

"How do I find the flaming sword from the Garden of Eden?" he asked suddenly, amazed his voice wasn't shaking.

Wallace Pointreid's jaw dropped, his glass soon following, slipping from numb fingers.

***

"You can't be serious!" gasped Wallace once he'd recovered enough to speak. He was sitting once more in the thick leather chair, a fresh glass of scotch in his hand.

"Unless you know of another way to go up against Abaddon. If you do, I'm all ears."

Wallace was shaking his head weakly. "There's no way. The cherubim won't allow any mortal access to the Garden."

"They'll have to, because I'm not leaving without it."

"But how will you get there? Nobody even knows where the Garden is!"

Jake grinned humorlessly. "That's your job."

"I... but –"

"You're the only person I've been able to talk to about all this stuff, apart from a priest who didn't believe me. There's no way I can do this without you, Wallace; I desperately need your help."

"I can't get involved.... I – I'm terrified of what lies beyond this realm. What if we fail?"

"We won't," replied Jake, amazed to find he actually believed what he was saying. "You need to trust me. We *have* to do this; we're the only ones who can. Do you think it's a coincidence I was led to your door? What are the odds something like that could happen? I glimpse a book and on a whim, come to a different country with practically no money in my wallet.... I mean, if it wasn't for a girl named Anael –"

"*Anael?*" gasped Wallace, gripping Jake's forearm tightly and staring at his face. "You met Anael?"

"Yeah," replied Jake, wondering at his host's sudden interest. "I met her at the airport. She gave me the taxi voucher to get here after I'd gotten off the bus at the wrong stop. Do you know her?"

"Anael is the name of an angel, sometimes called *Haniel*. Is this name more familiar to you?" Jake shook his head. "Anael is also referred to as one of the seven archangels in some scripts; she is supposedly connected to love and sexuality."

"Well, she certainly had something about her," mused Jake with a wistful smile, remembering the incredible beauty who'd helped him.

"If this Anael who helped you truly was one of the Host...." Wallace trailed off, deep in his own thoughts. A moment passed before his gaze snapped back to Jake's face. "As much as this terrifies me to say, I think I need to help you."

"Why the sudden change of heart?"

"If things have deteriorated as much as you indicate, it means my grandfather tampered with a great deal more than I'd thought. As the sole living adult of his bloodline, I'm the only one with any hope of undoing his work." Wallace looked utterly petrified as he spoke, but somehow more resolute at the same time.

"Do you really think the woman I met was an angel?" Jake asked.

"Yes, I do. And if there are angels wandering Vancouver just to aid you in finding me, the situation might be bordering on Armageddon. If I don't help you, the world might tip into oblivion, the entire universe crumbling as Hell consumes all that God created."

"So... no pressure then," said Jake, chuckling weakly, the sound humorless and swiftly dying.

"I said you might not like what you found if you decided on this course. This is only the beginning. If you truly want to go to the Garden and find the Flaming Sword, you need to be prepared to face horrors beyond imagination. Picture your most terrifying nightmares, and then multiply them by infinity. What I have discussed with you is merely the edge of the nightmare, something glimpsed from afar, through a muted lens. I just hope you are up for the task – I hope we both are."

"What about your family?" asked Jake.

"It's for my family that I do this thing," replied Wallace grimly, his face contorted with suppressed emotion. He took his thin-framed glasses off and began to polish them. "I don't want my boys to be consumed by Hell."

"But won't your helping me focus the attention of these... *Fallen*... toward those close to you?"

Wallace nodded, his attention seemingly still focused on cleaning his glasses. "I will send my wife and sons away. There is a place in Europe where they should be safe... for a while. The address is not easily located, should I be taken."

"I appreciate you offering, but your family is more important –"

"More important than what? The planet? The cosmos? Heaven itself?"

Jake had no answer, and shook his head dumbly.

"There is nothing more important than this, Mr. Hope, and there is nowhere we can hide," Wallace pronounced emphatically. "I warned you about the implications going into this because you needed to know, but there is no turning back now – for either of us. That one of the Host aided you in getting here; that you somehow have this ability to see through the guise of Abaddon; these things prove you have been chosen for this task. And you've come to *my* door for assistance; this means our destinies are to be intertwined forever."

"Well, that's not creepy," said Jake with a shaky smile, trying to lighten the mood. He self-consciously gripped his elbows, hugging his chest.

"This is not a joking matter," admonished Wallace.

"Sorry."

"You are welcome to stay here for the night while I make plans for my family, but we leave in the morning."

"Where are we going?" asked Jake.

"Rome."

"What's in Rome?"

"The Vatican hides the greatest secrets the Catholic religion has ever discovered. If there's a way into the Garden, they'll know about it."

"What makes you think they'll help us?" asked Jake. "I mean, they might just be like the priest I spoke to in Seattle who thought I was insane."

"They might, but we still have to go. That is, unless you can think of another option?"

Jake sat silently for a moment, pondering the issue. For some reason he couldn't define, heading to the Vatican felt wrong to him.

Something suddenly occurred to Jake. "I have no money," he said, shifting uncomfortably in the thick chair, causing the leather to squeak loudly, as if in protest.

Wallace smiled, lightening the strain upon his face. "Money isn't a problem for me these days, my friend – not since I moved in here. Beside other financial sources I've built up since that time, my grandfather left me a very hefty sum of money along with this house in his will."

"Okay, that makes things easier." Jake sighed, settling back in his chair once more. "But something doesn't feel right about going to the Vatican; I really don't think it'll hold any answers. Part of me feels drawn there, tugged almost, but I can't help feeling such an ancient and important treasure won't be so easily found. I've already had run-ins with clergy, and traveling across the globe to have more seems a bit pointless."

"There's nowhere else," huffed Wallace, exasperated, but then his face brightened. "Unless…."

Wallace rushed to the stuffed bookshelf and thumbed quickly across the spines of several volumes, finally grasping a huge volume and pulling it clear. Wallace brought it over to the low table and hurriedly opened it up. The book was titled *Cherubim Throughout History*. Mumbling softly to himself, Wallace flipped through the pages until he came to the one he wanted. Silently reading the passage, he finally murmured, "I don't believe it."

"What did you find?" Jake leaned forward in anticipation. An artistic rendering depicted what looked like a Spanish conquistador spearing a loin-clothed man, feathers gathered in his hair.

"Are you familiar with the invasion of the Americas by the Spanish in the 1500s?"

"Not really," admitted Jake.

Wallace sighed. "The Spanish came to Central America searching for gold around 1519. The details surrounding the why and how of this are not important, but what is important is *who* came with them."

"Who was that?"

"Roman Catholic priests," replied Wallace. "They came to convert the Aztec people to Catholicism. In the opinion of the Catholic priests, the Aztecs were merely a bloodthirsty race who committed murder, sacrificing humans to their pagan gods upon altars bathed in blood. There is a reasonable likelihood this was true – the sacrifices I mean – but the reasons behind them may be substantially different to what the textbooks specify."

"How so?" asked Jake, intrigued.

"This writing," Pointreid jabbed his finger at the book on the table, "relates to potential instances of cherubim throughout different periods of history. I've read it before, many times, and that's why I thought to look here for clues. Now, many of these claims are downright ridiculous, but in here it talks of the Aztec belief that Templo Mayor – the main temple of the Aztecs – guarded something incredible. They believed in some sort of horror beneath the temple, and that's what their human sacrifices were designed to appease. According to this, once the Spanish conquered them something very bad happened."

"Well?" prompted Jake when he paused. "What was it? Don't leave me hanging in suspense."

"It's not clear, but the book writes of something decimating the ranks of the Spanish when they attempted to penetrate deep beneath Templo Mayor. The ones who escaped the temple were rendered completely insane. Cortez, the leader of the Spanish, ordered the systematic destruction of the entire city of Tenochtitlan – including the temple itself. The only things remaining on the site are ruins."

"But how does this tie in with us finding a way to the Garden of Eden?" asked Jake.

Wallace rubbed his forehead, sweeping a hand through his receding hair, pushing it back over his scalp. "The scraps of language found carved into the temple, which the Spanish managed to document before their destruction, spoke of many things, but there was one phrase singled out just beneath a warning. Translated many years later, they discovered it spoke of the cherubim, the protectors of the Garden."

"Whoa!" breathed Jake. "Do you think...?"

"I think it's the strongest lead we have," replied Wallace. "I'll book our tickets immediately." He rose to leave. ·   .

"We're going there?" asked Jake.

Wallace paused, his hand on the door, and turned around to face Jake once more. "We need to go to the place where Tenochtitlan and Templo Mayor used to stand: Mexico City." Turning the knob he strode from the room, leaving Jake alone, unsure of whether he should feel relieved or terrified.

***

The plane jolted Jake awake, and his head snapped up. He stared around wildly, panic nearly overwhelming him. Whatever dream had been tormenting his subconscious disappeared in an instant, not even the remnants of its dark cloud lingering.

Wiping a thin line of crusted drool from the edge of his mouth, he took in his surroundings, recognizing the layout of the Boeing 747-400 and relaxing back into the business-class recliner seat. As stressed as he felt anticipating the coming events, he still enjoyed the feeling of not being cramped into one of the seats in the economy section of the plane. Yawning widely, he reached for his bottle of water, noticing Wallace still asleep in the seat beside him, a look of anguish etched into his slumbering features.

The parting from his family had been wrenching to observe, especially when Wallace's young boys – aged seven and nine – didn't understand why they had to leave their home. His wife had accepted it better, and Jake suspected she knew it had something to do with Wallace's family history. Still, her tears had been awkward to witness, and Jake had walked away to give them some privacy. They deserved it; if things were as dangerous as Wallace had made out, this might be the last time they saw each other.

The thought disturbed Jake, and he tried to shake it away, but it clung to his mind and wouldn't let go, like chewing gum enmeshed in his conscience. The warnings promising the damnation of his soul still echoed through Jake's mind, combining with the memory of his encounter with Abaddon, and making it extremely difficult for him to fall asleep. He stretched out and settled back into the comfortable recliner, shutting his eyes once more, determined to get some rest.

As soon as his lids closed, Jake's mind was assaulted by images so horrific he fought to wrench his eyes back open, only to find them locked. Scenes of children flayed alive, women brutally raped and abused, and men torn to pieces by the vehemence of a solitary figure –

Abaddon.

The dark, tormented form trod unhurriedly between multitudes of races; his long, clawed fingers seeming to merely brush their exposed flesh, unleashing torment as unseen attackers fell upon their fragile human forms. Jake struggled uselessly against the bonds locking him to the vision, soundlessly screaming out as his brain quaked, threatening shutdown against the horror it was being forced to witness. Crimson splashed across his mind's eye, and Jake found himself mercilessly dragged through Abaddon's wake, like an emaciated mongrel on a heavy chain.

Abaddon turned and stared malevolently at Jake, a blood-mist spraying from his slit nostrils with each exhalation, his blue eyes piercing Jake's soul like twin spikes of ice.

"I know who you are now, Legacy," growled the Fallen, "and I know what you plan. I have put my mark on you, and there is nowhere you can go where I will not find you. You should have taken the gift of your life, my mistake and your boon, and blindly lived out your meager measure of years as these other ignorant monkeys do.

"I was happy – as happy as one such as I can be – staying in my little section of this pathetic planet and creating a corner of anarchy, but now you have drawn me out, and I must follow you. I am a king in this world, possessed of resources you cannot even begin to imagine. I can shed my appearance at will, taking on another as it suits me. You will never know who or *what* I am. The pathetic shell you saw in Uganda is not the one which will come for you. It might be the form of someone you trust, maybe even the ridiculous one who thinks himself so smart and is now trying to wake you. Rest well, Legacy. Your heart will taste all the sweeter for the panic which shall surely fill it."

Jake gasped for air, throwing the figure atop him away like a rag doll. He barely had time to register the crowd of people and flight attendants surrounding his chair before realizing the person now sprawled on the floor of the aisle was actually Wallace.

"Wallace! I –"

The small man scrambled swiftly to his feet. "Don't say anything! These people don't need to know about your seizures."

Glancing hurriedly at the inquisitive faces surrounding him, Jake nodded. The plane had fallen completely silent apart from the whispering of those arrayed around him, whom the flight attendants were now thankfully ushering away.

Jake glanced out the small window beside his chair and saw the plane had landed while he'd been trapped within his vision. The people moving past were actually disembarking. Wallace was hurriedly thanking the flight attendants for their assistance and assuring them everything was now under control – all the while flicking worried glances back at Jake.

What the hell had just happened?

It had felt like a nightmare, but seemed so much more realistic than anything Jake had ever dreamed. He could still see the atrocities being committed upon the men, women, and children who had surrounded Abaddon, the wounds left by the invisible hands of unseen assailants clawing and slashing with horrible efficiency.

"Wallace, what was I just doing?" he asked once everyone had moved away.

"You were screaming fit to wake the dead," replied Wallace in a hushed voice. "I couldn't wake you, so I just told everyone you were prone to seizures. I think being business-class passengers helped convince them you weren't just crazy."

Jake could tell by his tone that Wallace himself wasn't too certain of his sanity at the moment, and was probably thinking he'd made a big mistake. Jake needed to somehow explain the situation, but felt afraid Wallace wouldn't believe him. Summoning his courage, Jake glanced around to make sure none of the disembarking passengers or flight crew could hear them.

"I saw Abaddon," he said.

Wallace's eyes narrowed behind his glasses. "In your dream?"

"I don't know what it was; it seemed too real to be a dream, more real than sitting here and looking at you even. I tried to get away, to snap out of whatever was holding me, but I couldn't escape."

"What did he say to you?" asked Wallace.

"He said he'd marked me, and would now be coming for me."

Wallace leaned back, concern etched across his features. "He *marked* you? How would he have done that?" He rubbed his chin quizzically.

"I think we need to get off this plane," said Jake, noticing they were almost alone.

Wallace glanced around and rose. "But we need to discuss everything you saw in this… whatever it was."

Jake nodded, Abaddon's final words reverberating through his memory. He would come for Jake, and he could come as anyone. Until this finally ended, Jake couldn't be sure who anyone truly was, and would need to be on the lookout for anything suspicious those around him might say or do. If he didn't, it might not only mean the end of his life, but also the loss of his soul, never mind the release of something horrific upon the world. The banished angel had previously been content with fermenting anarchy in Northern Uganda, but Jake had drawn him out with whatever threat he presented. Now one of the Fallen wandered the planet, filled with rage, destruction foremost in his mind.

All of which would occur *after* he'd destroyed Jake, of course.

Great.

\*\*\*

The taxi was potentially the worst Jake had ever seen. He hadn't led a sheltered life up until this point, but even the memory of Fletcher's mercenary trucks seemed a luxury compared to this rusted old Volkswagen Beetle – the rear seat smelled like a wondrous combination of stale urine and vomit. Even with the window rolled down as far as it could go, Jake tasted bile rising in his throat. His hand happened upon something tacky and stuck to the fabric seat cover. He suddenly felt certain his stomach contents would flee completely out his throat.

"How much further?" he gasped. An echo of inquiry, almost pleading, followed from an equally nauseated Wallace, who hunched on the other side of the back seat, sucking in air through his own window.

"Qué?" asked the driver, seemingly untouched by the stench bubble they were trapped in.

"How long to Templo Mayor?" yelled Jake over the roaring of the engine. "Er…." He rifled through the English–Spanish dictionary Wallace had bought at the airport. "Cuánto tiempo… Templo Mayor?"

"Uh. Abowt figh minutos," replied the driver in very broken English.

Jake shook his head and threw the dictionary back into his bag on the floor. The driver had initially offered to place their luggage in the trunk under the front hood of the car, but when he'd opened it, a stench like the bowels of Hell had smacked Jake in the face so hard he thought he might pass out. Brown and red smears on the inside lining of the under-hood trunk held mysteries Jake didn't wish to investigate, and just before he slammed the lid down he caught a glimpse of something rubber and balloon-like which did not appear unused....

That had been their first warning about this vehicle, a warning Jake shouldn't have ignored.

Both he and Wallace had packed light, so their bags didn't take up much space, but he still yearned to escape the coffin-like confines of the stench-ridden vehicle. The outside heat didn't help either. Under the pounding sun their cut-price Mexican transport became a fetor-filled pressure-cooker.

Just as Jake contemplated trying to slit his wrists with the buckle-less seatbelt, the cab pulled up to the curb. Jake and Wallace practically hurled themselves free of it, dragging their bags with them. Wallace hurriedly paid the driver, and the man drove the smoking bomb away in a plume of blue-gray haze.

Peering around, Jake saw nothing even remotely similar to a temple. He recalled what Wallace had mentioned about the Spanish destroying Templo Mayor along with the rest of the Aztec city. This modern city, constructed atop the site where the ancient one once sat, had aged badly, and appeared distinctly third-world, leaving it with a very tired feeling. The streets weren't filthy, but Jake saw garbage strewn about, a sickly-sour smell permeating the hot air. Cracks in the pavement were possible evidence of the occasional earthquakes the city suffered, or maybe just further confirmation of the localized poverty and neglect as compared to other, more prosperous, areas of Mexico City.

"Where do we go?" he asked Wallace.

"If there is some sort of entrance, my guess would be it might possibly be hidden beneath the ruins of the Great Temple situated beside the museum, Museo Templo Mayor."

Wallace indicated a large building just back from where they stood, a nearby sign stating the road was called Justo Sierra. They followed a trail of tourists down the cracked concrete leading toward the museum where, according to Wallace, many of the unearthed artifacts of the Aztecs were now housed. They walked for perhaps ten minutes, shuffling along among the tourists who seemed intent on making their way as slowly as possible, until Wallace indicated something over to Jake's left.

It was the Great Temple.

Jake felt immediately underwhelmed.

Even though he'd known it had been destroyed by the Spanish, in his mind's eye he'd thought there might be *something*. Where he'd been expecting a partially collapsed or eroded monolithic structure, there remained merely several flat expanses of ancient pavers, a few sets of stairs, and some stone carvings, all surrounded by fences and railings designed to limit public access to the ruins.

"Is that it?" asked Jake incredulously. He went to lean on one of the railings to get a better view, but retracted his hand before making contact. Jake couldn't identify whatever dripped from the barrier, but he got the distinct impression it might have been left by the previous occupants of their recent taxi.

"The entrance must be underground... somewhere. But how do we get there?" wondered Wallace.

Jake scanned the area, spotting the lower section he guessed must have once been the Great Temple where the Aztec priests had sacrificed so many to appease the hunger of their bloodthirsty gods. Wallace suspected these were actually the cherubim, set to protect the Garden against intruders. If such a thing were true, the sacrifices had been pointless, a wasted exercise cutting short thousands of lives, and as such were doubly tragic.

"Over there," he said, indicating the sacrificial area.

Wallace peered over and nodded. "Yes, I think that would have been where the Grand Temple resided. Let's get down there."

The sandy rock path scratched the soles of Jake's shoes as the two of them slowly pushed their way through the meandering crowds, down into the excavated area, eventually making their way to the rear of the site. Barriers and railings stood everywhere, preventing tourists from wandering from the designated paths and over the actual ruins. This in itself would prove an issue, Jake knew, when it came time to search closer for the doorway or whatever the hell was supposed to give them access to… to what?

"Over there!" called Wallace, barely concealed excitement thrumming his voice.

Shielding his eyes against the glare of the afternoon sun, Jake followed where Wallace indicated and saw a raised circular edifice on the ground, carved from light-colored stone and etched with ancient figures. Wide as a large dining table and perhaps a foot thick, the stone resembled an enormous coin lying flat upon the ground. They moved closer until they could get a better view.

"What is that?" asked Jake.

"I remember reading about it in the book I showed you. It's designed to depict Coyolxauhqui, a powerful female magician who attempted to attack Coatlicue, her mother and Earth deity. The stone is carved with the scene of Coyolxauhqui's execution after her failed attack, and her subsequent dismemberment. It was originally placed at the base of the stairs of the ninety-foot-high temple, and the dismembered bodies from the sacrifices were thrown down the steps to land upon it, supposedly so their essence could bleed out through the stone. If the entrance is anywhere, I think it might be there."

Jake gazed at the crowd standing at the railing surrounding the huge stone, taking photos. Sneaking to it unseen would be impossible.

"Follow me and try to look like you belong," said Jake.

Moving over to the side, he found a small alcove in the rock and casually pushed his backpack into it, pulling his passport out first and sliding it into his pocket, indicating Wallace should do the same. He definitely didn't want to lose his passport if someone chanced upon the hiding place and decided to make a grab for their bags. At least they wouldn't be gone too long, a quick dart closer and then back, but for what Jake wanted to do he had to look as little like a tourist as possible.

Once relieved of their bags, Jake moved back toward the stone disc, climbing casually over the railing and boldly approaching the base of the crumbled stairs. Someone called out something, and he turned and smiled, waving casually, pointing at the logo on the breast pocket of his shirt like it was supposed to mean something. The speaker – one of the local workers on the site – looked confused for a moment, and then waved back. Jake grinned at Wallace, and the two of them moved toward the stone.

When they were almost upon the disc Wallace said, "That's too perfect to be the original stone; it must be a replica, with the main one stored in the museum to preserve it."

Indeed, the stone disc looked completely unblemished and appeared to be made of cement. Jake wondered how that might affect their theory; was it the stone, or the location? Within seconds they had their answer.

The area around the circle began to glow an unearthly red which completely lit the cement replica from the interior, as though it were merely an empty shell filled with a tiny sun. Excited shouting rose from behind them, but Jake couldn't wrench his gaze from the disc, wondering at the marvel occurring before his eyes. The ground began to rumble and shake as a sudden earthquake hit the area.

A resounding crack echoed through the air, and the stone disc fractured down the middle and across as well, so that from above it looked like a huge cross had been stamped upon it. From the center of the cross it began to crumble, cement trickling away like sand, and within seconds the entire disc was gone, and a wide, gaping abyss beckoning.

"How did you do that?" gasped Wallace.

"I have no idea, but there's no time to think about it." The ground stopped shaking and people began shouting once more, even more fervently this time. Jake stepped toward the opening in the ground, staring inside; a circular stairwell spiraled down. "Let's go."

"But what if –"

"Move!" shouted Jake, grabbing Wallace and pulling him along behind him.

The earth began to rumble again as soon as Jake placed his foot upon the top step, and he struggled for balance as he raced down the first section of stairs, dragging the hapless Wallace behind him. They'd descended about ten steps when Jake noticed the stairs getting darker. Glancing up, he saw the disc reassembling itself, cutting out the light. Within seconds it was whole again, and the stairs were plunged into darkness. The shaking of the ground ceased once more, and a deathly silence filled the circular stairwell.

"What now?" asked Wallace, his voice echoing hollowly.

"I don't –" At the sound of Jake's voice, the entire stairwell lit up. An intense, but not uncomfortable glow shone out, seemingly from the walls themselves. The two men stared at each other in shock for a few moments.

"Why do I get the feeling this place was waiting for you?" whispered Wallace. His eyes flickered to Jake's birthmark, his expression unreadable.

"It's just a coincidence," replied Jake hurriedly.

"I don't think so. It was your approach which triggered the opening. Once you touched the first step it began to close. And now the lights come on when you speak? That's a bit too much for coincidence."

"Just lucky, then," said Jake, his stomach clenching. He didn't want to contemplate the implications of what Wallace insinuated.

"Templo Mayor was excavated in the 1980s. That's a long time to be sitting dormant with nobody happening upon this little stairwell for it to be merely luck. They would have done all sorts of scans since then to see if there were any hidden underground chambers, not to mention the replacement of the stone disc; this stairway would have certainly been discovered, which means not just anybody can find it. Who are you really?"

"I don't know what you're talking about," replied Jake hurriedly, descending the stairs once more. Wallace's footsteps echoed behind him.

"I believe you, but what just happened was nothing short of amazing, and I'm sure it had something to do with you. Is it merely a coincidence that your feet have been placed upon this course of restoring equilibrium in the universe? I can't help but feel there are vast amounts of serendipity at work here."

"Stop using big words, you're confusing me," replied Jake, trying to avoid the subject.

Wallace chuckled nervously, the noise echoing slightly as they continued their descent. "I'm sorry. When I get anxious I tend to become slightly pompous."

"I'm scared too, Wallace. But we don't have time to play guessing games. The door opened, and for that I'm grateful, but I'm not about to start philosophizing over the creation of the universe as a result."

"Who's using the big words now?"

Jake glanced back and grinned slightly. "I guess it's contagious."

The stairs continued on, seemingly forever, endlessly drawing them down, sinking ominously into the very mysteries of the Earth.

\*\*\*

Several hours passed. Long hours. The repetitive *crunch, crunch, crunch* of sand beneath Jake's shoes soon fell into time with the ache in his knees as they descended each step. There seemed no end in sight, no matter how Jake craned his neck to peer down the spiraling stairway. Jake's legs began to scream, and every step made him grit his teeth in anticipation of the pain about to shoot through his shins. The glow of the walls seemed restricted to the section they were currently on, illuminating perhaps fifty stairs above and fifty below, giving the impression they made absolutely no progress, no matter how fast they moved. It was like the Stairmaster from Hell.

"Did that book say how long it took the Spaniards to get to the bottom of this damned thing – you know, before they were all slaughtered?"

Wallace grunted behind him as he took another step down. "No, but if this continues much longer I think I'll accept death with open arms."

"Talk to me about something to take my mind off these stairs."

"What would you like to – *ow!* – hear?"

"What do you think about all of this? Was it mentioned in your grandfather's writings at all?"

"No," replied Wallace gingerly, and Jake could sense his mind was focused elsewhere, probably on not falling down the steep stone steps, "but it all seems to be falling into place."

"What do you mean?"

"Well, the near-fanatical attempts of the Spanish invaders to convert the Aztec people to Christianity, the razing of the city – all of it."

"Can you explain that a bit better?"

Wallace huffed slightly, but continued. "Why would they destroy the entire city? Many believed it was to find gold or other artifacts, while others thought it simply to eradicate any sign of the paganism which had occurred at Templo Mayor. But what if it were actually a search for the entrance to the Garden of Eden?"

Jake stopped so suddenly that Wallace almost crashed into him. "They were looking for this?"

"Possibly," replied Wallace. "I really wish we'd brought something to drink, my throat is rasping like sandpaper."

They both sat down, trying to get as comfortable as possible on the triangular stairs. Jake braced his back against the outer wall and sat sideways so as to look back at Wallace without difficulty.

"But why would the Spaniards have been looking to get into the Garden?"

Wallace looked at him incredulously. "Why would they *not*? The Garden contains the Tree of Life! To eat from the Tree of Life would be to live forever, cure any disease, any injury. If continually eaten, the fruit could mean immortality to the person or people who found it."

"You sound like you want to find the Tree yourself," said Jake softly, holding Wallace's gaze.

Wallace grinned self-consciously, dropping his eyes. "I won't lie to you, I would love to walk through the Garden and partake of its fruit – all of its fruits – but that's not why I'm here. We have to stop Abaddon at all costs, and now is not the time for dreams of immortality. Only with the Flaming Sword do we have any chance of fighting him; without it we're doomed."

Jake stared at him until Wallace looked up and met his gaze. Looking deep into Wallace's eyes, Jake trusted what he was saying, and nodded, rising to his feet again. Wallace groaned, but rose as well. The two once more began the awkward descent.

Another hour passed. Finally Jake glimpsed something below which caused his heart to double-beat – it was brightness separate from the illumination of the stairwell walls! Hope rose within Jake, but at the same time he dreaded what they approached; the Garden held unknown terrors which, according to Wallace, had either torn the Spanish invaders to pieces or driven them mad. The two of them may have just made such a mammoth descent only to die horribly.

At least they'd already be in a tomb, he chuckled to himself.

They continued down, adrenaline pushing aside the aches in their bones. Jake saw a final step, an open doorway the source of the external light. He approached the doorway warily; being on an angle, unable to see beyond the huge stone frame, anything might be waiting for them. The bright illumination bore heat and shone like sunlight, beams of radiance streaming through the entrance.

But they were miles beneath the ground... weren't they? There couldn't be any sunlight here.

The exit beckoned, and Jake cautiously approached it, peering around the edge of the frame....

And gasped.

Extending out before him, for as far as he could see, stretched a land carved directly from wonder. He emerged at the top of a hill. Vibrant, emerald grass carpeted the earth, flowing like water over small hillocks, broken only by the tree-line below. Far off in the distance towered mountainous ridges, higher than the Alps and yet untouched by snow, their jagged peaks curving in a razor-sharp ring the entire way around the land. The range linked to the left and right of where Jake now stood, like a colossal defensive wall, forming an immense crater. The basin appeared wide enough to house the moon, and yet at the same time Jake sensed he might be able to sprint across it in a day.

High above soared a cloudless sky, so blue it almost hurt to look at it, a beautiful orb of golden light, almost identical to the sun, beaming brightly from its unmarred heavens. Unlike the sun, however, this globe could be gazed upon without fear of hurting your eyes. A forest of giant oak trees, each at least three-times as large as any Jake had seen in the world above, stretched out before him. Birds colored like rainbows flitted between the trees, their song filling the air with such serenity Jake wanted nothing more than to recline in the lush grass and relax forever. Perhaps he would hike to that magnificent waterfall cascading down the mountains to his left –

"WHO ARE YOU?"

The voice seemed to come from everywhere at once, and an entire flock of birds took flight in terror. Jake stared around for the speaker, but couldn't see him.

"I –" he began, his voice cracking as he backed toward the stairwell once more. He could hear Wallace slowly descending the last few steps behind him.

"Wait!" called a much smoother voice, causing Jake to pause.

Emerging from the trees below stood a young man in his mid-twenties, long flowing hair so white it appeared to glow, cascading over his shoulders and surrounding a face of such intense beauty that Jake gasped. He wore a simple loincloth which seemed to have been spun from unmarred silk, his feet bare against the grass.

"I know you," said the young man, his voice like music, and he swiftly ran across the grass toward Jake, his feet seeming to float above the blades, not marking the lawn's splendor.

Jake heard a shuffle of footsteps behind him and turned, seeing Wallace emerge through the doorway, his look of weariness turning to one of wonder as he stared at the vista surrounding them.

And then it gradually changed into something else, something....

*Predatory?*

There was no mistaking the expression upon Wallace's face; he looked like a lion which had just slaughtered an antelope and now anticipated feasting upon its corpse. Jake felt like he was watching the man transform before his eyes, changing from the genial figure of Wallace into something much more sinister. The glint in his eyes as he gazed around the Garden contained a longing so much deeper than anything academic.

"Wallace —?"

"I told you I would come for you, Legacy," hissed Wallace.

Jake stumbled backward as Wallace smirked maliciously. Midstride, his appearance blurred, as though an enchantment had been lifted, and suddenly Abaddon stood before Jake, his charred skin swimming beneath the strange mist-like substance.

"Did you think I could not conceal my true appearance from you? You are pathetic. I took over your friend on that airplane as easily as slicing the flesh from a baby, but it was only thanks to you that I was able to get close enough to possess him. He trusted you, and lowered his guard when trying to help you escape from your dream. His soul tasted like wine." The fallen angel cackled hollowly.

"YOU!!!" bellowed a voice from behind Jake. He spun around to see the young man approaching them, a flaming sword blazing high in his hand.

A Flaming Sword!

Even amid the chaos, Jake realized what the man held.

Something suddenly smashed into Jake from behind. Unable to move, he glanced down. His ribs had blown outward, a horrific clawed hand emerging from his chest, something the size of a softball clutched in its grip.

"I told you I would have your heart," hissed the rank voice of Abaddon in his ear.

Jake sucked in a whistling breath, his broken ribs cracking further as he did so. Everything was fading. The world around him began to spin.

He breathed out….

And died.

-*CHAPTER 5*-
# THE INVASION OF EDEN

Awareness came slowly, and the first thing Jake sensed was birdsong, the sweet chorus of the birds he'd heard so recently in – where had that been? The beauty of the land aroused his senses, and Jake swam through the murk ever more swiftly toward the song. Within moments he noticed the blanket of grass beneath him and felt the crisp breeze, the wondrous scent of some elusive bloom drifting upon it.

His memory sprang back into focus, and Jake recalled the last thing he'd seen. It had been Abaddon's hand jutting through his chest from his back, the fallen angel's clawed fist squeezing... grasping....

His heart!

Jerking upright, Jake sucked in a huge gasp of air and clutched at his chest. It seemed remarkably whole. Momentarily bewildered, he stared at the hole in his shirt, blood crusted and drying around its edges.

"You are lucky Abaddon waited until you had led him to this place before he attacked you," said a silky voice behind him.

Jake spun around, ending up crouched on the ground, staring up at the handsome young man who had confronted him upon entering the Garden. Climbing warily to his feet, Jake remembered the sword, and wondered where the man had concealed it. He wore no scabbard, barely wore any clothing apart from his silk loincloth, and as such Jake doubted he carried it upon his person. Yet he couldn't take anything for granted.

"You may relax," said the man calmly, "Abaddon has been driven away. Perhaps he didn't expect to find me here as guard, or else his intentions were otherwise." The man's stunningly blue eyes fixed upon Jake's birthmark, and he nodded slightly.

"Wallace told me there would only be cherubim here," said Jake hesitantly, hoping to change the subject.

"*Only* cherubim. I fear your friend had no real concept of what cherubim truly are, or else he might have shown them more respect. But it would explain why Abaddon was so startled to see me here; possessing a mortal passes all their memories on to the inhabiting spirit, and as such Abaddon would probably have only known what your friend knew."

"What happened to Wallace?" asked Jake, though he feared he already knew the answer.

"His spirit has gone – whether on toward the light or consumed by Abaddon, I cannot say. But it shows your true measure in that one of your first questions would be about him and not yourself. Aren't you curious as to how you are still alive?"

Jake glanced down at his chest once more and stood up. Beneath the torn and bloodied shirt there wasn't so much as a scar, even the scar from his previous operation had disappeared. He ran his hand across the flesh, half expecting an illusion to rub away.

"It was no dream," said the young man. His voice sang like the birdsong surrounding them, inhuman and musical, beauty formed into speech.

"H-how did you know what I was thinking?"

"It is not difficult to guess what a mortal would be thinking at a time like this. Humans always try to discount what you don't understand as being *impossible*. Nothing is impossible, my friend. The universe is vaster than anything you could imagine, full of mysteries which would baffle humanity's wisest professors. What people think of as standard today was deemed witchcraft a thousand years ago, and yet the arrogance of the human race prohibits them from envisaging anything different. They still pride themselves as being the center of the universe, even though the universe itself contradicts such an obtuse assumption."

"Who are you?" asked Jake.

"My name is Uriel. I am what you would call an archangel."

The words were stated simply, so simply, in fact, that at first Jake didn't fully grasp their significance. As he stared at the figure standing calmly before him, he realized what Uriel had just uttered.

"I'm sorry, you're a *what?*"

"You see? Instantly your mind rejects what it does not understand. You are thinking about stories from your Bible and creatures with wings – and before you ask, no I am not reading your mind. You are as predictable as every other human I have had to deal with over the eons." Uriel's voice remained calm, but seemed all the more mocking because of it. It was like being lectured by an extremely patient teacher.

"Oh. Um… okay," stumbled Jake awkwardly. "Er – how is it I'm still alive?"

Uriel smiled, the expression lighting up his entire face, making it intensely beautiful, causing Jake to gasp slightly. It wasn't erotic beauty, more like seeing the purest sunrise after months of rain – a natural wonder.

"You are in Eden's Garden," stated Uriel. "This is where God's Tree of Everlasting Life blossoms. Its fruit can heal any wound."

Jake nodded, too stunned to talk, and then suddenly realized he hadn't asked the most important thing. "What happened to Abaddon? Did you kill him with your flaming sword?"

Uriel smiled once again, but it seemed slightly more strained this time. "Abaddon has existed since time began. One doesn't simply kill him. I did manage to fight him off with the aid of the cherubim. He has fled from Eden – for now. After learning the location of the Garden, however, he may seek to return with greater forces."

"It will take him a fair amount of time to get back up those stairs. Surely we could chase him," Jake urged. "You have to understand, he can't be left to continue on Earth unchecked; we *have* to stop him while we have the chance." Jake ran toward the stairway, but froze in his tracks mere steps later. A blank wall of rock faced him where before the doorway had opened. He scanned the area, certain there must be some sort of mistake, but there was no access – the stairs were gone!

"Abaddon did not leave via the route you both entered," said Uriel calmly. "He shed the body of your companion and fled ethereally. I have sealed the stairwell against his physical return, but he will, in all likelihood, discover another way to enter, and I must remain here to protect the Garden from him lest he revisit. I cannot aid you beyond this place; my bond will not allow it."

"Your *bond*? With who?"

"With God."

And there it was.

Jake knew he shouldn't be surprised; he *was* talking to an angel, after all. But the sudden introduction of God into the equation took this beyond a scenario where he could simply think of Abaddon as an immensely powerful creature with little to no moral partiality, and had to step outside everything he knew to be true. This was entering the next level of oddity, and Jake felt a desperate need to delay it.

"Where's Wallace's body?" he asked.

"It is gone. The Garden took it."

"What's that mean? Did you bury him?" asked Jake, looking around for some indication of a grave.

"It means he has been absorbed into the Garden. All of life is made up of energy, swirling and flowing throughout the cosmos. That energy never dies, it merely changes. This is how rebirth is possible, what humans might call reincarnation."

"Wait," said Jake. "You mean to tell me reincarnation is possible?"

"In a sense. The energy of the dead returns to the universal stream of energy, but is usually constrained to Earth before being absorbed through living creatures, eventually finding new life in some way, shape or form. Sometimes that life has consciousness, and the energy retains memories within that consciousness, a sense of being something before living, and in its new life that energy takes on certain traits from its former subsistence, recollections and skills aiding it throughout its new being. This is how humans have come to perceive reincarnation."

"So it's not just dying, and then being reborn into another body?"

"*Just* dying? Dying is one of the most complex things human beings will ever accomplish, and should not be trivialized in such a way."

Jake thought about what Uriel was saying for a moment, comprehension dangling tantalizingly close.

"So through death... we are reborn... but not necessarily as we choose. I might be reborn as a... tree?"

"Perhaps," replied Uriel patiently. "It is through this that life is fully experienced."

"Then you're saying that the Bible has it all wrong?"

Uriel frowned slightly. "Why do you say that?"

"Well... it says we die and go to Heaven. But if we're reborn that can't be true, right?"

"All things are true, as I told you before. This universe is made up of more marvels than even I have been able to witness; what hope has someone of your limited span of years to understand that which has been unraveling forever?"

This was like wrestling with eels. Every time Jake thought he'd grasped what Uriel was talking about, the meaning slipped away once more. Surely all of it couldn't be right, could it?

"Reincarnation – the rebirth of energy through new life – that's real, right?" he asked cautiously.

"In a sense."

"And Heaven is real as well?"

Uriel smiled. "It is if you want it to be."

"Why can't you just answer me?" snapped Jake before the calmness of the Garden soothed him once more, and he sighed. "Sorry," he murmured. Uriel smiled.

"I cannot *just* answer you because that is not the way knowledge is attained. *You* must come into understanding on your own, I can merely guide you."

"But why are you guiding me?" asked Jake. "Is it just because I'm trying to fight Abaddon, or is it something else?"

Uriel seemed to ponder the question for a moment. "That is something you will have to decide on your own when the time is right. I cannot simply tell you, because to do so would unravel the reason for my assistance."

Jake shook his head, frustration mounting within him once more, but he let it go, drifting away with the light breeze which kissed his neck. Thinking about it, he decided to change the course of his questioning.

"What is this place – this *Garden*?"

"This was to be the keeper of life and knowledge for the world above," replied Uriel, strolling along and indicating the beautiful valley spread out before them, trees layered to its farthest reaches.

"So the Bible is right? Did Adam and Eve begin life for humans here?"

Uriel smiled, somewhat forlornly this time. "Adam and Eve? Theirs is truly a sad tale."

"You mean they actually *existed*?" Jake couldn't believe it.

"Oh yes, they were very real. Over the centuries a handful of people have inadvertently stumbled upon this place – those with the appropriate disposition and makeup of positive energy."

"Like me?"

"Yes… but also no. The others were not intended to be allowed access, whereas you were."

"Me?" asked Jake. "Why was I allowed access?"

"So that we might have this conversation, of course."

Jake swallowed down his frustration, knowing that to follow such a line of conversation would ultimately get him nowhere. It seemed there were only certain questions the archangel would clarify directly, others would simply become leaves in a sandstorm.

"So what about Adam and Eve?"

"Adam and Eve gained access, and we welcomed them for the innocence they held within themselves. The only rule we gave them was they were not to eat from a certain tree –"

"The Tree of Knowledge of Good and Evil, right?"

"No. There is no such tree. Humans have possessed that knowledge within themselves since they crawled from the sludge of this newly-born planet. The tree I speak of contains an influence more terrible than good or evil; it bears a fruit which grants the one who consumes it immeasurable physical and intellectual power, but saps the energy of their spirit. With such a thing, humans could become elevated above their fellow man, but would become tyrannical in their power, creating disharmony with their hunger for more power. Such was it with the two you speak of, the ones you call Adam and Eve. They could not contain their curiosity at what the fruit might grant them, and gave up eternal life in this place in order to taste the power the fruit contained.

"We drove them from here, not as punishment, but because they posed a grave threat to the harmony of Eden. If they had stayed, the Garden would have died as the darkness within them grew and sucked all that is altruistic away from that which surrounded them. They returned to the world above, full of ambition, but with nothing to expend it upon. In order to elevate their station they immortalized themselves within the pages of what you now call the Bible, altering certain facts so as to make their blame appear less."

"Like the snake?" suggested Jake.

Uriel nodded, his visage soft, no condemnation in his gaze. "Yes. The snake was a metaphor for their greed and temptation – which also proved their undoing."

Something occurred to Jake. "What did Abaddon want with this place? He kept me alive in order to gain access, but why?"

"He wanted the fruit from that tree, along with the fruit from the Tree of Life. If he combined the two of these with his own dark energy, he'd be able to create an army of immortals so powerful and ambitious he could destroy nations."

"How can you be so certain that's what he was after? Did he tell you?" asked Jake.

Uriel shook his head. "Because that is what he managed to snatch before he was driven away. Luckily the amount he stole was negligible, but doubles the chance he will return."

Jake was aghast. "He got the fruit? How?"

"I am not sure. Abaddon does not seem bound by the laws which limit our kind on this plane of existence; he should not be able to act the way he does."

"How so?" asked Jake, the serenity of Eden not preventing his pulse from quickening.

"In order for me to exist in this realm, a body was created for me to inhabit. I cannot be on Earth in my natural form without weakening the corporeal sphere to the point where it might shatter. My body is stronger than yours, and like the fruit from the Tree of Life I do not age. Yet, given enough trauma to my physical form, I can be killed. My spirit – the energy which makes up that which you would call an angel – cannot die unless I decide to expend it. Do you follow what I am saying?"

Jake nodded hesitantly. "There are rules which you have to abide by here which you normally wouldn't, right?"

"Correct," said Uriel. "Abaddon seems no longer bound by these rules, and can travel from body to body at will, or leave human form completely and travel as pure energy. This shouldn't be possible, especially for one of the Fallen, who are completely barred from accessing this realm. They are bound within Hell, the universe's greatest prison, and the power required to break loose is unimaginable."

The mention of Hell brought something to the surface of Jake's memory. "Wallace – the man whose body Abaddon was possessing – said his grandfather was some sort of authority on the occult. I'm not certain, but I think he did something to grant the Fallen access to Earth. Abaddon somehow ended up in the body of Joseph Kony in Uganda and began creating as much torment there as he could… until I turned up. Since then, it seems he's decided to broaden his activities."

The archangel nodded thoughtfully, his eyes never leaving Jake. "He would have expanded his dark reach eventually; you were merely the catalyst which made him act," said Uriel casually. "But what you say about your companion's ancestor unlocking something to allow the Fallen through cannot be true, or else we would be inundated with them. It may be that he opened a crack, and Abaddon slipped through, but the power to do something like that would be inconceivable for a mortal."

"I don't know," replied Jake, "but the evidence is here. I mean, Abaddon is running around using people like they're finger puppets, right?"

Uriel shrugged. "This is true, and it would explain his actions up until this point."

"What do you mean?"

"By causing death and destruction, he weakens the ambient energy holding harmony together in a singular place – for instance, this Uganda you speak of. It may be that by creating anarchy, Abaddon is hoping to open a gateway to allow the other Fallen through."

"That would be bad," said Jake.

"I think bad would be an understatement," mused Uriel.

"What are we talking about – Armageddon?"

"Possibly."

The conversational way Uriel spoke was both calming and maddening to Jake. "What are we going to do about it?"

"I have told you before, my mandate prohibits me from leaving the Garden for any reason unless God instructs me to, and He will not."

"But why not? You already failed to protect the fruit."

"That is irrelevant," responded Uriel without resentment. "My purpose is to guard *this* place; that is my reason for being until another function is given to me. I cannot sacrifice that in order to aid you, regardless of how much I might deem your cause important."

"That was a really complicated way of saying no," muttered Jake. "What can I do? I'm just a man."

"Just a man?" Uriel glanced at him and chuckled, the sound golden, his eyes glinting with humor. "Have you heard nothing I have said? You must discover the way to your destiny on your own. If I were to tell you which way to go, your quest would be doomed to failure before your first step. You have not yet gained the strength to walk the destiny you are intended for."

"Then how am I supposed to know?"

"You start walking the path, and deal with your problems as they arise. You can sit around deliberating on the wisest choices or waiting for someone of greater intellect to come along and make the difficult decisions for you, but that would be a life wasted. You must begin, and then follow it through until you either fail or succeed. That is all you can do."

"So if I decide to take on Abaddon, I can't back out?"

"I think you're already beyond that point, wouldn't you agree?" replied Uriel.

Jake nodded, gripping his elbows and hugging his chest. Uriel stared hard into Jake's eyes, his gaze seemingly penetrating every inner shield Jake had ever built.

"You must conquer your own demons before you battle any others. Any weakness you possess will be a feast for one of the Fallen, and he will use all your fears against you."

Jake contemplated arguing, but there was knowledge in the archangel's gaze, so he merely nodded. They strolled toward the line of trees at the bottom of the hill. "Okay, so let's say I want to fight Abaddon. How do I do it?" asked Jake.

"That is something you'll need to discover on your own. The answer resides where your true strength will eventually lie: within yourself."

"Can I use your sword? Will that kill him?"

Uriel paused in his walk and extended his hand. Instantly a flaming blade appeared in his grip, extending three-feet up from the thumb-side of Uriel's fist.

"This blade is a part of me – my inner energy – flowing and controlled by my spiritual essence. It is not a weapon to be handed over like a human tool, any more than I can lend you my leg."

"Damn," muttered Jake. He thought about pleading with Uriel for more information, but knew it would prove futile. As human as the archangel seemed, there was something immutable about him which Jake knew wouldn't budge. "So where are we going now?"

"Where would you like to go?"

"What do you mean?" asked Jake, frowning.

"The Garden has many exits leading to different lands throughout your world, so where would you like to go?"

"Can I stay here for a while to consider things?"

"That would not be advisable," replied Uriel, his voice, as ever, irritatingly devoid of inflection.

"Why not?"

Uriel glanced toward the sky. "Because I believe Abaddon will return with those he has converted."

"But why?" asked Jake. "Why would he come back? He stole the fruit."

"He did not get all of it, merely some. But he will return for other reasons; by now he will know he failed to kill you, and will return to finish the job as soon as possible."

"*Me*? Why would he care about me?"

"Because you are more important than you can possibly fathom. There are many things you do not yet understand, Jacob, but they will become clearer in time – if you live long enough."

"That's a nice thought," muttered Jake.

"For now, you must simply accept that you are currently the most important player in a game which has existed since the dawn of time. Find those whom you can trust and keep them close to you; you will discover how to protect them from the machinations of Abaddon when the time is right. For now your most important function is to survive. Learn what you can as you progress along your path, and grow stronger as a result."

Jake sighed. "You realize that's about as clear as mud, don't you?"

Uriel gave him a grim smile. "I am forbidden to tell you any more than I already have. To do so would jeopardize everything we have worked toward since Satan was first cast out of Heaven. But we shall soon be meeting with one from your world who may be able to enlighten you further. He has travelled his own path, one much darker than yours, and one which is far from over. It may be that he can help you for a time. One thing is for certain, however, he has something within him which will prohibit Abaddon from possessing his body, and for the time being it shall mean you can walk with someone you will be able to trust."

"Who is he?"

"You will meet him when you choose which way you wish to go," replied Uriel enigmatically.

"But how is that possible? If I choose the wrong direction I'll never meet him."

"Some things are incontrovertible, and this is one of them. We shall continue across the valley, and during that time you will decide which path is truly yours. The information you have at your disposal is all you need, and when the time is right the other shall attend, though he does not realize why just yet. He is on a different quest to the one you are about to partake in, and will not be swayed from it, no matter the coercion. I warn you not to upset him, because though he may assist us in what we need, he may also see you as a threat, and no fruit will resurrect you from what he is able to assail you with."

"You make him sound worse than Abaddon," said Jake, his nervousness beginning to rise, despite the tranquility of their surroundings.

"In many ways he is. He carries something within him more powerful than anything Abaddon could ever hope to compete with, and he has faced down creatures much like those you now fear."

Jake looked up, seeing they had now reached the tree line. "Then he can help me fight Abaddon."

"You do not listen, despite what you hear," said Uriel, shaking his head. "He will not budge from his own quest, no matter what is said to him. He may help you for a time if it does not hinder what he needs to do, but do not expect him to follow you. His darkness would burn the purity within you, and though the path he walks may alter slightly, it will never, ever change."

"Who is this man you keep talking about?" asked Jake, frustrated.

"He is an enigma, a complete contradiction through his own actions. He hates and loves, kills and saves, all at his own whim."

"You do realize you're quite the enigma yourself, don't you?"

Uriel turned to Jake and smiled once more, the same dazzling energy radiating out through his expression yet again, unnerving Jake with its power. It was like looking at the most brilliant sunset over and over again, each viewing more incredible than the last.

"I am *supposed* to be an enigma, Jacob."

"I have so many questions, but you're not going to give me any answers, are you?"

"We need to travel through the Garden now; are you ready?" asked Uriel, ignoring Jake's query.

Jake looked at the towering woodland spread before them. It seemed unlike any forest he had ever seen, like something out of an incredible fantasy or fairy tale. The trees were similar to oaks, but infinitely taller, the shortest at least the height of a forty story building. Despite the magnificence of the forest, light still streamed through the branches and, as Jake had previously observed, the ground was bare of bracken, leaves or fallen branches. The effect was dramatic, making the forest seem more like a tranquil park. Birdsong filtered through the thin canopy, and Jake could hear the bubbling of a rippling stream somewhere off to his left.

"How is all this possible, Uriel?"

"What do you mean?"

"I mean we're under the ground, aren't we? How can the sun be here and trees and everything? It defies the laws of nature."

Uriel smiled softly. "And who created those laws?"

"Well...." He was about to say nobody, but then realized what Uriel meant.

A moment of clarity hit Jake like one of the rays of impossible sunlight filtering down through the huge trees surrounding them. He had to make a choice at this junction; a decision larger than anything he had ever needed to worry about before in his life. Uriel stood before him, within the Garden of Eden, a place he had formerly believed only a myth. Here Jake had been killed, his heart ripped from his chest by one of the Fallen, one cast out of Heaven by...

... by God.

This was what now confronted Jake in this place of unreal beauty. Did he believe in something which had created the universe, something which continued, even now, to watch over all of mankind?

Did he believe in God?

A part of Jake rebelled instantly at the thought, his inner child recoiling, screaming as it backed away into the recesses of his mind, the memory of male-sweat and bourbon-whisky-breath hissing out the commandments... particularly the fifth.

*"Honor thy father and thy mother."*

The mewling creature that had once been his smiling adoptive mother, sitting in the corner as the unshaven beast whipped her for her tears. She was supposed to be stronger. Jake would have liked her to have been stronger.

Tearing himself away from the memory with an audible gasp, Jake swallowed hard. Despite the calm of the Garden, he felt tears threatening and forced them away, a trick he'd learned long ago. Tears were for the weak, and God didn't tolerate the weak. Those who God refused to tolerate were punished brutally.

The bitter memories resurrected a need to help others, a burning sensation which drove all other fears aside in its quest to be sated. Had all of this, his entire life, been choreographed in such a way as to make him the tool of some divine force? Did God, or whatever pulled the strings of the universe, need him to be His tool, shaped through design and anguish in order to act exactly as He chose? If that were the case, Jake should rebel. Something which would impose such pain on someone so young should never be followed, and yet his nature told him otherwise. His memories of the malevolence wrought at Abaddon's bidding burned deeply, the spirit of the Ugandan boy urged him to fight when he wanted nothing more than to walk away.

Was this the trap he had been placed into? Would he both despise and crave the course set out for him? Could he follow a God who had abandoned him when his own calls for help had gone unanswered, forcing him to stop believing in any kind of loving deity? Did God even exist? Such a concept seemed impossible to him.

He gazed at the Garden surrounding him once more, his eyes widening and heart lifting as he tilted his head backward to peer up at the towering trees surrounding him.

Everything he was seeing of late seemed impossible in the eyes of science. His heart had been punched out through his chest! Yet now he found himself alive again, without even so much as a scar beneath his torn and bloodied shirt. Jake contemplated the possibility it had been a hallucination, but then remembered the agony, and the vision of his ribs thrusting out his chest, blood spraying from between them....

No, that had been all too real.

Jake thought back over his life, contemplating every choice and decision he had made. Had they all truly been his alone, or had something else been pushing him along in order to end up in this exact place at this exact time? He tried to shake the thought away, but it wouldn't budge. There was something far too convenient about all of this; it slotted a little too perfectly into what Jake had subconsciously been striving for his entire life:

To save the world.

The concept seemed colossal, and immensely arrogant, even in his own mind. But when Jake broke it down, this was exactly the choice he faced. The memory of Aadesh's prophecy so long ago in Pakistan came back to Jake with startling clarity, and a huge sense of responsibility seemed to weigh down on him.

"Uriel," he asked softly, "what was Jesus like?"

The angel smiled knowingly. "He was a man with tremendous courage."

"But he was a *man*, right?"

"What else could he be?" countered Uriel.

Jake stared at the ground. "They say he was the son of God."

Silence filled the glade where they stood, and even the birds seemed to have hushed. Everything in the Garden appeared to be anticipating Uriel's answer.

"Of course he was."

Jake breathed out an immense sigh of relief. "Thank goodness for that." He chuckled.

"Why do you say that?"

Jake glanced at him, noticing how Uriel's head was cocked in silent curiosity. "It's stupid really, but a man…. Actually, don't worry about it."

"The man said you were Christ reborn." It was not a question, but a statement.

"Yeah," replied Jake. "How crazy is that?"

"Why would you say that?" Uriel's voice was soft. The silence in the Garden suddenly seemed terrifying.

"I can't be… *him*. I mean… I mean… it's just not possible!"

Uriel shook his head softly. "Once again a man listens, but does not hear. Why am I not surprised?"

"I don't follow you." Jake's voice shook, just a tiny tremor, like the precursor of an earthquake.

"Energy. The entire universe is made up of energy which never depletes nor disappears. Christ was created using the same energy which you are now made up of, so why can you not be Christ reborn?"

"But you just said he was the son of God!"

"All humans were created by God," replied Uriel, "and as such you are all His sons or daughters... in one sense or another."

"But... but Jesus created miracles. He healed the sick, and... and rose from the dead."

"As you have so recently done," replied Uriel, his voice maddeningly serene.

"But that was because of the fruit!" argued Jake.

Uriel shrugged. "The how or the why doesn't take away from the fact your heart, potentially the most vital organ in the human body, was torn from your chest. You died within moments, yet now you are alive once more. Where is the difference?"

"I...." Jake struggled like a man drowning beneath incontrovertible fact. "But I've never healed anyone, I haven't performed any miracles."

"Doctors heal the sick every day. Charlatans perform marvels. There is much more to a miracle than these things, as you will no doubt learn."

"But I – I can't –" Jake was trembling so hard now that he stepped back and sat down on a massive tree root in order to stop from falling over.

"I remember Gabriel telling me about this sort of reaction by humans, but never thought to see it for myself," murmured Uriel. More loudly, he said, "How can you deny that which is in your heart?"

"This is too much, can't you see that?" pleaded Jake. "Jesus was – "

"This has nothing to do with *Jesus*."

"But you're saying I'm Christ reborn, or whatever."

Uriel shook his head, looking bemused. "Jesus was a man. What you hold within you is more than that, something which cannot be described in words. It is like hope without focus, life without conception, dreams without sleep. Do you understand?"

"I haven't the slightest idea what you are talking about."

"He had the courage and the dream to fight for what he believed in; that energy now resides within you."

Jake sat upon the root, unable to speak for a moment. Finally he stood again. "I can't do this – I'm not the guy for this job."

"This is not a *job*," replied Uriel, something akin to humor sparkling in his eyes. "This is who you are, part of what resides within your soul; your essence. You may deny it all you want, but eventually it will shine through."

"But what am I supposed to do?"

"Follow your heart. Do not try to be anything other than yourself, and trust your instincts, they will show you the way."

"That's great," muttered Jake, holding his head in his hands. He wasn't some spiritualistic guru destined to alter the world, he was just a man.

True, something deep within drove him to aid people wherever he could. His efforts – first through his misguided attempts in the United Nations, and then through his short-lived work with the Red Cross – had seen him travel into danger with little regard for his own safety. For as long as he could remember he'd yearned to help others, to aid people who couldn't help themselves, but this... this eclipsed anything he could have ever conceived.

Jake dropped to his knees and heaved. Vomit gushed over the pristine grass: a splash of impurity within its unspoiled beauty – just like Jake. He shouldn't be here, not with the corruption imprinted upon his soul. They had to have the wrong man.

Despite Uriel's assurances that nothing was expected from him, Jake knew what he was supposed to do. He knew what the second-coming of Christ heralded; he'd heard the gospel preached enough to almost recite it from memory.

Armageddon. The End of Days.

Jake looked up at the archangel. "I –"

A hollow explosion rumbled directly overhead, and Jake shot to his feet, staring through the branches at the incredible sky high above. He couldn't be sure if it was his imagination or not, but it seemed as though a crack had appeared within the seamless blue. Jake was reminded how long the walk down the stairs had taken and how many miles they must be underground. For something to be cracking the roof –

"It is Abaddon," said Uriel calmly, not even looking up. "He must have gathered a force and has returned to reap the rest of the Garden."

"What do you mean?" asked Jake, still staring worriedly at the sky.

"The fruit will enable him to create an army of undying warriors with which to destroy your planet. With enough death and chaos he will be able to weaken the chains which hold the rest of the Fallen in Hell, and then they will once more challenge God."

"What can we do?"

Uriel stared at him. "Have you decided on your path?"

"What do you mean?" gasped Jake. "How can I know where on Earth to go when this is going on above our heads?"

"I was never meaning your physical destination; I meant your path through life. This was always to be a journey of your mind to awareness, and acceptance of what you truly are. Have you decided which path your life will take?"

As another, even more devastating explosion sounded overhead, Jake suddenly understood. This was the moment where he had to choose his destiny. It wasn't written in stone, he had the option to walk away from it, from everything, and live out whatever life he chose.

He grimaced, all doubt instantly falling away from him. There really wasn't a choice, despite the illusion of one. This was who he was, not a man from another time, merely a man with the power to do something good in the world. He wasn't Jesus, and he wasn't God, he was Jacob Hope, perfectly imperfect, and that would have to be enough.

Uriel saw his reaction, and his radiant smile beamed once more. "You bring me joy, Jacob," said the archangel, "and hope. Your legacy sits well within you."

Jake recognized the incredible coincidence between Uriel's words and Abaddon's pronouncement. Was it merely a coincidence, or was there possibly more to it that he was yet to discover? Another jarring detonation shook the air around them, closer this time, and Jake glanced up, seeing the crack had widened.

"He is here," said Uriel, pointing through the forest. "The Dark Man."

Jake looked around to see who Uriel was talking about, and spotted an incredibly intense-looking man walking toward them. The trees, large as they were, seemed to pull away as the newcomer passed them, catlike and wary, but with a confidence bordering on arrogance. Jake's heart began to beat faster, beads of sweat forming on his brow despite the idyllic temperature of the Garden.

The stranger stood around six feet tall, give or take, his black hair cut short and neat, but lacking any particular style, as though it sat where it had lain since the man rose from bed. He wore black jeans and a t-shirt beneath a black leather jacket, suspicious bulges under each of his armpits suggesting the presence of handguns in shoulder-holsters. Their gazes met, and Jake's breath froze in his throat. The stranger's eyes were black as pitch, barely any white around the edges to denote his humanity, and they peered at him unblinking, hungry.

There was something very dark about the man, and not just his clothing or appearance. An almost palpable aura hung about him – similar to the miasma he had seen around the demonic form of Abaddon, but this remained invisible.

It reminded Jake of death.

"Who is that?" whispered Jake uncertainly in a low voice.

Uriel's eyes never left the form of the Dark Man. "Hopefully he is one who will aid you… for a time. Be careful not to upset him, for he is somewhat unpredictable, and not very trusting. In another life he killed and tortured people as an assassin, and despite a change of heart some time ago, his instincts often revert to the simplistic, darker

ones he used to harbor. His ultimate quest lies elsewhere, but for now your paths remain intertwined."

Jake swallowed heavily, looking back at the approaching figure.

"You're not Gabriel," uttered the Dark Man coldly, staring at Uriel, "but you look like him."

"Gabriel was my brother," replied Uriel.

The Dark Man stopped about twenty paces away from them, seeming to stand casually, but Jake noticed his hands discretely gripped the zippered edges of his jacket, very near to the two bulges beneath his arms. Cold eyes, offering the same emotional range as lumps of coal, raked roughly over Jake. He felt the sudden urge to take a step backwards, but forced himself to stand firm under the stranger's scrutiny.

"Hello, Vain," said Uriel.

"They told me Gabriel would be here. Who are you?" he demanded. His voice scraped like cold steel over ice.

"I am Uriel, and this is Jacob Ho —"

"I don't care about your boyfriend," cut in Vain. "I'm looking for someone, and my information led me here. Where's Sebastian Dunn?"

Jake gasped, drawing the dark eyes of the stranger back to him. "Do you mean Sebastian Dunn, the founder of the Martin Roberts' Foundation?"

"Well I sure as hell didn't mean Sebastian Dunn the pole-dancer. How does a little bitch like you know who Sebastian is?"

Jake's jaw fell open momentarily. "Um… I worked for the United Nations, along with the International Red Cross, and his work inspired many of us. Mr. Dunn's disappearance was a terrible loss."

"I bet you cried yourself to sleep every night for a month. Where is he? Tell me quickly so I can get out of this shit bucket full of weeds."

"He is not here, Vain," said Uriel softly. Another echoing explosion sounded overhead, but the newcomer didn't even look up; his dark gaze never strayed from Uriel.

"I suppose you're another angel," snarled Vain. "Are you going to annoy me as much as Gabriel did?"

"I cannot follow the same path as Gabriel, my fate lies here against other foes of our Lord. But Jake will accompany you for a time, if you will allow it."

Vain's eyes turned to Jake, his glare like black ice, looking him up and down, pausing momentarily at his cheek, but saying nothing.

"Do I look like a fucking tour guide?" Vain growled menacingly. "I need to find Sebastian. If either of you know anything, I recommend you tell me now."

Though the words were spoken casually, the hairs on the back of Jake's neck stood on edge, and his legs felt weak. Vain stood calmly, taking in the scenery, though somehow none of the majesty of this place seemed to touch the Dark Man.

"We know nothing of Sebastian, of that you can be certain. Jacob has his own quest which is of the utmost importance –"

"So you're the new messiah," said Vain coldly, his black eyes staring intently into Jake's. Despite blinking several times, Jake managed to hold the gaze.

"How do you know that?" asked Uriel, sounding shocked for the first time since Jake had met him.

"I met someone named Aadesh who told me some stuff. It was his information which led me here. Uriel, if this guy is the reincarnation of Christ –" Jake winced inwardly "– what does that mean for the Avun-Riah?"

Jake turned to Uriel, who appeared oddly discomfited.

"The Avun-Riah was always… a ruse," said the angel. "Every incarnation of the Avun-Riah throughout the ages was meant as a decoy for the true coming of the new messenger."

"So Sebastian was a decoy? All that misery we went through was for nothing?" The Dark Man still stood casually, but his posture held a distinct tenseness now. Jake's instincts screamed at him to run, but he forced himself to stand firm.

"It was not for nothing," said Uriel, attempting to retain his composure. "The battle against Sordarrah is of vital importance as well, but lies separate to the path which Jacob must now walk. The release of Sordarrah will wreak havoc upon the Earth, but was never

foreseen when the Avun-Riah was first initiated as a way to deceive those who might wish to destroy Jacob."

"Would you please just call me Jake? Jacob makes me feel like I'm about three years old."

"Who cares?" snarled Vain, but as Jake looked at him he seemed slightly more relaxed, as though the assassin had drifted from his murderous edge.

"Speaking of age," said Uriel, "how is it you have not grown older, Vain?"

"Don't you angels know all this shit? Or do you just run around manipulating people without any clue as to how it will affect their lives?" He glared at Uriel, and Jake was amazed at the archangel's ability to smile in the face of such controlled vehemence. "The Glimloche might have burned out of me, but apparently some residue of it remains deep inside, still wrapped around my soul. It stops me from aging. I also heal faster than usual and can do some fancy party tricks. But trust me, fairy boy, if I had all its power, I'd torch a few of your dainty feathers, just for fun."

"Then I am thankful you no longer can," replied Uriel.

Vain turned disdainfully from Uriel and stared at Jake once more, his gaze intense as the rumbling overhead sounded again, even closer this time.

"So I wasted my time coming here." For a moment the murderous glint returned to Vain's gaze, and it felt like a cube of ice had just slithered down Jake's spine. "You can tag along until Venice, but slow me down, and you're on your own. If you piss me off I'll put a hole in your head and leave you for the rats – messiah or not. Understood?"

Jake glanced at Uriel, and then nodded. He had no idea why they were traveling to Venice, but at this stage he figured he'd just keep moving until he got his thoughts together enough to formulate a plan. Too much was happening at once, too many dramas emerging for him to prepare some sort of strategy. He was still trying to come to grips with everything he'd been told.

The sky shuddered.

"How will you fight Abaddon, Uriel?"

"The cherubim will assist me," replied the archangel with a sweep of his arm. Jake peered around, but could see only trees.

Vain looked at the ever-widening crack in the sky, and then at the forest Uriel had indicated, grinning humorlessly. "Good luck with that. Let's go, blondie."

Jake wanted to thank Uriel, to ask him a million more things and offer to stay behind to fight at his side, but he knew he had to leave. Vain was already striding off in the direction he'd come from, and Jake had no doubt he'd meant it when he'd said he would leave Jake behind. Uriel gave him a calm smile, and Jake nodded before jogging off after the assassin through the trees.

He caught up with Vain shortly. "It's nice to meet you," he said, offering his hand.

Vain glanced at Jake's proffered hand and ignored it, returning his gaze ahead. His eyes roamed constantly, searching for hidden dangers. "You really don't want to get too friendly with me."

"Why not?" asked Jake.

"Because I might kill you."

Jake chuckled, but then realized Vain wasn't joking and abruptly stopped. "I'm sorry if I offended you."

"You sound like one of them," replied Vain, increasing the length of his stride.

"Who? Uriel?"

"Zealous angels with their pious attitudes. Even Gabriel used to get on my nerves, but in the end he turned out to be okay. Shame what happened to him, though."

"What happened?" asked Jake.

Vain glanced at him, his expression unreadable. "He died."

"You're talking about the Archangel Gabriel, the one from the Bible, right?"

Vain nodded.

"How did *he* die?"

"It's a long story."

"But –"

"This is the part where you shut up," hissed Vain coldly. "I agreed to let you tag along, don't turn into a whining bitch and make me regret that decision."

Jake stumbled mid-stride, Vain's casual insult catching him completely off-guard. A loud rumble from overhead drew his attention skyward once more. Through a gap in the trees he saw the crack was now more like a cross, pieces of rock and earth crumbling from it, crashing into the trees of the Garden. It was an odd thing to be staring at the sky – or what seemed like the sky – and seeing such violent cracks registered in it. Jake had to remind himself they were miles beneath the earth –

"Hurry up," growled Vain. The Dark Man was now about twenty yards ahead of him. Jake jogged to catch up.

The trees before them thinned, melting into a grassy knoll. Jake saw a steep cliff rising high in front of them, bordering the edge of the Garden like a prison wall. He stared at the rock incredulously – there was no way they could have crossed the valley in such a short time. Some sort of magic was at work here, aiding them.

"What now?" he asked.

Vain looked at him, his visage unruffled, his eyes unreadable. "I'm guessing they've closed off all doorways to this place while your fallen angel is trying to break in."

"So how do we get out?"

"We wait and hope an exit opens once the fighting starts."

"That's it?" asked Jake. "Shouldn't we look around for another way out?"

Vain crouched down on the grass, his steely gaze taking in everything around them with a glance. "That'd be stupid."

"Why?"

"I know this is the way out. We could run off looking for another way, while meanwhile that Abaddon dipshit breaks through, and we both get killed. So we wait here. If things get messy we'll move, but until then we wait. Sit down and conserve your energy, you might need it soon."

Jake sat cross-legged on the grass beside the former assassin. He glanced over and saw the black leather jacket Vain wore hung open slightly, the butt of a gun poking out. It reminded him of something.

"What's the Glimloche?" he asked.

"Don't you ever stop talking?"

"I'm curious. You mentioned it before; was it some kind of weapon?"

"It was a part of Satan wrapped around my soul. Now shut up and watch."

Jake's jaw dropped and hung slightly ajar, as much from what Vain had just admitted as from his casual attitude about it. The admission seemed honest enough, at least from Jake's point of view, but how was one to tell? Did he call Vain out as a liar and face a bullet from whatever handgun remained hidden within the assassin's jacket? And what if Vain were telling the truth? Jake would now be traveling alongside a man who was potentially more corrupted than Abaddon.

Vain couldn't be lying, he had no need. The Dark Man seemed above such things, as though whatever hellish past he'd survived had burned out his need for deception. Being so akin to Death might have made Vain more than just a man – or perhaps the blame lay in whatever clawed around his heart, maybe it had tainted him in such a way as to deftly cut him from humanity. And now Jake travelled at this man's side.

Smart move.

"So what's with the beauty spot?" queried Vain suddenly, disturbing his introspection. The assassin wasn't looking at him, still staring out at the valley. Searching.

"Beauty spot?"

"The thing on your left cheek."

Jake's hand rose self-consciously to his face. "Er, it's a birthmark."

"So it's a present from your father, then." Vain pointed toward the heavens. "Very subtle, I'm sure you'll blend right into the crowd. Nobody will ever recognize you. Be sure to thank daddy when the assholes chasing you ram a stick up your ass and roast you on a fire."

The truth of the statement hit Jake squarely. How could he ever hide with such a telltale mark? Perhaps he should have had it removed – but then he would have been left with a scar which might have been just as telling.

Staring out at the magnificent valley which embraced the fabled Garden of Eden, Jake contemplated the world he now walked through, a world most people had no idea existed. He'd been swept along ever since meeting Abaddon in Uganda, and now he found himself in the supposed birthplace of humankind, sitting beside a former assassin who'd just admitted to having a piece of the devil wrapped around his soul.

Gazing at the roof of the enormous cavern, he noticed the spider-webbed cracks growing ever wider. Soon the entire thing would come crashing down into the Garden. Abaddon would attack, apparently with the goal of stealing the rest of the fruit he hadn't taken. But Jake knew he was coming for something else.

To finish killing him.

Jake had been lucky that Abaddon had waited to attack him here, the one place where he could be resurrected –

*Resurrected.*

The reality of the word hit him hard, and Jake felt his heart – the one Abaddon had completely torn from his chest – begin to beat much faster. Part of him wanted nothing more than to rebel against the truth he'd come to understand, the truth of who he actually was, but he knew he wouldn't do it. For better or worse, Jake's feet were now set upon this path, and he would walk it until the end, trying to do the right thing along the way.

"Here they come," murmured Vain offhandedly.

Jake flicked his gaze back to the broken sky and saw the truth in Vain's statement. Boulder-sized chunks of stone tumbled from the roof of the cavern, leaving black gaps in the inexplicable sky. Clawed hands emerged, scrabbling against the rock, striving to drag the hidden invaders through.

A horn blared, deep and resounding, from within the Garden, and suddenly everything changed. The trees shifted, their forms blurring and altering, legs growing from trunks and tearing deep roots from the earth. These roots shrank upon contact with the air, the ground beneath them healing in an instant, reforming into pristine lawn once more. Each figure morphed and stretched, branches receding into muscular arms, their leaves blending with bark to become pale skin. In moments the forest was gone, replaced with something else.

An army.

The cherubim.

Shaped roughly like humans, though about twice as large, the cherubim bodies stood completely naked, their skin alabaster white, glowing slightly within the false sunlight of the chamber. Strange nodules budded and grew from each set of shoulders, expanding in a blink to become large black wings. But these weren't like the symbolic portrayal of angels' wings adorned with feathers. The wings of the cherubim were predatory and sleek, webbed like a bat's, tiny claw-like hands at the tips of the membranous skin stretched between bones.

Thousands of hairless heads, perfect in their uniformity, turned skyward. The gathered cherubims stared calmly toward the roof of the cavern, each a picture of serenity. Their muscular, naked forms appeared sexless, creating the semblance of an army of motionless marble statues, contrasted starkly by their near-bestial black wings. Their trunk-sized arms ended in long, fingerless hands, curved and bladelike, similar to sickles. Jake suddenly realized these were creatures designed for one purpose: killing.

More rubble began to tumble from the ever-widening hole in the sky. Movement flickered in the valley below, separate from the cherubims. Focusing on it, Jake glimpsed the angelic form of Uriel, walking serenely, still dressed only in his meager loincloth, the flaming blade extending from his right fist as he strolled toward the center of the army of cherubim. None of them appeared the least bit tense, but Jake's heart was smashing against the cage of his ribs, and his mouth felt completely void of moisture.

And then he saw something which had eluded him amid the amazing sight of the forest's metamorphosis....

Two trees – the widest in the entire Garden – stood forlornly alone in the exact center of the valley, their branches hanging low with fruit: one crop yellow, the other red.

The Tree of Life rose beside the unnamed tree Uriel had spoken of, the one laden with fruit gifting knowledge, but also sapping the soul. Both trees stood colossal, larger than any Jake had ever heard of in the world above, each bearing thousands of fruits the rough size of an apple or orange, their mysterious power glowing from within. The Tree of Life's fruit held a golden radiance which appeared warm and healthy, reminding Jake of a small child's smile, whereas the other's looked diseased and rotten, the tree itself a canker within the beauteous Eden. Yet something within Jake yearned to go forth and devour it nonetheless.

A thunderous rumble, louder than any so far, split the fracturing roof, and suddenly the entire sky collapsed. Boulders and tons of earth rained down, and thousands upon thousands of warped, horrific creatures fell through the hole. It wasn't until Jake saw the tattered remnants of a military uniform that he realized who these creatures truly were:

Soldiers of the Lord's Resistance Army.

The invaders' frames swelled, bloated and repugnant, huge festering boils spread over their corpse-gray flesh, flesh stretched taut across gnarled muscles, distorted far beyond anything human. The evidence of Abaddon's touch in their creation was obvious to Jake's gaze, wisps of the Fallen one's decaying aura occasionally flitting around their inhuman forms. Gigantic bestial mouths screeched in silent screams as they tumbled through the air, their horrific forms retaining only the barest vestige of their former selves.

Men, women... even children.

Staring at the warped mass of creatures, Jake was hit with the terror that similar deformation might strike him down as well. After all, hadn't he eaten the fruit too? He only exhaled when he remembered that these creatures had not only taken in the fruit from the Tree of Life, they'd also consumed the fruit from the Unnamed Tree, not to mention the influence of Abaddon's pestilential power. Still, staring at what could be done with such potency made him realize what sort of force he was thinking of challenging; something of this nature was beyond anything mortal, and he felt foolish imagining he could ever hope to stand against it.

They hurtled through the hole in the broken sky, making no attempt to stop themselves. In response, the cherubim spread their membranous wings and launched as one into flight, an unspoken command synchronizing the warriors in a way no human force could ever replicate. The falling invaders and soaring defenders clashed midair, the cherubim literally hewing through Abaddon's ranks, their sickle-like hands cleaving the corrupt flesh like axes hacking watermelons.

Jake's heart leaped. Body parts fell from the sky, almost as though it were hailing limbs. The invaders seemed certain to lose in moments. Surely Uriel would locate and defeat Abaddon as well. If that were to happen, Jake's role in this universal conflict would become superfluous, and he could perhaps return to some semblance of a normal life. In that moment he allowed himself a tiny portion of hope.

But he was wrong, so terribly wrong.

Chunks of dark flesh slapped to the floor of the valley and instantly began to writhe and twitch. Each part doubled and tripled in size, expanding so swiftly it became impossible for Jake to keep track of their growth. Within seconds the dissected army was renewed – more than renewed. Each individual piece of sliced flesh had turned into a new warrior, the invading force now filling the valley. Understanding struck Jake like an icy hammer driving a frozen spike down his spine as he suddenly recognized the power of the fruit Abaddon had stolen from the Tree of Life. The same fruit which had restored Jake to life, now granted the invaders invulnerability.

In the center of the mass of attackers, Uriel moved and flowed like a dancer, his flaming blade licking out around him and culling the warped aggressors, their bodies turning to ash as it touched them. His seemed the only effective resistance among the entire force defending the Garden.

Cherubim landed amid the mutated warriors and hacked and slashed, but the defense of the Garden seemed almost certain to fail.

If anything, the cherubim attacks made the entire situation worse, each slice creating another warrior. The more they cut down, the more rose to fight against them.

Soon the weight of numbers began to tell, and as more and more invaders dropped through the hole in the false sky, the cherubim slowly, but inexorably began to buckle. The slashing claws and rotting teeth of Abaddon's followers were gradually overcoming the cherubims' mighty frames. Within seconds of them dropping, they were torn to pieces, the once-human creatures snarling and snapping like feral dogs over their carcasses. The scene was terrifying to behold, but Jake couldn't tear his eyes away.

Within the swirling storm of nightmare, Uriel still fought serenely, his blade slicing easily through everything it touched, but the opposing force looked like an ocean now, and the cherubim were failing all over the field. Soon, the angel would be overcome, and the invaders would win.

But where was Abaddon?

Jake scanned the field, yet he couldn't spot the fallen angel among the combatants. Where was he now, during his moment of triumph?

Soon the last cherubim had yielded. The invaders seemed to pause around Uriel, and the archangel scanned the edge of the valley until he glimpsed Jake and Vain. His brilliant smile radiated across the space between them, and his flaming sword blinked before disappearing completely.

"Shit,' muttered Vain, standing up swiftly. "Time to go."

"Wha –"

"Trust me," said Vain, easily lifting Jake to his feet by the collar of his shirt.

Jake heard a low hissing noise. Glancing around, he saw the wall behind them shimmer, and then open, revealing a doorway similar to the one through which Jake had first entered the Garden. Beyond this entryway, however, there wasn't a towering stairwell, merely a short hallway with a rough wooden door waiting at the end.

Jake struggled free from Vain's grip and turned back to the battle. "I have to see this."

Vain studied him silently for a moment before shrugging. "Just don't expect me to give you a cuddle afterwards."

Jake stared across the valley to where Uriel stood alone, surrounded by corruption, an island of purity within an ocean of taint. The angel seemed frozen in concentration, and something pulsed out from his still form. To Jake's eyes it appeared to be some kind of bubble, writhing with energy. The bubble expanded swiftly, until the entire invading horde was covered, dropping to the ground like a net, ensnaring the malignant warriors beneath it. Not a single invader escaped the powerful trap, but it seemed to have done little other than hinder them for the moment; Jake knew they would soon break free if nothing else happened.

Once more his eyes met with Uriel's across the yawning space. The power of the Garden brought them together for one final moment, and Jake knew in that instant what Uriel was about to do.

"NO!" he hollered.

But it was too late.

A brilliant surge of power shot through the trap, flowing from Uriel at its center. The archangel appeared to flare slightly, and then exploded into fragments as force detonated through the ranks of invaders. It extended to the very edges of the bubble, frying everything in its path. Abaddon's invading horde was consumed in an instant – not one of the corrupted beasts escaped the vengeful assault, and their demise transpired with a resonating sigh of release. With a final thunderclap, the power disappeared and with it Uriel, his life-force spent, and his essence gone forever.

The Garden, now empty apart from Jake and Vain, echoed with the rolling of the thunderous blast. Jake stood upon the hill aghast. He had never imagined witnessing the destruction of one of the fabled archangels; he'd presumed they were invulnerable against all odds.

"Is – is he dead?"

"Probably," replied Vain, his voice devoid of emotion.

"But why?"

"So that you could escape is my guess. While you stood around gawping at what was going on, everyone who was fighting to secure our escape died. If Uriel's mortal body fell, that entire army would have caught us and killed us. So he expended his energy to ensure you survived."

"Oh no," whispered Jake. "He died for me."

In that moment Jake understood what the archangel had meant earlier. He could not die unless he chose to, and Jake had just witnessed an awesome sacrifice.

All in order to protect him.

It hadn't been for the Garden, which now lay open and unguarded. The sacrifice had been for Jake, to keep him safe from Abaddon's beasts. An archangel, a creature of unfathomable power, had given up immortality for him.

"You can break out the tissues later," growled Vain. "For now we're going to leave before this door disappears forever."

Jake turned on Vain. "Don't you feel anything?"

"Impatience springs to mind, so if you don't hurry up I might just leave you behind before something else turns up to replace the inbred Foreign Legion that angel-boy just got rid of. Are you coming or not?"

Jake shook his head in bewilderment, but moved toward the tunnel, Vain following behind him, glancing around to make sure nothing followed them. Jake twisted the archaic door handle and stepped through, the assassin following on his heels.

Just as the door began to swing closed behind them, Jake glanced back, glimpsing a figure dropping from the hole in the sky, shrouded by a dark miasma, its flesh burned and torn.

Abaddon had the garden to himself.

## -CHAPTER 6-
# VENICE

Jake squinted against the midday sun's glare. After the gentle glow of the Garden, the harshness of normal sunlight made his eyes water.

Three and four story buildings rose on both sides of the canal, some with doorways opening directly onto the murky water, boats moored before the front step. The cobbled path they stood on appeared centuries old, and Jake could sense the history which had seeped into the walls surrounding them. Peace and tranquility seemed to echo from the gurgling canal, bouncing from the walls of the dwellings, and Jake smiled despite the horror he'd just witnessed. He'd never been here before, but recognized Venice instantly, and found he loved it.

"I hate it already," muttered Vain.

"This place is beautiful, what are you talking about?"

"Easy to get trapped in a place like this."

Vain eyed the high windows of the buildings around them. Jake followed his gaze and imagined the scene as a lifelong killer might see it: a perfect setting for an ambush. He pictured Abaddon's corrupted creatures attacking them from those windows, surging out like blood from a wound, rushing down into the ancient canals, and suddenly Venice seemed much less enthralling.

"Okay, now you've ruined it for me," Jake said, chuckling slightly in an attempt to break the ice a bit.

Vain glared at him blankly. "You're really going to disappoint those idiots waiting for the Second Coming."

Jake felt like he'd just been slapped. Vain turned away without further comment, striding off down one of the narrow alleys, the shadows seeming to embrace the Dark Man as he stepped into them. Jake closed his mouth, a hundred retorts popping into his brain just a moment too late. He followed the assassin into the alleyway, knowing that at this point he really had no other option apart from wandering away on his own. Probably not such a great idea in a strange city surrounded by water with little knowledge of where he was going, or what he was doing.

Catching up after three or four turns, Jake tried to say something, but Vain held up his hand, silencing him. Not a moment later, two men stepped out in front of them from around a corner, one brandishing a club and the other a long, evil-looking knife.

"Back up," Vain murmured to Jake, his eyes fixed on the men barring their path.

Jake moved to comply, but a door opened behind him and two more men stepped from one of the buildings, both armed with knives as well. It was just as Vain had predicted: they'd been boxed into an alley barely wide enough for them to walk in single file.

"What do you want?" called Jake.

"Money. Give us now," snarled one of the muggers, the one with the club.

"Don't do this," Vain cautioned, his voice carrying an icy chill which echoed from the surrounding walls. "You still have a chance to avoid dying."

The man who had demanded money translated this for his companions, who laughed heartily, their bravado evident, still shuffling forward with their weapons ready. There seemed no compromise in their eyes, merely hunger for violence.

"Get down," murmured Vain to Jake, who instinctively dropped to the alley floor.

In a move of incredible swiftness which spoke of many years' practice, Vain drew two handguns from beneath his jacket, their barrels tipped with long silencers, and aimed them in opposite directions.

Four soft pops sounded, and four bodies collapsed to the ground, crimson staining the cobbles around them.

Jake scrambled to his feet as Vain smoothly holstered his weapons. "You killed them!" he burst out incredulously.

"It was their choice." Vain's voice held no emotion, untouched by the violence he had just wrought.

"How could you just kill them like that?"

"Why do you care?" countered Vain.

"What are you?" whispered Jake, gazing down at the bodies.

Vain stared coldly at him. "Let's get one thing clear; I'm not your fucking tour guide, your best buddy, or your future girlfriend. I agreed to let you tag along on a whim; the next whim I have might be to cut your balls off and feed them to the ducks in one of these reeking canals. Follow my directions and stay out of my way, and we'll get along just fine. Whine to me like a bitch, and I'll gut you here."

"But you can't just murder people!"

Vain's gun was in his right hand again before Jake knew it, the barrel pressed into Jake's Adam's apple, the circular tip of the silencer still warm. Jake stepped backward, his foot crunching down on the fingers of one of the dead men. He froze, his nostrils flaring as panic flooded his veins.

"I kill people. That's what I do," cooed Vain, his voice soft, almost seductive in its cold malice. "When I don't, I become weak, and then people get hurt. So I kill people, and will continue to take down anyone who gets in my way, you included, until I find Sebastian Dunn once more. Is that understood?" Vain's dark eyes never flinched, fixed to his own widened gaze, and Jake knew without a doubt the Dark Man was serious; he'd kill Jake swifter than a thought if he imagined he was slowing him down.

"I'm sorry," Jake replied. His voice choked as he tried to force the words past the silencer jammed into his throat.

Vain withdrew the gun, smiling coldly, and slipping it back into its shoulder holster.

"I don't like seeing death," said Jake, still holding Vain's ebony gaze, "even when the people possibly deserve it. These men might have had families: wives and children waiting for them at home. Now they'll never see them again."

"Or, they might have been child rapists and murderers," countered Vain, casually stepping over the bodies and continuing down the alley. "Now they're fertilizer. We can speculate all day, but their actions dictated their fate for them, and you shouldn't lose any sleep over it. I'm sure your *pure* little soul won't be stained too much from it, but if it is you can just go and confess it to your daddy and everything will be okay again, right?"

"Daddy? You mean God?"

"Nah, I'm talking about your pimp," snapped Vain. "Of course I mean God. Isn't that your purpose, to fulfill some glorious prophecy and step into the shoes of Jesus as the son of God or something? Go and have a chat with God about me, He seems intent on fucking up my life every chance He gets. Tell Him I said 'Hi... and to go fuck Himself.'"

Jake was completely dumbstruck by Vain's callous blasphemy, and he stopped walking completely. It wasn't that Jake had ever held any sort of love for religion, far from it, but the pure unfiltered hatred washing out from Vain as he spoke of God almost scorched Jake with its vehemence. The disdain seemed much more personal for the assassin, and in that moment of disclosure Jake had glimpsed past the mask, seeing the absolute fury hiding just beneath Vain's surface. The realization terrified him. Why had Uriel told him to travel with such a man?

Because Vain couldn't be taken over by Abaddon.

That was the simple truth of the matter; for the time being, Vain was Jake's safest companion. Their paths were pointed in the same direction and, for whatever reason, the assassin was apparently immune to possession. Vain had mentioned a piece of Satan wrapped around his soul, but surely that couldn't be true... could it?

"Come on, Jesus," hissed Vain, "Those bodies back there won't go unnoticed for long, and we need to be as far away from them as possible when they're found."

"I'm not Jesus," insisted Jake.

"Whatever," muttered Vain, leading the way through yet another alley. Jake jogged slightly to keep up with the assassin's swift pace, trying hard not to trip on the uneven cobblestones as he went.

"I might not know what I am, but I'm not the same Christ who was crucified. It's not like I'm walking around spouting gospel or battling repressed memories. I'm a completely different person to Jesus, and I don't care much about God either."

"You say that like I'm supposed to give a shit."

"Well... don't you?" said Jake. "You seemed pretty pissed off a minute ago"

"God just has that effect on me, I guess," replied Vain, his eyes flicking around, scanning for danger. "I don't like the idea of someone pulling my strings and making me feel guilty about living while His followers have sex with kids and condemn homos. That's not the kind of deity I'd like to follow, if you know what I mean." Vain paused and peered around a corner before advancing.

The assassin's words struck like a sliver of ice deep into Jake's heart, and for a moment he felt unable to talk, merely following dumbly as he tried to reassemble his thoughts. Why was he arguing this point? The assassin had already said he didn't care about Jake's opinions, and yet he still felt compelled to disagree.

"So you don't think religion does any good in the world?"

"I don't know; why not ask those idiots who flew those planes into the twin towers? What about all those cocksuckers back in the Crusades who chopped each other up over a piece of dirt? I'll wager they thought God was pretty awesome. Religion is simply a way of people blaming the shitty things they do on the will of something else, something larger and easier to blame than them."

"But you can't blame God for religious fanatics," said Jake.

"Why not? They're running around doing shit in His name, so why can't I blame Him? If He really is so almighty, why doesn't He stop them? Why let them run around making Him look like an asshole? Because it's a sham, that's why. Religion is the creation of selfish bastards who want to gain something while blaming a higher power. Even the so-called charity causes around the world are selfish, because they think that by doing good stuff they'll get into Heaven. It's all bullshit."

"And you know all about being selfless, I suppose," retorted Jake.

Vain ignored his remark. "If they were all as pious as they make out, they'd do it while admitting there's no ultimate reward. Do it simply because it's the right thing to do. But they never will, because all humans are selfish."

"That's rich coming from someone named Vain," muttered Jake.

The assassin glanced back at him. "That's how I *know* what I'm talking about. The only way to be truly selfless is to do something which will achieve absolutely nothing, or indeed something completely negative, resulting in consequences nobody would ever strive for."

"Like Jesus did, you mean?"

Vain paused, staring blankly at Jake, his dark eyes revealing nothing of his thoughts, and yet Jake had the sudden feeling he'd just lost the argument in his moment of triumph.

"I guess you've got some pretty big shoes to fill, then," mused the assassin. Jake's stomach flipped.

The Dark Man cut around another corner, and Jake, following behind, struggled to control his thoughts. The conversation kept turning over and over in his head. Had Vain just tricked him? Had he seen through Jake's shields and recognized his insecurities, especially those regarding God? The sensation he'd just been duped kept rising like acid in his throat, and though Jake forced it away, the words returned again and again.

Big shoes.

Had Jesus ever thought such a thing, or had he simply known all along what he was supposed to do, a plan of action laid out, predestined at birth with few choices for him to make along the way?

"What are we doing here, anyway?" asked Jake as they stepped from the warren of alleyways and onto a path tracing a large canal, trying to shake his mind free from the complexity of what Vain had just presented him with.

"I have to see someone for information, but he might also be able to point you in the right direction."

"Who is it?"

"A priest who apparently specializes in demonic possession and the various structures of Hell: a real party animal."

"Are you serious? They have specialists like that?"

"Well, the Church doesn't advertise them in the Yellow Pages," said Vain, "but yeah, they exist. How do you think they keep track of everything going on down in Hell? Facebook?"

"So where is he?"

Luke Romyn

"At this time of day he should be hanging out at Saint Mark's Basilica, about five minutes walk from here," replied Vain, swiftly crossing one of the footbridges over the canal. Jake followed, his own thoughts still jumbled.

In the chaos of what had occurred in the Garden, Jake had given no consideration as to what he hoped to do once they escaped. Now they were in Venice, heading toward a man who might be able to give Jake some answers, and his mind felt completely blank.

What was he supposed to say? That he was Christ resurrected? Yeah, that would go down really well with a Catholic priest. Very few countries still stoned people to death – especially for blasphemy – but Jake had a feeling that if he came out spouting he was the Second Coming they might take up old habits, just for him.

Maybe he could explain to the priest how an archangel in the Garden of Eden had described him as a container of the positive energies which had once made up Jesus Christ. Perhaps he should say how another angel had spotted him a cab voucher.

Maybe not.

Damn it. All he could do was talk with the priest, possibly following Vain's lead – if the assassin didn't kill the guy first.

Jake now understood Uriel's hesitation when speaking of Vain; the man wore death like a cloak. There seemed something very unapproachable about him, as though he'd buried himself within a shell of acid, locking his soul inside a bastion of rage, keeping his vulnerabilities safely hidden deep within.

They rounded a corner and suddenly the alleyway opened out onto a wide courtyard, thousands of pigeons strutting and pecking, hundreds of tourists acting similarly. From images he'd seen on holiday programs, Jake recognized this place as Saint Mark's Square. Buildings occupied three sides of the square while at the end of it, beyond the people and birds, stood a magnificent high-pointed tower. Directly behind rose broad arches, adorning the large, double-door entrance of a beautiful church, its roof crowned with domes and spires.

Saint Mark's Basilica.

138

Eagerness leaped up within Jake, counteracted by a deep sense of dread. Before him stood a place which could potentially give him the answers he so desperately needed....

But what if he didn't like those answers?

Dragging his feet slightly, Jake followed Vain around the perimeter of the square – the assassin apparently didn't like exposing himself out in the open, preferring instead to hug the shadows of the buildings surrounding the courtyard. Regardless, Vain moved with silent efficiency, and all too soon they were both striding over the light-colored stone pavers, toward the front entrance of the church.

"Hey, Jake," whispered a voice behind him.

Instinctively, Jake turned toward the sound of his name, only to see a blade glint in the sunlight. Jake stepped back in horror as the wielder stabbed the seven-inch knife forward –

It was Abaddon!

His murky rotting features swam in and out of focus. He launched himself toward Jake, murder glinting within his hideous eyes. The blade flashed for Jake's exposed throat.

But then he hesitated. For an infinitesimal moment Abaddon froze, his expression tentative. Time slowed, but Jake's thoughts raced. He noticed every cloud, every insect, every wisp of corruption floating around the body Abaddon had possessed.

Jake couldn't be certain, but in that moment he felt that Abaddon had paused for a reason. Perhaps he'd changed his mind. After all the scheming, the centuries of horror, perhaps his original essence was shining true. He had been an angel, after all. Maybe –

The horrific face exploded, the burned and disfigured flesh disappearing, replaced by the features of a man in his fifties, half his cheek blown outward, exposing several shattered teeth. Jake spun around to see Vain holstering his silenced handgun.

People had turned to stare at the commotion, and it took only seconds for realization to kick in. A woman screamed. Chaos erupted, and Jake stared at Vain, panic thundering through his veins.

"I can't take you anywhere, can I?" said the assassin casually.

"Wha –" began Jake, but Vain grabbed him by the upper arm, hauling him away, swiftly cutting down an alley beside the church.

Once out of public view, Vain paused. "I sincerely hope I didn't just kill a tourist offering to give you a Brazilian."

"It was Abaddon," gasped Jake. "He can take people over, possess their bodies. I'm the only one who can recognize his malignance."

Vain nodded, glancing back at the piazza. Jake followed his gaze and saw a crowd around the body; as yet there seemed no sign of any police.

Moving further down the walkway, Vain checked a door handle protruding from Saint Mark's rear wall, squatting in front of it and inserting two thin pieces of steel into the lock. He jiggled the lock-pick for a moment, and then turned the handle once more, smoothly swinging the door inwards.

"Through here," he hissed. "Quickly!"

Jake practically threw himself through the doorway, and Vain followed, silently closing the door behind them, squatting to lock it once more. As Jake tried to steady his breathing, he wondered at the coolness of Vain to think of locking the door behind them, reducing the chances any pursuers had of discovering their hiding place. They would expect whoever killed the man back in the piazza to run as far and fast as possible, not simply stroll fifty yards, enter the church through a side door, and then lock it behind them.

At least that's what Jake hoped.

"Let's find this damn priest before more boogiemen turn up," said Vain, leading Jake through what appeared to be some kind of storeroom for the Basilica, books, statues, and odd and broken things stacked in precarious and jumbled piles.

"Thank you for saving my life," said Jake softly, his nerves still jangling like a discordant orchestra within him.

Vain glanced at him. "Don't read too much into it. If he'd killed you it would have been just as much hassle as me shooting him, so I simply did the latter. We're not buddies now, and I'm not going to braid your hair."

Jake shrugged. "Thanks anyway."

"Whatever," muttered Vain. "Let's just see if we can find this priest."

"What's his name?"

"Father Abramo Costello. He's short, chunky, with dark hair and glasses. And he's probably a pervert like the rest of these cloistered bastards. Keep an eye out for a guy who looks like he's got a hairbrush jammed up his ass."

"You're not really into the whole politically correct thing, are you?" commented Jake.

Vain turned to him, regarding him darkly. "Maybe I should have let that asshole stab you," he murmured, opening a door and stepping from the storage room into the church.

Shaking his head slightly, Jake followed, frustrated. Despite his best efforts, he was beginning to appreciate the sardonic wit of his new companion. Vain strode boldly through the church, straight up to the first priest he saw. The assassin spoke in a hushed whisper, his words flowing in what sounded like fluent Italian. Jake tried to mask his shock. He couldn't understand what Vain said, but the simple fact a man so versed in death could converse in such a beautiful language seemed contradictory.

The priest looked at Vain oddly, but pointed to the other end of the massive church. Vain nodded curtly and glided away without thanking the man, his footfalls silent in the deathly quiet cathedral.

Glancing around, Jake stopped and stared at the majesty of the building. The domes were filled with mosaics, artistic images of angels and other archaic religious symbols, many unknown to Jake. Timber carvings were rife throughout the place, many coated in what appeared to be gold leaf, glowing with splendor.

Rather than being awed by the magnificence of the church, however, Jake felt something akin to anger beginning to simmer within him. The four men who had attacked them in the alley had been dressed in little more than rags, beggars and thieves who'd chosen the wrong target for the day and paid for it with their lives. What sort of religion could justify such magnificence when the people outside were living in squalor? Those men's lives were now forfeit simply because they'd been trying to get money, but this church had gold ceilings! Something within Jake snarled at the hypocrisy of such things. With difficulty he forced it back down, focusing instead on their purpose: he needed information, and this priest might be able to supply some. It would be better not to alienate him straight away, even though Jake's instincts screamed at him to confront the priest regarding the church's excesses.

They soon observed the portly priest kneeling before a statue of the Lady Madonna, his head bowed in prayer. Jake recognized the man immediately from Vain's description. Perhaps fifty years old, his dark hair receded heavily at the temples above his thick, horn-rimmed glasses. The priest's jowls wobbled as he whispered prayers to the effigy of Mary, his hands clasped together and his forearms resting upon his enormous belly.

"Father Costello," whispered Vain.

The priest's head turned, his welcoming smile freezing as he spotted the dark figure with the scowling countenance lurking in the shadows.

"Who are you?" he asked in heavily accented English, rising slowly to his feet.

"Father Armadeuso in Rome sent me. My name is Vain."

The overweight priest's face paled, and he reached out a hand to steady himself as his balance wobbled. Jake moved to assist the priest, gripping his arm to prevent him from keeling over completely in shock. With Jake's aid, the man was able to make his way to one of the nearby bench seats, dropping heavily upon it.

"I see my reputation precedes me," murmured Vain, sliding over. "Father Armadeuso really needs to keep his mouth shut."

"What do you want?" hissed the priest, glancing around to ensure nobody else could hear them – or perhaps he was searching for someone to call out to in case he needed to yell for help.

"Him first," said Vain, nodding at Jake. "I need privacy for my request, and I won't get it with him lingering like a bad smell."

The priest turned to Jake, sweat beading upon his brow. "And who are you to walk with a demon such as this?"

Anger flared within Jake. "This man has already saved my life twice today. If that makes him a demon, then I'd rather surround myself with demons than fat pigs like you who hide away in a church and judge others from afar!"

Vain chuckled, and the priest's eyes widened in shock. His shaking left hand removed an embroidered handkerchief from within the right sleeve of his robes, which he used to dab at his sweaty brow.

"I am sorry," apologized Father Costello hastily. "What you say is completely true, and I am ashamed of myself for it. 'Judge not, lest ye be judged'," he quoted from the Bible.

Jake swallowed his anger and nodded. "Father, I need your help. What do you know of Abaddon?"

"The fallen angel? He is the King of the Pit and Lord of the Locusts –"

"I don't need the Bible version, Father; I need some facts about Abaddon that I can't find in books." Jake stared into the priest's eyes, realizing he had to risk telling the truth. He didn't have the luxury of time, especially with police no doubt swarming around outside searching for two men matching their description. "Abaddon is here, Father. He's broken free from Hell – or wherever he normally lives – and is walking the Earth. I need to find a way to stop him."

Swiftly and without embellishment Jake explained what had happened up until their meeting, waving the priest to silence at various points when it seemed he might interrupt. The only thing he left out was any reference to his tenuous link with Christ – that really held no relevance at this point.

"And now there's a dead man outside those doors," he said, finishing his speech. "All because Abaddon chose to use him as a puppet. People are dying, and it's going to get worse if we can't stop him soon. Do you know of a way?"

Father Costello fervently wiped at his sweaty brow. His mouth kept opening and closing like a fish gasping for water. He finally shook his head as though trying to clear it, and looked up once more.

"You are telling me the truth?"

Jake nodded. Vain snorted in the background.

"There is no way... unless.... I have heard of a temple in the mountains above Beijing –"

"That's not an option," pronounced Vain with cold finality.

Father Costello glanced up at the assassin, speedily flicking his gaze back toward Jake to avoid the Dark Man's stare. "Then the only way is to open the Fallen One up to the power of God Himself. I had heard talk of a staff which could do such a thing, but this has been largely discredited as pure conjecture."

"Why?" asked Jake.

"It is the Staff carried by both Noah and Moses; each used a rod or shaft to direct the power of God from Heaven to do whatever it was they required."

"Can it kill one of the Fallen?"

"It is the only artifact I can imagine being able to do such a thing. With the Staff, Moses was able to part the Red Sea, visit the ten plagues upon the Egyptians, and see the Ten Commandments forged atop Mount Sinai."

"Did it truly do all those things?" asked Jake. "I don't have time to go off on a fool's errand searching for something which doesn't even work."

"With the Staff, Noah was able to control hundreds of creatures, loading them aboard his Ark, a vessel which could not possibly have contained such a vast cargo. This ensured they were not killed during the Great Cleansing of the Earth. If anything can aid you, it will be this relic.

Jake frowned, far from convinced. "Where would I even begin to look for it?"

"From what I have studied, Moses somehow discovered the Staff many years, perhaps centuries, after Noah wielded it. When Moses found it he became somewhat changed. He was, at the time, being raised by the Egyptian royal family, and one day he killed a slave master with the very same Staff, though this is less documented. After fleeing –"

"Can you just cut to the part where you tell us where the fucking stick is?" snapped Vain.

Father Costello gasped, wiping more sweat from his brow. Jake rested a reassuring hand on the priest's arm. "If the Staff is all that you say, it's urgent I find it."

The priest nodded. "It was buried with Moses. The location of his gravesite was kept hidden after the Archangel Michael battled Lucifer near it, possibly to protect the Staff itself. All that is commonly known is that Moses's body was interred somewhere in the land of Moab, overlooking the Jordan River."

"Well, that's helpful," snarled Vain, his contempt evident. Turning to Jake, he said, "Just jump on a bus and head for Moab, wherever that is."

"It's in Jordan, near Israel; I saw a documentary about it on the Discovery Channel," Jake muttered, his gaze unfocused, his mind pondering the dilemma. He snapped his attention back to the priest. "But how am I supposed to find Moses's grave?"

Father Costello stared deep into Jake's eyes, and then his gaze flicked down. For the first time, the man's eyes registered Jake's teardrop birthmark. Flinching slightly, as though glimpsing something he couldn't quite identify, the large priest nodded, somewhat spasmodically, his many chins jiggling as a result.

"Stay here," the priest whispered, climbing to his feet and hurrying off.

Jake sat in silence on the bench seat in the cavernous church, waiting, trying to remain patient, knowing each passing second saw more people at risk, the danger increasing, billowing on the horizon like a swarm of locusts. Vain paced like a caged lion, glancing at the main doors every few seconds and fingering the edge of his jacket as though yearning to draw his guns. Jake heard the shuffling steps of the rotund priest and turned, seeing him scurrying toward them, carrying a small, ancient-looking, leather-bound book. Father Costello sat down once more, his eyes fixed intently on the book in his hands.

"This is something I found many years ago whilst researching this very thing. It is the diary of Zipporah, Moses's Ethiopian wife."

Jake stared at the book, astounded. It seemed impossible he could be gazing upon something so steeped in history, but if he were to believe the priest, there it was before him, undeniable in its reality.

"Common belief is that the tomb of Moses lies in Nabi Musa, in Jericho; a large Muslim shrine has been built above the site where his body supposedly lays. This diary relays something entirely different. Zipporah's own words place the grave of Moses within the walls of Jerusalem."

Vain's dark chuckle sounded, cutting through the priest's words.

"You expect *him* to travel to Jerusalem. That should be an interesting bit of déjà-vu for you, don't you think?"

Jake swiftly understood Vain's meaning and grimaced. Jerusalem was where Jesus had been crucified.

Father Costello flicked his gaze between Jake and Vain with no idea what they were talking about. Jake simply shook his head, determined to gather more information without getting distracted.

"Does the diary say exactly where Moses's body lies?" he asked.

The priest looked suddenly uncomfortable, gripping the diary even tighter in his meaty hands. He peered intently at Jake, his eyes gazing deeply into Jake's own, searching....

"Who are you really?" asked the timid priest. "There's something about you which seems... I don't know."

Jake returned Father Costello's imploring gaze with one of open warmth, and he smiled reassuringly. "I think you know who I am, Father."

"Are you an American television personality? I sense something about you, something like fame, and yet you do not seem to hold the arrogance I would expect from an actor."

"No, I'm something else."

"Something? What do you mean?"

Vain, obviously exasperated by the exchange, finally interjected. "Look, he's Christ reborn, okay? Now, can we just get on with this?"

Instead of scorn or disbelief as Jake had expected, Father Costello simply gasped. Fumbling the sign of the cross he tried to kneel, but Jake caught him, holding him to the seat.

"B-but...." pleaded Father Costello. "Y-you're...."

"I'm a man seeking answers, Father, and having you act like a star-struck teenager won't get me any closer to my goal. Can you tell me where the resting place of Moses is? I need to find that Staff; this is urgent."

The priest swallowed heavily, his hands shaking as he opened the diary to a well-worn page, one he had obviously read many times.

"Z-Zipporah wrote... she wrote that his body was laid down and interred atop a mound of land I have traced to Golgotha, also known as Calvary. There is a church there now, built atop the old location, called the Church of the Holy Sepulchre. It is the site where…." His eyes darted up, his gaze pleading.

"Go on," said Jake reassuringly.

"It is the place where Christ was crucified."

Vain's mocking laughter rang out, echoing through the high domes of Saint Mark's Basilica.

\*\*\*

"Good luck in Jerusalem," said Vain dismissively. "Try not to get killed, but I don't like your chances. Now go away, I want to talk to this asshole alone."

Panic roared through Jake. "You're not coming with me?"

Vain half-turned and raised an eyebrow. "Why would I?"

Jake was stunned. He had known all along they'd eventually part ways, but he'd grown used to Vain's company. The man was amoral to the point of being evil, but there was something reliable about him, like a solid stone in the midst of a whipping storm, which Jake had come to depend upon in their short time together. Realizing they were now about to separate, that security was abruptly torn away, leaving Jake feeling alone and terribly vulnerable.

"What am I supposed to do?" asked Jake, hating his voice, the way it sounded like a beggar's.

"You're supposed to do exactly what you're doing," replied Vain. "This is something you have to do on your own, and nobody can carry that responsibility for you. You know where to go from here now, and when you get there, you'll have to deal with whatever comes your way."

Jake took a deep breath and suddenly realized something. "I don't have any money!"

Vain stared at him, his expression unreadable. "How the hell did you manage to stay alive before you met me?" he muttered, reaching inside his jacket and removing a thin wallet from which he pulled a card, passing it to Jake along with a few Euro notes. Jake turned the card over and fingered the name embossed on the front: *Martin Roberts.*

"It's unsigned, and there's no credit limit. Just don't go to Vegas and blow it all like an idiot," said Vain.

"But what if this Martin Roberts guy reports it stolen?"

"He won't. That card should look after you for whatever you need; just make sure you sign it as Martin Roberts and not your own name."

Jake pocketed the card. "Thank you."

Vain shrugged. "I've got others," he said dismissively. Once more the assassin moved to leave.

"Goodbye, Vain," said Jake, holding out his hand.

"Yeah," said Vain over his shoulder. Ignoring Jake's offered hand, he strode back to the priest, who still sat on the bench, staring at him, an expression of awe etching his features. Jake had a feeling Vain wouldn't have too much trouble snapping the man out of his shock.

Jake stood momentarily just inside the basilica's doors, delaying the inevitable moment when he'd have to exit into the open square. Their planned strategy had been to blend in with the various tourists coming and going from the church. Jake pretended to stare at one of the basilica's many paintings while waiting for a small group to exit.

He didn't have to wait for long. Soon a crowd of seven tourists, German from the sound of their speech, moved toward the large double-doors. Jake waited until they passed and inconspicuously tagged onto the back of the group, following them out of the church and into the piazza where a couple of hours earlier Vain had shot the man possessed by Abaddon.

Several Italian police were in the area, but the body was gone. The area remained cordoned off. Bloodstains had dried on the ground. Jake turned left and walked away from the scene, trying his best to blend in with those around him, hoping Vain was correct in assuming the police would never expect him to be so brazen.

What if a witness recognized him?

What if Abaddon possessed someone else and pointed him out?

What if...?

His pulse thundered in his temples, so loudly he feared the police might hear it and come running at any moment, but Jake forced himself to slow down, wishing Vain had decided to come with him. But he was alone, and no amount of wishing could change that.

Following the route Father Costello had suggested, Jake soon glimpsed water directly ahead. Turning left at the end of what he'd been told was the Ducal Palace, he saw the dock almost straight in front of him, the ferry only just coming into the jetty.

Perfect timing.

Casually climbing aboard the boat, Jake paid for his ticket out of the handful of Euros Vain had given him. Fifteen minutes later the ferry pulled away, and they were traveling down the Grand Canal, leaving the scene of the murder far behind, but at the same time filling Jake with such a sense of isolation he feared the world might be collapsing in around him.

*-CHAPTER 7-*
# THE TOMB OF MOSES

The plane jolted as the landing gear smacked down hard on the tarmac. Jake snapped awake, peering around groggily, his right hand rubbing the stiffness in his neck.

Nervous about using the credit card Vain had given him, Jake had only purchased an economy seat to Israel. Although the flight hadn't been overly long, it had been all the more draining because of the cramped seat and noisy passengers.

Not for the first time, Jake began to doubt the validity of what had been put before him. Tired and sore as he was, he felt like anything other than a religious figure. He'd never really thought about how it must have been for Jesus, but he was starting to wonder if the supposed son of God had been more human, more frail and flawed, than stories led people to believe. Had he felt the same fear Jake did? Jake stared at his hands, hands without calluses, and doubted it. How could a mere man have created such a phenomenal message, one to echo down through the centuries?

Without any luggage, Jake quickly slipped through Ben Gurion International Airport. The luck of having placed his passport into his pocket prior to stowing his bag in the ruins of Templo Mayor made him say a silent prayer of thanks – and he immediately felt confused as a result. It seemed hypocritical to do such a thing after a lifetime of doubt, of virtual hatred directed toward a deity which had seemingly ignored him for most of his existence. How many times had he cried out in the night for help and none had come? How many times had he heard the screams of his adoptive mother, verses of the Bible drowning her out, the Man screeching words designed for peace, but used instead as justification for his sins?

Was Jake supposed to pray?

The possibility he was delusional popped back into his head for the hundredth time. Ignoring it, Jake swiftly hailed a taxicab and, after a short moment of awkward haggling over the price and struggling to explain where he wanted to go, he climbed in, slamming the door shut behind him.

The city buzzed past his window, and Jake made an effort to pay attention to what was going on outside. Israel's relative prosperity was obvious, and Jake wondered about the people who stared coldly at him as his taxi drove past. He wondered about their dreams, their lives.

For the centuries of war Jerusalem had endured, the city appeared remarkably orderly and pristine. Three religions claimed the city as a holy place – Christianity, Judaism, and Islam – and battles had been fought inside and outside the city walls for almost as long as people had been there. Although Jake's knowledge of history was vague at best, he knew the Christian Crusades had lasted for almost two hundred years, during which time the city had been destroyed and rebuilt many times.

Something suddenly occurred to Jake. What if, during all of the activity and excavation that had likely taken place over the centuries, the Staff had already been found? Such a thought did not sit well with him, so Jake pushed the notion aside for the time being; a problem like that could be dealt with if or when it became a fact, and not beforehand.

Jake concentrated on not falling asleep. He was in a strange city, and the last thing he wanted was to get robbed after dozing off, waking up in a dark alley with no money, no passport, and no idea how to proceed.

Shaking his head, Jake felt disgusted with himself.

He wondered what Vain had gotten up to. Whereas Jake might have once condemned Vain as merely a callous killer, he now knew differently. Vain had given those who accosted them a choice, and they had chosen unwisely.

Such gray areas around morality confused Jake. Vain was so close to evil it almost hurt to be in his presence, but he was also selflessly looking to save Sebastian Dunn's life. Somehow Vain was integrally involved in the issues Jake himself was dealing with, and he couldn't shake the feeling something was going on with the former assassin which Jake could not fully understand. Instinct told him he hadn't seen the last of the Dark Man.

Part of him wished his return would happen sooner, rather than later. Part of Vain seemed almost elemental, as though he were more than just a man. Jake had seen him kill, and knew he should condemn such actions in his mind, but something inside him approved of what had happened.

He hadn't wished those men dead, and would have done anything to avoid it if left on his own, but the terror he'd felt when the muggers approached had been replaced by euphoria when Vain had cut them down. The reasoning part of him said it was merely relief at having survived, but something else lurked there, making him doubt his logic.

Was he glad? Had he enjoyed their deaths? Was he... *evil*?

Examining deep within himself, Jake sensed it wasn't true, and yet that thrill when Abaddon – or rather the poor man taken over by Abaddon – had been shot by Vain remained with him still. He knew remorse should have been paramount, but he couldn't help it. For that one moment in time Abaddon had been foiled, and he couldn't help but feel glad about it, even though it had cost an innocent man his life.

Some messiah he was turning out to be....

Jake shook his head sadly, staring at the strangers the cab sped past, and he sighed.

"What the hell am I supposed to do?" he muttered.

"Your best!" said the cab driver suddenly, snapping Jake out of his thoughts.

"Excuse me?"

"You must do your best, no matter what," replied the driver. "Left of center is sometimes the only path through a seemingly impossible situation."

"But what if my best isn't enough?" asked Jake, unable to resist questioning the stranger, his current mood driving him to seek answers, any answers, which might help settle his melancholy. Who knew, maybe this driver had some mystical insight into the secret workings of the universe? Jake suppressed a grin at the thought.

"It doesn't matter; all that counts is that you try. Success or failure is not measured upon whether you win or lose; it is simply how stubbornly you fight for what you truly believe in. Though the heavens themselves might rail against you, you must go forward into the unknown, trusting in God and luck."

Jake sat back in his seat, staring at the knowing eyes which gazed calmly back at him in the rearview mirror. *Blue* eyes....

"Who are you?" croaked Jake through a suddenly dry throat.

"I am your driver," replied the cabbie. "My name is Sabathiel. And now you must get out."

"Why?" asked Jake, alarmed as he realized the car had stopped.

"Because this is your destination," replied Sabathiel, pointing.

Glancing out the window, Jake realized they had arrived at the Church of the Holy Sepulchre, and suddenly he felt immensely foolish. Shaking his head, he reached for his cash, but Sabathiel stepped out of the cab, closing the door behind him.

Confused, Jake opened his own door and climbed out, glancing around for the driver....

Sabathiel was gone.

Jake looked everywhere, stopping short of searching under the car, but the driver had simply vanished. Jake remembered those blue eyes once more, so similar to those of Uriel in the Garden. Could Sabathiel have been here to simply aid him as the other one, Anael, had done in Vancouver? But Anael had been there when he'd needed money, what had Sabathiel been there for?

Maybe he'd merely been there to support Jake in a moment of need?

Jake stood beside the cab for a while, unsure of what to do. Should he stay with the taxi, hoping someone collected it, or could he just wander off? Eventually he pulled out a few Euros and threw them on the driver's seat, just in case the owner of the taxi appeared. Jake wandered off toward the high church, the large gray domes rising beyond the clustered buildings.

The walkway hugged tightly around him, but Jake didn't notice, trying to focus his thoughts on the goal at hand: investigating the holiest Christian structure on the face of the planet in an attempt to find the burial place of a prophet; stealing a staff which might potentially aid him in destroying one of the Fallen.

It seemed so simple when he thought about it like that….

Pushing aside the immensity of what he was about to attempt, Jake focused instead on the incredible entrance courtyard he'd just stepped into. The yellowed stone of the church walls, possibly carved from sandstone, had also been laid across the floor, blending the two and making the church seem less a building and more like part of the landscape. Large scaffolds attached to the exterior indicated some sort of renovation underway.

Jake strode across the courtyard, trying not to look nervous when he spotted several Israeli soldiers positioned over on the left, standing next to a faded timber door. Finally reaching the main entrance, he stepped into the church. As he passed through the doorway, he noticed the intricate artistry of the carvings around the doorframe. Several days, or perhaps even weeks, would have been needed to create each and every stone block around and above the lintel alone, never mind the rest of the entrance. How much work and time had gone into constructing the entire building?

As his eyes slowly adjusted to the gloom of the church interior, he peered around, wondering where he might possibly begin searching.

His eyes fixed on an object in the center of the room, widening in awe. Directly in front of him, stood something which made Jake freeze, stunned by his proximity to it.

It was the Stone of Unction, also known as the Stone of Anointing.

The Man had ranted about this place, swearing he would one day drag their unworthy asses across the planet on a pilgrimage here. Gazing upon the Stone now, seeing it right in front of him, Jake felt mixed feelings of exhilaration and dread.

This was the rock where Jesus's body had supposedly been washed after he'd been taken down from the cross.

Pilgrims crowded around the Stone, kneeling down just to touch it, or press their lips against the rock. Four tall candlestick holders, each bearing long scented candles, stood protectively at the corners of the rectangular slab, which was set into the ground with a protective lip around the edging. A brass bracket – similar to a large clothes hanger – hung over the Stone, eight frosted-glass lanterns suspended from it, each adorned with a crucifix, the flickering light of a candle illuminating from within.

A massive fresco stretched along the wall behind the Stone of Jesus's body, a painting depicting Christ's body after his crucifixion. Other figures graced the mosaic, but Jake only had eyes for the images of Jesus. His gaze flicked between the painting and the Stone, and the moment hit him like a claw hammer tearing at his stomach:

The eyes of the Christ in the painting met his in an indisputable bond. Jake's ribcage seemed to hug his heart tighter and he gasped slightly. And then the connection disappeared, the eyes of the painting becoming closed once more, leaving Jake wondering if he'd imagined the entire incident. The painting stood inanimate, it wasn't some interactive display direct from Tokyo where Jesus could reach out and let him know what he thought. It was a wall, just a wall with some paint on it....

Jake stared at it for a long time, but nothing else happened. Had the candlelight fooled him? How could such a thing have happened without anyone else seeing? It must have all been in his mind. But what if it weren't; what if it had truly happened?

Savagely thrusting the idea aside, Jake stared hard at the Stone, trying in vain to calm his haphazard pulse. Right now, in this place, the last thing he needed was to get overwhelmed by the enormity of what was going on. Tearing his gaze away from the Stone, he stalked off to the left, unsure of what he was really looking for. This entire structure had been designed as a holy representation of the final resting place of Jesus Christ; it had nothing to do with Moses, who had existed about a thousand years before Christ.

So why would Moses be buried here?

Jake had come here on a hunch. Through the conjecture of a Venetian priest and what he had been told were the writings of

Moses's wife, Jake had arrived at this point, and now he had no idea what to do or where to look.

He should have asked to borrow Zipporah's diary... but that would have been useless since he couldn't read the script – unless that was some miraculous skill he had, something which he was yet to discover perhaps?

Jake suppressed a chuckle. He'd been stressed for too long, and now he was beginning to think he possessed superpowers.

Stupid powers, more like.

Passing a shrine on his left, Jake strolled through a vacant area before skidding to a halt so quickly one of the people behind him almost crashed into his back. Apologizing hastily, Jake stepped to the side and stared at the majesty of the rotunda he had just entered.

Huge sandstone pillars, each the breadth of a forest oak, supported a large circular balcony with high stone archways facing inward. Above the balcony lay another two levels of arches before the inside of the majestic dome curved above it all, gold-layered carvings inlaid against the ash-gray stone.

But the structure did not seal completely at the top. The central tip of the towering dome was raised, like a nipple, the tip itself made of strengthened glass. The refracting effect was staggering, the sunlight from outside shooting through the glass, spotlighting the area with a ray of light from above, as though the finger of God were piercing the roof, reaching down....

The sunbeam illuminated the surprisingly thin crowd and a structure situated in the middle of the circular rotunda – a small chapel constructed from the same sandstone bricks as the church around it – but the outer walls remained bathed in shadow. It seemed to Jake as though he now stood upon an island within the room, an island created solely for him. Once more Jake's heart fluttered at the realization he now gazed upon something which might possibly be very close to him indeed.

It was the Tomb of Christ.

Jake couldn't stop himself from circling the small structure within the larger building, staring at it, unwilling to enter, and yet powerless to flee. He soon arrived at the entrance to the shrine and stared at the opening, a darkened maw yearning for his flesh, a trap, his heritage returned to ensnare him. His heart hammered in his chest, and he wanted nothing more than to run away from this entire affair forever.

But he couldn't do that. It was inexplicable, even within Jake's own mind. He had chosen this course in Eden when Uriel had sacrificed his eternal existence in order to see Jake safe, and there was no turning away from his fate now, whatever it might be.

He *had* to go inside.

Nausea threatened to rise up, but Jake pushed it back down and focused on the entrance to the tomb. It was faced with what appeared to be polished marble, surrounded by various adornments and candles, but Jake had little thought for these details. He focused on what lay beyond the entrance, the opportunity to discover some answers to his past... and potentially his future.

As he walked toward the doorway, however, he admitted to himself he had no sense of what to expect from this expedition into Jesus's tomb. Was he searching for an answer to his new-found role in life? Jake truly didn't know, but tendrils of curiosity drew him forward, like visiting the ancient grave of a never-known ancestor, and he felt the intense desire to discover what resided within the shrine.

Stepping over the threshold, Jake noticed a small, almost square, altar. A sign inside the door identified this as the Chapel of the Angels, stating that the altar actually contained a piece of the stone which had sealed Jesus's tomb.

Interesting, but not what he was here for.

Jake continued on, entering the next room and halting once more, this time to allow three tourists to exit the room, leaving him alone for the moment. He gazed around the tiny space, even smaller than the Chapel of the Angels. It seemed remarkably bare apart from a marble slab against a wall, surrounded on three sides by candles, a vase full of smaller candles sitting at one end of the stone. Reading the small sign explaining the slab's significance, Jake's jaw dropped.

Jesus's body had been placed on this stone after his crucifixion, the vase indicating where his head had lain.

As skeptical as Jake was about many things involved in this entire affair, this moment made him pause. It seemed unreal, somehow choreographed, like a play he had been haphazardly flung into. Here he was, alone in the tomb of Christ when normally it would be filled with pilgrims and tourists. All in all it felt like more than coincidence, it seemed more like fate.

He stared at the slab, watching the candlelight flicker –

*Flicker?*

How could the candles flicker in a tomb without a breeze?

Superstition momentarily gripped him, but Jake pushed the sensation aside with difficulty. Stepping closer, he held his open hand near the vase of candles and felt a soft breath of movement in the air coming from the edge of the slab. Leaning down he saw an infinitesimal crack in the stone, a tiny seam through which the breeze escaped. But if a draft was blowing from beyond the slab, that meant….

There must be a tunnel beneath it!

Now Jake was faced with a dilemma. He had come to the Church of the Holy Sepulchre in order to find the Staff of Moses, the only thing he knew of which might be able to defeat Abaddon. And now he had stumbled upon a seemingly hidden space beneath what was potentially the holiest relic in Christianity.

Staring at the stone slab, Jake felt the weight of the decision before him. This was not a mere historical tourist attraction where he could traipse beyond the regular boundaries and expect nothing more than a slap on the wrist. Arrayed throughout the Church of the Holy Sepulchre were no less than six separate Christian sects, not including the potentially zealous Brotherhood of the Holy Sepulchre, whose sole purpose, as far as Jake knew, was to act as guards for this holy place. That was a whole lot of religion to come crashing down on his head if this somehow went awry.

What was he thinking: *if* it went awry? How could it not?

Jake shook his head, unable to believe what he was about to attempt. He lifted the brass vase, placing it carefully on the ground. He studied the slab once more, noting that it was actually divided into several parts, not the single piece of stone it had originally seemed. Jake felt under the edge of the section where the vase had been, the part under which Jesus's head had supposedly rested at one time.

Boy was he going to be in trouble.

Fingers slick with sweat gripped the cold stone. Blood pounded in his temples, and he frantically glanced around once more to make sure nobody approached. Sadly, the coast was clear – he had no excuse. Jake hooked his fingers beneath the section of slab and heaved with all his might.

It lifted half an inch.

Returning it to where it had been, Jake stared incredulously at the tombstone. He'd expected it to be heavy, but as a sectional piece it shouldn't have been completely immovable. It felt like it was being held down from beneath. Every moment that passed saw a chance someone might enter the chamber, a chance of him getting caught. What possible explanation could he offer for his actions?

Glancing up at the gold-inlaid depiction of Jesus, Jake stared at the eyes of the image. "How do I get in?" he asked softly, frustration suffusing his tone.

The picture remained silent, and Jake turned his back on it, unconsciously leaning against the edge of the slab while he contemplated the problem.

The stone shifted.

It wasn't a major move, just enough for Jake to notice, and he spun back, swiftly gripping the edge once more and pushing with all his might. The section of the lid slid smoothly into the wall, the forward piece dropping down at the same time, revealing a stairwell plunging into darkness.

Footsteps sounded just outside the crypt. Without pausing to think, Jake darted down the marble stairs before anyone caught him. A shout sounded, echoing from the walls of the burial chamber, but he didn't stop. Descending beneath the floor level, a soft click whispered above him, and the stone lid of the tomb slid back into place silently, sealing him in, darkness consuming him completely.

Swallowing heavily, Jake now faced a choice: continue on or try to find a way to re-open the tomb entrance, probably getting caught in the process. Shrugging in the darkness, he felt for the next step with his foot and continued descending the stairs, clutching the wall as he slowly made his way through the inkiness.

Gradually, he realized the staircase wasn't really that dark. Within a few moments his eyes adjusted to the gloom, and Jake could dimly define the outline of his hand against the wall along with the stairs beneath his feet. Something further down the stairwell was generating a dull light, enough for Jake to negotiate the stairs without stumbling.

Cautious not to trip, Jake crept down the stairs, curiosity biting him more sharply with each descending step.

What would be waiting for him at the bottom?

Would the Staff of Moses truly be able to help him?

Would he ever truly feel adequate for the task facing him?

The last thought actually took him by surprise, and Jake slowed as he contemplated it, realizing how true it was. He felt completely unprepared for what he was going up against, woefully inadequate for the role he was trying to fill. Truth be told, it still scared him to death. He was walking a path only one man had ever trodden before him, and those were immensely large footprints to fill.

Uriel had spoken of him being energy reborn. He'd said Jake was a separate entity to what Jesus had been, but what he'd said couldn't be entirely true. If reincarnation – or whatever this was – were truly possible, surely more than just energy had to be reborn; what about love, passion, and purpose? Why had he always been driven to make life better for others, if not for the memories of the one whose path he was now following?

But then there were the contradictions. For instance, Jake wasn't religious, in fact he bordered on despising religion – that seemed a bit of a drawback for someone destined to represent a religious figure. How was he supposed to argue on the side of God, if he had silently blamed Him for all that had gone wrong in his own life? Despite his upbringing, this quest had marked the most time he'd spent in churches over his entire life, and now here he was desecrating the holiest Christian site on the face of the planet.

Jake continued down the stairs, his thoughts disturbed, his feelings confused.

The toe of his shoe snared on a cracked edge. He tripped, falling forward, tumbling down the steep staircase for what seemed an eternity, unable to stop or even slow himself. Tucking his head between his raised arms, Jake tried to roll with the fall, until he came to rest in a battered heap at the bottom, both cursing his clumsiness and thankful he hadn't shattered his spine.

Standing up tentatively, Jake began checking himself for injuries. Shaking off his bruises, he suddenly froze, stunned by what he saw. The stairs themselves had been immensely steep, and his fall must have brought him down further than he realized because where before there had been a dim glow, now he stood in a cavern filled with light.

The rocks of the walls and roof held some sort of iridescent quality. The entire chamber shone with unearthly brightness, glowing like some sort of perilous, subterranean theater. The floor of the hall appeared to be stone, smooth and somewhat shiny, almost polished in its beauty, but the walls and ceiling remained rough and jagged, the rock left natural and untouched, its rawness contrasting with the glossy floor.

Jake crept forward uncertainly, moving away from the base of the stairs and into the chamber itself. There seemed no real purpose to this place apart from serving as some sort of entrance hall, but an entrance hall to what? At the other end of the cavern stood a narrow doorway, seemingly innocuous against the oddity of the large glowing cavern, and Jake began to skulk toward it. Something nagged at his mind, however, and he stopped, uncertain. The area seemed too bare, too still, too… dangerous. Vain came to mind, and Jake wondered what the assassin might think of this room. The answer flashed into his mind: it was a trap!

Retreating to the stairway, Jake found a small rock and, on impulse, skipped it across the floor of the cavern. The stone, about the size of his palm, flipped and hopped across the shiny ground, bouncing slightly as it –

An enormous block thundered down, cracking the granite floor with its force and sending out a booming roar. The huge boulder left a substantial gap in the ceiling from which it fell, barely missing the skipping rock when it slammed into the cavern floor. The stone, little more than a pebble in comparison to its murderous brethren, skidded beyond the boulder, across the smooth floor and… vanished!

The seemingly solid stone floor had crumbled as the small stone touched it, falling away like eggshell. Jake listened, but he never heard the small stone hit the bottom of the chasm….

So now Jake was facing danger on at least two fronts. On one hand he had huge rocks falling from the ceiling, triggered by who knew what, and on the other a floor which might crumble beneath his feet at any moment.

Glancing around for another stone he could throw, Jake saw nothing. The entire area seemed bare of anything he might use.

*Think!*

There *had* to be a way across. The builders couldn't possibly have been so narrow-minded as to imagine the Staff would never be needed again… could they?

Jake's frustrated gaze flowed across the smooth floor and rougher ceiling and walls, searching for a solution. The whole thing seemed like an impossible situation.

Impossible situation…?

Why did that seem so familiar?

It suddenly came to him. It was the same phrase the taxi driver, Sabathiel, had uttered to Jake before he'd disappeared.

*"Left of center is sometimes the only path through a seemingly impossible situation."*

Jake had presumed the man was uttering nonsense; maybe it was a common Israeli proverb – how was Jake to know? But since then he'd come to believe Sabathiel was perhaps more than just a taxi driver, possibly even an angel sent to aid him – his disappearance into thin air had definitely added to that presumption.

Now Jake stared at the floor across the chamber with a new perspective. He'd thrown the stone almost straight across, the most likely route someone crossing it would take, and he had triggered two traps before the small rock had made it halfway. Glancing up, he thought he could make out several more boulders waiting to drop at the slightest pressure from below, but then again the entire roof now appeared treacherous. If his theory about what Sabathiel had meant were correct, if he took a route slightly to the left of the centerline of the room, he would pass through safely.

*Maybe....*

At the very least it would avoid the two traps he'd already triggered, so hopefully they weren't built side-by-side.

He stared at the boulder, imagining the crushing force of something so heavy landing on top of him, and shuddered. Placing his faith in mere hope seemed a ridiculous ploy, but what choice did he have?

Trying to dismiss the likelihood of Sabathiel just being a crazy taxi driver, Jake took a trembling step forward. His foot touched the glossy floor. He put his weight down on it.

Nothing happened.

Flicking a glance first up at the ceiling, and then back down at the floor, Jake couldn't decide which trap would be worse. Being crushed beneath a boulder would be horrific beyond imagining, but at least it would be over quickly. Falling through a hole in the floor might seem less terrifying, but he had no idea what lay at the bottom of the chasm; maybe it would simply prolong the terror –

*Cut it out!*

His feet began to shake even more, and his eyes started to water. He feared blinking lest he miss some crucial piece of evidence; a giant boulder falling on his head, for instance – that would be pretty crucial.

Jake angled his route to run about four feet to the left of where the boulder had landed. From where he stood, he guessed the room stretched about quarter the length of a football field to the opposite doorway – ninety feet of potentially horrifying, torturous death.

A drop of sweat flicked from the tip of his nose and hung motionless in the air for the barest of seconds – just long enough for Jake to register it. And then it fell, twisting and hurtling, a symbol of what would happen to him if the floor gave way.

The drip splashed upon the polished stone. Jake cringed, expecting a crushing demise from above at any second. The rock he had flicked had barely kissed the floor before the boulder had loosed, surely a drop of water might do the same.

Apparently not.

Breathing out, Jake took another tremulous step forward, listening for the telltale groan which had preceded the boulder's fall. All remained silent. No noise had emitted before the ground gave way, though, and so he trained his eyes on the polished stone, searching for evidence of cracks in the floor – *anything* which might indicate a fragile section. He couldn't see anything, but then again he hadn't noticed any difference in the floor before the small stone had disappeared through it.

Jake wiped sweat from his eyes, the salt stinging them and making it hard to focus. He carefully dried his hand on his pant leg. Realizing he was merely delaying his next step, a silent snarl flickered across his face, abhorrence at such weakness pushing him forward. After two paces he came even with the fallen boulder and again paused, but this time for a reason. Glancing up, he saw the gaping aperture in the ceiling where the rock had been hidden. He looked over the entire ceiling, searching for signs of anything similar, any tiny indication of another ceiling trap, but he could discern nothing. What he had thought before were dangling rocks were merely variances in the ragged ceiling. Or were they...?

Eyes narrowed, Jake stepped forward once more, creeping as swiftly as he dared. He tried not to think about the large cracks in the polished floor. A disturbing image of a watermelon beneath a dropped anvil flitted through his mind, and he savagely tried to thrust it away. Like a buzzing fly, it returned again and again: the seeds flying in slow motion through the air as the pulp of the melon sprayed outward, the seemingly tough outer skin shattered in an instant by the inflexible iron of the anvil. His treacherous imagination replaced the watermelon with his skull, replaying the scene once more....

Jake neared the section of broken floor, and he froze, his feet unwilling to obey him any longer. Like a horse ordered to jump over a canyon without sight of the other side, his legs refused to comply with what his mind ordered, and he stood immobile like a clothing-store mannequin, modeling panic instead of cotton.

With a wrench of determination, Jake stepped to the left slightly, away from the cracked and wrecked edge of the hole. This loosened his trepidation slightly, allowing a modicum of movement.

Sliding forward as though on ice, Jake's eyes betrayed him, his gaze flicking to the hole on his right, his mind noting the millimeter-thin shell which had crumbled, its surface indistinguishable from the rest of the polished granite. Distracted, he lifted his left foot, stepping forward and lowering it down... down.

Too far down!

His shoe met no resistance, his entire body tilting forward dramatically. Wobbling and off-balance, Jake struggled to steady himself as an entire portion of the floor unexpectedly dropped into eternity, the crust of the fake stone flaking away like ancient paint flecks. Arms wind-milling wildly, gravity tried with all its might to haul him into the midnight fissure, but Jake finally managed to tear himself from its grasp and regain his balance. Standing frozen once more, tears of panic threatened to burst loose, the only thing holding them back being the stronger fear that to set free such a torrent might release as yet unseen traps.

Jake swallowed heavily and gazed around, realizing he now stood on a bridge of secure ground about a foot wide between the two deceptive portions of disintegrated fake floor. The bridge curved slightly to the right, leading all the way to the room's exit, like a tightrope above the Grand Canyon.

Suddenly the giant boulder didn't seem so terrifying.

Battling the insistent urge to grip his elbows, Jake focused his eyes straight ahead, stepping forward on quavering legs, trying not to deviate from the slightly-left path he had chosen. Each footstep held the potential to be his last, each indecisive stride held the potential of death from above or below. The march stretched out like a marathon, but he finally neared the end, breathing a soft sigh of relief.

A groan sounded from directly above him, little more than a murmur, but enough to make Jake freeze a mere three feet from the exit. Surely the builders wouldn't place a rock trap above such a narrow escape route.

Surely.

Without pausing to look, Jake skipped clumsily across the remaining span of bridge, leaped forward through the doorway, and skidded along the ground. A thunderous crash erupted from behind, dust billowing all around him. Jake waited a moment, allowing the dust to settle before lifting his head from the ground and glancing around.

Another boulder, larger than the first, now sealed the doorway, huge cracks radiating out from its base. Simply looking at it told Jake the giant rock was immovable. There was no going back the way he had come; all Jake could do was continue forward and hope for another exit from this crypt.

Lifting himself up, Jake climbed slowly to his feet, brushed the dust off his clothes, and gazed around.

The same glowing rock from the last chamber shone here as well, but now it had been channeled, sections of the wall designed like bracketed lights. The floor once more resembled polished granite, impeccably finished, but now it curved beyond its edges, the smoothness continuing up the high walls, broken only by the black, half-cone brackets blazing with the iridescent stone, the cones directing the light upward, where it disappeared into shadows.

Jake felt his guard lower slightly and instinctively knew he shouldn't, not after what had just happened. While this chamber appeared only about half the length and breadth of the one before, the roof disappeared in the gloom above, bringing to mind that anything might plunge down from that darkness – perhaps the entire ceiling would simply collapse if he hiccupped or coughed. At this thought, Jake realized he was breathing shallowly, and forced himself to inhale and exhale as normally as possible, trying to calm his already traumatized mind.

Returning his gaze to the floor, he noticed the stone was set out in different shaded squares, almost like a checkerboard. That meant every panel was separate, and as such each one could work as a trigger.

*Drip.*

The spot of water hit Jake on the neck, and he absently stepped aside and wiped it away with his right hand while trying to figure out the best way to tackle the room –

*Drip.*

Annoyed, Jake once more wiped the water from his neck, wincing as his hand rubbed over raw skin.

But how could it be raw? He'd only just wiped away the other drop….

Jake quickly looked at his hand, noting how his palm now appeared red and inflamed, the skin already rising up in tiny blisters.

*Drip.*

This one landed on his ear, and Jake instantly felt it burning the more sensitive skin there.

*Drip – drip – drip.*

The drops fell all around him, and Jake suddenly realized they weren't water – they were some sort of *acid!* With every second that passed, more and more droplets tumbled from the darkness above until they fell all around him like a light rain. Either the dropping of that final rock in the previous room or one of the floor panels Jake had stepped on must have triggered some sort of trap.

Now Jake faced a dilemma, and each second he wasted analyzing it brought more peril from above. Did he run across the floor in front of him, unsure of what might happen if he did, or did he wait where he was, trying to figure something out while the acidic liquid slowly and horrifically burned him to death a tiny drop at a time?

Pressing himself hard against the back wall, Jake tried to edge under the doorframe he'd just leaped through, but it was completely blocked by the boulder, and he could find no shelter beneath the frame. Thinking furiously, he recalled the other thing Sabathiel had said to him:

*"Though the heavens themselves might rail against you, you must go forward into the unknown, trusting in God and luck."*

Oh well, better to die trying than cringing against a wall.

Jake bolted, sprinting across the floor just as an acidic torrent rushed down against the wall he'd been leaning against a heartbeat before. Unable to look back, Jake focused on the doorway ahead of him, running as fast as he could, the roar of the downpour growing louder and louder behind him. From the sound of it, the entire roof had opened, dumping an ocean of acid. If the liquid hit him, there would be no hope; even if he survived the burns, there was no way he'd make his way out of here alive with the injuries he was sure he'd suffer.

This thought spurred him on, pumping energy into already fatigued legs as he scrambled across the smooth floor. Breath burned in his lungs, or perhaps it was merely the fumes from the acid threatening to overwhelm him. He tried not to think of this possibility, straining forward, yearning to reach the doorway, but afraid the wave would hit him at any second.

It was too far, he'd never make it. Time seemed to slow as Jake's fear almost made him give in. He felt exhausted. Dizziness from the fumes made the doorway double in front of him, and he became unsure of which was the true exit. If he misjudged it he would slam into a solid wall right before drowning in the caustic flood.

Left or right, he had to choose.

Right.

Jake shot through the doorframe, the step just past the exit cracking loudly as his foot landed on it. A gigantic slab, perfectly cut to fit into the tightly-carved groove, smashed down into the floor like an emergency gate – sealing the doorway perfectly. Jake heard the ocean of acid smash into the rock from the other side. He waited, certain the stone could not prevent such a flood, but not a drop of the liquid seeped through… at least not yet.

He had to keep moving. The cavern Jake now found himself in appeared enormous, dwarfing any he'd stepped through so far. Again Jake spied the bracketed glowing rocks along the walls, but unlike the previous room, the ceiling of this area could be seen, carved from the same smooth granite as the walls and floor. This room had a touch of majesty about it, somehow enhanced by the sparseness of detail involved.

Preparing himself for more traps, Jake was surprised to look across the floor and see a staff… *the* Staff! It was lying atop a large rectangular marble block which looked suspiciously like a… like a….

A tomb.

Jake knew he shouldn't feel surprised; he *had* come here looking for Moses's grave, after all. He'd entered this place through the supposed grave of Jesus Christ himself, so nothing should have shocked him.

And yet this did.

The Staff confirmed who lay interred here. This cavernous underground crypt held the final resting place of the man who had saved the Israelites from the Egyptians, who had supposedly faced down the most powerful society on Earth at the time, because of his faith and desire to do what was right.

Moses.

Putting aside all the tales of mystical wonders involving God, Moses had performed some amazing feats on his own. The fact he'd accomplished all he did, the bravery involved in standing his ground against such powerful foes, put Moses in a league of his own. Some might argue that it was all mythology or exaggeration, but Jake stared at evidence the man had actually existed, and all tall tales sprung from some source of truth. Even exaggerated, Moses must have accomplished something incredible to be revered almost four thousand years after his death.

But for the moment, Jake couldn't worry about that. He'd travelled to this place for the staff, and he needed to put aside his awe and simply complete the task he'd come here for, and then try to find a way out.

Crossing the floor to the tomb, Jake felt confident there would be no traps in this room – the makers wouldn't risk damage to the tomb or the Staff with falling boulders and downpours of acid. His footfalls echoed against the stone walls and roof as he stepped toward the large sarcophagus, noting the design of the stone and its remarkable resemblance to pictures he'd seen in Egyptian crypts.

Egypt? But that meant….

Halting his stride, Jake suddenly realized who'd originally built the traps in the previous rooms – indeed, who had probably designed and created this entire place. The Israelites had been slaves to the Egyptians, and as such they would have worked for them on their pyramids and crypts. The traps in the other two rooms convinced him this entire place had been recreated from the construction of Egyptian tombs, right down to the traps designed to stop grave-robbers. The lack of hieroglyphs or markings would have been a direct rebellion against their former masters.

But the construction of this vault remained irrelevant now, and part of Jake realized he was merely stalling, fear of the enormity of what he was about to do delaying him when he had no real time to delay. Gritting his teeth, Jake strode forward once more, his eyes set upon the Staff. It rested atop two crescents set into the lid of the huge sarcophagus, raising it above the surface of the lid.

As he got closer, Jake could see the two brackets bearing the Staff were actually talons, like those of an eagle or falcon, and the claws were locked around the staff, grasping it tightly. He slowed his walk and approached more cautiously, unsure of how to proceed.

The Staff itself looked quite plain, carved from a wood-like substance and about six feet long. He thought of it as 'wood-like' for the simple fact that there was no way real wood could have survived this long, and as such it had to be something else.

But it sure looked like wood.

Leaning down, Jake could even see a couple of frayed splinters, as well as a worn section about four feet up from the base – around the same place a person would continuously grip such a staff. But if this were the *actual* Staff, how in the world could it have not rotted away centuries ago?

Jake contemplated it momentarily. If not for the stressfulness of the current situation and the imminent death lurking around every corner in this place, he might have laughed. Facing fallen angels cast from Heaven by God, he'd been shot through the heart, had this very same heart completely torn from his chest, been brought back to life by the fruit from the Tree of Life in the Garden of Eden, in the process conversing with at least one angel, possibly receiving help from another two.

And somehow he was worried about a stick that didn't rot.

As far as priorities went at the moment, that was pretty low on the scale of weird stuff.

Studying the Staff once more, Jake searched for traps or triggers, but saw none. The claws gripping it, however, were made of bronze and appeared far too sturdy to be pried apart. Their grasp allowed no space to even slip the rod out. There had to be another way.

Jake stared hard at the lid, discerning an ancient script which he couldn't understand. As he glared at the words and the lettering, the script seemed to shift around in his mind, as though his brain were somehow reorganizing the characters. The carvings themselves remained unchanged, but within a few moments, Jake realized he could decipher what they said.

His heart thundered a rapid-fire drumbeat in his ears. Something dramatic had just occurred, but he had no time to contemplate it; the phenomenon might disperse like mist at any moment. Jake held on to the image, focusing on each letter, willing his concentration not to slip.

*And you shall find yourself reading these words, and despite what you think, your soul will tell you who you truly are and the hazardous course you must travel. Your road will be long and full of doubt, but hold to the knowledge of who you are, not the One before, but the One yet to be. Your prize will be neither glory nor riches, but you will rejoice in it nonetheless.*

*This Staff awaits the walker of paths uncharted. Its wood has aided me throughout my life, but I was always merely a borrower, as were all those who held it before me. Its true purpose remains within your hands, oh One who is yet to be. I shall have this Staff interred with me in a place no other can reach, beyond the hands of greed and malice, and only your touch shall release its grip.*

*Good luck to you, stranger. I wish I could offer words beyond these which I have been allowed to utter, but this is all I know. Be comforted in the knowledge that the power of Heaven passes through the Staff, but it is not a tool of evil, and the task of evil shall corrupt the wielder, as I have sadly discovered. Fare well and strive beyond hope, for that is what you will require.*

Jake stepped back, stunned by the message carved into sarcophagus lid. His focus broken, the words snapped back to their original indecipherable script and try as he might, Jake couldn't compel his brain to understand them again.

Could the message have truly been meant for *him*? This revelation was immense, far beyond anything Jake had imagined. The script said only one person could get in here, and Jake had survived the traps to emerge into this room, but surely that was mere luck, wasn't it?

He suddenly remembered the lid of Jesus's supposed tomb in the Church of the Holy Sepulchre above, and how easily it had slid open for him. All the centuries of people investigating the site, the multitudes of pilgrims who must have touched the tomb – why had it opened so easily for Jake? Perhaps there was more to it than just luck. Maybe some of it was… destiny? The traps themselves may have merely been secondary precautions, the main deterrent being the entrance itself.

It didn't really matter now – he was here and only had one thing left to do. Well… *two* if he counted finding a way out of this place.

Jake reached out his hand, grasping the Staff at the portion where it was most worn, the wood feeling smooth and warm beneath his palm. He could have sworn it vibrated slightly, like a tiny shiver, before becoming still once more. The claws holding the Staff suddenly snapped open, and he raised it high, feeling a sense of purpose thrum through his body as Staff and wielder were united.

Bringing the Staff down, Jake gazed at it reverently, waiting for some great revelation. None came.

"Okay. Now what?" he muttered.

Jake raised his eyes once more, noticing distinct cracks of light around a door in the far shadow of the room. It might have been there before, but Jake hadn't noticed it in his excitement over having found the Staff, he couldn't be sure.

Striding toward the doorway, Jake glanced at the Staff in his hands. It didn't seem like anything special. Apart from looking like a functional tool for walking and possibly guiding animals, he couldn't imagine what else it had originally been used for. More importantly, he couldn't fathom what it could possibly do for *him* in his quest to defeat Abaddon. Maybe he could give the fallen angel a splinter.

Jake reached the door, pausing to check that it wasn't surrounded by traps. He took note of its simple latch and oak paneling before reaching out his hand….

He tripped!

How such a thing had occurred when he'd been standing still eluded Jake. It felt like the floor itself had lifted up, propelling him forward. Jake stumbled and smacked into the door, knocking it open and flying through to land as a lump beyond it, hearing the door slam shut behind him.

Darkness surrounded him, and the first thing Jake noticed was his fist stinging. He hadn't released the Staff from his right hand and had grazed his knuckles in the fall.

"Hey, you alright, man?" called a husky voice.

It took Jake a moment to realize the words were in English, and he sat up, stunned. Glancing around, Jake realized he was in an alley, but not in Jerusalem. This place looked more modern, more… American?

But how?

Dull footsteps sounded, and he glanced up to see a young black man, around twenty years of age approaching him. "I asked if you're alright, man. That was a nasty fall."

The man squatted down beside Jake, concern crinkling his features. Jake noted a scar running from his forehead, through both top and bottom lids of the man's left eye, and down his cheek. The orb itself, lay milky in its socket. Jake also noted the stranger's thick jacket, surely capable of hiding a weapon beneath it.

"Where am I?" croaked Jake, his throat dry.

The young man pulled a fresh, sealed bottle of water from within his coat and cracked it open, offering it to Jake. Sniffing it discreetly, Jake nodded thanks to the young man and took a swift swig from the bottle. The water was fresh and cool, and Jake suddenly realized just how thirsty he was. He guzzled down the liquid, draining the small bottle within moments. The young man grinned. The smile reshaped the young man's face amazingly.

"Feeling better?" he asked. "I'm Michael, and you're in Chicago."

"Chicago? How the hell did I get here?" muttered Jake.

"I got no idea, man. You just fell out that door and here you are. What were you doing in that place anyway?"

Jake stared at the door, cracked and peeling blue paint encrusting its surface, and oddly no handle on this side. The sign above the top of the doorway read:

## JEHOVAH RELICS
### NEW AND USED RELIGIOUS ARTEFACTS
### SERVICE ENTRANCE ONLY

"What the...?" muttered Jake.

"I know, man," replied Michael. "That sure is a weird-ass place to be robbing, but at least it looks like you got yourself a nice-looking stick." He laughed loudly.

Jake glanced at the Staff in his hand and grinned, sighing heavily. "More than you can imagine, Michael."

"Oh, I doubt that," responded the black man, giving Jake a knowing smile. "Now the question arises, what are you going to do, now you've got your pretty stick?"

"I have no idea," replied Jake. "But I must be in this place for a reason." He paused, realizing a subtle change had taken place in the stranger. Looking up, he stared hard into the one good eye of the man squatting beside him, noting how startlingly blue it was. "What do you think I should do?"

Michael chuckled. "I can't tell you that. This entire task is yours and yours alone; the rest of us are merely here to assist where we can."

Jake nodded. Disappointed as he was, he hadn't really expected anything more. "Uriel died, you know that, right?"

Michael's expression sobered. "We all know. But if he died to aid you, then it was worth it. Uriel was always a good soldier, and I will miss him, but there's a lot more at stake than the existence of individuals, and we can't afford to mourn him. There are things which you will face, things I can't discuss for fear of you coming to knowledge before you are ready for it, but rest assured you are not alone on this quest, and your path affects much more than you think. More and more of us are being brought to this plane by God, and even I don't know everything He has planned. Remember the words Moses left you, and continue on the course you now travel. Know that God loves you."

Jake opened his mouth to ask another question, but realized Michael was gone. Sighing, he rose to his feet, leaning heavily on the Staff and realizing how utterly conspicuous it was.

"It'd help if I didn't look like a damn shepherd," he muttered, wishing the Staff were smaller.

Jake felt a slight vibration in the wood, and suddenly he was no longer holding a pole, rather it had reduced in size to that of a walking stick carved out of smooth wood. The top had molded itself into a handle the shape of a cobra's head, mouth open, ready to strike.

Testing it out, Jake realized it was the perfect height for him, and felt completely natural in his grip. Staring at the marvel, he grinned at how such things were rapidly failing to amaze him. In the space of fifteen minutes he'd travelled halfway around the world, spoken to an archangel, and seen the near-mythical Staff of Moses transform into a simple walking stick.

And all without breaking a sweat.

Well… not really.

-CHAPTER 8-
# CAPTURED

"WHAT AM I SUPPOSED TO DO???" pleaded Jake.

Still in its form as an innocuous walking cane, the Staff remained resolutely silent, leaning casually against the end of the hotel bed, mutely taunting his inadequacy like a schoolyard smartass. Jake resumed his frustrated pacing around the room once more. He'd hoped once he held the Staff in his hands things would start falling into place, but if anything, the complete opposite was occurring.

The hotel room appeared decidedly unremarkable; merely a place to sleep and rest safely without fear of getting gnawed upon by rats. He needed to figure out why the fates had led him to Chicago of all places, and what in the world was he supposed to do next?

Frustrated, he slumped down into a chair and glared at the Staff, hoping for some kind of revelation. Nothing materialized, and he snarled angrily, leaning back and staring up at the ceiling.

It had been like this for three days, with no end in sight. What little sleep he managed seemed plagued with dreams of Abaddon drenched in crimson, Jake writhing atop a crucifix, his shredded flesh and exposed heart providing the blood for Abaddon's bath. Each time Jake would wake with the ghost of a scream still lingering upon his lips, grasping for the Staff and begging it soundlessly for the answer which refused to emerge.

He'd ordered room service several times, each time hoping deep down that the person delivering it might possess startling blue eyes and a cryptic message for him, only to be disappointed again and again. The temptation to pray had beckoned upon the edges of his consciousness, but the agonizing recollections of the Bible held by the Man licked across his memories like torturous flames, and his mind rebelled like a stomach retching poison.

He was in Chicago for a reason. It couldn't merely have been happenstance that the tomb had spat him out that door into the alley, nor that Michael had been there waiting for him when he'd emerged. If only the archangel had given him more information. If only the Staff would give him a clue.

*If only….*

Powerful words which rarely unveiled anything useful.

Jake strode over to the bed and picked up the Staff once more, sitting on the edge of the bed and examining the wood. What could possibly be in Chicago for him? He wanted nothing more than to charge off in pursuit of Abaddon, but had no idea where the Fallen's leader might be hiding, nor which body he now resided in. It would be like chasing the wind.

The other issue he now faced was that he had absolutely no concept of what the Staff could do. His knowledge of Moses was essentially limited to the Ten Commandments – of which Jake could only remember eight – and the parting of the Red Sea. Both, if he recalled correctly, had involved the use of the Staff, but Jake wasn't sure in what way. Despite his instincts screaming against him, he'd eventually forced himself to skim through the hotel room's Bible, searching for answers. His swift search revealed that the Staff had once been transformed by Moses into a serpent which ate the pharaoh's magicians' own snakes; it had also played a role in the plagues visited upon Egypt. Beyond that, Jake's ability to ignore the grotesque texture of the book began to fray, and he'd hurriedly returned the Bible back to the dresser drawer.

Heaving a great sigh of frustration, Jake shimmied back on the double-bed until his head was propped up by the two pillows. He grabbed the remote control, flicking the television on and skipping through the channels until he caught sight of something interesting. It seemed while he had been enmeshed in his quest for the Staff, a new president had been elected for the United States. His inaugural speech beamed live across the world, and Jake paused in his incessant contemplation for answers to listen to the man speaking.

The President's voice sounded rich and deep, his confidence obvious as he proclaimed a new era for the American people and –

*What the hell was that?*

Jake scrambled forward, kneeling on the bed, rushing to get closer to the screen. The President's speech hadn't faltered, and the screen had flickered for only a moment, but it was just long enough to show....

But it couldn't be.

No.

It did it again, and Jake dropped the Staff to the floor, his hands shaking beyond control. The face of the President had shimmered both times; the first could have been a technical glitch, and Jake hadn't really been paying attention, so he might have assumed wrong.

But the second time had confirmed it.

In that moment, Jake realized why he had been brought to this place. It was so he would end up in this room, staring at this television at this exact moment and see exactly what he had just seen.

For the minutest fraction of a second, the face hiding behind the confident expression of the new president had become visible to Jake, revealing that the most powerful man on the face of the planet was no longer a man.

It was Abaddon.

\*\*\*

The President of the United States of America.

No way.

It wasn't enough that this entire enterprise had seemed impossible from the beginning, or that Jake didn't have enough to deal with, now he had to find a way past this? Jake's target – a fallen angel with powers beyond anything this world or even this dimension could hope to yield – had now taken over the body of the most protected man on the face of the Earth.

Impossible was the word which instantly sprang to mind.

Trying to stop his hands from shaking, Jake picked up the Staff and moved to the door, opening it and stepping out, intent on fleeing this place, perhaps fleeing the entire affair. He felt tempted to leave the Staff behind, but something within him refused to let it go, not after what he'd gone through to get it. He just needed to clear his head, maybe go for a walk. Perhaps then everything would seem alrig –

Strong hands grabbed Jake and slammed him face-first into the wall. Stunned, he was unable to resist as his hands were handcuffed behind him, and the Staff was wrenched from his grip.

"Wait!" gasped Jake. "Don't take that! I need it!"

"Fuck what you want," growled one of his assailants. "We don't deal with terrorists."

"Terr – *What*? I'm not a terrorist!"

"That's what they all say. You're now under arrest for acts of terrorism under Title VIII of the United States PATRIOT Act. You have the right to remain silent...."

As the man read him his rights, and they hauled him docilely down the hallway of the hotel, Jake's mind began to swim.

Was this linked somehow to the inauguration of the new president whom Abaddon now controlled like a puppet, or was it something completely unrelated? His captors wore navy-blue jackets with FBI emblazoned across the back. Jake yearned to ask them what was going on, but some inner instinct advised him to shut up and simply find out where this whole thing was leading.

And so Jake remained silent, dropped his gaze, and simply stumbled along. The handcuffs dug deeply into his wrists, but he ignored the discomfort. Sweat dripped into his eyes, but he endured the stinging. As they walked through the mediocre hotel lobby, everyone stepped aside, and he felt like even more of a spectacle, but Jake kept his expression resolute, paying no attention to the murmuring voices and probing gazes of the people they passed.

He'd been arrested, presumably for some act of treason or terrorism, and for now he needed to discover who had set him up. In all likelihood Abaddon had a hand in all of this, but Jake needed to be sure before he....

Before he *what*?

It wasn't like he had a bunch of ninja skills with which to take out the – er – *eight* FBI agents who'd arrived to arrest him. If he tried to escape, at best, a charge of resisting arrest would be heaped upon whatever else they'd conjured up. At worst they'd beat him senseless, or put a bullet in his head while he tried to flee.

Jake figured he'd pass on that one.

Swiftly bustled into the back of one of the four unmarked Buicks parked in front of the hotel, Jake glanced over at the boxy, black police van. It probably concealed a SWAT team, waiting in case things got out of hand; lucky he hadn't demonstrated his non-existent ninja skills. Jake suppressed a humorless grin. This was hardly the time for mirth. He began to think, to prepare, to strategize…

… and came up with absolutely nothing of worth.

The cars drove away in a convoy, their hidden grill and windshield lights springing to life, and causing other cars to pull out of their way. Jake stared out the window, wondering what he was going to do now. The Staff had been taken by one of the agents, presumably as evidence; it wasn't like it could do Jake any good anyway. After all the trouble he'd gone through to get that stupid piece of wood.

He pushed aside his remorse with some difficulty. It wouldn't help to feel sorry for himself right now; what he needed was to plan for whatever might be coming.

But how could he plan when he had no idea what was going on?

Initially he'd wondered how Abaddon had known he'd been hiding out in the hotel room, thinking it had something to do with the 'link' the fallen angel had boasted about, but soon Jake realized it probably wasn't anything so complex. His suspicions were confirmed when one of the arresting agents referred to him as Martin Roberts.

Jake contemplated the situation momentarily, and then cursed. They'd tracked him down via the credit card Vain had given him. The name must have been flagged somehow, and they'd known as soon as Jake had checked into the hotel, probably maintaining surveillance on him for three days before getting bored watching him do nothing except talk to a stick.

Whoever this Martin Roberts guy was, he owed Jake – big time.

The lights flashed silently as the small convoy of FBI cars cut through the traffic, heading for whatever destination they planned for him. Wherever it was, Jake had a nasty feeling he wouldn't like it.

\*\*\*

"Rise and shine, asshole."

Jake peeled open his eyelids and peered around. It seemed their convoy had finally halted, and they were now parked within a basement garage of some sort, possibly beneath the FBI headquarters. Jake couldn't believe he'd dozed off, but days of stress, combined with the rocking of the Buick had conspired against him. He now had no real idea of where he was; they might have been in Vegas for all he knew.

Something suddenly prickled at his nerves, something beyond the obvious.

"Where are we?" he asked one of the two agents who hauled him, still cuffed, from the back of the car.

"You'll find out soon enough. Someone very important wants to see you."

They moved Jake over to a small set of steps leading up to a loading-dock with a raised concrete area. This was unexpected, but Jake guessed the FBI might need something like it for... for *something*. The motionless SWAT van had parked nearby, as had the other FBI vehicles, and Jake found himself staring down the barrels of at least a dozen guns gripped by nervous hands.

Whoever this Martin Roberts guy was, he sure had these men spooked.

"Hey, Mikey, why'd we nab this guy anyway?" queried one of the FBI agents. Jake noticed he was suspiciously wearing black tennis shoes – hardly federal issue. Jake's nervousness began to rise even more.

"Shut your mouth!" snapped the one named Mikey. "Tony said to get him, so we got him. You got a problem with that?"

"No! No way!" replied the other man hurriedly, obviously afraid. "I just thought... well... he must be kinda important for us to get dressed up like this, you know, like the FBI. Why'd we have to do that whole sham thing in the hotel, anyway? We could have just taken him; he hasn't given us any sort of fight."

"If he's the guy my brother's been lookin' for, he might be very important," replied Mikey grimly, "as well as being plenty dangerous. And we had to do that stuff. It would have looked a bit suspicious if we just dragged him out. The caps hid our faces from the CCTV cameras in the lobby and elevators, and the outfits stopped anyone hassling us. Now, if you have any more stupid questions, save them for Tony, because I don't wanna hear 'em."

Armed men stepped aside to allow the two talkers to guide Jake away, one on each side, his upper arms gripped firmly. They guided him up the five steps of the loading dock and through the doorway, entering a small, darkened room – some sort of basement from the looks of it. Dragging Jake to a heavy-looking timber chair with tough leather straps on the armrests and front legs, they forced him to sit down. It wasn't too hard, Jake wasn't even struggling – he was still too stunned by everything going on around him. More men entered the room, several stepping forward, gripping his upper arms, shoulders, one wrapping a thick forearm around his throat – all still training their weapons on his head. Mikey secured his legs with the thick leather straps, buckling them tight. Once they were locked in, Mikey ordered him pushed forward until his chest pressed against his thighs, then unlocked the handcuffs from behind his back. The men held each of Jake's arms tightly as they lifted his torso upright once more, securing his upper limbs to the armrests with the straps, buckling them firmly.

"Right," said Mikey. "Someone go get Tony. The rest of you guys get outta here, Tony wants to talk to this guy in private."

Mikey stared hard at Jake's face, his expression unreadable. He was short, only around five-feet, seven-inches tall, and looked to be of

Italian descent. Maybe thirty-five years old, but bearing the fatigued presence of a man much older.

"I'm sorry," he mumbled.

Jake stared up at him, nonplussed. "Why?"

"You deserve a lot better after what you done for me and Tony when we was kids. We just couldn't risk you killing everyone before we got to speak to you. That's why we nabbed you the way we did. You look different from what I remember, though. And I thought you'd be a lot older too."

"I'm not who you think I am," said Jake, but Mikey didn't hear him, he'd turned at the sound of footsteps.

Another man emerged through the door in the back of the room, tall with broad shoulders and a sharp, penetrating gaze. He stared hard at Jake for a moment, his features cold and implacable, his gaze flicking down to the crimson teardrop on Jake's cheek, and then he turned to Mikey.

"Who the hell is this?" he asked.

"That's Martin Roberts, Tony…. He – he's the guy!'

"This ain't the guy, Mikey. How could you not remember what he looks like after what he done for our family? Our guy never had no tattoo of no teardrop on his cheek."

"It's not a tattoo, and I'm not Martin Roberts," interjected Jake, "but I did use a credit card with his name on it. It was given to me by someone."

"And who gave you that?" growled the newcomer menacingly.

Jake paused, uncertain. On one hand there was the danger of Vain discovering he had mentioned him, possibly coming after him for retribution. On the other hand there was the much more immediate threat of these two brothers torturing and killing him for a name. Vain seemed more than capable of protecting himself, and he probably wouldn't have given Jake the card if he'd been worried about keeping his name out of things.

"His name was Vain."

Mikey inhaled sharply at mention of the name. Tony merely glared at him harder, fighting to keep his gaze fixed. Clearly they'd both met Vain before; only someone who had personally experienced the assassin would react in such a way.

"You'd better go and call dad," Tony said to Mikey, who nodded, turning and racing from the room.

Tony moved over to Jake and began unbuckling the straps holding his arms. Initially Jake thought this to be an extremely bold move until Tony's jacket flapped open, and Jake saw the grip of a handgun resting within a shoulder holster. A few moments, and Jake was free once more, standing and rubbing his wrists, forcing the blood into them again.

"Sorry about that," Tony apologized, looking ashamed, "but if you've met Vain you'll understand. He can be somewhat... unpredictable."

Jake ignored the statement. "Who are you guys?" he asked.

"Me and Mikey grew up with a guy named Sebastian Dunn after our stepfather and mom adopted him. But before that we were helped out by the guy named Vain; he gave us a heap of money and... well... he kinda cured our mom's cancer."

Jake stared at Tony, probing his features, waiting for any telltale indications he was joking or lying. Tony's straight-faced expression never flickered, and Jake instinctively sensed he was telling the truth.

So Vain had healed a woman's cancer when this guy was a kid? After all Jake had seen so far, hearing such a thing was hardly shocking. The dark-garbed assassin definitely was an enigma.

"So why would you kidnap the guy who helped you so long ago?" he asked finally.

Tony looked away, seemingly ashamed. "We couldn't be sure he'd want to come. Sebastian's disappeared, and the last thing our stepdad, Tobias, heard was that a man matching Vain's description was also looking for him."

"Yes, he is," said Jake.

"Is he looking to help him, or hurt him?" asked Tony, his gaze narrow, the words coming out in a rush.

"Oh, he's very much looking to help him, don't worry about that."

Tony heaved a great sigh of relief and slumped down into the chair with the straps on it.

"We couldn't be sure," he muttered.

"Why would Vain want to hurt him? The way he was talking, the only thing on his mind was saving Sebastian, to the point of refusing to help me. He gave me that credit card, which I'm now assuming was in his original name or an alias you knew about."

"Yeah, it's his name," said Tony, "but that's a whole other story. The thing is, there's something *inside* Vain, the same thing which helped him save our mom all those years ago, and we were scared it had somehow taken him over. But if he's looking to save Sebastian, then all of this –" he waved a hand around, indicating the room and chair "– was unnecessary. By the way, who are you, and how do you know Vain?"

"My name is Jake. I'm on a… a quest, I guess you'd call it. I crossed paths with Vain along the way."

"And you lived?" Tony raised his eyebrows. "I'm impressed. He almost killed me the first time I met him."

"So why were you looking for him? Just to make sure he wasn't trying to kill Sebastian, or is there more to it?"

"I want to help him," replied Tony simply.

"I'm no expert," said Jake, "but he seems to be a man who works better alone."

Tony grinned. "Yeah, I think you'd be right. But I had to try. Mikey was too young to really remember, but mom would have died without Vain's help, and he saved me too – after he almost killed me. I just want to repay the debt we owe him, that's all."

Jake nodded, understanding. "I think he's long gone now, though. And I doubt he'd be crazy enough to use a credit card which could be traced back to him in such a way. That's probably why he gave it to me – that way any pursuers would be tracking me instead of him. I guess it worked." Part of Jake objected to being used as bait in such a way, while another part silently appreciated such a simple tactic. He felt glad it hadn't been true enemies who had found him.

"How will you find him?" he asked.

Tony spread his hands wide. "I dunno. It was more luck than anything that we caught onto you with that credit card. We'd told one of the girls at the hotel you checked into to keep an eye out for that name and to call us if he ever showed up. We've got contacts like that around the city for all sorts of stuff. Outside the city we have a few leads, but nothing substantial."

"What is it you guys do? This whole setup seems a bit more professional than just a couple of brothers looking to repay a debt," said Jake.

"We run a private security detail, contracting out to businesses and… well… we don't ask too many questions. We got raised good, but some of my old habits from when I was a kid never really left me, and after mom died and Tobias took off looking for Seb, well, I needed to figure out a way for us to make money. We relocated to Chicago and have been in business here for about seven years now. It's not much, but we get by."

"So you're criminals, is that right?" Jake hadn't meant for it to come out so roughly, but the words escaped before he realized it.

Tony's expression hardened. "We ain't criminals. I don't break no laws… well, not really."

"You just abducted me while impersonating federal agents!"

"But that… it's just… well, we thought you was Vain, didn't we? How else was we supposed to get you? We don't always have a choice, ya know? We can't pick and choose who we work for so much. We can't afford to, we got no choice."

"Are you trying to convince me, or yourself," asked Jake, knowing he was pushing his luck, but determined to make his point.

"Who the fuck do you think you are?" snapped Tony, leaping to his feet. "You think you can just come in here and insult me like that?"

"I didn't *come* here; you kidnapped me. And it's not an insult unless you think you're doing something bad," replied Jake calmly.

Tony appeared torn between agreeing with Jake and smashing his face in. He was a solid man, with plenty of muscle, and it wouldn't take much for him to beat Jake to a pulp, but some instinct within Jake told him he needed to confront Tony on this issue before they went any further. Tony didn't seem a bad man, more a man torn by his deeds, a man searching for something. Jake doubted he could provide a solution, but maybe he could help Tony find his own way through the mire that surrounded his life – or maybe he'd get his kneecaps broken for trying to interfere in something that wasn't any of his business.

Tony glared at him, fists clenched at his sides, his breathing heavy. "I don't know!" he finally growled, throwing his arms in the air, turning away, pacing several steps, and then spinning to face Jake once more. "I started this group thinking it might help people out, but I learned real quick that the people who need help don't have any money! So we let our standards slip, a little at a time, but before I knew it we were protecting drug-dealers and pieces of shit."

"Is that the real reason you wanted to find Vain, to help you get out of this stuff?"

Tony appeared as though he was about to argue, but then slumped back down in the wooden chair, nodding.

"That guy was the only one who really seemed to give a shit about me and Mikey, you know? I mean, Tobias was a great guy, and he looked after our mom real good, but he was always worried about Sebastian; me and Mikey kinda blended into the background for him. I told him the story I just told you, the reason we wanted to find Vain, and he just accepted it. The truth is I really wanted Vain to come and... I dunno... help us get out of the mess we've gotten ourselves into."

"You don't need his help for that," assured Jake.

"What do you mean?" Tony stared at him, nonplussed.

"The power to change your life exists within yourself, not from some external source," said Jake, a sudden assurance filling him. "You can look to others for advice or support, but the true transformation has to come from deep inside, and when you feel it, you can act upon your desires and create a better existence for yourself. Until that point, it doesn't matter how much you want something, if you can't adjust the way you think about yourself, no amount of outside assistance will ever alter your life."

"You sayin' it's *my* fault?" asked Tony, his eyes narrowing.

Jake shrugged. "You said yourself that you slipped into this life because of old habits. Perhaps a part of you enjoys the power this lifestyle allows you, despite what your conscience wants to believe. Your scruples might be telling you this is wrong, but at heart you feel you're gaining something, some sort of recognition you revel in, that you otherwise feel is lacking."

"You sound like Sebastian," murmured Tony, staring at Jake. "He used to say stuff like that. Most of it went over my head, too."

Jake grinned, realizing how close he'd just come to preaching, yet knowing he no longer really cared. "It's not really that confusing. You just need to search within yourself, discover what you truly want, and then put every ounce of energy you possess into realizing that dream; every second you breathe, from the moment you wake until you sleep. Now what do you really want?"

"Redemption," said Tony reflexively, the word seemingly emerging from his mouth before he realized it.

"And how will you achieve that?"

"By helping others." Tony's face suddenly blossomed in comprehension. "You mean...? Aha! I get it now!"

Jake smiled even more. "You see? It's simple to see the target when your mind becomes clear."

"How did you do that?" asked Tony, standing up and staring at Jake incredulously. "I mean, it's obvious now. All this time... I... I know what I want to do. I want to help people! We started off with that idea, but somewhere along the line it got all messed up, and I just ended up organizing a bunch of thugs to do the crap jobs nobody else would do. That's why I started looking for Martin Roberts – before I knew he'd reverted back to being Vain. I mean, if he could come back from being Vain, surely there was hope for me and Mikey too. I was hoping... maybe... he could show us how, but now you've done it and... it's all so *simple*!"

"So what's your plan?" asked Jake, grinning.

"Well, that's easy," replied Tony, standing once more, a triumphant grin upon his face. "We're gonna help *you*!"

The smile disappeared from Jake's face.

***

"What do you mean?" asked Jake once he'd regained some modicum of composure.

"Well you said you were on some sort of mission or quest, and since Vain thought it important enough to help you, it must be damn important, so Mikey and me will come with you. Simple." There was no negotiation in Tony's voice.

"But you have no idea what I'm doing," protested Jake.

Tony shrugged. "Doesn't matter, I've decided, and now we're gonna do it."

"Mikey might disagree –"

"No, he won't."

"But –"

"You saying you don't need our help?" asked Tony, cocking his head.

"Well… yeah, I do, but… I don't know," said Jake finally. "There's a lot more going on here than you know; you might stand to lose more than you can possibly imagine."

"Okay then, lay it on me," said Tony. "Let me decide for myself how bad it really is."

Jake locked gazes with Tony, and seeing no give there, sighed. He launched into his tale, leaving out all references to his own significance, focusing instead on the threat of Abaddon, certain the mere mention of the fallen angel would be enough to make Tony think he was a liar. Jake figured he didn't need to heap the issue of being the supposed re-embodiment of Christ on top of everything else. Tony was certain to think he was crazy enough already.

At the end of the tale, Jake once more met Tony's gaze, surprised at what he saw there; it wasn't judgment or doubt, merely curiosity bordering on fascination. Jake realized Tony had been hanging on his every word, unwilling to speak lest he interrupt the flow of information.

"You're leaving something out," prompted Tony.

"What do you mean?" asked Jake cagily.

"Sebastian used to talk to me about... stuff, ya know?"

"I'm not sure I do."

Tony appeared uncomfortable. In fact, he looked exactly how Jake had felt right before telling his own tale – like he was afraid of being mocked.

"Sebastian told me... he told me he wasn't what people thought he was. He said he was like... I dunno... a distraction or something. He said there was someone else coming, someone way more important than him, and one day I'd meet the guy, when I didn't expect to. I reckon he was talking about you. Are you – are you the guy?"

Jake wasn't sure how to respond at first. His own self-doubts flooded in on him, and he almost faltered, but looking into Tony's eyes he gave a wistful smile.

"He knew?" Jake asked.

Tony nodded. "I think I'm the only one he told. Maybe he'd seen that we'd meet here; he sure as hell knew enough other weird shit. I mean – er – sorry about the swearing."

Jake chuckled. "That's okay, Tony. I'm not a delicate flower that'll shatter when you say 'shit'."

The conflicted expression creasing Tony's face caused Jake to burst out laughing. He could almost imagine what was going through Tony's mind: how was he supposed to deal with the supposed 'new messiah' swearing? Jake sighed. He wasn't going to start acting weird just because people expected him to behave a certain way; he had enough to worry about as it was – more than enough.

Jake folded his arms, wondering what to do about Tony's proposal. He could definitely use the assistance, but he didn't want to be responsible for anyone else. He figured it was probably best to leave it up to Tony.

"Do you still want to follow my little crusade now that you know who I am? There's a pretty strong chance we'll all get killed or have our souls turned into potpourri... without the nice smell."

Tony seemed to ponder the question, rubbing his jaw as he stared hard into Jake's eyes. He finally nodded and offered Jake his hand.

Pondering the odd union, Jake shrugged and reached out, grasping it, shaking it twice. It seemed such a small gesture for something so monumental, and he couldn't help wondering what Jesus had done upon meeting his first follower.

And in that moment, Jake brutally reminded himself that he wasn't Jesus – he was merely the man filling his shoes. What Jesus had done in his life didn't matter, what mattered was discovering a way to defeat Abaddon. If he spent all his time wondering what Jesus would have done in his place, he'd accomplish nothing. He had to do things the way he thought best, and right now the help of Tony, his brother, and potentially all their allies, would be a much needed boon. A small part of him wondered whether using such shady persons as partners was in some way contradictory, but consoled himself in the apparent sincerity of Tony's manner. The man's need for redemption seemed genuine, and what better way than to go head to head against an angel from Hell.

Jake swallowed at the thought.

Anyone around him could be Abaddon, he knew that. The fallen angel had already shown he could hide his true appearance from Jake's perception when necessary. There remained a real possibility he might be parading around inside Tony – or any of the guys who worked for him – just waiting for Jake to lower his guard....

Weighing his options, Jake realized he had little choice. He needed strong allies in the coming confrontation, and people who wandered around picking daisies and spouting scripture weren't likely to be much help when facing a creature bent on destroying humanity. Those people might have their hearts in the right place, but Jake knew that Abaddon would never be dissuaded by words, only deeds. For that he needed men of action.

He stared deep into Tony's eyes, recognizing the steely determination residing there, and knew he'd made the right choice. Jake nodded once, trying to convey a wealth of meaning in the movement, and he hoped Tony recognized it.

"I hope you don't regret this, Tony."

"Not a chance," replied Tony with a grin. "I reckon this is what I was born for."

Jake turned away slowly, hoping Tony wouldn't die for it as well.

-CHAPTER 9-
# NEPHILIM

"What the hell are you talking about?"

Jake grimaced. He'd known this would be the major snag in outlining his plan, and he rolled the Staff over in his hands, flicking it side to side, searching for the words to explain what he meant.

"The President has been taken over," Jake repeated, unable to phrase it any other way. "He's been possessed by a fallen angel named Abaddon, who has somehow escaped from Hell and hidden for years in the body of Joseph Kony in Northern Uganda – killing and raping people for no reason other than to create disharmony in the universe. His chains have been unfettered, and he can jump from body to body at will, possessing the flesh completely and controlling a person the way you would drive a car. He now has power over the most powerful man on the face of the planet, and we have to stop him."

"And how do you propose we do that?" asked the man, a belligerent-looking hulk standing several inches over six feet, his massive barrel chest and bulging biceps straining at the fabric of his dark-blue cotton t-shirt.

Jake shrugged. "I haven't figured that out yet, but I've got this staff –"

"What good will a stick do?!" thundered the man.

"Watch your tone, Alfonse," snapped Tony.

"Tony, you can't be serious about this guy. I mean, what he's saying is crazy, man. Demons and shit. You need an exorcist, not a damn *stick*. Actually, I reckon you need a shrink."

"He ain't a whacko. Everything he's sayin' is true," said Tony, fixing Alfonse with a steely gaze. Finally the man's eyes dropped. "We're the only ones who can do something about this, and from now on we follow this guy. Understood?"

"Seriously though, Tony," Mikey piped in. "I don't mean no disrespect, I don't think no-one here does, but this is all a bit far-fetched."

Tony went to argue, but Jake gripped his arm, silencing him.

"I know this all seems messed up," said Jake, "but I swear everything I'm saying is true. The man currently running the country is no longer who you think he is – he's been taken over by something malignant. Forget about talk of angels and demons; the thing controlling the President oversaw thousands of murders and the breaking of children through rape and torture in order to spread discord through a country which was already screwed up. Do you really want to see that happen here as well? I'm not lying to you! There's more going on than even I can imagine, and I've already seen and done things you would never believe. I can't do this on my own; I need your help."

The group of seventeen men remained silent for a moment before Alfonse nodded silently. "So what can you tell us about this stick?"

Jake grinned humorlessly before launching into the tale of how he had acquired the Staff once wielded by both Moses and Noah....

***

"Stupid computer," muttered Mikey, staring at the monitor.

"What's wrong?" asked Jake.

"Nothing serious," replied Mikey, "It's just this social networking thing; every now and then the site crashes, and it's a pain in the ass. What's up?"

"Do you mind if I use your computer when you're finished?"

"Go for it." Mikey stood up from his chair. "I spend too much time on the damn thing anyway."

Jake nodded his thanks and sat down in the chair, typing a search for anything under the term: 'The Staff of Moses'. Almost instantly the search engine discovered hundreds of pages of references to the Staff, and Jake settled down for what might be a very long search for answers.

He felt compelled to find out as much as he could about the Staff. Even though he now possessed it, he still had no sense of how to use it, only vague associations with both Noah and Moses. Indistinct references suggested both men had been able to achieve incredible things through the power of the Staff.

Wading through website after website – most full of nonsense – was a tedious task, but Jake needed to discover some way of using the power of the Staff to defeat Abaddon. Some pages linked the Staff to Aaron – a figure of great influence in Judaism – but these were even vaguer as to how Aaron had used its power.

Jake knew the Staff had power, he'd seen it transform before his eyes, but no matter what he did, no matter how he poked, prodded, or pleaded with the Staff, it did nothing other than sit innocuously, almost taunting him. For all intents and purposes it remained nothing more than a walking stick.

And now the internet, the supposed information superhighway, was contributing little in the way of information. Perhaps the wielders – Moses, Noah, *and* Aaron – had taken the secret with them to the grave.

The *grave*…?

Moses had left a message upon his crypt lid; Jake struggled to remember what he'd deciphered:

*"….Be comforted in the knowledge that the power of Heaven passes through the Staff, but it is not a tool of evil, and the task of evil shall corrupt the wielder, as I have sadly discovered."*

These words swam back through the murk of Jake's memory, and he shuddered. The Staff couldn't do evil. Did that mean he couldn't kill Abaddon with it? Would such a thing constitute an act of evil? Was destroying something as corrupted as one of the Fallen still considered wrong?

Crap.

What act had Moses committed, an act which had apparently backlashed against him, which had also made him discover he couldn't use the Staff as a tool of evil?

Jake searched his memory, tracing through every scrap of knowledge about Moses he could recall, but nothing came to mind which would explain the warning he'd seen etched upon the lid of the ancient sarcophagus. He knew that there'd been several threats and the –

The Plagues.

Moses had visited a series of plagues upon the Egyptian pharaoh in order to force him to release the Israelites from slavery. Jake couldn't remember them all, but the one which had always stood out most in his memory had been the last one.

The killing of the firstborn child.

His memory of the story had been watered down like so many other repressed moments he'd associated with the Bible, but Jake recalled that when all else had failed, Moses had summoned the Angel of Death to Earth – probably through the power of the Staff – and it had killed the firstborn child in every Egyptian house not marked with some sort of blood... or was it the ones marked with blood which had been visited? Jake couldn't recall, but he figured it didn't really matter; the end result had been the same. Moses had corrupted the power he'd wielded through the Staff, and something bad had happened. But what could it have been?

Right now he really didn't have the luxury of time to sit around and ponder the issue, so he turned his attention back to the latest website he'd brought up on the computer. This page was little different from so many others: some apparent expert describing his theory on the possibility Moses had actually been an alien, his displays of power simply the benefits of extra-terrestrial machines rather than anything divine.

Shaking his head, Jake closed the page and clicked on the next search result. Reading through the first few paragraphs, he swiftly realized this site was somehow different from the rest of the nonsense which had clogged up his time. This site included stories from the Bible, along with the Jewish Torah, but tried to decipher the truth behind the myths included in both books. There'd been much naivety at the time these books had been written, with many translation flaws occurring throughout the multiple versions. The author of this website had tried to read between the lines of these tomes in an attempt to discover the actual historical accuracy of the stories of Moses and his use of the power of God through the Staff.

The website was many-paged and complex. Jake didn't notice the time slipping by as he pored through the seemingly endless information. Some tended toward ridiculous conjecture, but there seemed to be some semblance of honest investigation behind it all. The author had actually travelled through Egypt and Israel, attempting to recreate the journey of the Israelites when they'd fled from the Pharaoh, but sadly there seemed no mention as to how Moses had used the power of the Staff apart from through God's grace. That was all well and good, thought Jake, but it wouldn't help him thwart a fallen angel.

"Work!" he barked at the Staff in his hands.

It didn't react – no real surprise there.

Muttering under his breath, Jake turned to the screen once more. As he moved the mouse to close off the page, he noticed something he'd initially skipped over. It was a description of a passage from the Torah where Moses – or *Moshe* in Jewish scripture – first realized the power of the Staff. Apparently God had instructed him to cast the Staff to the ground, and it had transformed into a serpent. Moshe had subsequently fled from the creature.

Jake knew a hazy variant of this story from the Bible, the memory of the Man's recitation echoing from the pits of his memory, and as such he'd initially ignored this one, thinking it the same story. Now, however, he realized the author had actually analyzed this section of the Torah and questioned why Moses, an aged and decidedly intelligent man, would run when the Staff turned into a snake. The serpent must have been extremely dangerous for him to do so.

Jake thought about it, wondering about the veracity of the author's analysis. Why would Moses, a man who had grown up in the desert full of snakes, panic so badly? Surely the transformation would be a shock, but the guy was having a conversation with God, why would a stick turning into a snake be such a big deal?

*Try it,* murmured a small voice in the back of his mind.

Jake grimaced, knowing such a thing was stupid, but his curiosity had indeed been piqued. He stood up, swiftly glancing around to make sure nobody was watching. Finding himself alone, he hefted the Staff in his hand and raised it up high before –

"What 'cha doin'?" said a voice behind him, causing Jake to almost drop the Staff in shock.

"Nothing!" yelped Jake hurriedly, spinning around and seeing Tony standing in the doorway.

Tony strode over, glancing quickly at what still shone on the computer screen before smiling broadly.

"Are you tryin' to get that stick to do something?"

Jake grinned sheepishly. "Yeah," he admitted, slumping back down in the chair once more. "I'm starting to feel desperate." He softly explained what he'd been about to attempt, realizing how stupid it sounded. Even if the Staff *had* turned into a giant snake, then what? How would he turn it back?

Tony chuckled. "Welcome to the human race, buddy. None of us know what we're doin'."

"What do you mean?"

Tony shrugged. "Since when does anyone understand what the hell they're supposed to do in life? We all just fumble around until something goes right, and then tell everyone it was part of some grand plan or something. You're just like everyone else."

"But I *can't* be… you know that."

"I know you're a person. You ain't no god or else you would have made your nose straighter and your ears less funky."

"What's wrong with my ears?" Jake's hands protectively moved to the sides of his head.

"And if you were God you wouldn't care about what was wrong with your ears. You're a man with the task of a god, and you just need to fumble your way through or bluff people until you know what the hell is going on."

"But I can't figure out how to use the Staff."

"What's it supposed to do?" asked Tony.

"All sorts of stuff, but Moses left me a message –"

Tony held up his hand. "Wait! Back up. Moses left *you* a message?"

Jake hefted the walking stick in his right hand. "This is the Staff of Moses, right?" Tony nodded. "What I left out when I told you about it was the message in a weird language etched into the lid of the sarcophagus. I somehow managed to decipher it even though it was in a language I don't know. It didn't name me personally, but it was like he knew I'd be coming. It said I couldn't use the Staff for evil."

"You ain't usin' it for evil," snapped Tony. "You're gonna kill that fuckin' Fallen guy, and that ain't evil – I mean, he's the bad guy, right?"

"I don't think it matters," mused Jake. "I think the act itself is what counts. If I try to do anything malicious with it, regardless of what I do it against, chances are something bad will happen – I don't know what."

Tony looked thoughtful for a moment. "How about –"

His words were cut off by the enormous explosion from the other end of the house. Its force seemed to rock the very foundations. Panicked shouting rang from everywhere as Tony's guys reacted to the blast, but behind it all echoed something else, something Jake couldn't quite make out. It seemed like shouting, but it was in some weird kind of language, words he couldn't understand.

A familiar figure suddenly appeared in the middle of the room; one moment there had been nothing, and the next a body stood before him. Jake tried to clear his vision, eventually realizing it was the man from the alley, his one good eye incredibly blue, the other a blind and milky orb in his left socket. He'd called himself Michael.

Archangel Michael.

"He is here," said Michael, his voice frustratingly calm.

Mikey ran into the room brandishing a pump-action shotgun. The younger brother took in the arrival of Michael in a glance. "Tony, what's going on?"

Tony ignored the question. "*Who's* here?" he asked the archangel. Jake noticed his voice wasn't anywhere near as calm as Michael's. "And who the hell are *you*?"

"I don't answer to you," Michael replied to Tony dismissively, his eyes boring deeply into Jake's.

"Michael's a friend," explained Jake. He turned to Michael. "Where's Abaddon?"

"He is near."

Jake gripped the Staff, but Michael shook his head. "This is not the time. He has the nephilim with him, and they will decimate all in their path."

"What's a neflin?' asked Tony.

"Originally, nephilim were created when angels mated with human women; their children possessed traits from both creatures. Abaddon has somehow recreated the process with his already zealous followers. It is actually quite extraordinary. He has combined fruit from the Garden along with his own corruption, feeding it to his deluded servants. They have transformed, becoming more than men, and are now halfway to being angels, but with a craving for flesh. Their bodies are large and immune to human weapons – even ethereal might will have little effect on them."

"But Uriel destroyed them all in the Garden," argued Jake.

Michael shook his head dismissively. "Abaddon was not with the invading force that Uriel defeated. The attack was merely a ruse, a diversion to allow Abaddon to gain entrance to the Garden and steal all of the remaining fruit. He now has an army of nephilim with which to do his bidding, and right now they are here to kill you."

A deafening crash sounded close by, followed by a staccato blast of gunfire. The noises of defense suddenly stopped, savagely cut off as though sliced in half.

"We gotta go," urged Tony, grabbing Jake by the arm.

"I can get you out," interjected Michael, his voice still maddeningly calm. "Gather near me."

"What about our guys?" asked Mikey.

"They are beyond my assistance," replied Michael.

Both Mikey and Tony appeared torn. Jake could almost hear the tormented thoughts clashing within their minds, feelings of betrayal conflicting with their own fear and need for survival. Eventually Tony nodded wrenchingly at Mikey, and the younger brother begrudgingly complied. Surrounded by the muffled screams of the dead and dying men in other parts of the house, the four figures gathered in the center of the room.

An earsplitting roar rose and an enormous beast – identical to the ones which had attacked the cherubim in the Garden of Eden – exploded into view. Its muscular gray body appeared bloated and covered in sores. It surged toward them, tearing plaster from the wall as it crashed through the doorway. All Jake could see were rotting teeth and dagger-like claws....

Everything spun. The room blurred, the air itself thinned, everything snapping back into focus a heartbeat later. Jake fell to his hands and knees, bent over, and retched, hearing similar reactions from Tony and Mikey. The cold night air felt good upon his burning skin.

"It is normal for your human bodies to react in this way to our mode of traveling," said Michael conversationally. "It has something to do with your ears."

"Where are we?" asked Jake when he had recovered enough to talk. Wiping his mouth on his sleeve, he rose slowly to his feet.

"I have taken us about five miles from where the house was. Further travel is not possible at this time, and so we must take other means of transport to retreat further."

Michael pointed, and Jake's eyes travelled up. A sign read: *El.*

It took him a moment and a bit of further reading to figure out that *El* stood for *Elevated* and it was actually a Chicago Transit Authority train line – elevated on tracks which ran above the street.

"Let's go!" snapped Tony groggily, taking the lead and staggering up the stairs.

Jake shrugged and followed him, Mikey and Michael bringing up the rear. Mikey still carried his pump-action shotgun, and Jake abstractly wondered how he hoped to get on the train without causing a panic. Even at this late hour, there would surely be passengers onboard, and even if by some miracle there weren't, there'd certainly be security cameras or guards. When compared with the horror chasing them, however, this seemed like a very minor issue indeed, and Jake had little trouble ignoring the problem for the moment.

They recovered swiftly from their previous sickness, sprinting up the stairs, Tony clambering over the turnstiles and indicating the rest should do likewise. Once beyond the barrier, they moved out onto the empty platform, Jake uncomfortably aware of the various security cameras staring at them blankly with their cyclopean black eyes.

The wait for the train proved tense. Tony constantly flicked his gaze around, and Mikey reloaded his shotgun – ready to blast anything at a moment's notice. Jake silently pleaded he didn't overreact and shoot a tourist by mistake.

Contrasting this nervousness was Michael. He watched the humans somewhat curiously, his bright blue eye blazing starkly against the dark skin of his face, his dull orb mutely accusing them of weakness within the thick, angry scar tissue surrounding it.

Michael's gaze flicked to him, and Jake dropped his stare guiltily, but swiftly looked up once more. "What happened to your eye?" he asked, more to make some sort of conversation than through any need to know. "Is it merely part of your appearance or did something actually injure it?"

For once Michael appeared discomfited. "It is a true wound, but do not worry, it does not impair my sight."

"How'd it happen?" asked Jake, fascinated. "I didn't think angels could be hurt."

"It occurred during the Great War of Heaven; I led the armies of God against those of Satan, and in the resulting clash, I was dealt this blow," he indicated his left eye, "by Satan himself. It scarred me on a level you cannot possibly imagine, and now that I have been returned to the flesh I must bear the physical mark of my wound as a result."

"You *fought* Satan?" asked Tony incredulously, Mikey was also staring on in wonder.

"Yes," replied Michael blandly. "He was once a truly wonderful creature, but something warped him on a level deeper than I could ever fathom. His jealousy of God became more than he could bear, and he rebelled against His rule – to his ultimate downfall."

"What was the war like?" asked Mikey, his nervous shotgun finally pointing toward the floor.

"Imagine a thousand stars imploding and exploding at the same time and you will comprehend just a tiny portion of the havoc wreaked. The very universe quaked as blows were dealt; the resulting violence destroyed practically all life on this planet. Your scientists claimed it was from the impact of a meteor or some such nonsense. They simply couldn't envision a world where the sun no longer existed, and as such they speculated… badly, as humans so often to do. Our struggle snuffed out all light in the universe, and the creatures of this planet died in the freezing cold of a world without warmth. And this was not the only world to suffer – many others expired completely as a result of Lucifer's scheming. They now lie as lifeless rock, floating throughout the cosmos like frozen pebbles for eternity."

"So there was life on other planets as well?" asked Mikey.

"Of course," replied Michael, gazing around watchfully, the action reminding Jake slightly of the wariness of Vain. "But not all were strong enough to survive the conflict. Some solar systems collapsed completely due to the war, and now exist as huge gaps in space where nothing can enter, not even light."

"How long did the war last?" asked Jake.

Michael shrugged. "It is difficult for me to speculate, time exists differently in other places than it does here – it is not always constant. But I would have to say that by your time system it was several centuries, maybe eons. As with the creation of the universe, for us a day would have seen millennia pass in this realm, and as such I cannot tell you with any surety how long it lasted. But it was *too* long, that is something I know for sure. Every moment saw horrors the likes of which the universe had never before witnessed, and it is a miracle anything survived. If such a conflict were to occur again, I would not be certain we could produce the same outcome."

"You mean Satan might win?" Mikey asked incredulously.

"I mean he has been growing stronger every moment since we defeated him. He is stronger now than during the original clash, and God has never been weaker. If such a thing were to happen now…." He left the thought incomplete.

"What do you mean, 'the Lord has never been weaker?'" asked Jake.

"Look around you; does His presence seem strong as you walk through this world? War is everywhere, death and corruption rule where once joy and happiness reigned. The very planet rebels against the horror it sees upon its skin. Soon will come a time of reckoning. I just hope you are ready when that moment arrives."

Michael's eyes were locked with Jake's, and if he hadn't felt enormous responsibility already, a mountain now toppled upon him.

"You mean Jake's supposed to stop the world from ending?" asked Tony incredulously. Jake heard Mikey gasp.

"I cannot be certain," answered Michael, "but something is definitely approaching, some great reckoning, and the only one capable of doing anything about it has been chosen. He now stands with you. Oblivion will arrive far too soon, and Abaddon's arrival is merely the first step on a course which may or may not determine the future existence of the universe itself."

"Holy shit," muttered Tony and Mikey in tandem as they each turned to stare at Jake, aghast. Jake struggled to keep his expression neutral despite the sudden wrenching within his stomach.

A rumble built to a scream as a train entered the station, the shrieking of its brakes sounding like the harbinger of his fate.

\*\*\*

"Man. That's like… *man*!" gasped Mikey, slumping back in the train seat, staring disbelievingly at Jake.

"Yeah, I know," murmured Jake. "Where are we going?" he asked Tony.

"No idea, I'm still getting over that angel guy just disappearing like that."

"That was kind of unexpected," agreed Jake. As the train had sped in to the station, Michael had simply blinked out of existence, leaving the three of them alone on the platform. "I guess he'd seen us to safety – at least for the time being – and figured his job was done."

"Safety? Where the hell are we gonna be safe?" snapped Mikey. "You heard what that angel guy said; the whole damn roof is gonna come down on our heads!"

"Calm down, Mikey," said Tony, but his expression betrayed his own powerful feelings on the subject.

"We need to keep moving," said Jake. "Now, where's this train taking us?" He got up and stumbled over to the map situated beside the door, rocking slightly along with the train's movement. Leaning against the door, Jake stared at the route. From what he could tell it made a giant loop around the entire downtown area, other lines branching off to separate sections of the city and along the....

"If only we had a boat," muttered Jake.

"Why's that?" asked Tony.

Jake turned around to see both Tony and Mikey staring at him.

"Well if we had a boat we could –"

Before he could finish, a blur of gray flesh shattered the glass in the door window and wrapped around Jake's neck, attempting to heave him out of the train. Even in his panic, Jake realized it was the arm of one of the nephilim. The Staff lay uselessly out of reach on his seat. He mightn't know how to tap into its power, but at least it could have been something to use against the brute force which now assailed him. As it was he'd been caught weaponless.

The limb felt as solid as a tree trunk, its putrid odor – like rotting steak – making Jake gag. In the space of a heartbeat it effortlessly hauled him from his feet and halfway out the broken window.

Beyond the panic roaring in his ears, Jake heard a shotgun blast. An explosion of meat and rotten flesh sprayed all around him. The arm fell limp, the huge shoulder disappearing through the window. Jake leaped away from the jagged frame and pulled the useless limb –

still grasping him – away from his neck, dropping it, twitching its final life force out, to the train floor.

His eyes darted about fervently. They followed the trail of smoke to the shotgun barrel, and then slid along the gun to Mikey's shaking hands. The moment felt like something out of an old Western movie. But this wasn't a Western. John Wayne wasn't about to ride in and save the day. This was very real, and very, very terrifying.

Tony held a small, black handgun and was aiming it at the same window. Jake scrabbled across the car and frantically grasped the Staff, determined never to let it out of his grip again. He wielded it like a baseball bat, part of his mind certain this must be some sort of blasphemy; the majority simply not caring. The wind whistled through the broken glass. All that worried Jake was defending against whatever might pounce through the window.

Nothing else appeared.

The trio stood motionless in the middle of the car for what seemed like an eternity. The *clakety-clak* of the train running along the tracks was the only sound apart from – what *was* that?

It sounded faintly like nails scraping down a chalkboard, and it was coming from the roof of the car. Tony and Mikey noticed it too, Tony adjusting his aim, pointing his handgun toward the roof. Mikey continued scanning the windows vigilantly, his shotgun up, pressed hard against his shoulder, the barrel yawning wide like an abyss, ready to spew forth leaden death. Jake stood between the two of them, feeling somewhat useless grasping the Staff – which was doing a great job of remaining completely stick-like. The noises on the roof seemed to divide slightly, indicating the presence of more than a single beast.

Nobody seemed to be breathing. The sound of the tracks became muted in the background as Jake strained to hear any change in the direction of their attackers.

The scrabbling abruptly ceased, and in the silent gap Jake suddenly remembered something. Swiftly dropping his gaze back to the floor, he was just in time to see the dismembered arm flip like a popcorn kernel, the skin mutating, bubbling and growing. A new shoulder emerged from the torn socket, expanding out into a thick, muscular chest in an instant. The torso complete, it took mere seconds before legs and a second arm formed, the head popping from the muscular gray neck like a disease-ridden bulb. The mouth yawned open revealing jagged teeth, perfect for tearing the flesh from the foolish men who stood frozen, watching it resurrect, instead of fleeing.

"We have to go," gasped Jake.

Tony and Mikey spun around to see the newly-formed nephilim rise from the floor at the same time as the train came screeching into another station. Mikey raised the shotgun to his shoulder, but Jake grabbed it, knocking his aim away. It discharged harmlessly against the interior wall of the car, tearing aside a poster advertising nicotine gum.

"Don't! They multiply when you injure them. We have to run. Now!"

The door slid laboriously open; the slowest Jake had ever seen doors move. The trio bolted through the exit just as the nephilim charged, its wide bulk momentarily blocked by the narrowness of the doorway. Mikey led the way, Tony running protectively alongside Jake as they sprinted down the stairs of the station. Jake glanced back, glimpsing four more nephilim leaping from the roof of the train before the platform was cut off from his view.

Heart thundering and gasping for breath, Jake ran with the brothers down the stairs and onto the street, the pounding of thunderous footfalls close behind them. Emerging onto the street, Jake glanced left and right before pointing left.

"This way," he shouted.

Jake could hear the beasts closing in behind them, but wasn't game enough to glance back.

"Here!" Tony yelled, running up another street toward a young woman with her car door open, just about to climb behind the wheel. Upon seeing the three men – two with guns in their hands – the woman froze, screaming.

"Take the car, just don't hurt me," pleaded the stranger.

"Get in and drive!" Jake ordered the car's owner.

The girl looked beyond them, and her eyes widened as the nephilim rounded the corner. Her mouth gaped wide, an inaudible scream yearning to escape her frozen vocal cords.

"Get in, ya stupid bitch!" bellowed Tony.

Whether from his insult or the order, the woman threw herself into the small silver sedan, fumbling for the ignition while Jake and Tony leaped into the back seat. Mikey bolted around to the passenger seat and climbed in. The engine roared to life, and Jake twisted in his seat to see the nephilim mere yards away.

"Hit it! *Go, go, go!*" he urged the driver.

The woman needed no such advice and clumsily slammed the car into gear, hitting the accelerator, and spinning the wheels dramatically as she popped the clutch and sped off up the street. Jake stared as the hideous creatures fell further and further behind. Blood pounded in his temples and – realizing he'd forgotten to breathe – he sucked in a huge gasp of air.

The car turned another corner, but none of the occupants thought for a second they were in the clear. The nephilim had somehow tracked them after Michael had teleported them through the air, so they held no delusions that a mere car ride would put the beasts off. Jake pictured the five massive creatures loping along in their wake, tracking their scent the way wolves would patiently pursue their prey until it ran out of strength.

Not a good thought.

"Thank you," Jake said to the driver, trying to keep his voice calm.

"What the hell are those things?" sputtered the woman, hysteria creeping along the edge of her tone.

"Bad shit," muttered Mikey. "Where can we go, boss?"

It took Jake a moment to realize Mikey was talking to him.

"Um… well I was thinking back on the train… if we had a boat, the best way to get away from these things would be if we could get across Lake Michigan. I don't care how invulnerable they are, I'm betting a long swim would slow them down."

"Sounds good," agreed Tony. "Hey, girl," he addressed the driver of the car.

"Er... yeah?"

"Take us down to the Chicago Yacht Club, would ya?" he asked. "I got a buddy with a boat who owes me a favor... even though he doesn't know it yet."

"Don't do anything illegal, Tony," said Jake. "The last thing we need is police chasing us as well as those things."

"Don't worry, it's all good. This guy's been using our – er – services for the last few months, and he owes me money. I'll take a small boat trip as payment for what he owes instead."

"Who is this guy?" asked Jake.

"Ah... nobody," replied Tony, avoiding Jake's gaze.

"Who is he?"

Tony looked at Jake sideways and sighed. "He's a drug dealer. I swear I only found out last week, and that's when I cut off communication with him. But he still owes me money, and I'm sure I can use that to make him take us out on the water. Hey, we need a boat, don't we? This is the best I can do."

Jake thought about it and begrudgingly agreed. They stood little to no chance against the nephilim unless they could get across Lake Michigan. The thought of traveling with a drug dealer made Jake cringe, and glancing down noticed he was self-consciously gripping his elbows, the Staff resting loosely between his knees. Prying his fingers open, he dropped his hands, clutching the Staff once more in his moist palm.

"Excuse me – er – s-sir," Jake heard the driver mutter. He noticed the girl was only young, maybe twenty years old, and she looked terrified, on the verge of tears.

"Um... yeah?"

"W-what's going on?"

"Sorry about all this. What's your name?" Jake felt obliged to at least try to ease some of her fear.

The girl glanced in the rear-view mirror, the reflection of her hazel eyes meeting Jake's. "My name's Alana."

"Hi, Alana, I'm Jake. And this is Tony and Mikey. Sorry about the guns." Even as he spoke, Jake realized how lame he sounded. "As you can see, we're facing some pretty serious stuff. Do you mind driving us to the yacht club? After that we'll be out of your hair, and you won't have to worry about us or those things again."

"What were those t-things back there?" asked Alana tremulously.

"Bad shit," muttered Mikey. "Real bad shit."

"It'd take a long time to explain, Alana," said Jake. "Just rest assured they're not after you, they're after us, and they'll leave you alone once we're out of your life."

The woman took several deep breaths, seemingly summoning her courage.

"Can I come with you?" she asked, the words tumbling out in a rush, and when she looked at him in the mirror her eyes were wide, as though she couldn't believe what she'd just asked.

The request stunned Jake so much he sat momentarily speechless, unsure of how to respond. A moment ago this girl had screamed upon seeing them, begging them not to hurt her, and now she wanted to come with them? Was she an idiot? Hadn't she seen what chased them?

"Why would you want to do that?" countered Jake.

"That was so cool! Those things were like something out of a movie!"

"This ain't a movie, ya idiot," snapped Tony. Jake gripped his forearm, and he desisted.

"What Tony's saying is true, Alana. What we're doing, well, it's really serious stuff."

"You think I'm too young to understand? Or is it because I'm a girl?"

Jake glanced at Tony who tilted his head, silently asking permission to berate the girl. Jake begrudgingly nodded.

"Hey, kid. Those things'll rip you to pieces. This ain't no fucking video game where you get a second chance, and you don't wanna get involved. Is that clear?"

Alana whimpered in response.

As much as Jake regretted Tony speaking to the girl in such a way, he understood his reasoning, and let the result be. To Alana it might seem like a great adventure, but the truth about the whole thing was much more terrifying. They couldn't afford to be weighed down with someone who didn't understand the consequences of getting involved. Jake felt bad enough having Tony and Mikey with him, but they at least knew what they were up against and had accepted it. This girl probably just wanted a few thrills in her otherwise dreary life. Maybe she thought the things chasing them were from a lab or something. Her ignorance could see them all killed.

Jake turned his attention to the darkened streets beyond the car windows, noticing the random people out walking in the middle of the night, oblivious to the evil now present within their city. All Jake could hope for was that the nephilim would indeed follow them and leave the other people alone.

And then he looked at the Staff.

*If only….*

Such a powerful phrase, and one so truly full of ensnarement. *If only* he knew how to use the power of the Staff…. *If only* he could stop Abaddon before he hurt anyone else….

*If only* someone else had all this damn responsibility….

And that was the crux of it all; Jake felt he wasn't living up to his part in this entire scenario. Despite all the good advice from people – and angels – who each had his best interests at heart, Jake still couldn't help but wonder what Jesus would have done in his position. His limited knowledge of the Bible didn't really help things either, and he wondered what his predecessor might have done.

Theoretically, if Jake were recreated from the same energy as Jesus – *reincarnated* from his essence – he should have had at least some sort of insight into what he was supposed to be doing, shouldn't he? Instead, it felt like he was running around blindly. It didn't seem he'd gained anything along the way, except a walking-stick once owned by Moses, a lot of cryptic advice, and two followers who might be more suited following his adversaries than pursuing any course serving God….

Jake cursed, silently rubbing the birthmark on his left cheek with the knuckles of his hand, the sensation of failure hanging heavily over him, like a blanket soaked in urine. He knew that his objective meant putting an end to Abaddon, but he had no means to accomplish it apart from the Staff, which so far had only revealed the minutest indication of power.

The car suddenly jolted to a halt, tearing Jake out of his reverie. He looked around and saw they had stopped at the Chicago Yacht Club, its innocuous buildings recessed away from the street lights, giving them a slightly ominous feel in the darkness. Jake shook the sensation away and climbed out of the car, thanking Alana for her help. The young girl mumbled something inaudible, quickly zooming off into the night.

"Huh. The bitch," muttered Mikey.

"Why?" countered Jake. "Because she wanted to help us and was upset when we refused? Be careful about condemning the people who try to aid us, Mikey; they're few and far between right now."

Mikey nodded and murmured an apology, resting his shotgun on his shoulder, reminding Jake yet again of the oddness of his supporters.

"I sent my guy a message to meet us here," said Tony, checking his cell phone. "He told me to go down to his boat. It's moored, um, off the jetty marked with an *E*. He said to wait for him there."

"So he's on his way?" asked Jake. "I don't know how much of a lead we have on those things."

"We could always just *take* the boat," suggested Mikey.

"That's what we're *not* going to do," replied Jake, following Tony toward the jetties. "I'm no expert on these things yet, but I'm pretty sure the new messiah, or whatever I am, isn't supposed to be stealing stuff."

They bypassed four fingers jutting out into the water, boats tied up to each, all bobbing lightly in the mainly-placid lake water. When they finally reached E-finger, Tony swiftly led their way down it until they reached –

"What the hell is *that*?" asked Mikey.

"That's a boat," said Tony.

"No it ain't," argued Mikey, "that's a boat!" He pointed at a massive fiberglass cruiser moored at the end of the jetty. "This thing's a raft. I reckon Tom Hanks wouldn't even ride in it with Wilson.

Those necrophile things won't have to catch us; we'll sink long before they even come close."

Jake hated to admit it, but he tended to agree with Mikey. Staring down at the most unlikely transport he could have ever hoped for, he felt his stomach lurch and his mouth run dry. The tiny yacht looked like an oversized bathtub, its single mast ready to snap at the slightest breeze. And then there was the obvious instability of the craft; if it were rocking this wildly at dock, what would it be like once they sailed to the center of Lake Michigan?

"It ain't that bad," muttered Tony, but Jake could see the skepticism in his eyes.

"I don't think we have much of a choice," said Jake, as the sun began to crest the far horizon. "We have to get away from the nephilim, and I don't think we'll be able to do that on land. I have a horrible feeling that they'll just keep coming, like a hound with a scent. Maybe crossing the lake will put them off that scent – at least for the time being."

"Couldn't you have been owed money by a *successful* drug-runner?" asked Mikey, forcing Jake to suppress a grin.

"Hey, Tony," called a voice from up the pier.

All three of them turned at the sound; a man approached them, limping heavily. He looked decidedly scruffy and unkempt – as though he had just woken from a bad sleep.

"Hurry up, George," replied Tony. "We got to go."

George limped along, his receding hairline looking slick with sweat. "But this wipes the slate clean, right? I don't owe you nothing now."

"Yeah, sure, whatever," replied Tony, somewhat reluctantly.

"Er, what's with the cannon?" asked George suspiciously, pointing at Mikey's shotgun. He stood frozen on the wharf, appearing torn between waiting for an answer and fleeing.

"Don't worry, we ain't here to whack ya. It's part of the reason we need to hurry," snapped Tony. "Can we go now, or do you want to ask another fifty questions?"

"Okay, okay," said George. He stepped over and undid the docking line, hauling the small yacht closer. It was barely the length of two small cars set end to end – a tiny vessel compared to any of the others lined up along the jetty. George climbed aboard awkwardly, his stiff leg hampering him somewhat.

Tony indicated they should follow and easily jumped aboard the vessel, Jake climbing somewhat less glamorously onto the rocking deck while Mikey scanned for any sign of the nephilim. Just as he was about to climb onboard, Mikey froze, staring hard at something in the dim light of the early morning.

"Oh shit," he gasped. "Here they come! Go, let's go!"

"Wha…." began George, looking up and seeing the monstrous nephilim loping easily toward them. "Oh my God."

"Not quite, George," snapped Tony. "Get the engine started and get us the hell out of here."

George didn't need to be told twice. He clambered rapidly to the stern, priming the engine and hitting the ignition.

Nothing happened.

"Damn it!" growled George.

"What's going on?" asked Tony, nervously watching the rapidly approaching nephilim while Mikey climbed aboard.

"Damn battery's dead," mumbled George. "Give me a minute."

"We don't *have* a minute, George."

The nephilim had spotted them, around thirty or so of the creatures now. Whether they had multiplied somehow or simply more had joined the original numbers, Jake didn't want to hang around to find out. The lead creatures let out an unearthly howl, charging directly toward them. Jake glanced at the cockpit where George stood fumbling with the connections of an engine battery under a floorboard.

"Crap!" hissed George. "It's totally corroded!"

Jake snapped his gaze back at the nephilim. They'd entered the parking lot of the Yacht Club and would be upon them in moments. Mikey cast off the lines holding the boat to the jetty and pushed them away; the boat lazily drifted several yards away from the dock, but it would not be far enough. In another minute the nephilim would be upon them.

They were screwed.

Swiftly skipping to the rear of the small boat, Jake leaped into the cockpit and stared over George's shoulder at the engine, hoping it wasn't as tragic as the boat's owner had made out. It wasn't... it was much worse. Frustration welled up inside Jake, a snarling, snapping beast. Why couldn't things be simple for once? Where was God now? Maybe Vain was right, maybe God relished the torment of mortals; perhaps this was all some sort of game for His amusement, a kind of TV show with billions of characters, airing for eternity.

Grasping the Staff in both hands, Jake swung it with all his might, hoping to snap it in his rage. In that moment he didn't care about anything, not this stupid quest, the world – nothing. He just wanted it all to end.

The Staff grew warmer in his hands, the wood beneath his fingers vibrating slightly in the moment he swung it. The tip of the walking stick cracked down against the engine block, the sound resonating with a dull *thunk*. Power rushed through his entire body – the raging need he'd felt in his heart poured through his hands, into the Staff, blasting into the engine...

... which exploded into life.

"Whoa!" gasped George.

Jake pushed aside his shock. "Get us out of here."

"You got it," replied George, gunning the engine – or rather, making it splutter as powerfully as possible. They drew slowly away from the jetty.

Too slowly.

The nephilim charged down the wharf, looking like a band of deformed gorillas, burned and mutated through some sort of nuclear mishap. They would reach the end of the pier before the small boat cleared it completely, and Jake had no doubt they would be able to leap the short distance to the deck. He looked around, trying to quell his panic and find a solution.

He had nothing.

Damn it! He'd somehow just used the Staff to –

The Staff!

Jake strode to the right side of the boat and waited, trying to calm his thoughts in the face of the terrifying nephilim, their corpse-like skin cracked and broken, their mouths filled with cracked and rotting teeth. They hurtled toward him like a wall of doom. Unstopping – unstoppable.

Focusing his thoughts, Jake fingered the wood of the Staff, trying to replicate what he had felt moments before. Channeling the energy of his spirit, utilizing every ounce of emotion he could muster, he raised the Staff high above his head. He waited for the enormous rush of force, power he felt certain would wash away this filth like a great, cleansing flood. Joy suffused him knowing that through his actions he could destroy this evil, this embodiment of all that had corrupted his life, twisting his thoughts, his memories, all those long nights where the screams rang out and the Biblical phrases thudded into him, the howling of the Man, the recollection of his rotten whisky-breath still clawing at Jake's flesh. Jake would destroy them all; all his bad memories would be obliterated with the Staff's annihilation of these creatures from the Abyss. Any moment now. Any moment....

Nothing happened.

His lids snapped open just in time to witness the lead nephilim reach the end of the jetty and leap high into the air. The jump was effortless, it's power phenomenal. The result of Abaddon's machinations would easily reach the yacht, and then they would all die. Its eyes – malicious little orbs of ebony – seemed fixed only on Jake.

Numb fingers dropped the Staff to the deck. It rattled hollowly, mocking his audacity.

A booming explosion cracked through the still air. The nephilim crumpled midair, folding double at the midsection as though it had been punched by a giant invisible fist. It dropped with a loud splash into the water, dark ripples closing over its head in an instant. A second beast had reached the end of the wharf and also leaped, only to be met with a similar fate as Mikey emptied the barrel of his shotgun into its snarling, warped face. It, too, sank like a stone into the murky depths.

"I can do this all day, you bastards!" shouted Mikey.

The beasts paused as one, each of the remaining thirty or so staring malevolently at the boat, apparently just beyond even their reach. Jake got the distinct impression the other beasts had sunk, not due to any injury caused by Mikey's shooting, but because the nephilim were simply too heavy to float. He hoped their imperviousness didn't go so far as to make them immune to drowning, but his luck couldn't possibly be that good. If the nephilim could survive being minced by the cherubim, chances were they could handle a dunking.

At least they had managed to escape the immediate threat, something he'd thought nearly impossible a moment ago. He stared at the dropped Staff, grimacing as he bent down to pick it up once more. Had he really started the engine, or had it just been a coincidence?

"What the hell were *you* doin'?" snapped Tony.

"What do you mean?" replied Jake.

Tony waved his arm at the nephilim still crowded upon the dock. "I mean standing there like some sort of open target for those things. Why not just tack a big red circle on your ass and tell 'em you're open for business?"

"I thought I might be able to use the Staff to stop them." Such defense sounded ridiculous, even to Jake.

"It's a stick, it can't do nothin'. You almost got yourself killed because of a stick!"

"It's more than that! I started the engine with it, didn't I?"

Tony stared at him incredulously. "Did you?"

"Well I...." Jake's voice trailed away, unable to think of any evidence to back his claim. With the memory of the event slipping behind them, what he had done seemed nothing more than a frustrated man bashing the side of a television to get reception.

"So you just risked all our necks because, at best, you used a stick like jumper cables?"

"I thought it might work," Jake defended. "I mean, the nephilim are evil, aren't they?"

"Was the engine evil?" countered Tony.

"What? It's an engine, it's not...." Jake's voice disappeared as he grasped Tony's meaning. "But surely the Staff will work against evil, won't it?"

"Guess not," replied Tony, wildly indicating the horde of creatures still massing upon the dock. "What I do know is you just about got yourself splattered because of a theory that proved wrong. Me and him," he pointed at Mikey, "are gonna try to protect you, but we can't if you make yourself a target, can we?"

Jake begrudgingly nodded, knowing that Tony spoke the truth. His task, or whatever it was, was too important to risk on guesses and hopes. He needed to know what he was doing before leaping into the line of fire.

"Er, can somebody tell me what's going on?" asked George, holding the tiller in his trembling hands, glancing nervously back at the jetty where the nephilim were starting to disperse. Several remained motionless, still staring balefully after them.

Tony looked from George to Jake and chuckled. "Well, George, you're not going to believe this…."

-*CHAPTER 10*-
# CLEANSING

George *hadn't* believed a word of it, a fact Jake found himself strangely grateful for. The last thing he wanted was another criminal tagging along. As much as he appreciated the help of Tony and Mikey, he found their casual attitude toward right and wrong somewhat draining.

Shame suffused him at the thought. Here were two men helping him when others would not, risking more than their lives to assist Jake on his quest without asking for a single thing in return, and all he could think about was judging them for their shortcomings. Disgusted, Jake silently berated himself. Who was *he* to judge? Shouldn't he be helping them amend their ways rather than condemning them without consideration? It was so easy to criticize them, with their crass speech and somewhat shady behavior, but the reality stood that these were good men, regardless of their past. Their actions were what he should measure them by, what they did *right now*, and right now they were selflessly aiding him.

"Hey, guys," he said to them all, including George who sat steering the craft, flicking nervous glances behind him, back toward the dock. "I just want to say thanks, you know, for everything."

Mikey and Tony nodded slightly, and George looked at him oddly – no surprise really after Tony had told him Jake was the new messiah. Tony said, "Yeah, no problem, boss."

"I'm not your boss," corrected Jake swiftly.

"Sure you are," argued Tony, his tone defiant.

"But I can't –"

"Yeah, you can, you have to. There's no other way. You gotta be a leader, someone above the rest, not just a friend, otherwise the people you come up against are gonna try to walk all over you. And I'm not talking about this Abaddon guy, neither, I mean people in general;

anyone you deal with might try to exploit any kind of weakness you show. So you gotta show them no weakness. That's the burden of leadership, the weight you now carry. I can't imagine how huge it's gonna be for you; it was hard enough for me with my boys, but you've gotta convince the whole damn planet." He chuckled mirthlessly.

"I hadn't thought about it like that," admitted Jake. Dread lurched up within him at the notion of stepping out in front of the entire world and revealing himself… or at least what others claimed he was.

Thus far he hadn't really demonstrated anything Christ-like – it wasn't like he'd healed any lepers or walked on water. The incident with the Staff flickered on the edge of his mind, but he pushed it away. He could never be sure if he'd actually done something to start the engine, or if it had been mere luck. If he had to stand up and claim to be the new messiah, people would demand he prove it, otherwise they'd think he was just another nut.

The sound of the puttering engine eased his mind somewhat. At least they'd escaped the Nephilim – for now. He stumbled to the bow of the rolling yacht and sat down with his feet dangling above the water.

Somehow, with no real knowledge of how he'd done it, Jake had channeled a kind of power through the Staff, managing to start the motor… or had he? At the time, it had felt like something was occurring, but when faced with the charging nephilim only a moment later, the Staff had remained inert. Was this why Moses had been so old when he'd acted against the Egyptians, because it had taken him most of his life to figure out how to use the obstinate Staff?

Thinking about it, trying to observe the memory from every angle, Jake slowly became convinced he *had* in fact managed to use the power of the Staff, albeit unwittingly. A part of him admitted that even though this might be true, it had still been pure luck, there'd been absolutely no skill involved on his part. Some leader he was turning out to be – he would basically be lying to everyone in order to get people to follow him, and he didn't want to do that.

Staring at the near-black water passing by beneath his dangling shoes, Jake turned the dilemma over and over in his mind, like clothes in a tumble-dryer, but still didn't know what he wanted to do.

Actually, that wasn't entirely accurate. Jake wanted to stop Abaddon; his need to do so had roots so deep it almost hurt him to ignore it. He wanted nothing more than to face the fallen angel and put an end to the evil he represented, especially after his failure in the face of the nephilim. How was he supposed to get close to Abaddon when he was posing as the President of the United States of America, the most protected man on the planet?

The scope of such a task staggered him.

And now he sat aboard the boat of a drug dealer with no real destination in mind and absolutely no plan of action. He'd stared at George's onboard map and randomly picked Benton Harbor as a destination; from there they could easily travel by rail or road to Grand Rapids, Michigan. After their last escapade on a train he figured he might prefer to travel by road for now. From Grand Rapids they'd have access to an international airport from which they could catch a flight and travel to....

Where?

No idea arose, no grand schemes formulated. No matter how much he racked his tired mind, Jake simply stared at the waves pushing out in front of the small boat, pondering the enormity of his chosen task.

If only he'd asked Michael where he should go next. That would have been the smart thing to do, but at that point things had been slightly crazy, and Jake had been more concerned about surviving their encounter with the Nephilim. He'd had no time to ask the archangel for directions.

The quarter-moon behind Jake's head silhouetted him against the water, and he gazed at the outline, wondering what Jesus had looked like, wondering what doubts might have passed through his predecessor's mind during his days walking the Earth –

The surface erupted, and a clawing hand, its gray flesh peeling and rotten, surged upward. The nephilim lunged for Jake's dangling legs, its open mouth seeming to crave his flesh. Adrenaline surged through him, aiding Jake's reactions, and he snatched his legs up to his chest. The beast splashed back beneath the bow-wave.

"Nephilim!" he shouted, scrambling to his feet.

"Where?" Tony asked. Both he and Mikey ran forward.

"In the water! It jumped up at me out of the water!"

Mikey scanned the waves, his shotgun up and ready to fire. The small yacht chopped through the lake, and the moon reflected against the ripples, making visibility beyond the surface virtually impossible.

"Are you sure?" asked Tony. "I mean, how could it get us all the way out here?"

"I'm sure," replied Jake, gripping the railing with both trembling hands. "It's not as though I'm likely to mistake it for a goldfish, is it?"

Tony begrudgingly agreed. Jake wondered wildly how the nephilim could have possibly caught up with them so swiftly – especially since they were probably close to the middle of the lake by now. The depth of the water ought to have proven too much for the beasts, or at least he thought it should have. How, then, had one of the creatures managed to almost grab him?

The two creatures which had leaped from the dock had been stopped just short of the deck by the blasts from Mikey's shotgun. He recalled how the creatures in the Garden had regenerated, no matter how much they were sliced up. Jake wandered down the length of the small boat, staring into the murky water, thinking hard.

Perhaps… perhaps a small piece, an infinitesimal speck of one of the nephilim Mikey shot had somehow latched itself onto the hull of the yacht, regenerating while hidden, and holding on until Jake came near. If that were so, not only were they dealing with a creature – or rather, *creatures* – which were virtually invulnerable, but the nephilim had also displayed a modicum of intelligence, or at least a hunter's cunning.

They weren't just mindless beasts.

And one was still attached to the boat.

"Tony! Mikey!" Jake called urgently. "Don't shoot it if you see it, whatever you do. I think even tiny specks might be able to regenerate."

Tony swore long and loud, a sentiment echoed by Mikey, and one which Jake could understand. He turned to speak to George at the tiller of the boat, only to discover the man was gone. Glancing around, Jake saw George port-side, his back against the stainless-steel railing, terror etched upon his face.

"George, it's oka –"

Jake's words were cut short as a monstrous hand whipped from beneath the surface of the lake and grasped George, completely enveloping his skull from behind, the long gray fingers gripping wide across his face. It hauled him overboard with a whip-like crack. Jake yelled out, rushing over to the railing, but he could see no sign of the boat's owner.

"Get away from there!" snarled Tony harshly, pushing Jake back and aiming his handgun at the water. The boat continued moving, puttering along, not knowing its owner was now fish food.

"This sucks so bad," muttered Mikey, pointing his shotgun nervously at the surface of the lake.

"Remember," said Jake, trying hard not to panic, "if you cut them at all, any bits of blood or flesh will turn into another nephilim."

"What are we supposed to do, then? Tickle it?" snapped Mikey.

"I don't know what we can do," replied Jake, "but I saw these things get diced into tiny pieces by an army of cherubim. Every piece regenerated into a full-sized nephilim. So unless you want that to happen here, I suggest you avoid shooting this thing… or things."

He saw his words had their intended effect on the two men who, while still holding their weapons, now aimed them away from the water. Jake scanned the night for an answer to their dilemma.

*How do you stop something which can't be killed?*

*Trap it!*

Jake's eyes were drawn to the thin, naked mast. It stood bereft of sails, only the small engine powering the boat.

Where were the sails?

Glancing forward, Jake saw a small hatch in the front deck and quickly darted toward it, hopping awkwardly over ropes and cleats and other potential deck hazards. Wrenching the hatch open, he peered inside the darkened hold. As his eyes adjusted to the gloom, he saw there were no sails. He'd originally hoped to somehow net the beast, but he spied something they could use… or at least he *hoped* they could use it.

Jake reached down, hauling up a small, four-pronged anchor attached to a thick nylon rope. Larger boats often used the bigger, dual-pronged anchors more for weight, but smaller boats, such as this one, preferred the four-prongs for one reason: four prongs meant four chances it might catch hold.

It looked like a grappling hook, but one designed for underwater. Jake wasn't sure if this would work, but he had to try; they were barely halfway across the lake, and he doubted the nephilim clinging to the hull of the boat would simply leave them in peace until they reached their destination. It might have been willing to bide its time and hope to catch Jake unawares, but Jake felt sure its primal instincts would be telling it the time for hiding was over.

Swinging the small anchor overboard, Jake let it drop a couple of feet below the surface of the water before gripping the rope and swinging the anchor back and forth along the side of the hull like a pendulum. His hope was to somehow latch onto the nephilim, and then… well, he hadn't really thought it through beyond that.

The rope cut through the water, rubbing the side of the boat as Jake attempted to keep it as close to the hull as possible. If this plan had any hope of success he'd need to catch the nephilim under its armpit or something.

Not that this really looked like it had any chance of –

The rope unexpectedly stopped, snagged on something. Peering over the side, Jake was suddenly wrenched forward, almost launching over the boat's railing. Tony grabbed him by the belt and managed to haul him back. The anchor line sizzled through his hands, burning his palms, but Jake refused to release it. This might be their only chance.

Clamping his fists closed, Jake gritted his teeth against the pain and propped his foot against the railing, snapping the line taut. His shoulders felt as though they were about to pop from their sockets as Jake strained to hold the rope against the tremendous strength seeking to drag it clear of his grasp.

"Tony…" he gasped, "the winch… quick!"

Tony instantly understood and grabbed the end of the rope, clumsily wrapping it around the small electric winch attached to the foredeck of the boat, designed to drag in the anchor-line. The winch's tiny teeth-like notches locked the rope in place, gripping it while Tony raced back to the cockpit and hit the switch to start it up. Jake continued gripping the anchor-line, unwilling to risk letting it go yet. Within moments a tiny whine emitted from the winch as it tried to retract the line wound around its circular roller.

A motorized moan rose. Splintering echoed across the deck, and Jake realized the anchor-winch just wasn't powerful enough – the nephilim proving far too strong. Hauling with all his strength on the rigid length of rope, Jake called out to Mikey for assistance. He sprinted to help, dropping his shotgun and gripping the line. Tony also returned to the front of the boat and grabbed a hold. The three of them, along with the protesting electric-winch, managed to slowly, inch-by-inch, haul in the resistant line, groans and gasps escaping from each of them.

Hands bleeding and raw, eyes squeezed shut, Jake refused give in against the horrendous strength pulling against the line.

A loud crack echoed. The line hissed through their hands and snapped tight once more, causing Mikey to curse loudly and turn around –

"Oh… shit," murmured Mikey.

Jake opened his eyes, only to be confronted with the seven-foot-tall nephilim gripping the anchor in its left hand. This was the first time Jake had actually had a chance to study one of the beasts in detail, and he wished more than anything that it were something he could have missed out on.

"Make no sudden movements," he ordered softly.

Both men complied, though Jake remained unsure whether their stealth came from his order or from sheer terror at being so close to one of these beasts.

The creature towered above them, quivering slightly as if from cold, but Jake doubted such a mundane thing as cold water would affect the beast. Its flesh appeared on the verge of falling rotten from the bones. In contrast, the sores covering it seemed alive with pestilence. Naked, the nephilim stood unashamed, curiously without genitals. Its huge, muscular arms fell semi-relaxed near its sides.

And then Jake looked at its face.

The same dead skin covered the hairless cranium, and the beast's face appeared almost devoid of any sort of human features; only the black, emotionless eyes retained any vestige of humanity. The middle of the 'face' bore what appeared to be a massive cross carved into the flesh, the edges ragged and torn. As he stared, however, the mouth parted and four sections opened wide in a yawn-like gesture, revealing row upon row of shattered teeth disappearing into the cavernous maw of the nephilim.

Jake's first thought was of the Staff, but it was sitting in the cockpit – a million miles away for all the good it could do him right now.

"What do you want?" he asked, not really expecting an answer, but hoping to perhaps confuse the beast.

The nephilim cocked its head to the side, dropping the anchor to the deck with a hollow clunk. The winch swiftly dragged it, scraping across the deck. Mikey once more held the shotgun in his hands and made to raise it, but Jake signaled for him to freeze.

"I hope you know what you're doing," murmured Tony.

Jake stepped forward, closer to the creature, his head barely reaching the level of its broad, heaving chest. The nephilim's shivering increased dramatically and it appeared torn between fleeing and wrenching Jake's head from his shoulders.

"I can help you," said Jake, with a confidence he didn't truly feel.

The beast stared down at him through its beady eyes, the weight of that glare bearing heavily on Jake like so many unspoken utterances. Its trembling increased immeasurably until finally the nephilim collapsed to its knees before him, its horrific face looking slightly up at him as if in supplication.

Jake's mind went blank. All thoughts of the Staff or their quest were gone in an instant as he realized what the creature was begging him for. Fighting against whatever controls Abaddon had over it, the nephilim was pleading with Jake for some sort of release from the torment of being in this warped, corrupted body.

Laying his hands upon the diseased forehead, nothing happened. Quelling his rising panic, Jake breathed in....

Exhale.

The crisp breeze seemed to stall, the night air stilling. Nothing around Jake mattered in that moment, and he felt immensely peaceful. Jake wanted to smile into the beastly face before him. With a jolt, he suddenly felt every ounce of its torment, the burning of its corrupted flesh, the screaming of a mind torn between what it yearned to do and what it had been ordered to do. A cry escaped Jake's lips, but he held on, wrestling for control, searching for a way back to that peace he'd felt only moments ago. It was a hard fought journey, both sensations clashing within Jake's mind and chest, but he finally sensed a repression of the disharmony within the nephilim.

A surge of force exploded through Jake, blasting into the flesh of the nephilim directly through his hands, and without the Staff!

Joining with the mind of the nephilim, he shattered the coercions and boundaries locked in place by Abaddon's corruption like they were tissue paper, forcing his way into the core of the creature's mind. Once there he witnessed the mind of a young boy, kidnapped into Joseph Kony's army in Northern Uganda, and dragged into the corrupted ranks of Abaddon's minions along with hundreds of other innocents. The boy was screaming, begging for release from within the disfigured shell of the nephilim. Somehow Jake could sense that when the nephilim had been split apart by Mikey's shotgun blast, so too had the boy's torment, but instead of halving, the agony had been doubled.

Such was the fate for Abaddon's army.

Jake wept at the boy's pain, and each tear that fell turned into a torrent, falling upon the immense body, scouring it like acid. At first Jake panicked and tried to stop, but beneath the corrupted flesh he could see virgin tissue – the unblemished tissue of a dark-skinned child. The tears continued, but gradually the tempo of the downpour transformed from a theme of sorrow to one of incredible joy, and when Jake next looked, there lay upon the deck not a monstrous beast, but a boy no older than fourteen-years, the final vestiges of infection disappearing like muddy stains.

The tears ended, drying up as though evaporating in a desert, and the power dissipated, the last fragments fading away, soon becoming mere wisps of memory. In moments even these faded, leaving him bereft once more. Jake stared down at the naked boy, unable to believe what had just happened.

"Mikey, see if there're any clothes in the cabin," he said softly. Mikey darted away without question.

The boy roused just as Mikey returned with a large, dirty-white t-shirt bearing a big picture of Mickey Mouse on the front and a pair of blue elasticized pants. He handed them directly to the youth, who put them on without a word and stood, eyeing them all warily.

"Are you okay?" asked Jake.

The boy looked startled at the sound, and his hands shot up to his ears. Jake looked quizzically at Tony and Mikey, but both just shrugged.

"We mean you no harm," said Jake.

The boy appeared on the verge of panic and stared around him wildly, taking in the small boat and the wide expanse of water all around them.

"Who... you?" croaked the youth, his voice cracking.

"We're friends," said Jake, keeping his words simple. "We help."

Once more the boy jumped slightly at the sound. Jake began to suspect he knew why, and his heart began to hammer.

"Me... hear. How?" asked the youth roughly.

Jake swallowed heavily. It had been as he'd guessed; the boy had been deaf – possibly some sort of ear infection after he'd learned this smattering of English – and he'd been healed when Jake had....

What the hell had he just done?

Tony, seeing his discomfort, stepped forward. "It's a miracle," he said softly to the boy.

The boy appeared to think about this, and then nodded, accepting the answer without question.

"What your name?" asked Jake.

The youth stared hard at him, seeming to gauge his sincerity. "Me... Kibuuka."

"I'm Jake," he said, placing his hand on his own chest in demonstration. He figured he'd leave the other introductions until later when the boy wasn't so jumpy. "What do you remember, Kibuuka?"

Kibuuka at once appeared fearful, but stood his ground, raising his chin, and staring Jake in the eye. "My family... we... stolen by soldiers. Me become... soldier. Then... general come. Strange fruit.... Then here."

Jake nodded, understanding beyond the simplistic explanation what had actually happened to the boy. His family in Uganda had been forced into slavery by Joseph Kony's army, Kibuuka being made into a soldier. After that, things would have settled into nightmarish routine for the boy until he'd been given the fruit from the Garden, at which point he had been transformed into one of the nephilim, blurring his memories until Jake had revived him.

Something suddenly occurred to Jake, and he looked worriedly at Kibuuka. Tracing back over his rapidly fading memory of what had happened while he was inside the boy's mind, he remembered the boy being split, his form here on the boat growing from the piece of nephilim flesh which had reformed after Mikey had shot it. His soul, for want of a better word, had been divided when the nephilim had separated and reformed.

Was his soul still divided?

"Kibuuka," began Jake, "It's very important. Do you feel – er – *whole*? Does your... inside... feel right?"

Kibuuka cocked his head slightly, frowning at Jake's words, trying to understand what he meant. Then he suddenly seemed to comprehend, or perhaps remember, and nodded vigorously, a wide smile forming, displaying immaculately white teeth framed by his dark face.

"You fix," said Kibuuka enthusiastically, rubbing his chest. Jake let out a sigh of relief.

However it had happened – whether the other beast made from Kibuuka had died or simply existed now as an empty shell – Jake felt satisfied the boy was no longer split inside.

Something else flitted into Jake's mind which made his stomach churn. A single nephilim had been destroyed, restoring Kibuuka to humanity, and his deformation had been created by a combination of the Fruits from the Garden along with Abaddon's own power. Did that mean all of the nephilim were somehow tethered to Abaddon? If so, did Abaddon now know of the force Jake had just revealed?

Peering toward the far shore, Jake silently willed it to draw closer. He had the distinct feeling things were about to get much more dangerous. He'd very likely just been promoted from a minor annoyance in Abaddon's mind to a serious threat, and the fallen angel was unlikely to take such a threat lightly.

And then there was the other thing. Only moments ago he'd exerted a power he could never have previously dreamed of, felt it flowing through him without the use of the Staff, transforming a monster into the youth standing before him. Nothing else on the planet could do such a thing – well, nothing he knew of, anyway. Jake should have felt confident to the extreme after such an accomplishment, but nothing could be further from the truth. He felt terribly, horribly alone in his fear, despite the power he had discovered. Even given the ease with which he had drawn upon the glorious energy, Jake had absolutely no idea how he'd done it.

***

Mikey jumped up to the dock, securing the bow line. He stared back down at Jake. "You seriously don't know how you did it?"

Jake shook his head sadly. "I feel like a man without sight who miraculously catches a glimpse of the sky before blindness takes over once more. The power was there, but now it's gone."

"So you don't know if you could do it again?"

Jake simply shrugged; what could he say? He'd experienced a moment of absolute clarity, a wonderful combination of peace and purpose. To have it so suddenly wrenched away felt like one of his limbs had been torn off. In that instant, he'd held complete mastery of his mind and spirit, and had possessed more knowledge than he could have ever imagined possible.

And now it was gone.

After questioning them, he knew the two brothers hadn't seen exactly what had occurred. All they knew was one moment the nephilim was kneeling in front of Jake, and the next it was gone, replaced by the form of the unconscious boy. In a way this had been easier for Jake; he didn't need to explain the sight of his tears washing away the corrupted flesh smothering Kibuuka. But nor could he explain the end result. Kibuuka, too, had seemed confused. Exhausted, the boy now rested in the single cot below decks within the yacht's tiny cabin. All Jake could say for sure was that he had, in that instant, tapped into something which had sealed itself the moment he'd used it, and he wasn't sure if he would *ever* rediscover how to use it again.

Tony had simply accepted this statement, but Mikey had been more probing, certain there was something Jake had left out. There wasn't, at least nothing that Jake could remember. It had been nothing short of a miracle, but seemed slightly tainted through his inability to recreate it at will.

A huge sense of expectation weighed upon him, a great deal of it self-induced. The only answer Jake could come up with was that some other physical or ethereal force had used him for a purpose, and then discarded him. This notion disturbed Jake even more than the idea of never having access to that power again – it wasn't nice to think of himself as a tool to be exploited without his control.

And now they were here, Benton Harbor, the destination Jake had chosen on a whim simply because he had no other idea. Some leader he was turning out to be.

Jake clambered off the boat, striding over to where Tony stood, his pistol gripped so tightly in his hand that his knuckles glowed white in the dim light.

"So," said Tony, "what are we gonna do with the kid?"

"He said he wants to go home to Uganda. He's hoping he might be able to find his family or at least other people from his village. I still have Vain's credit card, I'll get a ticket for him with that."

"What about his passport?"

Jake cursed softly. He hadn't thought of that.

"There is a guy in Grand Rapids I know who owes me a favor," suggested Tony.

Cringing internally, Jake decided not to ask who this man was, or why he owed Tony a favor. "Can he set him up with a passport?"

Tony shrugged. "I reckon so, that's what he's best known for. It should only take a couple of hours."

Huffing slightly, Jake said, "I guess we have no choice. I'm not going to just dump Kibuuka at some consulate, and there's no way we'll be able to answer any of their questions if we go in with him." Was this how Tony had slipped so far into crime: a tiny need at a time?

"So we're stuck with him until Grand Rapids," grunted Tony, seemingly annoyed. He started slightly upon seeing Jake's reaction. "I don't mean it as a bad thing, but haven't you considered that Abaddon might still be able to – you know – track him? He might be able to send those other things after us too, using the kid to follow us."

"Yeah, I had thought of that," admitted Jake, "but it makes no difference. We're responsible for him, and regardless of the repercussions, we need to ensure his safety – the best we can, anyway."

"Well my job is to protect you –"

"No, it's not," snapped Jake, exhaustion making him short-tempered. "It's to do what I ask you to do, and I'm asking this. This is the right thing, and I don't need to justify it to you or anyone else."

Tony's impassive expression suddenly broke into a wide smile. "Now you're getting the idea… *boss*."

As Tony strode back toward the boat, Jake grimaced at the truth of what he'd said.

Jake couldn't simply be a friend to these men; he had to be more than that. He would be leading them into things beyond normal human comprehension, and only a leader could instill the confidence he'd need if he wasn't going to do it on his own. Jake knew he needed the help of men like Tony and Mikey. In truth, perhaps he'd require a bit more help than just the two brothers.

Slowly, ever so doubtfully, Jake raised his gaze skyward….

\*\*\*

The bus trip to Grand Rapids went mainly without incident – apart from the rather large lady who sat beside Jake and fell asleep on him, shuffling over to rest on his shoulder, her open mouth close to his ear. Her snoring continued echoing in his ears long after the trip was over. Jake hadn't been allowed into the passport-forger's dwelling, but true to Tony's estimation, he and Kibuuka were out within two hours, complete with a brand-new, slightly worn, fake passport.

"Gerald. R. Ford International Airport," called the driver, the doors of the bus swooshing open.

Jake clambered up, catching an unexpected whiff of his own body odor and wondering how long it had been since he'd last showered. Making a silent promise to remedy the issue at his next possible convenience, he made his way to the front of the bus, nodding his thanks to the driver. Exiting, he met Tony and Mikey – both minus their weapons, which they'd begrudgingly left behind – on the sidewalk. Kibuuka stood slightly apart from the brothers, staring hard at Jake.

"We're going to send you home, Kibuuka," said Jake, coming to stand in front of the Ugandan.

"I will destroy you," snarled Kibuuka, his English perfect, his voice sibilant.

Jake stepped back in shock, noticing for the first time that Kibuuka's hands were clenched into fists at his sides and quivering slightly, as if he were straining heavily against something. He glanced around, unsure if the brothers had also heard the boy's statement. Tony and Mikey tensed, their shock as evident as Jake's.

"This peasant might be able to resist me since you freed him," spat the voice manipulating Kibuuka's mouth, "but I can still speak through him, and I tell you this: You will fall at my feet before this is over. You are not who you think you are; you're just a puppet being used by a god who cares nothing for mankind. You were created for his amusement, nothing else, and when you fail to provide amusement anymore he will let your entire race crumble. I can promise you your failure will be epic, as will your agony. All of humanity will know you for the fool you truly are: the man who would be messiah – what a pathetic worm you are!"

Recovering from his shock, Jake realized the voice belonged to Abaddon. With great difficulty, he managed to retain his composure and stared evenly into Abaddon's eyes; dark orbs glaring balefully at him out from Kibuuka's face.

And he laughed.

The effort tore at Jake, but he forced himself to do it, and as he continued, his laughter became less forced and more genuine. The sound was infectious, and within moments Jake heard Tony and Mikey behind him start to snicker uncertainly, gradually breaking into full, raucous laughter.

The sound echoed all around them, and Kibuuka shook with Abaddon's rage, but the fallen angel seemed unable to move within the boy's body. His mouth twitched furiously, silently opening and snapping shut, like a shark chomping at feet on the deck of a boat after being captured, but their laughter only became louder at the sight.

"I *will* –" began Abaddon.

"No you won't," said Jake, breaking out of his laughter in an instant. "You're pathetic. Your master is pathetic. You've tried to kill me twice and have failed both times. Your monsters come after me, and I cleanse them of your contamination. I'm coming for you, Abaddon, and I can see in your eyes that you're afraid." This was a bluff, but Jake felt it sounded convincing enough. "So why don't you run back to Satan and tell him how badly you've failed – I'm sure his punishment won't be too nasty."

"I.... I –"

"My strength is growing every day, Abaddon, while yours obviously wanes. You can't even overpower a young boy; how do you think you'll be able to stand against me? I'll change your nephilim back to their former selves, and you'll be alone once more. The truth of your terror lies in your need to hide within the form of the President – yes, I know where you are – and there you cower behind the walls of the White House. But even that won't stop me, Abaddon. I'll find a way to get to you, and then I will *end* you. I have the Staff of Moses, but the power now flows directly through me, and it will cut its way through you as easily as Moses cut through the Red Sea. What do you have to say now, braggart?"

"You will fall –"

"You've already said that."

Kibuuka's possessed face abruptly flared with such intense rage that Jake had to fight his instincts against stepping backwards, but then the expression fled, and Kibuuka staggered, raising a hand to his face. Jake stepped forward and aided him before he fell. Tony and Mikey also came closer.

"What happen?" asked Kibuuka, terror etched upon his features.

"Don't worry, Kibuuka," replied Jake soothingly. "It's okay now."

A glance passed between the brothers, and Jake could almost guess what they were thinking, because he was contemplating exactly the same thing. Was it truly okay, or had Jake's bluff just made things much, much worse?

\*\*\*

After they had seen Kibuuka off on his flight home with a pocket-full of cash and instructions on how to get back to his village, Jake bought some deodorant and sprayed himself thoroughly, much to the amusement of Tony and Mikey – until he'd pointed out how badly they reeked as well. The next thing he knew, both brothers were asking to borrow his spray. Jake chuckled slightly at the sight before contemplating his next task, a task which just seemed to keep re-occurring, no matter how many twists and turns this expedition took.

Leaning heavily on the Staff, Jake stared at the flight board, searching for some sort of inspiration. Nothing materialized. No burning bush with glowing instructions, no tablets etched with wisdom.

This should have been the easy part. He had angels appearing every time he turned around, he'd tapped into some incredible source of power and transformed a horrifically mutated young man from a beast back into a human being – he'd even been resurrected from the dead – but he struggled to figure out something as simple as which flight to catch.

Jake absently rubbed the birthmark on his cheek, his eyes skipping down the list of departing flights on the board. He suddenly froze. Where else should he go, but to the people who were supposed to know more about this stuff than anyone else on the face of the planet?

Rome: home of the Catholics.

The plane was not overly full, which was an incredible boon to Jake. He desperately needed some sleep and hoped to catch a few hours before they landed. Jake reclined his chair slightly, closing his eyes. Surely this was the right path to take; if anyone on the surface of the planet knew how to combat Abaddon, the Catholics would have a clue.

The memory of the first priest he'd approached warred with the recollection of the aid he'd received in Venice: two men from the same clan with completely different perspectives. What would the Vatican, a city filled with men like these, be like?

The rumbling of the plane's engines drowned out the rest of Jake's thoughts, and he drifted away into oblivion.

## -CHAPTER 11-
# FATHER ARMADEUSO

"You've gotta be shittin' me!" Mikey barked at the cab driver.

"Try to be nice, Mikey," cautioned Jake softly.

Mikey threw his hands up in the air in frustration. "But do you know what he's trying to charge us?"

"We can afford it. Right now we don't need to be making waves. Agreed?"

"Sorry, boss."

Jake shook his head. They were going to have to figure out something else to call him, something which didn't make him feel like some sort of dictator, but for now they had bigger issues. Jake stared up at the enormous white structures before him.

Vatican City.

They'd been dropped off at Saint Peter's Square, and, gazing around in awe, Jake attempted to take in the sheer magnificence of the place.

The circular courtyard of the basilica was colossal, soaring pillars arrayed in a horseshoe for two-thirds of its circumference. A towering, white obelisk stood in the middle of the courtyard – square at its base and tapering to its peak – topped with what appeared to be an ornamental crucifix, the anodized copper contrasting green against the sandy-gray of the obelisk. Beyond the paved courtyard, Jake saw Saint Peter's Basilica; the enormous, domed, cathedral-style structure drawing every eye to it.

"What are you doing here?" demanded a familiar, icy voice behind them.

Jake spun around only to be confronted by Vain, standing casually, his arms by his sides. Tony and Mikey apparently recognized him as well, but rather than a tearful reunion, they stepped back, unease evident upon their faces. Jake was on his own.

"Hello, Vain," he said cautiously.

"What are you doing here?" the assassin repeated, his voice dangerously low.

Jake contemplated lying, but then sighed in frustration. "I don't know. I discovered some information regarding my purpose, and I know where Abaddon is, but... I guess I came here searching for direction."

"Can't you just do some of your God shit?"

"I wish," muttered Jake, dropping his eyes. "I managed to do a couple of things, but since then, nothing."

"So you ran here to ask the Catholics what to do. You've come whimpering to a bunch of closet maggots with their heads up God's ass to ask them for advice."

"What are *you* doing here, then?" countered Jake.

"What I'm doing is my business. Who are you going to see?"

"I...."

Vain chuckled darkly. "You've got to be the most ignorant messiah I could have ever imagined. Jesus would have seriously kicked you in the balls, you know that?"

"You think I'm not aware of that fact? But I'm doing my best, and rather than standing there ridiculing me, I'd really appreciate a little help."

"I think I might just ridicule you a bit more," retorted Vain. "Have you met any other metrosexual angels yet?"

Jake sighed. "I've met a couple."

"And they couldn't offer you any pearls of wisdom?"

"None I can recall."

"So if an angel can't give you any advice," said Vain, his tone somewhat more measured now, "what makes you think a bunch of crusty old farts locked up in this marble palace can help?"

The logic of what the assassin said was undeniable, and Jake cursed.

"What should I do?" he asked, his voice soft, almost pleading.

"Only *you* can know that," replied Vain, staring at him, his eyes like coal. "But in the meantime you might as well come and meet someone. He might be able to help. Just be warned, though, he's a priest, and he's old."

"Why would that matter?" asked Jake, confused.

"Well, if you're who they reckon you are," replied Vain, "he might keel over from shock, and I won't be the one giving him mouth-to-mouth."

The assassin turned and strode off down the street, away from Saint Peter's Square and down a side lane. Jake hesitated, remembering what had happened the last time he'd followed Vain down an alley, but he couldn't miss this opportunity. Signaling to Tony and Mikey, he followed the Dark Man as quickly as possible.

"I thought you guys knew Vain," he hissed at Tony.

"We did – once. That's why we're afraid of him," replied Tony. "Our stepdad was one of the biggest and most physically-formidable guys you'd ever meet, and even he spoke about Vain with awe. I think the two of them had some sort of fight one time, and dad came off second best. He never spoke about it, but he always said if there was anything he was more scared of than Vain, he hadn't met it yet."

"Well, that's comforting," Jake muttered.

Vain walked warily, catlike in his movements, and as Jake stared at his black-clad form he found himself marveling at the way the assassin seemed constantly vigilant and aware of his surroundings while still appearing completely casual about it. Straining his ears, Jake couldn't hear the faintest sound coming from Vain's movements; even his jacket didn't seem to rustle, and his eyes were at all times scanning everywhere, but never noticeably. He might have just been a curious tourist, albeit one with a palpable aura of death draped around him. It was an odd contradiction, and all Jake could think was how glad he felt that the assassin was on their side.

"Are you gonna stare at my ass all day, Jehovah?"

It took Jake a moment to realize Vain was speaking to him; the assassin hadn't turned and couldn't possibly have noticed Jake studying him.

"Um… what?' Jake asked, bluffing for time.

"You know," said Vain, chuckling icily.

"I was studying the way you watch everything around you so casually."

"Whatever helps you sleep at night," replied Vain without turning.

"I'm telling you the truth," snapped Jake, reaching forward to grab Vain by the shoulder.

Instantly he was on his back on the ground, his right arm trapped under Vain's armpit, his left flapping uselessly like a chicken wing. Gasping for breath, he realized the assassin's knee was pressed into his throat. Tony and Mikey moved forward, but Vain had a silenced handgun out and trained on them almost immediately, freezing the brothers in their tracks. The entire incident had taken only a fraction of a second. Vain raised his knee slightly for Jake to get air, but still left it low enough that he could drop it back down in an instant, crushing Jake's throat like a grape.

"What do you think you're doing?" asked Vain conversationally.

"I was – I was only trying to get your... attention," gasped Jake.

"Well now you've got it. What can I do for you?" The handgun aimed at Tony and Mikey didn't waver, and Vain never once dropped his eyes from the two brothers, confident in his absolute dominance over Jake.

That confidence was not misguided; Jake was trapped, unable to move an inch, and he suddenly felt extremely foolish. He'd ended up in this predicament because of his rash action – not just in trying to grab Vain, but in coming to Rome to start off with. What in the world had he been thinking; that the Pope would sit him down and have a chat over tea and scones about him being the resurrection of Christ? Maybe the Pope could have instructed Jake how to destroy a fallen angel with the Staff of Moses.

That would have been nice.

"I'm sorry," he croaked from the ground.

Vain finally looked down at him, shaking his head slightly in disappointment.

"How are you going to defeat something like Abaddon when you give up so easily?" he asked, holstering his weapon and standing up smoothly.

The two brothers rushed over to aid Jake as Vain stepped away, moving backward and leaning against a wall, but never dropping his gaze from Jake or the brothers.

"What could I have done?" gasped Jake, climbing to his feet. "You had me trapped."

"And so you just decided to surrender?" mused Vain. "I can see the universe is in safe hands, then. No wonder you came running to the Catholics when you ran out of answers; you're a moron."

The words were stated simply, but each sliced deep into Jake's confidence, like a verbal razor.

"Then what should I have done?" he snapped, his control slipping as the weeks of frustration began to make their weight felt within him.

"I don't know," replied Vain casually. He indicated Tony and Mikey. "They don't know. The fucking Pope sure as hell won't know. Only *you* can know for sure what to do because this task was appointed only to *you*, and it was given to you for a reason, a reason nobody else will ever know. Somewhere deep inside you hides the answer, and all the running around you do won't find it until you're ready to face it. Don't put your faith in sticks or gods – they're useless; have faith in yourself, and let God do whatever the hell he wants."

"Do you believe in God?" asked Jake.

"*Believe?*" said Vain. "No, I don't believe. I *know* he exists, so I don't have to believe. I wouldn't say I like him – although he's gotta be better than Lucifer – that guy just sucks."

"You've met the Devil?"

"Yeah," replied Vain calmly, "a couple of times – you could say we were close at one stage, but he's a real asshole. I don't know if this God of yours is any better, but I know enough to know all that shit is real. When you ask if I *believe* in Him... huh... I believe in *me*. That's all. God can suck my dick."

Jake was utterly stunned by what Vain said; every piece of it, from admitting he'd met Satan to his casual dismissal of God. It was all so incredibly unbelievable, but the assassin left Jake with no doubt he meant every word – one look into his dark, brooding eyes told Jake this was not a man likely to embellish the truth.

"I'm trying –"

"Don't try. Losers try… and then they whine about how unfair the world is and how it wasn't their fault they failed. As soon as you put the thought of *trying* into your spongy brain, the possibility of failure emerges. Do what you have to do, and if it all goes to shit, you do something else again and again and again until you succeed. Or else you might as well just give up now and go cry over how you're not as good as Jesus."

The words hit hard, amplifying Jake's anxiety, insecurities hidden from the light lest they weaken him even more. Every single word Vain uttered rang true, and Jake suddenly realized how naive he'd been. Searching for answers elsewhere, he'd wasted time when he knew all along what he needed to do.

He needed to stop Abaddon.

It was as simple as that. There was no magic answer, nothing another person could tell him that he didn't already know – Abaddon was the problem, and Jake needed to confront him, for good or ill. Perhaps the fallen angel would defeat him as simply as a newborn babe, but at least Jake would have tried; better than all this scurrying around from place to place coming away with wisps of information which he couldn't really piece together. Jake raised his gaze back to Vain, and the assassin regarded him emotionlessly, finally nodding.

"And now you understand," said Vain. "Took you long enough."

"I can't believe I was so naive. Thank you."

"Let's go and see Father Armadeuso before you leave. The old fart might have some information you can use." Vain turned his gaze to Tony and Mikey, his smile disappearing. "You two ought to be ashamed of yourselves. I thought Tobias would have raised you to have bigger balls than to stand by and watch while I did that to the guy you're supposedly protecting."

"We – ah…." began Tony. "You remember us?"

"Unfortunately," replied Vain, but the semblance of a grin tugged at the corners of his mouth, and Jake knew he was toying with the awestruck brothers. "How's your mother?"

"Good," replied Tony swiftly. "She –"

"That's great." Vain turned and strode off once more. Jake stared incredulously at the assassin's back and –

"Remember what happened the last time you were ogling my ass, God-boy," remarked Vain without looking around. "Hurry up and follow."

Jake grinned despite everything and motioned to the two still-flustered brothers before jogging slightly to catch up.

***

"You can't be serious."

"Do I look like I'm joking?" replied Vain.

The priest regarded him sideways. "Hmm... good point." He returned his gaze to Jake, seated across the table in the ancient priest's tiny kitchen. Tony and Mikey had remained outside the small tenement block, nodding at Jake's request to keep an eye out for anything unusual, knowing he referred to the nephilim. "So... the Avun-Riah was a ruse. Ah well, there are worse ways I could have spent my life than waiting for a deception." He glanced coldly at Vain. "And I suppose it did help *you*."

"Yeah, you were awesome," snapped Vain. "I remember that whole time I was in Hell how you never left my side. Remember that? Oh, that's right, you can't, because you never left *here*, you miserable old bastard."

"Nice to see your attitude hasn't changed – nor has your age either, it seems," said Father Armadeuso with an air of casual familiarity, something Jake would have never imagined someone could possess around Vain. As though reading his thoughts, the old man turned to Jake. "I'm close enough to death now, so this murderer doesn't scare me as much anymore. How is it, Vain, that you look like you haven't aged a day?"

"I've been moisturizing. Can you help Jesus?"

"I'm not Jes –" began Jake.

"Whatever," snarled Vain. "Can you help him?"

Father Armadeuso stared hard at Jake, his wispy white hair and wrinkled visage set around a pair of gray eyes which were impossibly clear for someone so old. The priest's gaze flickered to Jake's left cheek, fixating there for a moment, his brows narrowing.

"Is that a tattoo?"

Jake shook his head roughly. "I was born with it – it's a birthmark."

"It's shaped exactly like a teardrop. How unusual."

"Not to me," replied Jake, grimacing at the conversation he'd experienced many times throughout his life.

The old man's eyes flicked up, staring hard into Jake's for a moment, slowly traveling around his face, scanning him, assessing his weakness and mortality. "So you think you're the new messiah," murmured the priest, his voice doubtful. "I thought you would have been taller." He chuckled mirthlessly, the sound raspy. "At least the Avun-Riah looked the part, even as a child."

Jake frowned, irritation roiling within him, momentarily pushing aside his self doubt. "I am what I am, and judgment from you won't change the fact. You look at me, but you don't see what I am, you see what I'm not. In your mind you imagined a mirror of Jesus strolling across oceans heralded by angels and surrounded by light – you didn't expect a man, a mortal man, with a god-like challenge placed before him. This is what I am, and any help you can give would be greatly appreciated."

Father Armadeuso sat back in his chair, nodding, evidently impressed by Jake's words. "I'm sorry… my Lord," murmured the priest.

Jake shook his head. A part of him reveled in the new-found respect he saw reflected in the old priest's eyes, while another part cringed, wondering at this responsibility he'd just accepted. With these words he'd fully taken up the mantle of Christ, and knew what he had to become. He had to be more than a man, more than a leader; he had to become a beacon, a symbol of all that was good in the world.

Well, that shouldn't be too difficult.

Yeah, right.

As Vain had pointed out, however, he accomplished nothing whining about it.

He had to either do it, or simply give up now – there would be no more excuses or fumbling around while waiting for someone else to make the hard choices for him. Now was the time to fully accept who and what he was, and accept the title bestowed upon him.

"Father Armadeuso," said Jake, leaning forward across the kitchen table and cupping the old priest's hands under his own, "I am the Christ reborn, and my task here is crucial. Can you aid me in defeating Abaddon?"

The old priest collapsed.

"Great," grunted Vain. "You killed him. Well done."

"He's not dead," muttered Jake. "He just fainted."

"At his age it's pretty close to the same thing." Vain pulled a dagger out and began cleaning under his fingernails with its tip. "I guess this isn't really an impressive start to your coming out of the God closet, huh?"

"I guess not," agreed Jake, sitting back in his own chair and looking across at Vain, who sheathed the knife in a move so swift Jake didn't even see where it disappeared to.

The assassin pulled something from one of his pockets, and Jake heard a crack; a moment later an incredibly pungent scent hit his nostrils, making him recoil violently. Vain leaned across Father Armadeuso, and Jake saw him holding a glass ampoule under the priest's nose. A second later the priest awoke with a start, snapping upright so swiftly Jake winced, certain the old man would hurt himself in the spasmodic reaction.

"My own formula," said Vain with a malicious grin. "Smelling salts to awaken miserable old assholes – works every time."

Jake really didn't want to know who else Vain had used the smelling salts on over the years. He pushed the thought aside and focused instead on Father Armadeuso.

"Are you alright?" he asked.

The elderly priest glanced around, startled, but apparently unharmed. "Have you awakened me, oh Lord?"

"Here we go," muttered Vain.

Father Armadeuso ignored Vain, his gaze fixed completely on Jake. Shifting awkwardly in his seat, Jake sucked in a huge gulp of air – preparing himself for what he had to do next.

"Can you give me any information which might help me, Father?"

Father Armadeuso stood up, bending awkwardly in an odd move which confused Jake. It took him a moment to realize the old priest was trying to kneel before him in an act of genuflection.

Jake leaped up from his chair and darted around the table while Vain stood by laughing mockingly. Jake stopped Father Armadeuso before the old man had gone too far down and wrestled him lightly back into his seat.

"You don't need to kneel before me, Father."

"But – but you're...."

"I know who I am,' replied Jake, with what he hoped was a reassuring smile. "But right now I need you to focus. What can we do to stop Abaddon? I need to find something soon or it might be too late – he's getting stronger all the time."

"Abaddon?" croaked the priest, as though hearing Jake for the first time. "He's here?"

Out of the corner of his eye, Jake saw Vain shake his head in disgust.

"He's here," said Jake patiently. "How do we stop him?"

"How did he get here?"

"He caught the fucking bus, what do you think?" Vain said, chuckling hollowly.

Jake ignored the assassin's comment. "That's not important right now, Father, the fact is he's here, and he can possess almost anybody he wants, controlling them at will." Jake thought it best not to reveal to Father Armadeuso who Abaddon was currently controlling, the old man seemed to be under enough stress already. "How do we stop him?"

"Only through the power of God can you oppose one of the Fallen. It was through Him they were created, and through Him they will be defeated."

"But didn't the angels fight each other somehow? How did they do it?"

Father Armadeuso shook his head. "That was on a different plane of existence. If they were to battle here the entire universe might be destroyed. The fact Abaddon seems to be unfettered is extremely unsettling, to say the least," the old priest continued, his voice sounding slightly less tremulous. "If God were to send one of his angels to oppose him, the results would be catastrophic. We are talking about powers beyond human imagination here, not merely people with wings."

The priest took a deep breath, his gaze growing steadier the longer he spoke. He still stared at Jake with awe, but now his eyes twinkled with purpose. "Angels are described as power of the purest kind – think of them as a nuclear reactor containing only positive energy. If two such reactors clashed, the results would be globally disastrous. Now imagine if those reactors contained more energy than a hundred of our suns." Jake frowned, his brow creasing heavily imagining the power Father Armadeuso described. "Even this is a moderate estimation," said the old man.

"There must be some way," argued Jake. "I have to stop him – there's nobody else."

"Rather arrogant of you," drawled Vain. "Isn't arrogance a sin? Everything else seems to be."

Jake ignored him.

Father Armadeuso's eyes never left Jake, his gaze piercing. "You must have it within you to somehow combat this threat, or else you would not be here. I sense you carry much doubt, and this is understandable considering your situation, but you will need to put your doubts aside and trust in God if you are to prevail."

Vain snorted. "*God?* All that asshole seems to do is sit on the sidelines and dictate who lives and who dies. And you priests are like his cheerleaders – where are your pompoms?"

Father Armadeuso merely shook his head sadly. "After all you have seen, why must you still mock Him?"

"Because after all I went through to save Sebastian, your God still took him away again – and that's after he'd fulfilled his purpose of pretending to be this idiot." Vain waved a hand at Jake. "Where is the boy now? Maybe you should ask your God that?"

The priest's eyes narrowed. "They still took Sebastian when he was merely a decoy?"

"His death can still unlock things for Sordarrah, apparently," snarled Vain, his frustration evident. "But that's all beside the point – we're here for God-boy. Is that all you can tell him; trust in a God who does nothing?"

"What else is there? Do you want me to pull out a magic talisman or something? You of all people should know better than to look for something like that, Vain."

Jake saw the assassin grimace and self-consciously rub his hand against his chest. "It's gone now."

"Not all of it, judging by the lack of lines on your face."

"How do I tap into this power of God?" asked Jake, breaking back into the conversation in an attempt to keep it on track. He lifted up the walking stick in his hands and showed it to Father Armadeuso. "Do you have any idea how I can use this? It's the Staff of Moses, but –"

"The Staff of Moses?" gasped the old priest, and Jake feared he might pass out once more. "How did you find that?"

"Beneath the Tomb of Christ, inside the Church of the Holy Sepulchre, in Jerusalem," replied Jake. "It's a long story, but I can't seem to channel the power of God through it in the way I expected."

"Well of course not," said Father Armadeuso. "It was designed as a conduit for a mortal man, not someone like you."

"But I *am* a mortal man," retorted Jake.

"You are far more than that. If you haven't realized that already you need to… and soon."

"But Moses left a message for me on the lid of his sarcophagus," argued Jake.

"I'm sure it told you exactly what you needed to know at the time, in order for you to progress further along your destined path," said the old man. "But, as I'm sure you already know, Christ never carried such a staff, nor did he require any sort of conduit to invoke the power of God – he merely needed faith, both in himself and in the Holy Father."

"Then why can't I do anything?" asked Jake, his frustration rising.

"Are you saying you haven't, not even once, tapped into something without the help of the Staff?"

"Well… yes. But that was just a freak incident."

"There are no freak incidents," replied Father Armadeuso stoutly. "Whatever happened was all part of God's plan."

"What about Catholic priests fiddling with little kids? Does that fit into His plan?" asked Vain coarsely. Jake's chest tightened.

Father Armadeuso sighed heavily. "Is there no end to your bile?"

"Apparently not," replied Vain with a malicious chuckle.

Turning his attention from the assassin, Father Armadeuso returned his gaze to Jake. "How did His power reveal itself?"

Jake paused, gathering his thoughts. He looked hard at the frail priest, gauging the strength of the man and his ability to see beyond his teachings. Despite his mocking, Jake sensed Vain had respect for the priest – why else would he bring Jake here? If a man who seemed to detest everything actually trusted someone like Father Armadeuso, maybe Jake should trust him also.

Maybe.

"One of the nephilim attacked us," said Jake hurriedly, the words tumbling out in a rush before he could change his mind. "I cried an ocean of tears while the world around us froze. My tears washed away the corruption surrounding the nephilim and revealed a Ugandan boy whom Abaddon had transformed."

Father Armadeuso's eyes widened. He turned his gaze to Vain who simply shrugged.

"I didn't see it," replied the assassin to the priest's unasked question. The old man nodded and turned back to face Jake, frowning, his eyes zeroing in on Jake's left cheek, focusing on the bloody teardrop.

"What does it mean?" Jake heard Father Armadeuso whisper.

Unsure whether the man referred to the situation or his birthmark, Jake reacted defensively. "If you don't believe me, the two brothers outside your door saw the whole thing. I can't explain it either, but it was incredible, like nothing I've ever seen before."

Father Armadeuso appeared to be coming to terms with something; Jake could almost see the cogs of the old man's mind at work. Under any other situation he might have grinned at the calamity shrouding the priest's face.

"So," said Jake finally, unable to resist any longer, "do you know what's wrong? Why can't I tap into this power all the time?"

"I think –"

The ceiling collapsed in an explosion of gray skin and thick muscle. At first, Jake thought it might be one of the nephilim, but this was much larger and much faster than one of Abaddon's creatures. Even Vain, with his almost supernatural reactions, seemed completely caught off guard as the huge creature tore through the roof, crashing squarely atop Father Armadeuso, pinning him to the floor with its feet. Saber-length claws decapitated the priest, a bloody spray spurting high.

Vain grabbed Jake and spun him away in the same instant as Tony and Mikey burst through the door and froze. Jake hadn't glimpsed much of the beast, but judging from the mute horror etched upon Tony's face, he didn't want to see any more.

"Get him out of here!" ordered Vain, thrusting Jake toward Tony. Twisting back to confront the beast, Vain kicked the door closed behind him, shutting them out.

"*No!*" screamed Jake, struggling to get loose from Tony's grip. Mikey joined in, and the brothers swiftly dragged Jake away, out of the building and onto the street. Deafening crashes shook the old priest's home. Whatever was happening inside, Vain wasn't giving up without a fight.

"We gotta go!" shouted Tony.

"I can't just let him die! I have the Staff, I can help… somehow."

"Vain has seen more shit than you can even begin to imagine. I don't think that thing's got enough in it to take him down unless he's gotten really soft in his old age."

Jake stopped struggling, realizing how ridiculous it would be for him to charge back inside.

"But... I have to do something," he pleaded.

"You can live," said Tony, grabbing his face with both hands and staring into his eyes. "That's why he's fighting that thing, to give you a chance to escape. Don't make it mean nothing."

Jake nodded, flicking his gaze back to the building, its roof partially collapsed, the cacophony of demolition still echoing from within.

"Let's go," he whispered.

The three turned and jogged swiftly up the street, away from the clamor – which slowly began drawing a crowd into the street. Once a safe distance from the building, all three slowed to a brisk stroll to avoid drawing attention, scanning for a cab as they went.

"Where are we going, boss?" asked Tony.

"We're heading back to America," replied Jake, regretting how wasteful this entire trip to Rome had actually been.

Tony and Mikey exchanged a look just as a taxi pulled around the corner and Jake hailed it.

"What are we gonna do back in the States?" asked Mikey hesitantly.

Jake looked at them both while the cab pulled up beside them. "I'm going to confront Abaddon and try to stop him. One way or another, this entire thing has to end; it's gone on far too long. I've wandered around blindly. I'm going to do what I should have done a long time ago – face him and do the best I can. There are no easy answers; there isn't a magical weapon I can use to stop him. This" – he indicated the Staff in his hand – "has some other purpose, something I'm yet to discover, but for now it's all up to me. If nothing else, this trip has shown me I need to be confident in myself. I just hope that's enough."

Jake opened the door to the cab and climbed in, thinking the doubt on the two brothers' faces mirrored what he felt in his own heart.

*-CHAPTER 12-*
# AN UNCOMFORTABLE ASSEMBLY

"Mister Hope. You need to come with us."

They'd only just exited through airport customs, and Jake stared at the two men in suits standing before him, Tony, and Mikey in the arrivals lounge of Dulles International Airport in Washington DC.

"Who the hell are you?" snapped Mikey.

Like mirror images, the two men smoothly pulled out and flipped open their badges and corresponding identifications.

"Agent Webster and Agent Foster from the FBI. You gentlemen need to stand aside; Mister Hope is coming with us."

"Bullsh –" began Mikey, but he was silenced by a movement from Jake, who had just noted four more men in suits edging into his field of vision.

"What seems to be the problem?" asked Jake, discretely passing the Staff to Tony who took it without comment.

"You need to come with us, sir," replied Agent Foster. "We'll explain it all down at the bureau." Handcuffs were out and ready in his left hand, his right resting close to where Jake imagined a gun holster might be kept hidden on his hip, beneath his dark-gray jacket.

"Okay," replied Jake, trying to calm the situation before things got out of hand. Turning to Tony and Mikey he said, "It's okay, guys. We'll meet up later on after I get this thing sorted out, alright?"

Jake's hands were pulled behind him, and the icy steel cuffs snapped into place around his wrists. Mikey was visibly angry about the whole thing, but Tony kept murmuring softly to him, his hand gently gripping his brother's arm – quietly reminding him not to do anything crazy. Jake gazed intently at them both, trying to convey what he was thinking. Tony nodded slightly, indicating he still held the Staff, and Jake hoped that meant he understood.

Abaddon had to be behind this, nothing else made sense.

Jake knew he should have seen something like this coming, but after the attempted attack on them in Rome by whatever that huge beast had been, he'd thought only of what he would do once they got back to the United States.

The main problem wasn't the fact Abaddon was immortal, nor was it the way he posed as the President and stood protected from virtually any imaginable threat. No, the problem was saving the man trapped behind the fallen angel's possession.

Jake had to keep reminding himself of that; behind the horrific machinations and manipulations of the former angel stood the President, an innocent man, who had been taken over for no other reason than to be used in the same way a puppeteer might pull on a marionette's strings. Even if Jake somehow stopped him, Abaddon would simply move on to someone else, and Jake would be left trying to explain why he'd tried to attack the President of the United States of America.

The FBI agents bustled him into the back of a black sedan, climbing into the front and swiftly pulling out into traffic. They didn't use sirens, but the agents were definitely in a hurry. Cars whizzed by on either side as Agent Foster calmly negotiated his way through the Washington DC traffic.

"Can you tell me something, Agent Webster? Did word come down from the President's office regarding me? Is that where you received your information from?"

Jake noticed the instant tension between the two agents. Foster – his eyes fixed on the road, his hands casually gripping the wheel – hurriedly glanced sideways at Webster.

"Why would you ask that, Mister Hope?" asked Agent Webster.

"Just a hunch. Something bad is going on in the White House, and you guys are caught up in the middle of it all." Jake chuckled to himself, imagining what these two agents would say if he told them what was going on in his life.

*Why not?*

The thought struck him like a casual comment overheard in a crowd, and he grinned, imagining their faces as he told them he was the new messiah. The idea stuck, however, and as he chewed it over in his mind it grew stronger and stronger. It seemed a very odd compulsion, especially since they were complete strangers, but Jake felt he should just go with it, abandon all common sense and blurt out what he was feeling to the two men likely speeding him toward his doom.

"Does the name Abaddon mean anything to you guys?" Jake asked conversationally, grinning and waiting for them to tell him he was talking nonsense.

Once again the two FBI agents exchanged a look, but for some reason this glance appeared slightly different to the earlier one.

"It's definitely him, then," said Foster. "You'd better do it now."

"What, in the car?" replied Agent Webster.

"We can't afford to take any chances."

"Excuse me guys, but what are you talking about?" asked Jake, suddenly uncomfortably aware how unlike a Federal car their transport actually appeared. There was no CB radio, no bizarre touch-screen GPS array like in the movies: none of the toys they always seemed to have. This car looked nice, clean, but disgustingly ordinary.

Jake's panic flared a moment before Agent Webster turned around in his seat, pointing the muzzle of the handgun directly toward Jake's chest.

"Nothing personal, Mister Hope, but we're backing the other side."

Jake glanced from the gun to the cruel look in Webster's eyes. "You guys aren't really FBI, are you?"

"Well, they said you were smart, but that's just incredible," Webster mocked sarcastically.

Foster laughed cruelly from the driver's seat. "What an idiot. Shoot this guy, already."

Webster pulled back the hammer on the revolver, the sound echoing ominously within the confines of the car. Jake kicked out, hoping to knock the gun from his hand, but Webster snatched it out of the way just in time, laughing at the near-miss before re-aiming once more.

Jake swallowed hard, his throat suddenly dry. Only a miracle could save him now.

And from the corner of his eye, he saw it hurtling toward them, crashing into the side of the sedan a fraction of a second later. Jake barely caught a glimpse of the other car's brown hood as his entire world tilted crazily and he was sent tumbling in the back of the overturned vehicle.

The entire car flipped sideways. Jake's handcuffs grew hot in an instant. A gunshot sounded, and Jake saw blood spray across the windshield as Foster's head sheered apart, impacted by the bullet from Webster's flailing revolver. The back of Jake's head crashed into something unyielding.

And the world went black.

***

"He... ar... ay?"

Jake heard the muted voice as if from a great distance, and he struggled up through the murk toward consciousness. Pushing aside the fog cottoning his brain, he opened his left eye and entered a world of pain. His right lid was sealed shut, and raising his hand up he felt congealing blood there before he lost all strength and his hand flopped back onto his lap.

He had a vague sense of being in motion, and it took him a few moments to realize he was once more in the back of a car – a different car.

"I asked if you're okay?" a familiar voice inquired.

Groggily, Jake turned his working eye with effort and saw Tony seated beside him, supporting him. Tilting his head slightly, Jake registered Mikey in the front passenger seat and another figure driving, someone whose profile also seemed somehow familiar....

"Aadesh?" croaked Jake.

"Yes, sir," replied the driver.

"What's going on?"

"Sorry, boss," Tony answered, "but there was no other way. This Aadesh guy turned up right after those guys took you, and he told me and Mikey they weren't really feds. By the time we caught up, that guy had pulled a gun on you and looked like he was about to shoot, all Aadesh could do was ram the car and hope you'd be okay."

"He is watched over by angels. He cannot die," said Aadesh.

"Yeah?" said Mikey. "Well those angels didn't stop his head going through the side window and almost getting squashed like a cantaloupe on the asphalt, did they? You almost killed him, you fu –"

"It's okay, Mikey," intervened Jake. "I'm okay… I think. My head just hurts a lot. Who were those guys?"

"They are supporters of Abaddon," replied Aadesh, suddenly swerving the wheel. "And it seems they do not give up easily."

Jake foggily remembered the other men in suits at the airport and realized what Aadesh referred to. Not only were Foster and Webster imposters, the other four suits were in on it too and, judging from Aadesh's current hazardous driving, they were now being pursued by those same mysterious men – followers of the Fallen.

"Do they know what Abaddon is, or do they think he's actually the President?" asked Jake.

"You can ask them if they catch us!" snapped Mikey.

"Good point," croaked Jake.

With what felt like a superhuman effort, Jake reached up with his right hand and peeled open his sealed eyelid, wincing as shards of pain shot through his already tortured brain. Once his eye was opened, however, Jake was able to see much better, and looked around wearily. Two cars darted between vehicles slightly behind them as Aadesh weaved through traffic on the freeway. The cars were almost identical to the one Foster and Webster had taken the handcuffed Jake in –

Hang on.

"Where are the handcuffs?" asked Jake.

"What handcuffs?" asked Tony. "You mean the ones they put on you? I thought they must have taken them off or something, 'cause you didn't have 'em on when Mikey dragged you clear of that car."

Jake probed his cloudy memory. "No, they were still on right up until...." Something flashed into his mind, and he recalled the intense warmth in his wrists just as the car had flipped... but then the memory slipped away.

Could he have done... *something*? Was there some way he'd instinctively tapped into his innate power? He remembered feeling the intense need to cover himself with his hands, and then the warming sensation had occurred....

Nope. The memory was gone again. Whatever had transpired, it must have happened right before his head crashed through the window. But the thought niggled at him, and something inside him just wouldn't let it rest. He needed to understand what had occurred with the handcuffs. There was some key piece of the immense puzzle surrounding his existence which he should have easily grasped, but his pounding head could hardly focus, and he had to put the problem aside for the time being. The answer to the riddle would have to wait for now; he just felt glad they were gone.

"Where are we heading?" Jake rasped, the inside of his throat feeling as though it had been hit with a belt-sander.

"I will take you to meet the rest of the followers," replied Aadesh, his voice seemingly calm despite the harrowing situation they were in, though his eyes kept flicking up nervously to check the rearview mirror. He seemed incredibly controlled, and Jake remembered the first time he'd met the –

Wait a minute.

"What followers are you talking about?"

Aadesh turned his head slightly. "Your followers, my Lord."

"Don't call me that," replied Jake reflexively. "How is it that I have followers? Apart from a few others, you guys are the only ones who know what's going on."

"I have gathered them for you, my... er...." Aadesh seemed unsure how to address Jake.

"We just call him boss," suggested Mikey.

"Okay... boss."

"How are you here, Aadesh? Is this another psychic thing?" asked Jake.

"Nothing of the sort. I have gathered people for your cause ever since we last met, and we have been awaiting your return. We have contacts in airport customs who notified me as soon as your plane landed. I hurried, but arrived just in time to see them remove you."

A violent impact jarred Jake to the left as they smashed into something on the driver's side of the car. He glanced out the rear window and saw one of the sedans pursuing them veer away slightly after the collision, but judging from the determined expressions on the men's faces, they weren't finished yet.

"Sorry, boss," said Aadesh evenly. "They were getting a bit too close."

"I'm not your boss," mumbled Jake, shaking his head and instantly regretting it. It felt like his brain was sitting in a vat of acid, and he'd just stirred it up. "Who are these people you've gathered, Aadesh?"

"They are good people, ones needing hope and guidance. They will provide a good base of followers for you."

"How many people are we talking about?" Jake asked, thinking there couldn't possibly be more than a dozen or so.

"I lost count at about four hundred and thirty," replied Aadesh calmly, swerving the car slightly. "I have been gathering them for several years – long before I first met you."

"Wow," said Mikey. "I guess you've got a fan club, boss."

"I guess so," muttered Jake, forgetting for the moment about the cars chasing them.

What the hell was he going to say to all those people? Jake had barely come to grips with his role in this entire convoluted mess, and now he was supposed to be some sort of deity-figure to a bunch of random strangers? He still recalled the massive lurching he'd felt inside when Aadesh had called him 'my Lord'; there was no way he was ready for any of that stuff.

It wasn't even true. Jake was just a man – he wasn't God or Jesus or anything! Sure, he'd done some things which defied explanation, but they might as well call him Harry Potter.

He could see it now; these people would have come expecting to meet some sort of divine being who would forgive their sins and heal the blind and lame. The cars clashed again, jolting him forward, but Jake hardly even noticed, so consumed was he by the prospect of what they were racing toward.

Part of him had known this point would be inevitable. Each time he'd spoken to someone and convinced them of his role in this world, he'd seen a look of hope mixed with disbelief in their expression. Would the people waiting for him be expecting some sort of circus sideshow, complete with walking on water and raising the dead?

He couldn't think about that right now.

*Then when?*

The world outside appeared to fade away. Jake slipped into an introspection so deep even his hearing seemed to shut down.

He'd stepped onto this treacherous path somewhat naively in the hope of doing something good in the world, but now things were beginning to mount up, and he began to feel the pressure more and more with each step he took toward his goal. All he wanted, all he hoped for, was to stop Abaddon, but so much more came attached to the mantle he had donned.

Like a 'fan club', as Mikey had so eloquently phrased it.

In some distant corner of his mind, Jake had always known he'd eventually have to go public with who he was, what he represented, but he'd hoped to deal with Abaddon first before having to worry about it. He'd been so focused on the job at hand and grappling with his own misgivings that he'd dismissed the issue of what the public at large might think of him when he finally divulged his identity – his *true* identity, whatever that meant.

It would be nice if he knew who he was before he had to explain it to anyone else.

And now they were racing away from people who wanted him dead, while speeding toward people who would, in all likelihood, want him to be God.

Which was more terrifying?

The car slid to the right as one of the pursuing vehicles smashed into the side panel yet again, and Jake snapped out of his reverie. Glancing at Tony beside him, Jake saw he was peering around behind them, his right hand clenching and unclenching as though yearning for some kind of weapon with which to defend them. In his left, he still clutched the Staff.

"Can I have that please, Tony?" croaked Jake, indicating the Staff.

Tony looked down at the Staff before passing it over to Jake. "Can you use it to stop these guys?"

"Maybe I should part the Red Sea and drown them behind us," snapped Jake, the lack of energy in his statement reducing its acidity.

"I – I didn't mean it like that," replied Tony.

"How did you mean it? Everyone expects me to fix everything, but I'm more lost than any of you guys."

"Sorry, boss."

"And stop calling me boss," grunted Jake.

He glanced beyond Tony, looking left out of the car window. A face mere feet from his own, in the car hurtling along beside them, contorted from a livid frown to a grin as the man drew a pistol from within his suit jacket.

Jake instinctively raised his hands to cover his face. In the same instant the gun went off, the bullet shattering the window beside Tony and showering him with glass. Time seemed to slow down all around Jake. With infinitesimal detail, Jake envisioned the bullet piercing the glass and spiraling through the air toward his face.

And then it slowed even more.

This wasn't the same slowing of time as when he'd tapped into his power on the boat to reverse the corruption of the nephilim – this was something different. Jake witnessed the bullet hitting the Staff in his hand, freezing in place, and then flinging backwards at the car pursuing them, hitting it in the side. The car flipped violently sideways through the air, crossing three lanes before crashing dramatically onto its roof.

Jake slowly lowered his hands, glancing through the rear window at their attackers' vehicle, lying on its crumpled roof, smoke drifting lazily from the hood. As he watched, two figures struggled through the shattered windshield and groggily stood. The second car screeched to a halt.

"What the hell...?" Jake murmured, staring at the Staff.

"How did you do that?" gasped Mikey incredulously.

"I'm not really sure." Jake glanced at Tony and shrugged. "I couldn't find a sea to part, I guess."

"Thanks, boss!" said Aadesh in his heavily accented English.

Tony stared at the demolished car falling further and further behind them. His laughter rose from a nervous giggle, gathering in strength as first Mikey, and then finally Aadesh, joined in

Jake remained mute, his brow creased as he stared at the unmarred wood of the Staff, powerfully aware he'd had no control over what just happened.

***

"H-hello… er… hello everyone," began Jake, the hall full of faces undulating like an immense ocean before him.

Chatter had ceased the moment he had stepped to the center of the small stage – his island – and all eyes stared, glared, peered, and leered at him, different expectations radiating from each gaze, and yet all of them here for the same thing:

To see the man claiming to be the new messiah.

He froze. Muttering ran through the crowd, and Jake suppressed a grimace. This was exactly how he'd feared it would be, with almost five hundred people crammed into the hall all waiting for the freak show to begin. He wiped his sweaty palms against the sides of his jeans.

"I… I suppose you're all wondering what we're doing here today." What the hell *were* they doing here today? What was Jake doing? "We're here to –"

"Can you speak up?" yelled someone toward the back of the crowd.

"Uh – yeah. Sorry." Jake cleared his throat. "I'm Jake Hope and – "

"Where's Jesus?" called out a rather large woman with bouffant-styled red hair near the front. "I came here to see Jesus."

"Well… that's kind of difficult to explain."

"The guy who looks like a Muslim told us Jesus had returned," shouted a balding man wearing thick glasses to her left. "Why are you here? Where's Jesus?"

"The world is made up of – of energy," began Jake tremulously, trying to remember Uriel's speech in Eden. "And this energy –"

"Is that a tattoo on your cheek?" called someone in the middle.

"Energy binds us all, and it has memories, and it... it...." Jake sighed. "The truth is... I don't really know the truth," admitted Jake. "I'm not Jesus – this I know for a fact, but I also know –"

"Can you cure my arthritis?" shouted a wizened, old woman almost directly in front of Jake. "I came here for a miracle; it hurts me to move. Can you cure me?"

"I can't cure you, but –"

"Then what good are ya? I'm here for my arthritis, not to hear some fool prattle on about energy. Is this some sort of con?"

A general murmuring of displeasure rumbled through the room, and Jake gritted his teeth in frustration. He hadn't thought it would be easy, but this was turning into a downright disaster! Several cell phones aimed at him, as terrifying as sniper-scopes, the holders no doubt recording this auspicious event to upload to the internet the very first chance they got.

*Look at the idiot who calls himself Jesus.*

"Folks!" called Jake as the murmuring increased in volume. "Please listen to me! I'm not Jesus – he was a man, just as I am, with a –"

"He was the son of God!"

Oh boy, here we go.

"Jesus was –" Jake began, but he got no further.

The deafening splintering of wood sounded from the side of the hall, and hundreds of heads spun around, the gathered mass screaming at the sight of the beast now glowering down at them. Jake's gaze snapped up, tracing the long, curved claws in dreaded recognition.

The same claws he'd last seen decapitating Father Armadeuso in Rome.

"GET OUT!" hollered Jake, pointing toward the side door furthest from the creature. The people needed no second urging, and the crowd surged toward the exit.

The beast appeared in no rush, however, largely ignoring the crowd, and Jake finally had a chance to examine it properly.

Crouched on all fours, its back still scraped the ceiling of the hall – and that was at least nine feet high! Thick, sinuous muscle rippled through broad shoulders and down long forelimbs as well as up through the neck. Its smoky gray hide, rather than fur or skin, seemed to be small, interlocking scales which shimmered slightly in the hall's receding sunlight. The last of his assembled 'followers' were finally escaping via the exit, but Jake saw several teenagers standing outside, hands pressed tightly against the windows, their cell phone-cameras aiming through the glass, still recording everything.

"You guys should go too," Jake admonished Tony, Mikey, and Aadesh.

"We ain't leaving you, boss," replied Tony. There was no negotiation in his voice.

"Then wait here," said Jake, wishing he hadn't left the Staff behind the hall. Despite his inability to control whatever power the ancient artifact possessed, it would have greatly increased his confidence to be gripping the Staff in his hands while facing such a monster. He stepped down from the stage toward the creature, which casually slashed at the timber floor, gouging the thick flooring while it waited for him.

"You cannot think to challenge it!" called Aadesh.

"I can't let it hurt these people,' replied Jake, indicating the onlookers still crowding outside.

"It is Behemoth," said Aadesh, fear evident in his voice. Jake noticed he used the word as though it were a name, not a title. "It cannot be stopped by any hand other than that of God."

Jake stared at the beast, its eyes like burning coals within the canine features. The face looked very much like that of a pit-bull, with the thickened and powerful jaw, its lips drawn back in a silent growl. Around its neck flicked a mane of stout, cord-like strands, each as thick as one of Jake's fingers. A long, chunky tail whipped out behind its muscular hind legs, and Jake thought he could discern sharp, razor-like ridges running down the length of it. He pictured what would happen if the tail, as wide as his leg, lashed into him, those ridges slicing through his skin....

And he pushed the image aside.

"It is Behemoth. It cannot be stopped by man, only God, you must believe this!" repeated Aadesh, as though this would make Jake understand him better.

In that moment, as if triggered by Aadesh's words, Jake once more felt a trickling sensation, a calm, cooling moment of absolute clarity piercing his mind, pushing aside his terror. Every smell in the room seemed magnified, every nuance of flickering light landed upon his lids with new definition.

Everything made sense in that one calm moment. Turning toward the windows, he grinned at the young men standing on the other side of the glass as though it were a shield, men who would glory in their bravery later when recounting this tale, showing their videos as proof of their daring. Differing from the other occasions Jake had tapped into his strange latent talent, this time the outside world carried on, not slowed at all by what was happening. As he moved toward Behemoth, he could sense everyone – the two brothers, Aadesh, and the twenty or so people outside the building staring through the windows – still moving at a normal pace, watching his actions with perfect clarity. But Jake no longer cared.

Tilting his head back, Jake stared at the colossal creature towering before him and felt no fear. The snout of the creature snorted, a plume of spray erupting in a show of domination, but Jake knew if this beast wanted to kill him, he'd be dead already. Behemoth was not like the nephilim, not something created by the evil of Abaddon. It was something else entirely: almost pure in its raw power, and as such Jake realized Aadesh was entirely correct in what he'd said. Jake would never be able to defeat a creature such as this with strength, not even if he funneled all the energy of the universe through his mortal frame and hurled it against the beast. Such an act would be futile; Behemoth stood beyond mere energy.

He grinned at the creature, sensing its uncertainty as he strolled calmly across the hall. Stepping up to the beast as though it were merely a puppy, he felt its fetid breath wash over him, putrid as ash. The immense claws, the same ones which had so easily slashed through Father Armadeuso's neck, twitched nervously, clattering against the wooden floor, but Jake's heart didn't tremble, his knees didn't shake. He raised his arm up and allowed Behemoth to sniff his knuckles, the way one would introduce himself to a strange dog. The beast snorted again, spraying Jake. Wiping his face clear, Jake chuckled softly.

*Hello*, he said silently, speaking through his thoughts in a way he'd never imagined possible, but which now seemed entirely logical.

*You talk?* The beast's thoughts came through as simplistic, but Jake sensed an immense intelligence behind the primitive words – it seemed more his comprehension of what Behemoth said which was flawed.

*Yes*, replied Jake. *Why do you attack us?*

*No choice. You enemy of he who have power over me. Me must fight.*

*But you are pure*, argued Jake. *How can he have captured you?*

Behemoth snorted once more, shaking its mane and rattling the cords. *He strong, and hold my brothers Leviathan and Ziz. If I not do as he say, they never be free.*

*But he'll never free them while you do as he says*, said Jake within his mind. *Can he destroy them?*

*No. Only One-God can do that. But he hurt them if I not obey.*

Jake paused, uncertain how to proceed. *Do you know who I am?*

*Your smell... familiar. Who you?*

*I am Jacob Hope.*

At the mention of his name, the beast flicked its fiery eyes to his left cheek and took a step back in shock. *Is it time already?*

Jake frowned, uncertainty slipping beyond the shield of his confidence. *What do you mean?*

*Time. You come at the end. The End of Days. Has it come?*

The question rocked Jake, and his calmness threatened to flee completely, but he grimly hung on to the vestiges of it, clawing it back, drawing it around himself once more like an immense cloak.

*I don't know about that, I'm just here to face Abaddon. But I'm not your enemy.*

*This I know*, replied the creature in the strange mind-speech. *You must live. I help you.*

Jake smiled, feeling the warmth of the expression glowing through him. *Right now all I need is to know that you won't try to harm us, but at another time I might need to call upon you. Can I rely on that?*

*I serve you now. You command me*, replied Behemoth. And then it did the strangest thing Jake could have imagined: the huge creature dropped its front legs down while keeping its hind ones straight…

… and bowed to him.

Without another thought, the beast turned and was gone. It was as if the air around Behemoth opened up and absorbed the creature, and in that instant the fabric of space around Jake shifted. His feeling of confidence dissolved like a balloon thrust upon a rapier-tip, leaving him once again ignorant as to how he'd managed to tap into such a power in the first place. The sense of loss left him feeling totally bereft, and he paused, barely controlling the urge to cry out in frustration.

Finally, he looked around. Tony, Mikey and Aadesh stood frozen, staring at him, awe evident in every fiber of their beings. Turning his attention to the windows surrounding the hall, he saw every gap was filled with faces pressed up against the glass, camera-phones still recording, nobody daring to move.

"Well… that went well," said Jake dazedly to the trio still standing on the stage.

"Whoa," muttered Mikey. "How – how in the world… how did you do that?"

"I wish I knew. What did it look like?"

"You just seemed to stand there, face to face with that thing, and then it sniffed your hand like a puppy," replied Tony. "Did that thing *bow* to you?"

"I think so."

Tony looked at the crowded windows and the cameras. "Well, I guess the world's gonna know all about you soon. It might not be what Achmed had planned –"

"My name is Aadesh."

"– but I think it worked out in the end."

Jake glanced at Aadesh, seeing the Indian man looking the most unsettled. He was used to Aadesh seeming so controlled and composed through almost any situation. It made Jake pause.

"Is everything okay, Aadesh?"

"I always knew – I knew you would one day arrive. That day I saved you was one filled with conflict for me. I felt sure you were the one I had waited for all my life, but at the same time my self-doubt and human nature conflicted with me and made me disbelieve what I knew to be true. I have just seen a man compel a beast created through God's own strength to bow down before him. You truly are the one I have waited for my whole life, and now I fear what will come next."

"What do you mean?" asked Jake.

"I have striven for years to reach this point – this exact moment – and never looked beyond it. Now we are stepping beyond it, and I find myself heading toward an uncertain future with dread in my heart. Such a future leaves me uncertain, and uncertain people are apt to do foolish things – such as gathering an audience of people who want something you are not, and for that I am truly sorry."

Jake shook the mistake away; that was the least of his worries right now. "So what do we do?" he asked.

Aadesh appeared hesitant for a moment, and then his confidence seemed to return, sliding like a veil over his countenance. "We continue on, regardless of the outcome."

"That's what I thought you were going to say." Jake looked around at Mikey and Tony, motioning them closer, still painfully aware of the faces and cameras outside the windows. "We need to find out where the President is going to be in the next few weeks."

Aadesh raised a querying eyebrow.

"Abaddon has possessed the President," explained Jake.

"I thought a guru like you would already know that," mocked Mikey.

Aadesh ignored the taunt. "I heard that your president most recently visited Los Angeles, but I think he will return to Washington DC in a week."

"Okay, then, we've got a week to prepare."

"Prepare for what, boss?" asked Tony.

"We're going to confront Abaddon," said Jake, amazed at how calm his voice sounded compared to the thundering of his heart. "And if everything goes to hell, we need to be ready for a war."

The three men on the stage stared at Jake, and then at each other, finally returning their gazes to Jake again.

"Oh dear," muttered Aadesh.

"You got that right, Abdul," said Mikey.

"My name is Aadesh."

"Hey, boss, whaddya mean we're gonna go to war? Not literally, right?" asked Mikey.

Jake nodded somberly. "We have no other choice if it comes right down to it. I'm going to confront Abaddon. I need to stop him becoming any more powerful than he already is. And that may mean war."

"But how will you fight a war?" asked Tony. "We ain't got no army or nothing."

"We'll have an army if we need one. Isn't that right, Michael?"

As though he'd merely been waiting in the next room, Michael suddenly blinked into existence. There was no puff of smoke, no theatrics. Simply one moment the archangel wasn't there, and the next he was, still dressed in his casual street clothes, his one blind eye staring out milky-white within the scar splitting his dark-skinned face.

"It would be preferable if such a battle could be avoided," said Michael conversationally, idly fingering his scar as though recollecting the clash which had disfigured him. "But yes, you will have support if it is required."

"What other option is there?" asked Jake. "In the space of a few months, Abaddon's plans have accelerated dramatically. I have to follow my instincts, and they're telling me to confront Abaddon, for good or ill."

Michael shrugged. "I am limited in what information I can relay to you. Just remember how your actions have already fashioned events in such a way as to bring us to this point."

"What do you mean?" asked Jake, his brow creased. "Are you saying I *shouldn't* do this?"

"Not at all, but such decisions should not be made simply because you cannot find another solution. You need to be absolutely sure of what you're doing; such a choice will hold repercussions for all of us, not just for humanity."

Jake remained silent for a moment, searching through his feelings and thoughts. Whenever he came to one thought, his heart seemed to leap. He studied the emotion, trying the rationalize it, but no matter how he looked at it he came back to the same conclusion:

There was no other option; he had to face Abaddon.

It had been a wild and crazy road to this point, but Jake suspected he knew why things had happened in such a way. If he'd simply rushed ahead and fought Abaddon, he would have been annihilated by an enemy who considered him a mere annoyance.

But now Jake knew he was more than that. He might not have a clue how to control the powers he wielded, but his confidence was growing, and he no longer felt like a naive little farm boy stepping out in the big city for the first time. He'd seen and done things no one on the face of the planet could even dream of doing, and he now needed to step up for his greatest challenge. He was going to kill Abaddon.

All he had to figure out was how.

Jake had a sneaky suspicion this wasn't going to be resolved with rivers of tears or conversations within his mind. No, this had the feel of something far more ominous, and he wanted the support of Michael. Jake had acquired the aid of Behemoth through dumb luck, to call on if needed, but he felt unsure of its allegiance, even after its show of submission. Something about what it had said of its brothers' captivity left Jake hoping he wouldn't need to test the strength of their tenuous alliance.

"I will avoid a war if at all possible," Jake finally said to Michael, "but if it comes down to it, I need you there to help us, along with the cherubim – if any are left after the massacre in the Garden."

Michael nodded somberly, giving away nothing of his thoughts. "There are more cherubim we can call upon if needed, along with other forces, but such a war will likely see this world turned to ash. Humanity will never survive such a clash, but if you fail in all else, or if you die, Heaven's forces will once again wage war in this realm. Are you absolutely certain you wish to travel down a path that might lead to such a conclusion? There can be no turning back."

Jake blinked heavily, his mouth running completely dry. He glanced at Tony and Mikey, seeing his own thoughts and fears mirrored on their faces. Up until this point the culmination of all his endeavors had seemed almost entirely theoretical, but with Michael's words the finality of the situation was hammered home. If Jake pressed this and things went awry, chances were every single person in the world would die, and it would be entirely his fault.

But what choice did he have?

There was always another choice, but whichever one Jake made, he would have to see it through to the very end, for good or ill. The confidence he'd experienced a moment before in his communication with Behemoth now seemed like something from a fairy tale, and he wanted nothing more than to leave these problems for someone else to figure out.

"We have to do this," said Jake, shaking his head stubbornly. "I'm sick of wasting time. We're going to find the President and stop Abaddon before he does to America what he did in Uganda. Can you imagine those atrocities taking place here? No. I have to put a stop to this now."

"But how?" asked Tony.

"I'm not sure yet," replied Jake, still painfully aware of the people with cameras in the windows, glad their video couldn't capture the uncertainty of his words. "But I have to trust my feelings on this, and they're telling me to hit Abaddon head-on, rather than screwing around anymore."

Jake thought he saw Michael's expression flicker, but he was turning away and couldn't tell if he seemed pleased or astounded at his decision. When he glanced back, the look had disappeared.

"Can you get us out of here, Michael?" he asked.

The archangel bowed his head slightly in acknowledgement of the request. "Are you ready?"

Jake looked around at the people in the windows before nodding. As Michael gathered them close, Jake had a fleeting moment where he wondered what the world would make of the videos about to emerge showing a man facing down a demonic beast, then disappearing into thin air.

What would the world's population make of their supposed messiah?

One last, fleeting glimpse of the cameras in the windows, and then he felt himself dragged away by Michael's power. Whatever happened from now on, Jake was definitely no longer going to be a secret.

-CHAPTER 13-
# THE PRESIDENT

Jake stood on the pavement amid the horde, self-consciously pulling the edges of his hoodie tighter around his face, adjusting his sunglasses for the umpteenth time, intensely paranoid someone might recognize him. The whole incident with Behemoth had swamped the internet, taking mere hours to go viral, and news programs had swiftly picked up on the story of the mysterious blond man with a bloody teardrop who had calmed the monster. The whole world now knew his face.

What a mess. If he weren't so preoccupied with what needed to be done, Jake might have found the entire situation amusing. Theories were exploding globally regarding what had occurred, everyone from theologians to basement crackpots weighing in with their own opinions about who Jake might be and what had actually happened. Some came scarily close to the truth, while others were wildly off the mark – speculating he was some sort of alien, here to take over the planet in the guise of a human being. But Jake didn't have time for any of that.

Michael had promptly disappeared without comment after transporting them away from the hall. The week of preparation had ended up consisting of Jake predominantly hiding out in a run-down motel in Washington while the others ran around doing menial errands. What else could they do, buy rocket launchers?

And now, today was the day, the day where Jake would ensure mankind's survival or demise. He swallowed heavily at the thought.

Jake had told Tony, Mikey, and Aadesh to spread themselves out in the crowd, a crowd made up of fans and protestors alike. A horrible feeling sat in his gut, like a bloated toad belching noxious wisdom. If they were all seen together it might spark some kind of recognition.

So now he waited alone.

Within the crowd, Jake felt a momentary sense of panic. His blood thundered in his temples, and he realized this must be how it would feel waiting for an assassination target. What he was doing – or at least trying to do – was theoretically different to what an assassin might attempt, and yet the setup proved the same. His clammy hands gripped the Staff tightly, and he struggled to calm his pulse. Thinking about it simply made things worse.

Jake's mind weighed heavily on the problem, so much so, that he almost missed the rising excitement as the man he'd been waiting for appeared. The crowd around Jake surged forward, leaning over the steel barriers erected along the roadside to keep the people back. He stepped forward with them, shouldering his way to the front.

They had come to see a man; Jake had come here for something else.

Glancing nervously at the Secret Service agents placed among the regular police along the roadside – their reflective sunglasses making them look more like terminators than men and women – he once more tightened his grip on the Staff, calling to it for strength. None came. He felt certain the agents would be able to hear his heart hammering and recognize the sheen of sweat upon his brow despite the chilly air. Every glance seemed to pierce through the shroud of his hoodie, every touch felt like the cuffs that would steal his freedom.

As the presidential vehicle rounded the corner, Jake self-consciously pulled his hoodie closer around his face once more. He realized he was holding his breath and exhaled, sucking in a huge gasp at the same time as the vehicle stopped. Two agents moved to the rear door, opening it for the man who led the free world. But this wasn't truly a man; Jake knew it was something else entirely.

The calm he'd been hoping for hadn't emerged yet; the confidence still concealed itself from him. Jake began to breathe shallowly, panic threatening to overtake him. He grappled with the Staff, his hands slick with sweat.

What the hell was he doing?

Dread consumed Jake's mind as the President strolled down the line of spectators pressed against the barriers, Secret Service agents glowering from behind their reflective glasses at the crowd. Jake wondered if they had already been tainted by the power of Abaddon. He couldn't detect the miasmic aura of corruption around the form of the President, but Abaddon had already shown he could disguise himself.

If he were cloaked, he must be expecting Jake.

Perhaps this was all some sort of trap, a way of luring Jake out and capturing him. Every set of eyes in the crowd seemed to be boring into him, and he felt exposed before them all. The intense desire to flee as swiftly as he could became close to overwhelming.

Nobody would know what he was doing here; they'd feel certain he was trying to attack the President. They'd attempt to stop him, maybe even try to kill him.

*What then?* thought Jake.

He'd be faced with the choice of hurting innocent people or being taken down, probably thrown into an asylum if they didn't blow his brains out. Then he remembered the videos circulating the internet....

Nope, no asylum, then.

He'd be taken and dissected piece by piece – either anatomically or psychologically – and he'd be left broken, a husk.

But that was only if Armageddon didn't arrive before they sharpened their scalpels. Michael had sworn the next war would obliterate mankind. If Jake failed here today, every person on the face of the planet was going to die.

The President loomed closer, strolling casually down the line, shaking hands and kissing babies. This was a press moment: designed for the papers to show the leader of the country as a man of the people, riding the euphoria of his recent election win.

Jake frowned. Abaddon would surely be more concerned with his own plans than being here.

Wouldn't he?

There was no time to follow the thought. As the President stepped close to him, Jake thrust out his right hand, clutching the Staff in his left like a club. This was not a conscious action on Jake's behalf, more a chance circumstance, but it almost sealed his fate.

His right hand snaked out, grasping a hold of the President's bicep. The Secret Service agents reacted instantly. Indistinct shouting rose behind Jake. The outside world closed off, becoming bogged-down and slow. Jake and the President fixed gazes.

The President gaped at Jake in shock, and Jake unconsciously brought up the Staff before freezing. This was not right, not at all. Something was intensely wrong with this entire situation. What was he doing?

"You're not Abaddon!" gasped Jake.

"Who are you?" asked the President.

In a whirlwind of confusion, the world turned. The scene outside their bubble remained frozen; the grip of Jake's hand contracted against his will, and their gazes locked even tighter. The President's pupils became tunnels, yawning wide like the mouth of a great whale, and power flickered between them like bolts of electricity. Jake couldn't be sure if the energy drew from within him or the Staff, but the result remained the same.

Jake fell, but not to the ground. He tumbled end over end into the President's consciousness, just as he sensed the President falling into his. Their minds merged, becoming one, similar to Jake's connection with Behemoth, but much more intense. In an instant, Jake saw everything, every single action, every word, every breath, which had shaped the President's life up until this point. At the same time, like a secondary display of his consciousness, Jake knew the President was experiencing his past.

The two men remained locked within this bubble of time, frozen in each other's memories. The situation endured for only a second, but it was a second which lasted an eternity. In that moment, so many things tumbled into place for Jake, but among the answers rose a myriad of new puzzles, things he needed to push aside for the time being while he dissimilated the most important fact this grand vision imparted.

This was indeed a trap set by Abaddon, but not in the way Jake had initially imagined. The fallen angel had played Jake for a fool, orchestrating the illusion on the television in order to lure him here, drawing Jake into an attempted attack on the President – a feat he had almost accomplished, and one which would have seen him seal his own doom. No, this was indeed the real, untainted president, but for Abaddon to have known when to spring the illusion on Jake he must have been close.

Tony's men had crashed into the hotel room right after Jake saw the footage of a corrupted president. They'd known he was there.

Jake dropped his hand, and the connection instantly snapped, the bubble shattering, the rest of the world closing in, crashing upon them forcefully like a resurging wave. Screams sounded and people fled from Jake as the Secret Service agents drew their guns, roaring at Jake to drop his weapon: the Staff.

"Lower your guns!" ordered the President, his voice steady, his gaze still locked with Jake's. The President's expression was one of awe. The Secret Service men hesitated, but realizing Jake no longer presented a direct threat, they reluctantly complied.

"This man is coming with us."

"But Mr. President –"

"Let him through. *Now*." There was no compromise in the President's tone, no chance for argument. Police moved to separate the barriers.

"I need my friends," said Jake, finding his voice with difficulty.

"We're here, boss!" shouted Tony, pushing through the crowd, which no longer fled, instead staring at the events occurring before them. Aadesh appeared a second later.

Jake waited, staring around in hope.

"Where's Mikey?" asked Tony, finally realizing his brother had not yet re-emerged.

Jake swallowed back his sorrow, accepting in that moment what he already knew. "Mikey's gone, Tony," he said softly. "I'll explain it all on the way."

"What do you mean? Hey, Mikey, quit foolin'," he called into the crowd. "MIKEY!"

People peered around, waiting for someone to emerge from their number.

Nobody appeared.

Tony's brow creased, and Jake could see he was close to panic. He gripped the older brother's shoulder, but Tony remained silent. Jake could see he still didn't fully grasp what had happened, and he dreaded telling him.

How was he supposed to explain that the man's brother might have already lost his soul?

\*\*\*

"I am unsure of your intentions, young man," began the President, sitting opposite Jake in the back of the presidential limousine – a stretched black Cadillac. "Just as I am unsure of what happened when you grabbed hold of me back there. But I saw things in that moment, and they disturbed me immeasurably. Why don't you try to put into words what just flashed through my mind?"

Tony and Aadesh had been escorted into the back of another car driving in front of them. Jake sat alone with this heavy task. He let out a heavy sigh and stared at the Staff in his hands, searching the stained wood for some sort of inspiration, but finding nothing. How could he tell this man what was going on if he didn't fully understand it himself?

He launched into his tale, leaving nothing out. Every scrap of information from the beginning of his journey – the perils he'd fumbled through – came flowing out of Jake like a confession.

A strange lightening of his burden seemed to occur as he told his story. This was the one person he *could* say everything to, because this man had already glimpsed it through the merging of their minds. The President wouldn't be able to disbelieve him or think he was crazy, because he had relived those memories in the moment they'd touched, just as Jake knew every secret the President kept hidden within the vault of his mind. And there were indeed many things hidden by the man who governed the most powerful land in the free world, both good things and gray, but Jake had received the impression of a man struggling to do what was right against what was often a mountain of immorality. Deep in his core, Jake knew he could trust him.

Jake's tale stretched startlingly long, and at the close of it he found himself marveling that such things could have happened in such a short space of time. It seemed the President agreed with this silent sentiment, and Jake could see the man struggling to come to terms with what he now knew; not only with who Jake was, but also the notion of Abaddon's evil lurking within the country the President had sworn to protect.

"What can I do to help?" inquired the President finally.

The words came as a surprise, despite what Jake had seen in the President's mind. The man had been through much in his life and held a core of steel, but politics had worn away at that steel, causing the President to often discover himself at odds with his own beliefs. Jake's dilemma, however, stood beyond such things, and the man had made up his mind swiftly.

Jake now had a very powerful ally indeed; Abaddon's plan had apparently backfired.

At least that's what Jake hoped.

Perhaps the Fallen, having suffered for eons, planned beyond mere chess moves. Maybe Abaddon had incorporated this possibility into his strategy, the two men now simply slipping their necks into a greater noose.

"We need to prepare the country for what's coming – whatever that is," said Jake. "I'm not sure what Abaddon's planning, but you can be confident he'll have some scheme ready to spring into action once – well – once he's gotten rid of me."

"You? Why would that be so important? Surely he could implement his plans around you, especially if he's been with you the entire time in the body of this Mikey character."

Jake grimaced. Hearing the words out loud felt like a sledgehammer to his guts. It shouldn't have made it any more real, but somehow it did, and Jake felt the full sting of the betrayal. Mikey might not be in control of his body, but Jake still felt like an idiot. The end result would be an innocent man manipulated like a puppet.

What would he tell Tony?

Ignoring the issue for the moment, Jake raised his gaze to look at the President once more. "I'm not sure why Abaddon's waiting. In my mind it would make more sense to start building his armies. He's definitely got enough fruit from the Garden, and I'm sure he'd be able to find enough people... unless...."

"Unless what?"

"He knows I can transform the nephilim back to their human form; I did it on the boat. Granted, I have no real idea how I did it, but there's a chance I'll be able to tap into that power once more if the conditions are right. Abaddon only has a limited amount of fruit from the Garden, and I doubt he'll be able to restock – at least not in a hurry. He probably wants me out of the way just in case I can destroy his army in the same way I stopped that single nephilim. The chances are slim, but a sliver of doubt might be enough to warrant his hesitation. And then there's this." Jake held out the Staff. "I don't think Abaddon knows what this thing can do any more than I do. Maybe he's scared of it."

The President sat back in his chair, his expression thoughtful. Rubbing his chin slightly, he peered at Jake, his gaze piercing. "I think you're right," he finally said. "Which means my role is to see that you remain safe until we can find him and deal with him."

"You can't deal with him," replied Jake. "Only I can do that. It's what I'm here for."

"I think you're here for much more than that," murmured the President, his unfathomable expression reminding Jake how this man had seen into almost every corner of his mind. "This is the first step, and you need to focus completely on it before you worry about anything else, but don't fool yourself into believing this is the only issue at hand. I think I may have seen more when you grabbed me than you realize. I may know pieces of you that perhaps even you don't know about, but we'll discuss all that at a later date – after you've dealt with Abaddon."

Jake smiled humorlessly. "Don't you mean *if* I deal with Abaddon?"

"No," said the President, leaning forward and staring directly into Jake's eyes. "Because I've seen what will happen if you fail."

"This sucks," muttered Jake. "I bet Jesus didn't have these problems."

"You mustn't have read much of the Bible."

"Why is that?"

"Jesus went through all sorts of trials before his final one," said the President, "and you are facing but one. If I'm correct it will be the first of many, and probably far from the hardest."

"Well, you're just a bucket full of smiles, aren't you?"

The President burst out laughing, the sound reverberating through the back of the limousine, and Jake smiled despite his anxiety.

"You know my grandfather used to say that exact same thing," said the President, wiping his right eye.

"I know," replied Jake.

The President's humor drifted away. "That's right. You do know, don't you? What about the rest of me, do you know as much about me as I think I know about you?"

"Probably more," admitted Jake.

"You realize what an incredible security risk this is, don't you?"

"Feel free to lock me up," said Jake, exasperated. "I could use the break. Good luck with Abaddon, though."

"Hmm. Excellent point," admitted the President. "Now who are these other two with you?"

"You must know already."

The President shrugged. "You know as well as me that some of the details are foggy. I remember Tony is related to the guy who's gone missing – brothers, aren't they?"

Jake nodded.

"But I don't really know who the other one is; it's like something's clouding the memory."

"He's a bit of an enigma," said Jake. "His name is Aadesh, and I met him in Pakistan – it seems like a lifetime ago now. He saved my life when some militant extremists were going to execute me. It was Aadesh who first told me who – or what – I am."

"But how did he know?"

"Hence the enigmatic part; I really don't know. He said God had told him in a dream when he was five, and the moment he saw me he knew I was the... well... you know. He called me the One. He also referred to me as the Christ and got upset when I thought he meant Jesus. He made a very big point of telling me he meant something completely different than the man, that I was more like a beacon, not a clone. Am I making any sense?"

The President nodded. "Yes. It links the fragmented images together within my mind, and I now understand what they mean. Well, kind of, at least." The President stared out his side window for a moment, finally turning back to Jake. "Do you realize how utterly unbelievable all of this is?"

"You're kidding me, right?" said Jake, aware of the familiarity he now felt with statesman. The joining had brought them closer than brothers, and he felt a kind of symbiosis, much like identical twins supposedly had.

The President reached over and poured a glass of scotch on ice which he offered to Jake. "I know you don't drink much, but figured this might be one of those rare occasions."

Jake grinned and accepted the glass, taking a sip. "That's nice." He sighed heavily. "What the hell am I going to do now?"

"You know I can't answer that for you," said the President, settling back in his seat with his own drink.

"Yeah, I know. But sometimes I really just wish someone else had been chosen to do this."

The President nodded. "Me too."

"You? But you campaigned for your role."

"That doesn't mean it's any easier, simply because I *wanted* to do it. And don't forget you've been searching your entire life for something meaningful, some way to make a difference in the world. Now's your chance. I'm probably the only person with any inkling of what you're going through, Jake, and I feel for you, I truly do. But you have responsibilities which set you apart from the common man, and you don't have the luxury of being able to sit back and whine about their unfairness. Get over it, and get on with the job."

"I know you're right," agreed Jake, "but I'm following in the footsteps of someone who changed the world, you know?"

The President raised an eyebrow. "I know exactly what you mean. All you can do is push forward and use your best judgment as each situation arises. From what I can tell you've done alright so far."

"How do you figure that?"

"Because you're still alive," replied the President, taking a sip of his scotch. "The crap you've gone through, you've probably been too busy staying alive to truly appreciate it, but that's some serious shit, Jake. I mean, we're not dealing with the average, run-of-the-mill situations here, are we? And you're still breathing, so you must be doing something right. Self-doubt is normal; you're only human after all." He grinned lopsidedly.

Jake chuckled, feeling the warmth of the alcohol slipping through his body.

The President chuckled. "If you think that's scary, you should try explaining the budget to Congress."

Jake's laughter filled the back of the limousine. "Okay, I'll give you that one."

And in that moment, as their laughter filled the bomb-proof Cadillac, two of the most important people on the planet became mere men once more.

***

The White House proved much larger than Jake had expected, and they were ushered into the Oval Office with little preamble. Soon he, Tony, and Aadesh were seated on the President's side of the Resolute Desk, potentially the most famous desk in the world. The antique ship's timbers had seen many of the world's most important decisions since being given to President Rutherford B. Hayes by Queen Victoria, way back in 1880.

Along the way to the Oval Office, Jake had explained to Tony what he suspected had happened with Mikey. He was surprised by

Tony's reaction – or rather, his lack of one. There had been no shrieks of denial, no demands to go rescue his brother. Tony had obviously been shocked, but he'd pushed it aside with a visible effort and simply nodded, accepting the fact, though not before turning away from Jake and the President to conceal the emotion brimming in his eyes.

Several very official-looking individuals swiftly attended the Oval Office, and soon there were eight other people standing or sitting opposite them. Quick introductions were thrown around, but Jake felt too flummoxed to really take any of it in. The President briefed everybody in the room, leaving out certain awkward points – such as the mental joining between him and Jake. When he stated who Jake was, surprise turned to scoffing disbelief, and several voices grew louder in argument, but the President waved them all to silence, promising to fill them in on the details at a later time.

"Now," began the President, talking to Jake this time, his tone business-like, not at all like when they had been in the car. "What are your plans? I know you have nothing definite, but is there anything you have in mind?"

Jake shook his head, glancing at the Staff in his hands as though it might answer for him. "We need to stop Abaddon, but right now I have no idea where he might be or how to find him. We know he's been hiding in Mikey's body up until now, but he could be anywhere – indeed, he could be *anyone*."

"Gentlemen," the President addressed the men arrayed opposite them. "What can we do to help Mister Hope achieve what he requires?"

"Mister President," said one of the suited men, his bald head speckled with liver-spots, flaring out against his wrinkled and pale skin, "I mean no disrespect in this, but is this some sort of joke?" A general murmuring of agreement from the others followed.

The President grimaced. "I had thought my own National Security Council would have faith in me, but since there seems some doubt about my credibility, I invite you to watch the latest viral video on the internet."

A few keystrokes and the President spun his computer monitor around for them all to see. Shining brightly on the screen flickered obviously amateur footage, showing Jake and Behemoth at the hall, its running commentary including a lot of background noise, swearing, and unanswered questions uttered by the holder of the camera. The entire episode lasted barely a few minutes, but even Jake felt awed by the show. He glanced around at the National Security Council members and saw several jaws gaping in amazement. Others appeared to have seen the footage already, but hadn't realized it starred Jake, and they shot querying glances between his face and the screen, as if to verify what they were seeing. The image of his birthmark shone clearly at several points in the video; there was no disputing it was him.

When the video finished, silence filled the room, a stillness the President let grow until the council members shifted uncertainly. Finally, the man with the liver spots spoke up.

"How do we know that's real?" he asked. "I mean, it might be fake; we should have it tested."

"There are at least a dozen more like it online from many different cameras," said the President calmly, glaring at the man, daring him to continue disbelieving.

Jake could tell from most of the expressions around the room that they'd been convinced by both the President's word and the video evidence, but liver spots wasn't finished yet, even though he couldn't meet the President's icy glare.

"This is just all so inconceivable –"

"You really are a dumbass sometimes, Joe," cut in the President. "I mean, you're my Director of National Intelligence, and yet you stand here showing very little intelligence. Think of Jake as a foreign ambassador if you have to, but we don't have time to get caught up in petty atheism or superstition. I don't know how this is happening, but it's happening, and we need to prepare. No committees we set up will come up with answers in time, no policies we put in place will help us against the threat we now face. Whether this is the first step on the road to Armageddon is uncertain" – he flicked a glance over, and Jake knew the President held no such uncertainty – "but what we do know, is that a very real alien threat has invaded our land, and the only one who can oppose it is the man sitting beside me. We need to do everything at our disposal to help him or else an epic scourge might cripple our populace. I come to you in open honesty with the hopes you will all aid us in cutting through some of the bullshit we'll have to endure in Congress. Understood?"

There was a general murmuring of agreement, and Jake noticed the director nodding dully, as though his head were being jerked by a piece of string.

"All right. Now what assistance can we provide for Jake?"

Several suggestions were forwarded and rejected until liver spots finally spoke up. "I think the first thing we need to do is locate this individual, this *Abaddon*." He said it as though the name were acid upon his tongue. "And then ascertain his true strength. You have described his followers, the *nephilim*, and their supposed supernatural powers, but we know nothing of their numbers, nor do we have a location of their assemblage point. If he is gathering a veritable army, he must have a base with which to keep them hidden; they can't simply blend in with society."

"Welcome back, Joe," said the President warmly, and liver spots grinned fragilely, as though afraid the grin might break his face at any moment. "Alright, let's get to it, people. I want full intel of this issue on my desk ASAP. Let's use Homeland Security, the CIA, FBI – hell, let's incorporate the girl scouts if we can. Tell them we've received information of a possible terrorist strike or something, you all know the drill. Everyone got that?"

Once again there was a murmuring of acknowledgement, and the Council began to file out of the Oval Office. Finally all others had gone, leaving only the Director of National Intelligence.

"What is it, Joe?" asked the President.

"Are you really him?" asked the director, his voice awed as he stared at Jake. "Are you really Christ reborn?"

Jake paused, his natural instincts pushing him to shake off the reference or dull down his association with the new messiah.

"Yes. Yes, I am," he said softly.

A mountain of doubt suddenly lifted from Jake's shoulders. In acknowledging his legacy, it seemed he had eased his uncertainty. Not totally, of course. There were still too many unknowns lurking for Jake to hold any sort of confidence about his role, but in this he felt slightly more comfortable. It was a title, a name he went by, much like when he was a senior advisor for the United Nations. And just like then, he had a job to do – some might claim it an insurmountable task, but complaining wouldn't change the fact that the task was his and his alone. Running from it would accomplish nothing, because it was part of what he was, and no one can run from their true self – not for long, anyway.

The director swallowed heavily, dropping to his knees before Jake. Jake instinctively leaped out of his chair, thinking the man had fainted, only realizing an instant later that the director was genuflecting. Uncomfortable with such reverence, Jake bent and raised him back to his feet.

"Don't kneel to me, Joe," said Jake adamantly. "I'm not Jesus, I'm not your God; I'm just a guy. I've got stuff to do, and I need your help, but I'm not here to be worshipped."

The director nodded, but Jake could tell by the way the man refused to meet his stare that he wasn't convinced. The director swiftly scurried from the room before Jake could say anything else.

"You'd better get used to it, Jake," said the President. "These people are going to think you're God, whether you like it or not."

"But that's not right! I'm not a god, and I'm certainly not *their* God!"

"That's not the point," said the President. "You're filling the role of someone incredible from history, a man who pretty much changed the entire world. They're going to expect you to be all-knowing and all-powerful."

"That is foolish," interjected Aadesh, surprising everyone. "The role of the Christ is not to supersede the One God; he is the absolute servant of God in the realm of man. To say otherwise is blasphemy."

A sudden understanding bloomed within Jake. "But it's also human nature to need something tangible to worship," he said. "Maybe Jesus never intended to be seen as God. Maybe he just wanted to help people, to spread a message of peace and harmony, but the memories and words of people have warped what he truly was. It's much harder to believe in a deity you can't see than to worship a man with the powers of a god."

"What are you saying?" asked Tony. "Jesus wasn't the son of God?"

"That depends on your interpretation of God," said Jake, the memories of the Man's almost chant-like Bible recitations resonating within him like the echoes of a scream. "If you think God's a wizened old man who stepped down from Heaven to impregnate Mary, then no, I don't think Jesus was his son. But if you think God is the universe, that every speck of dust throughout the cosmos is God, every piece of floating energy and every hint of physicality, then yes, of course Jesus was the son of God. We all are. Every one of us is a child of the universe, born of the power of the universe, and as such we are all children of God. Jesus understood this. Unfortunately, the people of his time had no comprehension of what the universe was, and as such they translated his words literally."

Doubt flared within Jake as he realized what he was saying. Was this merely his own rebellion against the beliefs of the Man, or did he truly trust the words he now said? Searching within his heart, Jake realized the talons of the Man had slipped slightly, and even though they were very much still there, they no longer controlled him in the way they once had.

"I have no doubt Jesus said he was the son of God, but the people listening took him literally, creating an idol where there was only ever a man. The power Jesus displayed was not his own, just as the power I have doesn't come from me: it comes from elsewhere, and as such doesn't act when I want it to. It only emerges when the universe chooses to let me touch it."

"Does that mean you have no control over it?" asked the President.

"It all makes sense now!" remarked Jake, ignoring the President's question for the moment and pacing back and forth in his excitement. "Moses's Staff, the same staff I now carry, had a similar function. The inscription on his tomb said it could not be used for evil, which he discovered through some blighted attempt to redirect the power toward something contemptible."

"You mean like when he killed all those kids?" asked Tony.

"Yes! Or even after that, when he caused the Red Sea to drown the pharaoh's army. These were all deeds which would be considered evil. Perhaps they somehow corrupted him and... maybe they even killed him in the end. I don't know. But all of that is beside the point. The power isn't mine, just like it wasn't the Staff's – it comes from another source."

"Where from? God?" asked the President.

"That's one name for it," said Jake. "But whatever you call it, the result is the same, as our friend Aadesh here once said to me. It is a force of absolute benevolence in the universe, and for Moses to have twisted that power meant the corrupting influence came from within himself, not from the power he wielded, and as such it was *he* who suffered the consequences."

"So if you can't use this thing to kill Abaddon," said Tony, "what the hell are you gonna do?"

"First we need to find him," replied Jake cagily, "and then I need to save your brother."

Stunned silence filled the room, and Jake finally sat back down, staring at nothing, feeling certain for the first time, hoping he wasn't deceiving himself.

## -CHAPTER 14-
# THE HAPPIEST PLACE ON EARTH

"Mister President, we've found him!"

Liver-spotted Joe, the Director of Intelligence, handed a portfolio to the President across the Resolute Desk. The man's hands were shaking slightly, and Jake wondered if it were the enormity of the situation or frayed nerves over the delay in obtaining any usable information rattling him.

The President scanned through the documents for several moments, finally peering over the portfolio at the director, his eyes dangerously narrow. "Are you certain?" he asked.

"Yes, sir. One hundred percent."

"You know what this means?"

"Yes, sir," replied the director.

Jake was almost jumping out of his plush leather, high-backed chair in anticipation – it had been a long, drawn-out six days – but he managed to hold still until the President turned to him. Aadesh and Tony were absent from this meeting: this was only for those directly involved. The American government didn't want too many people to know for fear that the information might somehow get loose. After Mikey's possession, nobody could really argue against the precaution. Finally, the President turned his attention toward Jake, throwing a single photograph across the desk to him; Jake picked it up hesitantly and stared at it.

"It can't be," he murmured.

"It is," replied the President.

There, in crystal clarity within the photograph, was the distinct image of Mikey walking hurriedly toward the one place Jake would have never, in a million years, imagined Abaddon hiding.

The happiest place on Earth.

"You can't be serious!" said Jake, staring up at the director.

"I'm afraid so. The location was identified two days ago, and we have since verified the information twice. These photos came in from an agent in the field. He has not been heard from since."

"So, not only is the enemy situated within our borders, he's based himself – and potentially an army of these nephilim creatures – inside one of the most famous theme parks in the world," said the President grimly. "It seems this Abaddon is not without a sense of humor, dark as it may be. Has the order to evacuate the park been given yet?"

"No, sir. Such a move might have tipped the target off."

"Good point," replied the President. "Do we have troops ready to deploy?"

"Yes, sir. All units of the military are currently being briefed of a large terrorist sect harboring a substantial cache of weapons of unknown origin or capacity – I believe there'll even be hints at a local nuclear or chemical weapon threat during the briefing. This will be a major offensive – the first on US soil since, well, Pearl Harbor, I believe."

The President stared hard across the desk at Jake. "You're on your own from here, Jake. I can't go with you."

"I know," replied Jake, his voice cracking slightly as nerves rattled within him.

For the past six days he'd been chomping at the bit for some sort of information, and now that it was here he wished he could delay longer. Abaddon had presumably concealed the nephilim in the park, knowing he was hiding within a shield of innocents, more than willing to destroy every person there at the slightest indication something appeared to be going against his plan.

The fallen angel seemed invulnerable, not even constrained to one body. If they killed his possessed victim, Abaddon wouldn't be injured in the slightest.

Jake had incredible backing in the President of the United States, but Abaddon was millennia old, possessing a potential army of thousands of near-invincible creatures which multiplied upon injury. What chance did the armies of men have against odds such as these?

Thinking back, something about the convenience of meeting the President niggled at Jake. Why would Abaddon lead him to attack the man when the outcome had proven so beneficial to Jake's cause? Jake had initially thought it a trap – a ploy to get Jake killed – which had simply backfired.

But Abaddon was with him the entire time in Mikey's body; he could have killed him whenever he wished.

No, it was nothing so simple as a trap. He'd wanted Jake to meet the President for his own reasons, and Jake feared what those reasons might be. In this game of misdirection, Abaddon was a master, making Jake feel like a fumbling child.

Abaddon had already attempted to kill him twice, and it was only through luck on both occasions that Jake had survived. Perhaps the fallen angel had simply hoped to confuse Jake, to make him second-guess himself at every turn. If that were the case, he'd succeeded.

Every way Jake looked at it, the odds were stacked against them. Abaddon could create chaos in no time and destroy everything, possibly shattering the universe itself with his anarchy. The words of Behemoth came back to him like a lurching precursor of doom:

*Time. You come at the end. The End of Days. Has it come?*

Jake remembered little from the Bible, but he did recall something about the End of Days from the frenzied, drunken preaching of the Man, holding his Bible high like it was the Sword of God sent to condemn the heathens. Within the frayed bindings of the religious tome resided the tale of the end of the world – one of the Man's favorites – describing how the planet would crumble, and fate itself would rest upon the shoulders of one person.

Christ.

Jake.

He had no idea what Jesus had seen mankind through. Perhaps society was merely upon the edge of tearing itself apart, and he had been there to pull humanity back together… for a short time.

Now the task had fallen into the hands of Jacob Hope. Glancing down, he saw his hands were shaking. He clenched them into fists.

"When do we leave?" Jake asked.

The President looked to the Director of Intelligence, who said, "We're just waiting on your word, sir."

"You have it," replied the President. "Mobilize everyone, and get that park cleared of civilians as discreetly as possible so as not to tip Abaddon off. General Hammond will be in charge of the military, but nobody is to make a move unless Jake gives the word."

The director stared at Jake, and Jake got the distinct impression the man was about to drop to the floor and prostrate himself once more. To forestall this, Jake moved swiftly to the door, nodding acknowledgement to the President, who grimaced in return. Stepping beyond the room, he heard the footfalls of the director beside him. Tony and Aadesh appeared in the hallway from one of the many side rooms.

"Hey, boss," said Tony. "Is it time?"

Jake nodded, noticing the tension around Tony's eyes. Despite his efforts to appear casual about the entire affair, the stress of the situation was beginning to take its toll on the older brother. The fact it was Mikey they were going up against made him look close to breaking.

"Why don't you –" Jake began.

"No, boss," said Tony adamantly. "I need to do this. If there's a chance of helping Mikey I want to be there, but if there's no other choice, we'll have to just… you know… take him – take him down, I guess."

Jake knew exactly what he meant, and simply nodded. He didn't want to insult Tony's intelligence by denying the possibility they'd have to stop Abaddon by destroying the body he was using.

Mikey's body.

A helicopter was waiting to transport them to the airport where a private jet would fly them to Los Angeles, the next stop on their journey toward… toward what, exactly? Annihilation? Or merely avoiding one threat before another was somehow conjured. Was Jake here to prevent the Armageddon, or to ensure it came to pass?

He hadn't thought of that possibility before. Perhaps that was why Abaddon had pushed Jake and the President together. On his own Jake could do very little, but with the aid of the President he now had the force of the greatest army and most devastating weapons at his disposal. Even Behemoth, a beast once controlled by Abaddon, had bowed to him.

What if he wasn't here to save mankind? What if his role were to destroy the world?

Or what if Abaddon simply wanted him to think that…?

Jake shook his head. Down that road of thought crept insanity, and right now he didn't need that.

*Some messiah you are,* he thought bitterly.

Jake grimaced at the thought as the huge turbines powered up and the large helicopter lifted easily off the ground. He had a feeling this might be one of the President's own transports, but had no time to admire the opulence of the layout; his mind locked to other issues, namely how he was going to confront the Fallen.

Plans flipped and turned through his mind, just as they had for the past six days, each studied thoroughly before being decidedly thrust aside. Jake grew so obsessed, so caught up in his chaotic thought processes, that he barely noticed the transition from the helicopter to Air Force One. Complete with its jet fighter escort, Air Force One was potentially the safest plane in the skies, with countermeasures which could combat most airborne attacks.

Food arrived, but he ate mechanically, gnawing each mouthful slowly as he chewed through his ideas. Whereas he swallowed the food, he spat out the ideas, one after the other. Some were bitter, leaving a sour taste in his mind after he'd thrust them aside, but he churned on, determined to develop some sort of strategy.

The final result left him cold, terrified beyond belief, and desperately alone, but it was the only real option. Every other alternative ended in death, not just for himself, or the people following him, but potentially all of mankind.

Jake kept recalling the invasion of Eden by the nephilim, how they'd clashed midair with the cherubim, sliced to ribbons by the awesome power of the angelic creatures, only to reform again and again. Each piece of nephilim had become a full beast, multiplying their numbers infinitely until they'd completely overwhelmed the more powerful cherubim through strength of numbers.

A similar result would occur if he used the military against the nephilim. He couldn't take the risk that something would go wrong – the results could be disastrous. If the armies of Heaven led by Michael intervened, the archangel had promised that the powers unleashed would destroy the fragile humans.

No matter which way he twisted and turned the facts in his mind, Jake kept returning to the same result – he had to face Abaddon's force… alone. Jake's stomach flipped yet again at the thought. Jake was the only free number in this horrible equation.

But was he free?

Jake was an unknown entity in this entire conflict. The tears, the purity he had somehow released in order to cleanse the corruption of the nephilim away, were the only thing he could think of which could combat their scourge, but on this scale, such a task would surely prove impractical.

He had, through some miraculous happenstance, tapped into a power beyond himself, and that power had destroyed the corruption whilst saving the boy trapped inside it. How could he use this against the multitudes of corrupted beasts Abaddon had at his disposal? Kibuuka had wanted to be healed; how could Jake know such a power would work if the nephilim involved didn't want to be changed?

But he had to try; there was no other way.

Jake had heard talk from one of the military colonels about using napalm against the creatures in an attempt to burn them to ash, but Jake had a suspicion such an act would do no more than cutting them to pieces had. Despite the effectiveness of Uriel's flaming sword, it had been an ethereal weapon, not mere fire. A vision struck him: an entire field of ash budding, each flake of the cremated nephilim developing into a new creature until the horizon swelled with the beasts. Their hunger would be insatiable, their power overwhelming, until every speck of life on the planet crumbled under their combined assault.

Adding to such a disastrous outcome, Jake recalled that many of the nephilim were child soldiers kidnapped by Abaddon in Uganda. The thought of watching the diseased nephilim forms writhing, knowing that within the pestilent skin were trapped multitudes of children, was nothing short of abhorrent.

So napalm was out.

He could almost hear Abaddon's laughter mocking his ensnarement.

Chewing on his lip, Jake found himself still searching for alternatives as the plane landed, anything less harebrained than going forward alone, but nothing evolved. They disembarked, bustled into black sedans by serious-looking men wearing black suits. A sudden image of UFOs and bug-eyed aliens passed through Jake's mind as he sat in the leather back seat. This conjured the thought of Will Smith turning up to help him. A slight grin creased Jake's face… and then it vanished, the problems of the day consuming him once more. The next time he looked up, the convoy of cars was halting.

They had arrived.

Troops massed everywhere: armored vehicles of all descriptions, tanks and personnel carriers. Several vehicles bore missile launchers attached to their backs, arrayed beside numerous vicious-looking attack-helicopters. Huge, solid-looking barriers had been set up blocking roads, rolls of razorwire cutting off entire lanes, narrow gaps allowing troops to move between the rows if necessary. Curious pedestrians and complaining drivers lined the outsides of the barriers, kept back by the silent threat of the soldiers' automatic weapons. Some called out for answers. None were given.

Jake gripped the door handle tightly as he stepped out of the car, biting his lip while his heart thundered inside his ribcage. The trembling wouldn't stop. Knowledge that somewhere deep inside him resided a power that might contain this imminent disaster didn't help, and Jake felt the weight of every set of eyes as though each person knew what a fraud he really was. Someone important-looking waved him forward, and the chopping sound of rotary turbines brought his gaze skyward momentarily in time to see several more attack-helicopters swooping over the park.

So much for discretion.

Jake ignored it. Sooner or later, Abaddon would have known they were here, anyway. Sucking in a huge breath, Jake gazed anxiously toward the park entrance, half expecting the fallen angel to be standing there, mocking him. The entrance remained vacant.

This was the moment; there could be no more delays. Everything had been a lead up to this point, and now that he'd arrived, the fear of failure weighed heavier than ever upon his shoulders, each step feeling like a march toward the gallows. Each breath seemed to fill his lungs but not exhale, and the pressure in his chest just kept building. As if on cue, Aadesh touched his arm, his grasp steady and reassuring.

"Don't worry. God walks with you this day."

"Let's hope God knows that," muttered Jake.

Aadesh's hand dropped, leaving Jake bitterly alone once more within the crowd of people. Glancing around, Jake saw that it was more than just a crowd – it was a massive accumulation of people, hundreds of civilians, news crews, and reporters standing beyond the barriers. Some stared at him, no doubt wondering what his role in this military exercise might be. Some apparently recognized him – possibly from the videos with Behemoth – pointing fingers at him, and then indicating their own cheeks as they convinced comrades. Some went a step further and pulled out phones to check the video itself. Jake found himself wondering if Abaddon watched YouTube.

Glancing back at the gates of the park, he winced inwardly. From a childhood fraught by anguish, this site had nurtured dreams of hope and love. To have it the location of such a military operation seemed almost sacrilegious in itself.

*Says the guy claiming to be Christ*, muttered his own inner voice, causing Jake to grin humorlessly.

A very powerful-looking man wearing camouflage fatigues approached Jake, and he guessed this almost certainly had to be General Hammond. The general walked straight over to Jake, a frown creasing his heavily wrinkled face, features carved from stone set beneath short-cropped silver hair. Time or life had not been kind to the general, his emotionless eyes regarding Jake without the slightest hint of welcome. This was a man of action, of war, not some political general placed in front of cameras as the face of the military in times of peace. Here stood a warrior born.

"Son," said the general, ignoring Jake's proffered hand. "I don't know who the fuck you are, but I'm not used to having to bow and scrape to bureaucrats, and to be honest with you, I just don't like it. But when the President calls me directly and says I have to bend over and get shafted by you if that's what you want, I have to drop my pants and touch my toes – but don't expect me to smile and wait for your kiss."

The stress of the moment clashed with the blunt rudeness of the general, and Jake's anger flared momentarily. "Well, that's not going to happen, General. If anything, your biggest issue today will be how many sugars to have in your mochachino. So if it's all the same to you, I'd rather save the pissing contest for later, because I have more important things to do."

The general's expression lightened slightly, and he seemingly reappraised Jake before nodding slightly. "Well said. Point made."

"Good," said Jake, calming his nerves. The last thing he needed was to piss off the general in charge of the entire campaign.

"He is here," said a serene voice behind them.

Recognizing the voice, Jake spun around. Leaning casually against a military truck parked on the edge of the road stood Michael.

"Hi, Michael," said Jake, amazed at how calm his voice sounded. "Do you know how many nephilim he has?"

"No. He has cloaked the area, preventing me from spying, but in doing so, he also confirms he is here. Such an act of power cannot be done from afar, and as such Abaddon must be within."

"Who the hell is *this* guy?" snapped the general.

"He's the Archangel Michael, commander of Heaven's armies," murmured Jake absently, his mind occupied with the implications of what Michael had said. General Hammond stared at him incredulously for a moment before spinning his gaze to Tony and Aadesh for confirmation, only to see the two of them nodding in affirmation.

Jake gazed at the entrance, yearning for a better view. He walked toward the park, the rest of his party silently following, striding through the congregated military personnel for several hundred yards until they stood in the middle of an enormous courtyard, the theme park on one side and the secondary park – the adventure one – on the other side of the expansive square.

Nope, this view sucked even worse.

Peering around, Jake realized they could get absolutely no view of inside the park from anywhere nearby. His gaze travelled along the front of the park, past the turnstiles and finally fixed on something.

"General, please tell me that can be accessed from outside the park."

General Hammond's gaze followed to where Jake pointed and nodded. "Of course," he said, somewhat emphatically, like it was the most obvious thing in the world. "You can board it at the hotel."

"Is there someone there who can operate it for me?"

"I believe so. We locked them down from there, so they should be able to be restarted there also."

Jake nodded and moved to leave.

"Don't you want us to come with you, boss?" asked Tony.

Stopping, Jake turned and regarded the entire group, searching inside himself. He would have liked nothing more than to take the entire military force inside with him, hide within their might like it was an enormous shell, but he knew such a show of force might be suicidal. If anyone else accompanied him there was a chance Abaddon might take them over. As it stood he only had to worry about Mikey, and that was worry enough.

"This is something I have to do alone, Tony, but thanks for offering. General, I need you to keep everyone out of the park until I contact you. If you don't hear from me in three hours you'll have to assume I've failed and I'm... dead. If that happens, Michael will be your best source for information, and I urge you to listen to him. Goodbye."

Jake didn't wait for a response. He simply turned and strode toward the hotel. The thought of asking for a lift crossed his mind, but he discarded it, preferring to walk, the action giving him purpose. Every moment he remained inactive saw his resolve trickling away, along with his nerve.

His singular hope was the look he'd seen – the expression of satisfaction – which had flitted across one face when he'd announced he was entering the theme park on his own. Everyone else's features had dropped in stunned amazement – all but one figure's – and those features belonged to the one ally he valued most right now.

Michael, the archangel who commanded the armies of Heaven.

If an archangel showed relief at his choice, surely he'd made the correct decision… right?

Glancing up at the forlorn tracks of the park monorail, his decision didn't seem so smart after all.

***

"Are you sure you want to do this on your own, sir?"

Jake nodded stiffly at the technician, stepping into the monorail car with a determination he didn't truly feel. The Staff felt slick in his hand, and he leaned on it momentarily before feeling guilty, the sense that he was acting disrespectfully growing too strong. He lifted it from the ground and carried it in his right hand once more.

The doors slid shut with a soft pneumatic hiss, and Jake grabbed one of the chrome railings to steady himself. Jake stood totally and utterly alone as the monorail made its near-silent journey toward the theme park. Passing over the outer wall, Jake glimpsed rides and attractions drifting by beneath him, but saw no sign of movement at all. For just a moment his heart lifted. Maybe the information had been incorrect. Perhaps the President's men had mixed things up.

But then he remembered Michael's ominous warning, and the hope was shattered. Abaddon was here. He was waiting.

And so were his monsters.

Jake stared at the map of the park attached to the car wall. It felt silly to call the nephilim monsters, but in Jake's heart that's what they were. It seemed like every childhood fear he'd ever known was rising up from his subconscious to swamp him in a tidal-wave of panic. Nausea threatened to engulf him, the telltale trickle of bile warning that he might soon vomit, but Jake forced the sensation back down. The time had passed where he could afford the luxury of fear, now was the time for him to step up and face his demons – almost literally, as it were.

The monorail kept gliding on, an eerie transport toward Jake's final destiny. But was it *really* his final destiny? Something inside Jake whispered that this might be only the beginning, and if that were indeed true, then what in the world could something so momentous be a prelude to? The words of Behemoth edged back into his mind once more, but this time he thrust them away; he had no time to worry about the future – all he had was *now*, and now consisted solely of his quest to thwart Abaddon.

Thinking about Behemoth, Jake suddenly remembered that the last time he'd seen Vain was when the assassin had stayed to confront the beast after it'd killed Father Amadeuso. He hadn't appeared since, and Jake wondered what had happened to him; maybe he should have asked Behemoth, but in that moment he'd had other things on his mind. There seemed no way Vain could have survived, but something within Jake's mind strongly urged him to believe the assassin wasn't finished.

Vain seemed beyond death, and Jake had a feeling he would see the assassin again. Even Abaddon would be hard-pressed to defeat the Dark Man easily.

With a slight lurch, the monorail drifted around the curve of the track, sliding into the station and stopping lightly at the platform, the doors whooshing open. The exit beckoned, urging Jake to step beyond the safety of the monorail car and out into the unknown, like an open vault full of gold bullion – a vault filled with hidden snares ready to annihilate the unwary.

His legs trembled, and he sought the inner calm, but it remained elusive. He sought anger to quell the fear, but it, too, hid from his scraping search.

*Isn't this what I'm supposed to do?!* he silently demanded. *What else do you want from me?!*

Stumbling through the doorway, Jake's right foot tentatively touched the platform, amazement gripping him when the beasts from his nightmares didn't erupt through the very ground. Swallowing heavily, his left foot stepped clear, and he completely left the monorail. Peering around, he jumped slightly as the doors closed behind him, and the monorail departed back the way it had come – one of the safety precautions he'd discussed with the technicians – precautions he'd momentarily forgotten, which had seemed so sensible at the time, but now felt like a terrible idea.

They didn't want to offer the nephilim any sort of easy route out of the park. As it was, there were close to twenty thousand or so troops placed around the perimeter of the park, with every road for miles closed to the public, so if anything emerged over the walls it would almost certainly be spotted.

Except Abaddon, of course.

No, the fallen angel could depart at any time he wanted, simply by discarding the body he currently inhabited – Mikey's body. Jake had no idea what would happen to Mikey after Abaddon left him; he hoped things would return to normal, but he wasn't completely sure. Perhaps Abaddon would somehow damage Mikey's mind when extricating himself. The trauma of having such a powerful creation filling a mortal frame might somehow overload the frail human physiology. Jake hoped that wouldn't be the case. Wallace Pointreid had been killed, but had that been a malicious act on behalf of Abaddon, or had it simply been the body giving up after such intense violation?

Descending the steps from the station one at a time, Jake's senses tingled on edge, waiting for the attack he knew lurked around each corner.... With each footstep, Jake expected hordes of nephilim to emerge, and he held the Staff ready, as if to swing it like a sword, but nothing happened.

The park waited, eerily quiet, as Jake walked from the monorail station, his footfalls echoing menacingly off nearby walls and attractions. Even the normal city noise beyond the walls seemed muted, and as a result Jake felt all the more isolated. A deathly silence had fallen over the place, and part of him wanted nothing more than for something to happen, if for no other reason than to break the tension.

The greater part of him wanted nothing to happen. Nothing at all.

It wasn't only that Jake was afraid of Abaddon, he felt just as scared of fully accepting a role which had been waiting for him for centuries, maybe even since the world had been created. Behemoth had hinted Jake's coming heralded the end of the world. He swallowed heavily at the weight of such a concept and walked on, each step hesitant, as he anticipated the nightmares waiting to pounce.

*The end of the world.* What would such a thing mean? Did it mean the planet's actual destruction, or merely the death of all mankind? And how? Would it be nuclear warfare as everyone feared, or some biological agent created in a top secret labori –

*What the hell was that?*

Something had definitely moved. Jake peered at the section of bush until finally the culprit emerged. A fat, gray...

... pigeon. Bloated on fries from the looks of it.

Jake forced his arm to lower the instinctively-raised Staff. He stared around frantically, certain that at any moment the nephilim would come swarming out.

Nothing.

Perhaps they were merely playing with him. What if, even now, they stared at him, drinking in his fear the way one might swallow a can of soda? Anger flared within Jake at the thought, and his stride became more resolute, peering into each nook and recess for signs of gray flesh, until he finally stopped, frustrated, and then grinned mirthlessly. Why should he search for them? Why not make them come to him?

Spotting a nearby bench seat, Jake sat down, staring at the sunset, his heart full of melancholy. It was like watching a vibrant metaphor of this moment, the sun representing Jake's life up until this point, its sinking a symbol of the end of his old existence and the change he was going through. He crossed his legs and settled down, part of him hoping it would be for a very long wait, the rest just yearning to see an end to this nightmare.

Time passed with agonizing slowness, and Jake began to wonder if he'd made the right decision. Perhaps, while he'd been sitting here, Abaddon had marched the entire army of nephilim out through the front gates. Even now, they might be engaged in combat with the military outside. If that were the case, Jake had a feeling the muffling of the sound around him might prevent him from hearing any sort of conflict. He would never know until it was too late.

Or perhaps the nephilim weren't even here; maybe Michael had somehow gotten it all wrong and even now Abaddon rampaged across the country, crushing flowers and kicking puppies, every step drawing humanity closer to the demise of the universe. Everything within Jake screamed to get up and begin searching once more, but he refused to acknowledge the fear, forcing the inclination away. He would stay here and wait for Abaddon to come to him. Abaddon had to come... he had to....

The sun sank further, dropping swiftly beneath the replica of an enormous tree housing a large fabricated house, cutting out the light. The park came alive with shadows, and Jake's doubts began to double and treble. Lighting flickered on automatically around the park, whether by timer or sensor, Jake couldn't tell.

Why was he just sitting here when people might be dying? What kind of man was he to do something so... so cowardly? Was that what he truly was? A coward too afraid to confront Abaddon?

Jake became so consumed in his own thoughts that he didn't pay attention as some of the shadows detached and patches of darkness began to slink silently toward him. Whether through a trick of Abaddon's atmospheric shroud or simply his own distraction, Jake didn't realize something crept there until it was almost too late. Even then, it was only luck that saved him.

Luck... or something else?

A light, one of the many automatic spotlights set up around the park, suddenly swung loose from its moorings and spun around, shining directly on the nephilim as they snuck up on Jake from the left. Jake's heart shot to his throat, and he leaped to his feet, holding the Staff before him in a defensive gesture, adrenaline roaring through his veins.

As if on cue, the Staff suddenly expanded and unfolded, converting of its own volition, instantaneously shifting from the walking-stick it had been back into the full-sized, six-foot rod he'd retrieved from Moses's tomb. Jake stared at it, nonplussed for a nanosecond until the events around him jolted his attention away once more.

Movement from his right dragged Jake's gaze around. More nephilim – hundreds more – materialized from behind one of the many attractions. As if on cue, the creatures began emerging from everywhere – attractions, rides, food stalls, and restrooms. Like ants scouring a kitchen for loose sugar, the beasts moved purposefully, drawn toward his soul. Jake whirled from one direction to the next, confusion and terror intermingling within him. It wasn't supposed to be like this; he was supposed to be overwhelmed with calmness, and then everything would turn out alright.

He didn't feel that way at all.

And then he spotted it – a way out! Leaping over the bench and stumbling through the small flower garden behind it, Jake gathered his feet beneath him and sprinted, cutting through the rapidly meeting lines of nephilim and running as hard as he could toward the futuristic area of the park.

In the back of his mind, Jake recalled the map of the park he'd seen inside the monorail. It'd shown the park segregated into four sections, each representing a different theme. The one he'd just bolted into was based upon what the creator imagined the future might behold.

The lighting was minimal, various spotlights shining upon the attractions he ran past, some of the buildings glowing from within. Jake needed to be careful, almost tripping several times on unseen obstructions. Shadows became snarling nephilim in the blink of an eye, crawling over and under everything to get to him. Panic lent strength to his limbs, and he pushed himself harder, the slapping of naked feet pounding the pavement just behind him. Jake couldn't risk turning for fear they might grab him at any moment. Obstacles seemed to leap out of the darkness in front of Jake, trash cans and potted plants yearning to hinder him, as he dodged through the nightmarish conditions, searching for somewhere, *anywhere*, he could gather his thoughts for a moment and calm the terror coursing through his veins.

But there was nowhere. The nephilim emerged wherever he went.

Every single corner only unveiled more lurching, horrific shadows. The park became a veritable maze of attractions and shops, lifeless rides and tangled rope-lines leading to nowhere. Jake was rapidly running himself toward a dead-end – almost certainly a literal dead-end if the nephilim got their hands on him.

Sprinting through the exit of the futuristic part of the park, Jake's haphazard flight continued unabated for several more twists and turns until his body threatened to give in, his breath no more than juddering gasps, his heart a jackhammer against his ribcage. For once he heard no footfalls at his heels, and he flicked a glance around, seeing no immediate threat.

Slowing his mad run momentarily to suck in a couple of ragged breaths, Jake peered around, searching for salvation. Frustrated by the pointlessness of the endeavor, he tried to think of another option, but his panic-stricken mind could come up with nothing. He was trapped within the happiest place on Earth, hunted by creatures which could only be vanquished through a power he had no control of.

Power.... Control.

Jake's gaze dropped to the tall Staff he still gripped in his slick palm, its gnarled wood seeming to beseech him, calling silently for him to unseal its secrets. He might not be able to control the power he needed, but maybe....

Behind a grove of palms, Jake spotted what looked to be a massive artificial waterway, complete with a giant replica paddle-steamer sitting motionless against its bank. But the ship wasn't what grabbed Jake's attention.

He ran to the edge of the waterway just as thousands of nephilim poured into the area, surrounding him and cutting off any escape unless he swam through the murky river behind him. Jake wasn't about to try that, he had something else in mind.

The nephilim paused, possibly anticipating their kill, tasting his fear upon the still evening air, or perhaps they were waiting for Jake to plead for mercy, maybe even fall to his knees and cry.

And indeed he did cry.

A single tear fell, running swiftly from his left eye and down his cheek, sliding across his crimson birthmark, the two tears becoming one for a split second, before it slid away, reaching his chin and dropping onto the wood of the Staff.

Nothing happened.

Jake stared at it, rubbing the liquid into the wood with his left thumb. He shook the Staff. It remained inert, mocking his failure.

Whatever power the Staff answered to did not come from Jake. Just as he seemed a tool for some other entity at times, so too, apparently, was this stick. Jake felt the overwhelming urge to grip the Staff in both hands and snap it across his knee.

He refrained – with difficulty – thinking it would probably shatter his knee if he tried.

If the nephilim possessed the capacity to laugh, Jake sensed they might have been howling at his failure. His one hope – the belief that the force of his emotions and the power of the Staff might combine into inexorable purification – was quashed in an instant. The gray figures loomed closer, preparing to tear him limb from limb.

Jake readied himself, suddenly realizing the thought of death was not what scared him. He'd never been scared to die. He had always been terrified of failing, but now, in his moment of consummate failure, he suddenly realized that it was okay, because he'd tried, tried with all his might. The accomplishment was not what mattered: merely that he'd attempted a task worth doing. In that moment, his terror – his long-term companion – washed away, replaced by a strange peace which even the memories of the Man could not spoil.

A trickling sensation began in his fingertips, an almost electric sensation running through his hand and up his forearm. At first, Jake couldn't grasp what it might be, but soon understanding boomed within him, and a sly grin spread across his face.

The water behind him suddenly surged as though a bomb had exploded within its depths. Raising the Staff high above his head, Jake allowed the calmness to envelop his soul, aware that the water he couldn't see churned higher and higher behind him. Confidence poured through him in the same way the power flowed through the

Staff, forcing the water of the artificial river into complying with his will.

The thousands of nephilim stood frozen in place, their malicious faces now contorted into something akin to terror as they watched the wall of water rise before them.

Within seconds the wave changed, a soft glow illuminating the foaming liquid, lightning-like flickers flashing within the churning mass. It was more than power; it was passion, righteousness, and love all intermingling with a sense of purity which seemed to come from somewhere else, something entirely external to himself or the Staff. All of it gushed into the wall of water, and Jake smiled, consumed by peace, no longer feeling harrowed or afraid. Empathy toward the tormented figures consumed him. He no longer saw them as the monsters of nightmares, but more as prisoners within themselves; he yearned to set them free.

Jake dropped the Staff forward and instantly the entire wall of water – tons and tons of power-enriched liquid – surged over Jake and crashed down upon the nephilim like a starving predator. Even if they felt the inclination, the beasts had no time to flee as they were hit with the full force of the wave. It seemed to seek out every single figure within the mass and grasp it, cocooning each within the force incorporated into the liquid.

The effect was immediate. As before with the single nephilim on the boat, the liquid purged their infections, and within seconds Jake began to glimpse signs of humanity beneath the grotesque flesh. Several writhed silently, but the corruption was no match for the purity which scoured it, dissolving it like acid and leaving the flesh beneath – the human skin – untouched and pure. The result was incredible, and Jake gasped at the beauty each exposure revealed. Not beauty in the same terms as society might dictate, rather an almost divine cleansing which overcame the thousands of figures, leaving them untainted for perhaps the first time in their lives.

Through the power coursing within him, Jake could see what the water truly took away: it wasn't just the diseased flesh of the nephilim, but also the corruption of the people's lives from before they were converted by Abaddon. No matter how they had ended up as nephilim, either willingly or by coercion, their souls were somehow purified in a way Jake couldn't fully comprehend, but his senses recognized it as miraculous.

Was this God?

Savoring this moment of victory, Jake wondered, not for the first time, if the power he tapped into actually came from the deity everyone – including supposed angels – claimed existed, or could it be something else? He himself had argued that God might simply be the universe personified; a scientific perspective to an incalculable equation.

But Jake was no scientist. He possessed no answers. In those moments of clarity he heard no voice telling him the secrets of the universe, and when the moments passed, they left Jake as bereft of understanding as before. Distant dreams remained in his memory longer than his experiences within those bubbles of confidence, and this in itself confounded him as much as anything, for in losing such a gift he felt doubly bereft, and awesomely alone. He raised his right hand up and swept it through his hair, pushing his blond fringe away from his –

Realization suddenly occurred to Jake, and he looked down at his right hand, the one holding the Staff – it was empty! He flicked his gaze to his vacant left hand, and then all around, hoping he'd merely dropped the ancient relic, but the Staff was nowhere to be seen; it had disappeared completely.

The peace he'd just experienced shattered in an instant. Panic gripped him as a sense of utter nakedness swept down his spine. Jake searched once more for the Staff, tears unlike those of cleansing threatening to weep, but he forced them back, determined not to break, despite the realization that the one thing he'd been counting on to see him through all this had disappeared.

After several moments, Jake gave up searching, accepting that the Staff was gone. Whatever task it had been designed for had happened, and in a way felt strangely anticlimactic. He'd risked everything to find the relic, carrying it with him through distant countries, allowing it to see his greatest weaknesses and accomplishments –

In that moment something clicked. Perhaps the Staff had needed to be with him, absorbing his essence in some way, his joys and fears, accumulating them like a battery to be a tool when he needed it most. Uriel had been forced to expend his entire angelic essence in order to destroy the nephilim in Eden, how much more energy would be needed to cleanse an army such as what Jake had met?

The riddle suddenly unveiled itself. He recalled Moses's warning:

*Be comforted in the knowledge that the power of Heaven passes through the Staff, but it is not a tool of evil, and the task of evil shall corrupt the wielder, as I have sadly discovered.*

If the Staff merely absorbed the energy of its holder, for Moses to create evil he would have had to become evil – it had nothing to do with the Staff itself!

Taking a deep, shuddering breath, Jake wondered at the complexity of it all. Did this mean that everything had been preplanned? Had every step he made along this harrowing journey been thought out thousands of years ago by a strategist beyond comprehension? Moses had known Jake would need the Staff for this exact moment, a moment when nothing created on Earth could assist him, and he had interred the relic in a place only Jake could access.

All the pieces had fallen into place. Jake had imagined this to be a game of chess with Abaddon as the master, but he now suspected someone else was moving pieces with far greater skill than the fallen angel. The only question remaining regarded Jake's role in the game: would he be a knight used to battle for the entire contest, or was he a mere pawn to be cast aside once his task had been accomplished?

He shrugged. That would, in all likelihood, be something he had absolutely no control over, and as such he pushed the thought from his mind. At this moment he had greater problems, and the day – or rather night – wasn't won yet. There was one more foe still to be vanquished, and now Jake had to face him empty-handed.

Abaddon.

Moving to the first of the naked figures on the ground Jake kneeled beside him. The man had pale skin, looked perhaps forty years of age, and appeared severely overweight.

"I don't have time to explain," said Jake swiftly. You have to gather these people and get out of here as quickly as possible. Do you understand me?"

The man nodded unquestioningly, but he didn't move, his eyes gazing hard at Jake, as though he knew something Jake hadn't told him. Maybe it was a residual memory: something Abaddon had implanted in them as nephilim. Or perhaps a lingering memory of the power which had so recently cleansed them? Slowly, all the waking figures, both male and female of all ages and races, turned and stared at Jake with the same expression as they gradually rose to their feet.

Jake smiled uncomfortably, aware of the nakedness of the figures standing unashamedly in front of him. Muttering something utterly inane, Jake turned and walked hurriedly around a corner, cutting off the staring flock, hiding his awkwardness.

Once clear of the naked horde, Jake paused in his flight, frowned and glanced around, wondering where Abaddon might conceal himself. Jake doubted the fallen angel would come at him in the open, especially after such a furious display of power, and his eyes raked his surroundings for the most likely place Abaddon might hide.

Wandering through the park, Jake searched for inspiration. He felt certain no nephilim had escaped his torrent, and so all that remained was Abaddon.

Something within the gloom drew his focus closer until his gaze fastened upon it. The sealed entrance seemed to mock him, and Jake groaned at the irony. As Jake made his way toward the attraction, he could already hear the haunting and repetitive iconic song echoing through his mind. Everything in his soul yearned for it not to be, but some inner instinct told him Abaddon hid inside, waiting for him. Such sick absurdity played perfectly into the fallen angel's disposition.

The echoing words, a timeless message known around the world:

It really was a small world after all....

## -CHAPTER 15-
# CONFRONTATION

Just as Jake feared, after prying open the doors to the attraction, the only way he was able to turn on the lights in the place was to also turn on the mechanized dolls dancing to their monotonous, cyclical soundtrack. Boats designed to carry observers also began to move on their train-like route, but Jake chose the walkway running alongside the water course.

If there were ever a worse location for such a confrontation, Jake couldn't begin to envision it. The light was deceptive, often flickering. He kept stumbling on hidden objects, the next step trying to dodge something which didn't exist: mere shadows cast from one of the many singing puppets. The robotic chanting monstrosities were set up to represent different countries and their cultures, and as such Jake was unable to see anything beyond the next region.

And then there was the melody.

While the song the robotic midgets repeated was one of joy, under the circumstances it sounded haunting and somewhat nightmarish; as though Jake had stepped into the bizarre dream of an acid tripper.

"You can still leave, you know," boomed a voice over the music. It dripped with malice, seeming to come from everywhere and nowhere all at the same time.

"You can still stop doing what you're doing as well," countered Jake, calling to the shadows.

No response.

The song went on.

Jake lifted his leg high to step over the shadow of a dancing Scandinavian girl near the water's edge, cursing halfway when he saw it wasn't a solid object. Only now he noticed the song was no longer in English; judging by the dolls he guessed the words might be in German or Swedish.

Movement from his left caused Jake to jump slightly and clutch for the Staff, realizing remorsefully that he no longer possessed it, but when he spun around he saw only an empty boat, and he clenched his hands back into fists. His palms felt slick with sweat.

Mocking laughter cackled above the song, echoing from the walls all around him.

"He lied to you, you know," hissed the voice of Abaddon. "There is no Heaven; it's all a trick to get you stupid monkeys to worship Him."

"I don't care about that," called Jake, ducking through a small doorway into the next room. "All I care about is stopping you."

"Why? What possible good can come from you facing me? I will destroy you in an instant, and then God's tool will be gone once more. Wasted. Is this the fate you yearn for, human? Do you truly wish to die for a God who cares nothing for you? I was there at the formation of the universe, I know why he made everything as he did; wouldn't you like me to tell you?"

"No," responded Jake firmly. "I know whatever you tell me will be warped beyond reason, just as your mind is warped, Abaddon."

More laughter echoed through the tunnel, but Jake sensed it might be slightly forced now. "Bah! What would you know, you stupid mammal? I was eating the souls of your kind before your predecessor thought to deface the world with his arrogance. Because that's all it was: arrogance! He reveled in the adoration of the crowds, gloried in the attention it brought him, but he was nothing special, just as *you* are nothing special. You think you are God's tool, His instrument upon the Earth, but He despises you all. I know this; I was with Him at the beginning!"

"So you keep telling me," replied Jake, stepping into Africa, sensing he drew closer to the lurking fallen angel. "But you haven't told me about how He threw you out of Heaven – or didn't that happen either?"

"YOU DARE???" roared Abaddon. "I have existed for millennia – "

"Blah, blah, blah," retorted Jake, cutting him off. "Stop telling me how awesome you are and answer the question."

Silence filled the air as Abaddon seemed to contemplate Jake's insolence. "He was a fool. Lucifer was right to challenge Him."

Jake paused, convinced he heard something new there, some tiny fragment of uncertainty. "So you admit there is a Heaven, and thus everything else you said is a lie?"

Abaddon's roar filled the cavernous attraction, cutting off the song completely as though someone had abruptly slashed the singers' throats. Chunks of the ceiling rained down around Jake. For one terrifying moment, he feared Abaddon might simply bring the entire structure down, crushing him beneath tons of steel and cement; but slowly the bellow ebbed and the structure settled, though the song did not resume.

"COME TO ME!" screamed Abaddon. "I will feast on the juices of your eyeballs and suck the marrow from your bones before I destroy this petty planet!"

"How are you going to do that?" asked Jake, stepping through an entryway, its door hanging broken from a single hinge. "I've reversed all your nephilim, made them human once more. Unless you've got another source of fruit from the Garden, I doubt you can create another army."

"I will rejoice in your suffering, Legacy."

"And yet you're still hiding from me? Why is that, Abaddon? Are you afraid of this little mammal who destroyed your nephilim?"

So saying, Jake stepped through a final doorway.

Any further taunts choked in Jake's throat, and his false bravado dried up in an instant. The body was Mikey's, but the crazed, demonic look in the eyes seemed far beyond anything mortal. He held the aura of madness on a biblical scale: immortal and immutable, yet utterly damaged. Abaddon wasn't only a fallen angel, cast out of Heaven; his visage wore a mantle of depraved insanity. Deep scratch marks penetrated either cheek where he had clawed his face. His hair stood out in huge clumps, as though he'd been constantly pulling at it.

"You destroyed my children," hissed Abaddon, his fingers hooked into talons.

"They didn't seem to mind," replied Jake, grateful he didn't stammer, and carefully keeping a large mountain replica between them.

Jake's mind frantically searched for some way to outthink or even trap Abaddon, but his thoughts came up blank. The Staff had disappeared, and no overwhelming calm materialized to aid him. Instinct and hope had driven him to this point, but he hadn't seen beyond it, apart from some flimsy vision of somehow defeating Abaddon.

"Your God is pathetic; you know that, don't you?" growled Abaddon. "He sends *you*, a mortal, to confront me, a being even his most powerful angels fear to face. Do you know why He has done this? It's because He is afraid, Legacy, just as he has always been afraid. He forced Michael and his archangels to fight against us during the War while He hid behind the gates of His precious kingdom, too scared to come out lest Lucifer smite Him. Your God is a coward of the most colossal kind. He never cared for us. He used us as tools to do His bidding, and then cast us aside when we no longer served a purpose. I despise Him. "

"But you loved Him once," retorted Jake, peeking around the edge of the mountain, staring deep into Abaddon's eyes. "What changed your mind?"

Abaddon stared back, and Jake realized his mistake a moment too late. A stabbing needle shot into his brain, and he felt the former angel rummaging inside his mind, tendrils of acid digging around like a clumsy child searching in the mud for earthworms. The fingers jabbed deeper, causing Jake to cry out and fall to his knees. Despite being hidden from Abaddon's sight, the connection did not break; they were locked together like two bulls clashing horns, and Jake felt grossly overwhelmed by the power of his foe.

"When has God been there for you, Jacob Hope? I can see your nightmares, I know your pain. The Man hurt you, flinging words from that pathetic book at you, whipping your mind while he tormented your body. Can you smell him now, Jacob? Does his breath caress your neck?"

"STOP IT!" screamed Jake, fighting back the memories battling to break loose, trying in vain to sever Abaddon's hold.

"You cried out for salvation. Do you remember that, Jacob? You cried and screamed for someone to save you. Where was God then, Jacob? I'll tell you where. He sat upon his gilded throne and laughed at your agony, relishing your anguish. And yet you come against me in His name, doing His bidding without question. Why?"

Jake gripped his skull with both hands, trying to physically hold back the torment his mind seemed unable to constrain.

"He is using you, as he used the Fallen, Jacob Hope, and if you fail He will simply find another. Look at Christ, screaming upon his cross for a release your God never delivered. I was there; I stood and watched as Christ cried like a coward, while piss and shit ran down his legs. He was not so divine then, after I had hoisted his crucifix –"

"*You*?" Jake clung, gasping, to the thought as though it were a log in a flood. "What do you mean?"

In his mind, Jake sensed the fallen angel's smirk. "I stood there, momentarily free from my eternal imprisonment, a whisper of what I currently am, but powerful enough to coerce Pontius Pilate into condemning the beloved Jesus to be nailed upon that cross. Little did I know that by doing so I was creating a martyr. Who could have predicted the stupid human would not break and renounce his God? What should have been the greatest triumph of the Fallen turned into our biggest failure since the War. But that will all change with your destruction. Alas, I cannot kill you here, bereft of witnesses. No, even in your short time you have gained recognition throughout the world. If I were to smite you in the shadows, your legend would merely grow, just as your predecessor's grew. I must depart, but you will have no difficulty in finding me, I can assure you of that, messenger of God!"

The import of his words took a moment to sink in, and Jake knelt, frozen in pain, delayed in his reaction. Too late he realized what Abaddon meant. The connection snapped. Jake leaped up, staggering around the replica of the mountain – the obstacle he thought he'd been using to keep Abaddon away, but now realized the fallen angel had been utilizing to delay *him* until he was ready.

Jake crashed into the body of Mikey, and they both toppled to the floor. Staring into his opponent's eyes, he saw the last vestiges of malignance drift away.

Abaddon had escaped.

But why? He could have killed Jake at any time, so why had he fled? He spoke of fearing making Jake a martyr, but Jake sensed there was much more to it than just that. The behavior of the fallen angel seemed so unpredictable that if Jake didn't believe him completely insane he might have thought him....

What? Troubled by a conscience?

Jake might have laughed at such a concept under different circumstances. A being that had tormented souls for centuries, and Jake wondered if he'd somehow developed morals.

"Wha – what's going on?" groaned Mikey.

Cursing softly, Jake stood, bending to help Mikey to his feet.

"Mikey, what's the last thing you remember?"

Mikey peered at him as though from a long distance. "We were on the boat. No… wait. We were off the boat… and you'd just healed that nephilim thing."

Jake's stomach lurched, suddenly aware it might have been his healing of Kibuuka which had gathered Abaddon's attention. But why hadn't Abaddon tried to attack him until now? The illogic of such a tactic merely made Jake's nerves scream even more.

"But I been having some kinda… I dunno… blackout things. I mean, I don't even remember when we grabbed you, man. I didn't wanna say anything, thought I was goin' nuts."

So it had been before Kibuuka. Abaddon's depth of planning delved ever-deeper.

"So… so that *thing* was controlling me the whole time?" Mikey gasped, looking as though he might vomit.

"Pretty much," said Jake, hurrying toward a glowing red exit sign. "Now he's gone, like some sort of ghost, but he reckons we won't have trouble finding him. From the sound of it, whatever he's planning, it's going to be huge."

"Like what?" asked Mikey.

"That's what scares me," muttered Jake. "What would an insane, immortal, former-angel do if the restraints constraining him were slipped? He could do pretty much anything."

Clambering through the exit, they were met by hundreds of guns, laser sights aimed directly at their chests. Spotlights illuminated the entire area like mini suns, blinding them instantly.

"WHOA! Hold on, it's us!" called Jake, shading his eyes with one hand, trying to see beyond the blinding beams.

Several orders were yelled through the ranks of the surrounding soldiers. The lights dimmed, and guns clattered as they were hesitantly lowered. A shout sounded, and suddenly Tony was charging through the barriers and razorwire toward them, grabbing Mikey in an intense bear hug. Tears streamed down the normally stoic brother's face.

"I take it your mission was unsuccessful," stated a voice Jake quickly identified as General Hammond. The man strode forward from behind the lights to stand opposite Jake.

"How do you know?" asked Jake.

The general held out a computer tablet with what appeared to be a live video feed displaying on it. An image of horrific devastation shone out from the screen. The occasional movement of something red-black darted across the tablet every few moments, but the cameras couldn't seem to focus on it properly.

"Where's this?" queried Jake. "What's going on?"

"I was contacted about fifteen minutes ago. It seems something has attacked Beverly Hills."

"*Something*? What kind of something?"

The general shook his head. "We're not sure. Nobody that gets close to it survives. But if I were a betting man I'd speculate it had something to do with you."

Jake stared at the screen numbly. "I need to get out there as quickly as possible."

General Hammond nodded, calling to an aide and murmuring something Jake couldn't hear. Turning back, the general asked, "Who are those naked civilians you sent out here? Most of them couldn't speak English, and the one guy who could simply rambled something about the power of God."

Jake grimaced. "They're innocent and need help. Some might not be from here, others might seem to act strangely; all I ask is for your people to treat them gently, they've been through a lot."

The general nodded, obviously unsatisfied with the explanation, but resigned to operating in partial ignorance for the moment. Jake guessed the man had been given notice to do whatever Jake asked, and as such, now treated him as he would a superior, even though he seemed unhappy with the prospect. Such things must happen regularly in the military, thought Jake. Probably why the term 'need to know' got thrown around so much. For the moment he felt glad he didn't have to explain himself too thoroughly.

"You'll be transported via Apache attack helicopter," advised the general, pointing toward a sleek, jet-black helicopter bristling with armaments, including what appeared to be a rotating single-barreled machine gun under its belly. With its pointed nose, the Apache looked more like a ravenous wasp than an aircraft.

"It's the fastest thing we have on site. Unfortunately your companions will have to travel with the rest of us in one of the Super Stallions; the Apache's cockpit is only a dual-seater, and the rest of our airborne force has already been deployed in an effort to combat the threat in Beverly Hills."

"Thanks," said Jake hurriedly, rushing toward the aircraft, part of him in awe of the power which seemed to drip from every inch of its frame. Under any other circumstances he might feel invincible flying into battle in such a machine. As impressive as the Apache appeared, Jake had the distinct feeling it would be like a toy compared to whatever they were going up against.

Who was he trying to kid? He knew exactly what they were heading toward. Abaddon's power was unconstrained, even angels had said that. Now, either the fallen angel had found a body strong enough to withstand flying through a building, or perhaps he had chosen to create a body for himself, something invulnerable, a form Jake stood no hope of destroying.

His instincts told him the latter was most likely, and Abaddon no longer hid behind a human façade, converting his natural form into flesh. Such a creation – as far as Jake knew – had never occurred throughout history. Angels' powers were always stunted in physical form, leaving them weaker than when they were ethereal. That would not be the case now.

Through whatever process the author of *Precursors of the Final Conflict* had incorporated into the ritual used to bring Abaddon to Earth, he had also stripped away the restrictions placed upon the fallen angel. In effect, Abaddon had been left unfettered by the rite, leaving him open to uninhibited power, rather than just a portion of his being like Michael or Uriel.

As Jake was strapped into the cockpit of the Apache, he pulled the flight helmet on, wondering what such a thing might truly mean. What could a fallen angel be capable of in an unrestrained state? He doubted even Abaddon knew the answer to that question. It seemed something completely foreign in his existence; he was only now beginning to test the limits of his ability.

But before he could test himself fully – stretching the wings of his power – he had to dispose of the one obstacle in his way, the single thorn in his side.

Jake.

For some reason, Abaddon had fled from the relative safety of Mikey's body during their last confrontation. He now attacked Beverly Hills in order to gain Jake's attention, a move which undoubtedly made perfect sense to the mad angel, but outside his sphere of insanity it seemed impossible to understand.

The Apache's rotors began to whir, and within moments Jake and his pilot were hurtling through the air, shooting toward Beverly Hills. Jake sighed heavily. Would this madness never end?

Jake grimaced within the combat helmet, shaking his head. For years he'd yearned for a way to make a difference in the world around him, yet now, when he had the opportunity to save humanity, he was longing for something else. Would he ever be satisfied with what was laid out before him? Perhaps that was the secret to human existence; to never be truly happy. To be absolutely content would mean an end to aspiring for something better, and was that not merely another form of surrender? To be simply content with life seemed to be just awaiting death. Without goals or yearning, life itself seemed somehow empty.

Staring through the thickened glass of the Apache's cockpit as they shot through the air, Jake found himself wondering. He possessed no desire for riches or fame, but deep down he'd always felt the driving need to help people. This wasn't something he recalled with pride, just the way things were. In the same way, he didn't think less of anyone who did a job some might call menial. So long as they were happy, or at least content, who was he to judge? If everyone did exactly the same things the planet would –

Electronic beeping blared within the cockpit, slicing through Jake's contemplations like a bullet to the brain. He glanced around worriedly for the cause of the alarm, but couldn't see anything.

"*Hold on, sir.*" The controlled voice of the pilot echoed through the headphones in Jake's helmet. "*We have incoming.*"

The pilot's voice seemed eerily calm for such a horrific statement, and Jake peered ahead over the seat in front of him, straining to see what the pilot referred to. He had the feeling that ordinarily the pilot would sit in the rear with the gunner in the front, but with Jake unable to help, the pilot had to manage both jobs from the front seat.

Jake finally managed a clear view of what the pilot was talking about. A millisecond later the chopper veered to the left, and a burning vehicle hurtled past the right side of the craft. Another shot by on the left.

They were under attack from flying cars!

Abaddon must have spied them and now been attempting to bring down the chopper before Jake could get any closer. Whether or not he knew Jake traveled in the craft was irrelevant; if he destroyed the helicopter, Jake was finished, and Abaddon would then be free to run rampant. The only thing which might stop him were the angelic forces led by Michael, but if what the angel had said was true, their interference would be worse than leaving Abaddon alone to turn the world into a charnel house. The clashing of the ethereal powers within the physical dimension might cause all of creation to unravel – destroying the universe completely.

Definitely not an outcome to be desired.

Another car, a Volkswagen from the looks of it, hurtled past, terrifyingly close as the pilot jolted the craft to the right, steering them ever closer to the source of the projectiles.

"*Should I fire missiles, sir?*" called the pilot over the intercom.

Jake thumbed his own microphone. "No! That'll just piss him off. Get me as close as you can, and then set down – hopefully behind some sort of cover!"

"*Copy that,*" came the calm reply as the pilot dodged left.

Suddenly a deafening crash impacted the right side of the craft. More warning sirens started blaring and several instruments flashed alarmingly on the console arrayed in front of Jake.

"*We've been hit! Bastard doubled up on that last shot. We're going down. Too low to eject.*"

The calmness in the pilot's voice seemed to be fraying. Jake's nerves screamed, heart thumping, palms sweating, stomach clenching. The Apache shuddered heavily, and Jake could see smoke billowing from the right side. Despite the pilot's valiant attempts, they appeared to be dropping fast.

Their descent slowed enough that they didn't smash into the road like a meteorite, but they still crashed hard. The wheels absorbed some of the impact, as did their seats, and as a result they didn't die.

However, the threat of the unseen member of the Fallen still lurked outside the stricken craft, and Jake had no time to rejoice over their safe landing.

Fumbling with his harness, Jake swiftly released himself while the pilot opened the cockpit canopy, raising it easily on the pneumatic risers. They leaped from the crashed Apache and sprinted to the edge of a partially demolished building, the pilot pulling out a handgun and chambering a round as they took cover.

"I don't think that's going to help much," said Jake drily. "Did you manage to get a look at what was attacking us?"

The pilot shook his head. "There's too much smoke, looks like the entire area is on fire."

Jake glanced around, taking in the wrecked buildings, some reduced to rubble. Cracked roads, broken signs, blazing cars – devastation lay everywhere. Abaddon certainly hadn't wasted any time. It took Jake a moment to realize they were actually standing on Rodeo Drive, one of the most iconic strips in Beverly Hills. The place looked like a warzone. Jake saw another crashed Apache helicopter not too far away, the occupants not as lucky as Jake and his pilot had been.

"You need to find somewhere safe to hide," Jake instructed the pilot.

"But what about you, sir?"

"I have to stop that thing… somehow," replied Jake. "But I can't face him and try to watch out for you at the same time."

The pilot appeared to appraise Jake before shrugging, unconvinced. "You're the boss," he said, holstering his weapon and sprinting away in the opposite direction.

"That's what they all say," murmured Jake softly.

Sucking in a deep breath and trying to summon his courage, Jake glanced up at the crumbling building he sheltered behind. It had previously been some sort of ritzy fashion store – three floors of clothes Jake would need to live five lifetimes to be able to afford. Now it was one and a half floors of dirty, dust-cloaked garments homeless people might snub their noses at. Shuffling to the corner, Jake peeked around the edge.

A scene of devastation spread before him, a veritable landscape from Hell. Buildings stood shattered like boxers' teeth and fires blazed everywhere. Flipped and crushed cars lay scattered like throw pillows – civilian vehicles, police cars, and military units alike, none had escaped Abaddon's wrath. Nothing remained of the Beverly Hills Jake had seen on television. Smoldering palm trees added a haze to the air, black smoke wafting down the street and intermingling with the various building and vehicle fires. Even the blue sky above appeared somehow tainted by the devastation, as though the hellish scene sickened the heavens in some way.

And then Jake saw it.

It had to be Abaddon, there could be no other explanation. Carnage incarnate, far worse than anything he could have ever imagined, as though all the bile in the world had taken form and tried to look like a man. For a moment Jake hoped his mind had finally cracked under the pressure, and this thing he saw was merely an image conjured by his tortured imagination. It would be lovely to slip into insanity in this moment and discover he had imagined the larger portion of his adventure to date; there were no angels, he'd never touched Moses's Staff, he was no messiah.

His mind floated on this dream for the minutest of nanoseconds, right up until his arm scraped across a piece of metal protruding from the damaged facade of the building. The sting of the graze snapped him back to reality, crushing the hopeless daydream of insanity. It was all real, and he had to stop it.

Staring up once more, he focused on the cause of the mayhem.

Gliding through the air flew something roughly humanoid in shape, as tall as a two-story house. Broad, jagged wings spread from its back, swathed in scorched and blackened feathers. Large clusters of plumage were missing along the wings, as though torn out or diseased. The flesh beneath appeared leprous, covered in weeping sores and scabbing tissue. The creature's torso looked burned, charred flesh peeling away and regenerating as chunks fell to earth. Each spot of ground touched by the falling tissue burst into flames, as though hit by teardrops of napalm.

The head looked like a jackal's: cracked, ebony leather stretched over the skull, vibrant blue eyes full of frenzied rage sitting deep within blackened sockets. Human teeth sharpened to points filled the beast's jaws, and a shredded tongue flickered out between them, tasting the air like a snake.

"YOU!!!" roared Abaddon, spotting Jake. "Come to me, Legacy! Your petty opposition ends here!"

"No," muttered Jake through gritted teeth, throwing himself back behind the wall.

It couldn't end like this; there had to be some other answer. He held no Staff, possessed no otherworldly power which might stand against a beast such as this. All he had was what resided within his soul, and that would have to be enough.

Icy certainty filled him with determination. Not some otherworldly strength or a supernatural confidence, just the desire to vanquish Abaddon, no matter what the cost. Jake couldn't give in to this thing, couldn't run any longer. Stepping out into the devastated street, Jake squared his shoulders and met the fiery blue gaze of the fallen angel hovering in the broken street ahead of him, wondering that a beast such as this could still retain such beautiful eyes.

Abaddon waited, motionless in the air. His wings didn't flap, he seemed held aloft by some other power, and Jake guessed the feathered limbs might be more a contemptuous adornment than for any practical purpose. The former angel seemed to relish the tension in the air, drinking it in like a fine wine. The torn tongue flickered out yet again, and a hideous grin spread across the canine face of the beast.

"I can taste your fear, human."

"That's the taste of your own defeat," retorted Jake, stalling for time. Frustration caused rage to bubble up within him, but he pushed it back. Fighting a creature such as this with hatred in his heart would achieve nothing other than failure. He needed to keep a clear head.

"Has the little puppy learned how to bark?"

Jake paused, unsure of how to reply. When would the confidence fill him, taking away his doubts and leaving only the answers he required so badly? Surely this was the moment – faced with his greatest adversary – that the power of God or whoever or whatever it was would shine out through him, vanquishing his foe.

"You can't win, Abaddon," called Jake, struggling to delay things, maybe even to bluff his opponent. "You know the power that runs through me is too strong –" Jake suddenly remembered something and broke off his bluff. "Why didn't you kill me?"

Abaddon's gaze narrowed, obviously suspecting some sort of trap. "I could have killed you at any time, you pathetic –"

"That's right," replied Jake, so consumed in his consideration of the problem that Abaddon's threats ceased to intimidate him. "You *could* have killed me at any time, so why didn't you? Granted, you shot me in Uganda, but that was before any of us knew who I was and what I represented. Since then you've held a myriad of opportunities, and the only one you took was in Eden, where you must have surely known Uriel could revive me with the fruit. Every other attack has been pathetic – you walked right beside me for an age in Mikey's body and didn't try a thing! Why haven't you killed me now while I'm talking?" A bursting notion jabbed into his mind. "Why are your eyes still blue?"

For a split second, Jake thought he glimpsed something other than malice in the beast's gaze. Could Abaddon perhaps –

"Are you – are you looking for redemption?"

"I seek nothing from you!" bellowed Abaddon.

Jake leaped at the hope. "Why don't you join me? Help me fight against what's coming. I can help you. I can bring you back from wherever it is your soul now resides."

For a fraction of a moment, it seemed Abaddon considered what Jake proposed, and he wondered if the renegade angel would acquiesce. Instead the fallen angel shrieked, the sound full of anguish. He reached up with both clawed hands and gripped his face, tearing away the cracked skin. Mesmerized, Jake watched it heal almost immediately. In this action, Jake suddenly realized why he'd thought the fallen angel appeared insane. He was tormented.

"There can be no succor for one such as I. We are the Fallen, condemned by God. What can a stupid, pathetic simian like you do to help me?"

"I have the power," replied Jake with a confidence he didn't entirely feel. "I can bring you back –"

"FOOL! I *am* suffering – I am devastation. I yearn to tear this insignificant planet apart for the mere gall of it to bear inhabitants who would turn their backs on God –"

Jake caught hold of what Abaddon said just as the member of the Fallen cut himself off. "Do you still love God?"

Abaddon spat contemptuously, a wad of fire smashing into the concrete. "He discarded us like filth. Why would I care about Him?"

"You just seem… confused. Like if you had a chance to go back, you would have chosen a different side. Would you?"

For another fraction of a second – the tiniest stutter of a heartbeat – Abaddon's malicious gaze softened slightly, and an expression Jake could only liken to remorse flickered across the bestial features. And then it was gone, covered by a snarl.

"I despise Him, just as I abhor his pitiful apes. There is no confusion in me, you nauseating simian, I am merely savoring your demise, taking pleasure in the hope I see growing within you. Your terror amplifies with each moment your precious power hides from you, and it tastes like wine to my senses."

"If you know that, you also know I can save you," argued Jake, desperate to prolong the conversation. "I can stop your torment. I can bring you closer to God again."

The fallen angel stared at him, for once his expression dropping completely, and Jake saw beyond the madness for the first time. "You can't," replied Abaddon, his tone almost one of regret. "My fate is set, and I am what He has made me."

"I can save you."

The fallen angel cursed Jake, long and viciously, in what seemed like several languages, several voices, all at once, flowing out in a single iteration. Finally the flood of words ceased, and Abaddon dropped to the ground, scooping up a car with one clawed hand as easily as a child would lift a plastic toy. In one smooth action, Abaddon flung the car with all his might directly toward Jake.

The vehicle hit Jake squarely with the power of a freight train, punching him from his feet and crushing him like a bug. He felt his bones shatter under the impact as it skidded along the road, its weight dragging Jake beneath it. The car finally flipped clear and exploded somewhere behind him in what must have been a spectacular display.

But Jake was in no position to appreciate it.

It seemed a miracle he remained conscious; his body lay broken beyond anything a mortal should have been able to bear. Perhaps it owed to a lingering trace of the fruit Uriel had given him in the Garden, but now it seemed more a curse than a blessing. Agony flowed through Jake even as his precious lifeblood poured from his many wounds, and he found himself begging silently for death, just to stop the agony which beset him.

He sensed more than heard Abaddon approach, and when the fallen angel gazed down on him, his blue eyes shone with scorn.

"So tell me, *savior*," spat Abaddon, "tell me how you'll save me."

Jake coughed and a gush of blood sprayed from his mouth. He couldn't breathe. The world began to close off, darkness swirling all around. Panic filled his chest, washing away the foolish belief which he'd held only moments before, the hope that he might win.

He was dying.

Jake's vision closed off even more; the last thing he witnessed before passing out was Abaddon's jackal skull twisted into a mask of confusion, and the muted cursing of the fallen angel....

\*\*\*

Oxygen!

Jake heaved in a huge, painful gasp, his hands instinctively reaching for his bruised throat, finding the skin raw and damaged, as though it had been burned.

"Stupid ape! Your pathetic soul deserves the Abyss. Everything about you, from your stench to your stupid chimpanzee face, makes me want to retch."

Abaddon's jackal skull twisted and reshaped into the features of a man in his mid-twenties, black hair falling to his shoulders. Only his eyes remained unchanged; irises of pure blue blazing from within the beautiful features of the once-angel. His body remained as corrupted as before, his diseased wings continuing to shed charred feathers while the flesh of his body still dripped malice, but the flames fell nowhere near Jake. With a move of abject frustration, the fallen angel flung something toward him, something which smacked softly into the concrete beside Jake's head.

Jake twisted his neck, a neck he'd felt snap like a chicken bone, and saw the empty husk of a yellow fruit lying on the cracked concrete road, its shape a reminder of what he surely must have looked like only moments ago.

"I have used this," growled Abaddon, pointing at the empty skin, "the last of the fruit I took from the Tree of Everlasting Life, to heal your pathetic form. And now I don't know why."

"You... you saved me?" wheezed Jake.

Abaddon turned his head and spat, the impact causing the ground to crack. "You fumble around with elements you have no comprehension of like a child playing with poison," he hissed. "I want nothing more than to tear your body to pieces, and yet...."

"You need me," murmured Jake incredulously, rising to his feet.

The towering form of the former angel shuddered, and his dark eyes gazed down at Jake imploringly. "I cannot take this torment any longer. Most of my brethren have gone insane – yes, even immortals can become bereft of reason – and yet I have battled on for what you would class as centuries, holding onto my mind through sheer force of will, though at times I feared I had lost the fight. My singular hope was to one day redeem myself in the eyes of God – a foolish dream for one such as I, but it has helped me retain my sanity more than once. My choice to side with Lucifer should never have condemned me to the torments I have endured, but my repentance is true."

Jake sensed the sincerity behind the words, conflicting against the vehemence contained within the fallen angel. Rage, black and eternal, poured through every sinew and vein of Abaddon like blood; he seemed almost totally consumed by the malevolence inside him. But in the midst of it all, within the seething mass of spite, a tiny glint of what he must have once been glowed weakly like the last ember in a dying fire. This spark had made the fallen angel bring Jake back from death. This minute light within the darkness of Abaddon was the one glimmer of hope, and the only thing to have sustained him for the millennia he had endured in Hell.

"I can help you," assured Jake softly, knowing the words he spoke were true.

Rage and hope seemed to compete briefly within Abaddon.

"Please," grated the member of the Fallen from between gritted teeth.

Abaddon dropped to his knees and bowed low. Jake's hands stretched up and clasped the top of Abaddon's head, the black hair slipping in between his fingers. Jake waited.

And waited.

He sensed no power, no calmness. Would he be left here at this moment of victory only to fail?

Jake yearned to cry, but despite every effort he seemed unable to shed a single tear. Fear gripped him and his hands dropped.

"I don't know…."

There were no words. He expected Abaddon to rage, to tear him to pieces, but the former angel stayed motionless, his head still bowed.

"I'm sorry," Jake heard the corrupt figure whisper. He knew the words were not for him. Tears, each drop a thimble-full of liquid, fell from behind the mass of black hair which draped Abaddon's face, hiding his features. "I'm so sorry."

A jolt struck Jake in his chest like he'd been smacked with a baseball bat in the sternum. Unsure of what was happening, he hesitated, his hand rising uncertainly to the point in the center of his chest he'd felt it. Suddenly, intense power surged from the point, pouring down his arms, rushing up behind his eyes. Hurriedly, he clasped Abaddon's skull in both hands, raising it up to face him, and he gazed deep into the blue eyes filled with tears, knowing in an instant what he had to do.

An explosion of force tore through Jake, more intense than anything he'd ever experienced. It poured from his eyes, smashing into Abaddon's orbs, forcing an audible gasp from the fallen angel. Power strong enough to tear continents to pieces – perhaps even throw the planet completely off its axis – coursed through Jake, plunging into Abaddon.

An unearthly howl filled the air, and it took Jake a moment to realize the sound was uttering from his own lips. He had unconsciously opened his mouth as well, and even more power gushed from it, hurtling into Abaddon with a force beyond reckoning. The ground around them began to glow, the concrete melting under the pressure of the energy pulsing through them.

The darkness within Abaddon surged, battling against the golden flow, trying to snuff out the brilliance of the power. The darkness was strong, terrifyingly powerful in its ferocious struggle to survive, and several times Jake thought he might fail. Wisps of the malignance slipped past his defenses, and he tasted its bile, his heart cringing at its ferocity. He wondered how anything could retain the smallest amount of sanity while trapped within such an entity. Instinctively, Jake fought back against the toxicity, pouring more and more of himself into the fray in an attempt to overcome the evil defense.

His howl became a bellow, determination gripping him, aiding him, pushing the corruption back. The darkness, its strongest attack thwarted, slowly crumbled. It disintegrated, like a dike shattering against the onslaught of an enormous tidal surge, and Jake's power smashed through Abaddon, searching out the remnants of the darkness and destroying the malice from within.

Time passed by unnoticed. Minutes, hours, days, weeks, months – Jake couldn't tell, his mind totally suffused in the task at hand. There seemed no end to the corruption within Abaddon, like a bottomless well of vitriol, but he continued his healing. Eventually, after a lifetime of struggling, the end came into focus.

With a final wrenching burst of force, Jake smashed the remaining darkness to shards. The power filling Jake immediately fell silent, leaving him gasping, and he stared incredulously at the figure kneeling before him.

The colossal, diseased body and broken wings were gone; in their place laid a naked man in his mid twenties, the same black hair and features Abaddon had sported so recently adorning his hanging head. The man raised his face and opened his brilliant blue eyes.

"What have you done to me," gasped Abaddon, gazing at his hands. "I feel... unusual; somehow less... and yet more at the same time."

The answer came to Jake instantly, and he was amazed he hadn't guessed it sooner, but he'd been so shocked by the transformation that his brain had been slow to react.

"You're human," said Jake softly. "The corruption was too much to heal fully – you can never be an angel again, so you've been brought back halfway. You're human."

"Human?" asked Abaddon incredulously, standing up and staring down at his naked form. His voice was soft, trembling slightly. "That explains the smell." His self-conscious grin took any real chagrin away from the statement.

Jake chuckled. "I'm sure there are quite a few things you'll have to get used to."

The former fallen angel raised his azure eyes, deep emotion brimming within them. "You healed me," said Abaddon simply. "I feel the clash of emotions within me, but nothing like the all-consuming wrath I have experienced since being swept from Heaven – and nothing like the blissful clarity I knew before that event. My emotions are now... conflicted. I *must* be human to feel this confused."

"Must be," agreed Jake with a grin.

"But – wait! Everything is becoming foggy. Memories I have held for eons are fading even as I think of them."

Jake realized what was happening and cringed. In a similar fashion to the fading of his own confidence and knowledge after every passing event, the same was now happening to Abaddon, but on a much grander scale. Centuries – nay, millennia – would now be disappearing from the former angel's memory, leaving him bitterly alone.

"It's all... gone!" gasped Abaddon. "I know it was there, but can't recall anything."

"How far back can you remember?"

Abaddon stared at him, something akin to terror echoing in his gaze. "I remember getting dragged here in that moment of ritual along with my brethren. We wandered, formless, until finding bodies. I snatched the soul of Joseph Kony from his body and have since lain in wait for the final days, the time of Armageddon."

Jake's heart lurched, the world seeming to crumble around him as he heard what Abaddon said. Could it be true?

"Who else came with you, Abaddon?" he asked hurriedly, afraid that even this information might fade.

Abaddon's haunted eyes stared back at him. "All of them."

All of them.

All of the Fallen.

Here on Earth.

Uriel had been wrong when he'd said it couldn't be done. Jake shuddered at the idea and stared around at the devastation Abaddon had wrought on his own. What would a hundred – a *thousand* – such creatures do to the world? As if reading his thoughts, Abaddon shook his head slowly.

"Not just the Fallen," he murmured, his voice horrified, "all the beasts of the Abyss, everything from Hell, was released in that incantation. They lie in wait, hidden, each with its own purpose, its own job to aid toward the End of Days, just as I had mine."

"What was yours?" asked Jake.

"My task," croaked Abaddon, "was to keep *you* occupied long enough for our plans to come to fruition without your interference." His eyes were moist with tears. "I'm sorry."

Jake's reality threatened to crumble at the revelation. How was he supposed to stand up to such opposition? If all of Hell had been released onto the Earth, what was he supposed to do to stop it?

Gritting his teeth, he looked back at Abaddon, forcing himself to smile. At least he had one victory for the day, and he had gained something more. Although he couldn't control the power within him, Jake now felt more confident of it, guessing that in time he might learn to access it when absolutely necessary. The rest of the time things would be left up to him – as a man. There was no way he could rely on it to come at his beck and call. For the most part he remained human, but at least he knew it would be there when he truly needed it, and for that he felt grateful.

"And what of you, Abaddon?" asked Jake. "What will you do now that you're mortal?"

Abaddon looked down at his naked frame and grinned self-consciously. "I think the first thing I'll do will be to clothe myself." His eyes strayed to the nearby shops of Rodeo Drive, and he grinned before looking back to Jake, his expression becoming suddenly deadly serious. "But for the rest of this life my loyalty is now to you. Make of that what you will, but you have delivered me from torments I cannot remember, but whose scars will mar me forever. For that I am eternally indebted to you."

Jake didn't know what to say. The last thing he'd expected from this encounter was to end up with Abaddon as his follower, but upon reflection he realized there was no other way it could have been resolved. Despite all the power Jake seemed capable of, he'd only conquered the darkness because Abaddon had yielded.

If he couldn't defeat one fallen angel, how could he hope to stop an army?

Putting the problem aside for the moment, Jake strolled alongside Abaddon, heading toward one of the damaged stores, secure in the hope that no matter what else arose, he had some powerful allies supporting him.

Jake's eyes wandered to the cloudless sky, and he smiled.

## -EPILOGUE-

Jake sat on the grassy hill, leaning against a tree, and breathing in the sweet air. Mikey had recovered fully from his experience, Abaddon admitting he had deliberately left the younger brother undamaged, subconsciously hoping it might gain favor with Jake. Both brothers, along with Aadesh, had begrudgingly – after some argument which Jake had swiftly quashed – accepted the former angel's new-found allegiance.

The politicians had been harder to persuade, but with the President's support, Jake finally convinced everyone. It wasn't just Abaddon's physical transformation which left Jake so convinced, it was something internal, something undefined, yet as solid as granite.

News reports varied widely as to what had happened, but the government released a statement backed by several seismic reports indicating a large earthquake as the cause of the devastation in Beverly Hills. Independent theories were dismissed as the preserves of crackpots, and the media soon swallowed the story, focusing instead on the mysterious blond man with a blood-smeared cheek who had faced down a monster in Washington DC – videos of which had received over forty million hits online.

Jake had thus far avoided being recognized as the man in the clip, but it was only a matter of time before people began realizing it was him. His birthmark – the bloody tear – showed clearly in several of the videos. There were at least five different versions Jake knew about, and probably more would surface at a later date, but he couldn't be concerned about being discovered at the moment. He had much bigger issues at hand, the first of which involved finding out more about the demonic sleeper-cells.

Luckily, he had the full services of the United States Government at his disposal, and as such the most intricate intelligence network in the world now searched not for terrorists, political espionage, or threats from foreign nations; they hunted solely for information leading to the discovery of more of the Fallen.

The future would be difficult beyond anything in humanity's history. Jake knew this, but he headed toward it with a faith he'd never before known. Whatever he had to overcome would be horrific, and he wasn't looking forward to it, but with a little luck they might pull through.

God willing.

Made in the USA
Lexington, KY
21 May 2019